Selected Praise & Reviews
for
MATTHEW MATHER

"BRILLIANT...."
—*WIRED Magazine* on *CyberStorm* series

"Mather creates characters you've known your whole life."
—*BOING BOING* editor Jason Weisberger

"Relentless pacing...bombshell plot twists."
—*Publishers Weekly* on *The Dreaming Tree*

"Another home run for one of the genre's top authors."
—Washington Post #1 bestselling author Steven Konkoly

"Prepare for the most thrilling ride of 2021 in *CyberWar.*"
—New York Times bestseller Nicholas Sansbury Smith

"A wakeup call."
—Brent Watkins, FBI Cyber Special Agent *(retired)*

Published by Pallas Publishing

isbn // 978-1-987942-16-3 // e-book
isbn // 978-1-987942-17-0 // paperback
isbn // 978-1-987942-22-4 // hardcover

first edition

CYBER
WAR

Also by Matthew Mather

The New Earth Series
Winner of "Science Fiction Book of the Year"
Nomad
Sanctuary
Resistance
Destiny

World War C Series
Now in development with NETFLIX
CyberStorm
CyberSpace
CyberWar
Darknet

The Atopia Chronicles
Atopia
Dystopia
Utopia

Polar Vortex
Standalone novel now in development as a limited TV series

The Delta Devlin Novels
The Dreaming Tree
Meet Your Maker
Out of Time

CYBER WAR

A CYBERSTORM BOOK

MATTHEW MATHER

PALLAS
PUBLISHING

Acknowledgements

There are many people who helped in the development of this novel. In particular, I would like to thank:

Barry Matsumori
Vice-President, SpaceX *(former)*
CEO, BridgeSat

Brent Watkins
FBI Cyber Investigations
Special Agent (retired)

Richard Marshall
Global Director of Cybersecurity
US Department of Homeland Security

CYBER WAR

Prologue

Welcome to Pleasant Shade, Population 563," announced a black-and-white sign as Jolene and Travis swept past in the hissing rain.

"That's wrong," Jolene said. "At least two dozen people moved away this year. When are we going to move out? You said we—"

"Get your feet down from there." Travis hated it when she stuck her feet up on the dashboard. He leaned over the steering wheel and squinted into the foggy distance. What the heck was that up there? The edge of the tree line shimmered. "Goddamn, Jolene, what did I say?"

She pouted but slid upright in her seat, then held up her phone. "When are we going to get service back? It's gotta be against the law to cut us off like this."

"It's out of their control."

"'Their'? You mean, the government?"

Travis nodded.

Two days before, GPS service had gone down after a flurry of anti-satellite launches by India and Pakistan. Travis had been in hourly contact with his old special ops unit swapping theories and stories right until the internet and phones stopped working.

"And why ain't the TV working no more?"

"I told you. The anti-satellite attacks."

Taking Fox News and HBO and Netflix away at the same time as cell phones? It was like someone had pulled the cord from everyone's brains the last few days.

Jolene switched topics. "Did you see how many birds there were on that electrical wire back there? Like hundreds. You ever seen that before?"

"Might be the rain. Can't be easy to fly in."

The drizzle let up, but the humidity clouded the windshield. Travis leaned forward over the steering wheel to wipe the condensation away from the glass again. Birds ahead? There was a huge flock in the distance, tiny dots in the air.

"X says that it's not the anti-satellite attacks," Jolene mused. "He says the Indians are right. They didn't launch those attacks. It's our own government, they're—"

"Don't listen to that garbage, Jolene." Even with the internet down, somehow the conspiracy theories still flourished. Where was she getting this stuff? She hadn't stopped talking about this guy "Xenon" the whole day. "Our government is doing all they can."

"Can we pull into Todd's?" Jolene asked. "I need some Marlboros."

The Marathon gas station was as close to a center of town as Pleasant Shade had. Three other cars parked out front. Travis flicked on his indicator, slowed, and pulled his pickup next to a Buick—had to be old lady Mel's—near the entrance. Jolene got out and sauntered in through the door, swinging her butt in her cut-off jeans the way Travis liked. He smiled and leaned his head back and closed his eyes.

The staccato stutter of automatic gunfire popped in the distance.

Travis sat upright and looked left and right. Another weapon discharged, a shotgun, and much closer. Someone yelled. Through the fog in his driver's-side window, a man sprinted out of a house two doors down, dressed only in a robe and slippers. A gun in his hand.

"Jolene!" Travis yelled.

He swung around in his seat and reached for the AR-15 and magazine in the rack at the back. He never went anywhere without it. Couldn't even sleep—the little he could get—without it nearby. He kicked open his door and dropped to the pavement. The man in the robe had turned to run backward and was firing his handgun indiscriminately at his own house.

Automatic weapon fire stuttered again from multiple directions in the foggy distance.

Travis yelled again, "Jolene! Get the *hell* out here."

Or should he go inside? Were they under attack? Here? In *Tennessee*? By who? He inserted the magazine, gave it a solid whack, then tugged on it to make sure it was seated. Pulled the charging handle back, then let go. The bolt slipped forward and stripped a round from the magazine into the chamber. Flipped the selector to fire.

Jolene banged out through the gas station's door. "Travis!" she cried, her voice high and squeaking. "What in God's name is going on?"

Travis half stood from his crouch, using the open driver's-side door as a shield, and held out a hand to her. "Get over there. Get in the—"

She was halfway to him, running as best she could in her sandals, when a wet spray spattered across Travis's face and blinded him. With his left hand, he wiped the muck away in time to see Jolene's headless body flopping onto the pavement.

Chapter 1

A keening wail cut through the rain as images of Moscow filled the screen.

"Sorry, Mr. Mitchell," a Secret Service agent said. "I got her."

The man had my daughter, Olivia, wrapped up in his left arm while his right held his submachine gun and its long, curved magazine high and away.

Olivia's feet levitated a foot from the ground as he picked her up.

She wriggled to get free, her arms stretched out to me for help. To her, the heavy military-style encampment of Secret Service around the senator's house was just another opportunity to make new friends, and she ran between the agents, shrieking as they reached out, smiling, to grab her and try to slow her down.

They knew it was a game, but their business was still serious.

Those terrorists were still somewhere out there, maybe some of them still on American soil—even if all indications were that they had gone to sea to escape under cover of the hurricane two days before.

"Honey," my wife Lauren said to Olivia. "Come here and sit down. We're trying to watch something." She opened her arms and beckoned our daughter to the couch in the sitting area at the end of the dining room, where Luke and I sat too.

Olivia relented and made a serious face.

The agent released my daughter, and she walked haltingly to the couch. The Secret Service man—now blank-faced—returned to scanning the tree line beyond the river. It was dark outside, even at midday. Pregnant clouds skimmed the treetops. Rain continued over Virginia and DC as the straggling remains of Hurricane Dolly, which had obliterated Virginia Beach less than forty-eight hours before, finished churning up the Chesapeake.

"This footage is remarkable," said a Fox News anchor, a sandy-haired man with glasses and a sharp blue suit. "From a camera crew doing a promotional shoot just an hour ago..."

Floodlit, the red-and-green and blue-and-white striped onion-shaped domes of St. Basil's Cathedral painted a striking foreground to the twinkling lights of Moscow and an indigo night sky beyond. The drone rose higher and the brightly lit red-brick walls of the clock tower beside it came into view, the snaking black belt of the Moskva River just visible between the streetlights in the distance. Tourists milled about in Red Square.

The entire image on the TV screen went blank in an instant, but not because we had lost the signal. A beat later, emergency lighting clicked on to illuminate the base of St. Basil's, and even through the drone's mic, we heard the urgent panic as the crowd of tourists was plunged into darkness. The drone continued to rise, and in the clear distance, whole grid-patches of lights across greater metropolitan Moscow snapped off one by one until the entire city was dark to the horizon.

"I thought Russia had cut off their internet to us," Chuck said. "How did they get this footage over so quickly?" He perched on the edge of a tan leather recliner that matched the couch Lauren, Luke, and I—and now Olivia—cuddled on.

"Half of everything in geostationary orbit," Senator Seymour said, "the communications birds way up there, is still intact, and land-based fiber optic lines aren't affected. The

Russkies opened up comms when we regained control of the situation over our heads."

"*Is* it under control?" I asked.

"The threat from the GenCorp constellation is over, thanks to our friend." The senator nodded to his right, where Damon was talking to some FBI agents in the kitchen nook about fifty feet away and a half level up.

Not exactly talking to them. He was being interrogated.

Damon was the one who hacked into GenCorp and sent the kill command resulting in the fiery destruction of the ten-thousand satellites in their fleet. The few that were spared were rendered harmless as they burned out their reserves of fuel.

A Chechen terrorist group identifying itself as the Islamic Brigade had used a cyberattack to gain control of GenCorp's satellite base stations and TTC—telemetry, tracking, and command—of thousands of communication satellites in orbit. They used them as projectiles traveling at seventeen-thousand miles per hour to batter into hundreds of other satellites, destroying almost everything up there, from military birds to scientific imaging equipment.

As a result, growing massive debris fields of tens of millions of fragments were continuing to spread and engulf entire regions of space above our heads, wrecking what satellites remained in their path.

It was a nightmare scenario long dreaded by military planners—the Kessler Syndrome—in which a series of collisions in orbit created a runaway cascade of debris that would eventually destroy anything in orbit. It might be a generation before we could get any satellites back up, although the Russians were already trying.

The most damaging had been an attack on geopositioning satellites, GPS from America, GLONASS from Russia, the Galileo system from Europe, and more. The loss of positioning data was bad enough, but the loss of timing signals had brought down almost all the global mobile networks and wreaked havoc on any terrestrial systems that needed timing signals or mobile networks.

The power grid was one of them.

Without coordinated time-keeping maintaining the patchwork of national grids in phase with each other, the event had triggered overloads and outages—not just in America, but around the world. It was as if the entire planet Earth, already on a hair-trigger, had been short-circuited.

The whole world was falling apart out there.

"This year," the Fox news anchor said, "was already shaping up to be one of the worst on record for billion-dollar natural disasters. Costs for the CyberSpace attack, as pundits are now calling it, might run into the hundreds of billions or even trillions of dollars. And there had already been twenty-four individual billion-dollar-plus natural disasters in the months before that. Hurricane Dolly was the fifth hurricane of the season to make landfall in America. A massive heat wave in the western and central United States through the summer and fall killed hundreds."

Chuck returned with another beer and sat down.

"Add to that the massive wildfires in Appalachia and California that are still burning out of control," the news anchor continued. "With emergency services hampered by communications and GPS being knocked out, these disasters are going almost unchecked. The full scale of the loss of life is still unknown. For more on this, we go to our correspondent in Kentucky..."

Which made me think. I asked Chuck, "Have you talked to anyone at Farmer Joe's place?"

"Oscar is on his way up to our cottage right now."

"Oscar?"

"He's delivering our Mini." My friend grinned. "And he's supposed to be going with your brother Terry."

We'd left Kentucky in what seemed to me like another lifetime, but in reality, was only a week ago. With the fires pinning us down, we had gotten a boat out onto the Ohio River and then, on the other side, borrowed an Escalade truck from Oscar's cousin. The deal was that Oscar and a friend would drive up the Range Rover and Mini that we'd had to abandon at Farmer Joe's place.

However, the government had swept in and taken the Range Rover, because it had belonged to the terrorists. They almost took apart the Mini, too, Chuck said, but the guys had fixed it up.

I couldn't imagine my gorilla of a brother Terry jammed into a Mini with Oscar for the drive all the way from Kentucky up to the house in Shenandoah. I bet Oscar was already explaining for the tenth time how it was just bad luck that he had to crack me—Terry's little brother—in the head with the butt of a rifle. "They're on their way now? We'll meet them there?"

Lauren said, "You're feeling well enough?"

Our plan was to leave for the return trip to the cottage tomorrow morning. "I'm good."

She squeezed my leg. "I think we all need a vacation. Some time off."

"Yeah, like a year."

"We could do that. Maybe we should. A long trip?"

It was something I had always dreamed of. Taking a year off, traveling around America or maybe even the entire world with the kids. It was just idle daydreaming, but the way Lauren caught and held my eye, she looked like she meant it.

Chuck's wife, Susie, and their two kids were still up at their cottage, now with a security detail sent up there by the senator. Chuck talked to Susie every couple of hours over the landline, and it sounded like Susie and his kids were having a great time.

Smoke from the fires over the other face of the mountain was getting thicker, though. Might be a month before they could be put out, or a heavy rain might do everyone a favor.

Rural areas of America had been in an almost total communication blackout over the past two weeks, which meant that most of the United States outside of the big cities was in chaos—and would be for the foreseeable future. Not even any TV in many areas, which, with the loss of the internet, landlines, and cell service had to feel like being propelled back into the Stone Age.

Combined with the blackouts and loss of emergency services, the country was still in the grips of what felt like world-ending spasms. It was no wonder we ran into a Kentucky militia when we passed through. The chaos had forced towns and villages all over the country to take matters into their own hands to protect themselves from an unknown enemy.

The senator stood behind Chuck's leather seat, watching the Fox News broadcast. The coverage changed to a story about the terrorist attack and how many satellites had been lost in the past few hours. A long list.

"Any updates on where they are?" I asked the senator. "Have you caught them yet?"

"Last status I received, we're tracking a freighter that left from Pier Two at Norfolk International Terminal. We found that semitruck you saw being loaded at an abandoned house. It's our guess they're somewhere out in international waters by now."

"No satellite imaging, I'm guessing?"

"Not much. We've got the Navy, Coast Guard and Air Force fanning out over the eastern Atlantic looking for them. Should zero in any minute. The Russians are cooperating and providing their own overflight imaging from the area. We've got pictures of what we believe are the terrorists loading onto this freighter. The Russians hate these guys even more than we do."

"You're getting intel from the Russians?" Chuck said, raising his eyebrows. "Same Russians who just invaded the Baltic states and Ukraine last week? And Kyrgyzstan, too?"

"Same Russians that flattened most of Chechnya the last two weeks," the senator replied. He waved a hand at the TV, where it had returned to a replay of the Moscow blackout. "The Red Army was as blinded as we were by this, and they preemptively rolled over borders as a defensive measure. That's the line from their consulate, anyway."

"You don't believe them?"

"I'm not sure this is an appropriate response."

"I notice we haven't invaded anyone," I said.

"The Russians are sharing some timing signals with our military," the senator said. "They still have six operational GLONASS birds up, more than the two GPS we have left working so far. The European Galileo system is totally down."

"Not the Chinese, though," Chuck said.

I said, "Not the Chinese what?"

"They haven't opened up that Great Firewall of China yet."

The internet had become the splinternet in the past two weeks. Dozens of countries had literally disconnected themselves from the global network—sometimes even physically, by destroying optical ground cables.

Chuck continued, "And China just invaded Indian territory in the Himalayas and sent warships around Taiwan."

The senator said, "We're just lucky this has triggered no major conflicts—"

"Tell that to the Lithuanians."

"Things are calming down," the senator replied.

"And isn't the NATO Cyber Defence headquarters in Tallinn? That's in Estonia, right?"

The senator nodded. "Still operational, from what I've heard."

"But under Russian control?"

"You need to stop watching TV, son. They're cooperating. I'm staying on their ass, we're passing a resolution through Congress to go up to the Security Council to censure them for the Red Army's antics. They assure us they will roll the tanks back."

"Sure, worked great the last time."

"Last time?"

"Start of the Cold War."

I said, "The Chinese Baidu geopositioning satellites are mostly intact, aren't they? Are they sharing their signal?"

"Our Chinese friends are not sharing as much as a chopstick," the senator replied.

"That's exactly what Xenon is telling people on the networks."

"'Xenon'?" the senator asked.

"X-e-nonymous, Xenon for short," Chuck said. "He or she says they are a high-ranking official in the Department of Defense. Social media's been on fire the past two weeks, ever since this started. They've been bang-on with every detail so far."

"Conspiracy theorists?"

"Seems like more than that."

The senator sighed, "Can't we get the goddamned social media shut down?"

"Now that sounds autocratic."

"I'm just saying we don't need any more problems."

I said, "Most of it is being spread through Damon-net. Talk to him." I motioned with my half-empty beer at Damon, who was still being grilled by the FBI.

The black image of the metropolis of Moscow loomed in the eighty-inch screen as the Fox anchor continued talking of power outages in India, and another talking head appeared on the screen saying that they were the ones responsible.

Chuck asked, "Any sign of Tyrell Jakob? If that guy's not dead, he's in on it, I guarantee it."

"Where do you get that?"

"I've been reading."

"This Xenon guy?"

"Could be a woman, don't be a misogynist."

The senator said, "We've found no trace of him, either at the Mississippi HQ or online or anywhere else, we don't—"

Lamps beside the couches flickered.

The halogens in the ceiling blinked out just as all the other lights flashed off. The room was cast into a somber gray light. The humming sounds of the machines went silent. Someone shouted in the distance. The Secret Service men beyond the patio doors tensed, lowering their bodies while raising their submachine guns.

Chapter 2

A moment later the generator kicked in. The lights came back on.

"Just a power outage," an agent called from outside. "Other lights in the neighborhood have gone dark." The man's voice sounded like he was trying to be reassuring, but Secret Service agents were still scurrying past him across the grass embankment outside. "We're calling Dominion Energy right now."

I assumed that was the local power company.

Everyone was still on edge. Coming to this house was literally returning to the scene of the crime.

Bricklayers were already at work outside, repairing the entrance wall that I had nearly demolished when I thundered through it with the BullyBoy truck-tank two nights before. They must have cleaned off the driveway pavement by the entry, because the last time I'd seen it, it had been smeared with the blood of the Chechen terrorist I had landed the truck on top of.

It wasn't just the bad guys that had suffered casualties here—one of the Secret Service had been killed, and Agent Coleman was still in the hospital recovering from multiple gunshot wounds.

I had only just gotten out of the hospital myself the night before.

After two nights in there, the thing I wanted the most was to get out. Admitted into the intensive care unit, I had recovered fast. My major injury was that my lungs had filled with water. I also sported an enormous bruise in the center of my chest, where the ballistic vest had stopped the bullet fired by Terek, one of the terrorists who had befriended us, or pretended to.

Or Pyotr, or whatever his name really was.

Chuck was worse off than me. His left arm was in a sling, as much as he said he didn't need it. He took a round in the shoulder, which he said was mostly a flesh wound. At least it wasn't his right. That one held a beer, which was already empty again.

He eyed the lights. Satisfied they wouldn't go out, he said, "You want another?"

I shook my head and wrapped my arms tighter around Luke and my girls.

When the power had tripped off, the TV had shut down. The lights came up, but the TV remained dark. The room was silent. Luke was to my left and had his big-boy face on. I was half afraid he was going to ask for a beer to fit in with the guys.

"Should we turn it back on?" I asked Lauren.

She had Olivia in her arms, curled up like a little monkey. "She's scared," my wife whispered to me. "Why don't we leave the TV off for now? Go get that beer with Chuck. Take Luke with you."

I couldn't argue with that.

Everything on the cable news was disheartening, and they specifically designed their coverage to make it even more scary. Trust the TV news to turn an already frightening situation into something apocalyptic. Fires. Satellites falling from the sky. Entire cities and countries going dark. Images of warships and airplanes. We could all use a break from an already incessant news cycle whipping into a frenzy.

"Yeah, why don't you get a beer with Chuck," the senator said. "I'll join you in a second."

I rose from the couch, leaned over to kiss Olivia and then my wife on the forehead, and strode through the dining area toward the kitchen, which was a short flight of three stairs up. Luke followed me.

In hushed tones, I heard my wife and the senator talking. I couldn't quite hear what they were saying, but it sounded as if the senator was asking her about legal opinions. I didn't know they were working together, or that she had anything to do with his office. I let it go and decided to ask her about it later.

Through the floor-to-ceiling windows to the side of the dining room, looking out over the Potomac River, I spotted gardeners raking up the first of the fall leaves. Two of them dragged huge clear plastic bags toward the garage at the rear of the house.

"How many times have you been to the GenCorp headquarters in the past year?" I heard one of the FBI agents asking Damon. "Would you say you are friends with Mr. Tyrell Jakob?"

Damon looked up at me as I passed him and rolled his eyes. This new team of agents had tried to take him into a private room, but this time he refused. He said he would cooperate, but he wanted to remain with everyone else. It was well past 2 p.m., and this was the third round of questioning today.

This time, though, they wired a lie detector machine to him.

One of the men who had questioned Damon that morning was still here in his suit, along with a new colleague, but a third man had joined them. This guy was much more casual, in jeans and a T-shirt, short-cropped hair, dark ochre-brown skin, his face weathered and creased. Two-day stubble on his chin. They were all seated at the round kitchen table in the nook at the end of the large kitchen, which occupied most of the split-level at this end of the mansion.

I patted Damon on the shoulder and walked over to join Chuck by the fridge. He handed me a beer. I popped the top off and it hissed. He handed Luke a bottle of fizzy water.

"Dad," Luke said after taking a sip. "I'm kinda tired. Can I go take a nap?"

I ruffled his hair. "Yeah, but stay in your room, okay?"

He gave Chuck a high-five as he passed by and slid away around the corner.

"Leo," Chuck said, "you want one?" My friend was now on a first-name basis with the senator.

Leo held out his hand and accepted the offered brew.

"Who's that guy?" I indicated the man with the weathered face.

The senator said, "He's not FBI. He's more"—he searched for the right word—"off the books."

"Do you know this man?" one of the FBI agents asked Damon as he held up a picture.

It wasn't anyone I recognized.

"That's Damon's buddy." Chuck whispered low enough that the men at the table couldn't hear. "The one who worked at GenCorp. You remember, he was telling us he had a friend who worked there?"

Damon nodded that he knew the man. He explained exactly how they'd met when they had studied together at MIT, and said that he had communicated with him at GenCorp in the past two weeks. Or he thought he'd been communicating with him. He explained again how he had been duped, the same way they fooled the authorities into believing that his friend was still alive, when it was an artificial intelligence program that was responding to their emails.

"Don't they already know all this?" I said to the senator. "It's gotta be the tenth time I've heard them asking the same questions."

"They're doing their job," the senator replied.

"Any more details on what they found at GenCorp?"

"A lot of dead bodies. Wrecked equipment. Forensics is working the scene right now."

"I'm assuming they didn't find Tyrell?"

"I assure you, son, you'll be the first to hear."

"Like I said, one way or the other, that guy was in on this." Chuck raised his beer and took a sip. "Stubble-face over there is special ops or something? CIA? Why would somebody like that be questioning Damon?"

"Every three-letter agency is in on this," the senator replied. "Active foreign shooters on our soil. Half of America somehow doesn't believe it's true, think this is some plot by our own government. We're about to invoke the Stafford Act and bring active military onto the streets of America, but you can imagine how—"

I left the conversation and walked along the kitchen island with some intention of returning to the couch, but then stopped and made like I was playing with my phone.

"You destroyed twenty billion dollars' worth of equipment," I heard the second FBI guy say. "A lot of that was government-owned."

"Leased," Damon said. "Tyrell was renting some of those satellites to the government. And it was more like forty."

"Satellites?"

"Billion. Dollars. What those ten thousand satellites in the GenCorp constellation cost. I had to destroy them. It was the only way I could figure out to stop Terek—"

"Terek?"

"Pyotr, whatever you guys are calling him."

"This was your friend?"

"Is this a stupid game you need to keep playing?"

Both agents paused and looked at each other. Finally, one of them said, "We know he wasn't your friend."

I decided that had to be the one playing good cop.

"Thank you."

"But you destroyed most of the evidence. Everything at GenCorp HQ is ruined."

"I had nothing to do with the HQ in Mississippi, I told you that."

"We mean, the satellites."

Damon said, "I only did what I did because you guys were totally failing at doing *anything*."

The agents looked down at their notes.

"Are you being serious?" Damon said. "I saved your ass on this."

"You lied to federal officers," the other FBI agent said.

That had to be the one doing the bad cop routine. I understood why Damon was getting frustrated.

The agent held up a tablet screen and played a video. A grainy image of Damon's face appeared, in what had to be footage from a body camera on one of the police officers we'd encountered at a checkpoint a few days ago. The video revealed Damon, his voice scratchy, saying that he knew Terek, that they had gone to MIT at the same time, and that he had known him for years.

"They fooled all of us," Damon said.

"You had been in contact with him for a year, correct?"

"That's right."

"And you are the one that gave him access to your 'Damon net'?"

"I didn't give him free reign. He inserted an exploit. Created a back door."

The two FBI officers leaned back in their chairs and looked at the guy in the T-shirt. He shrugged, got up from his chair, and walked away down the flight of stairs toward the main living area.

The FBI guy to Damon's right held up the tablet screen again. "You know this man?"

They noticed me looking, so I turned away and went back to playing with my phone. I'd just seen a picture of a Chinese man on the FBI guy's tablet. Nobody I recognized.

"I don't know him," I heard Damon say.

"What about these phone calls?" The FBI agent produced a sheaf of papers.

"No idea what you guys are talking about," Damon said.

"Sir," the closest FBI guy said, "you have to answer us in more detail. You have no idea who this man is?"

Damon muttered, "I should've seen it. I should be able to see all this. This is all my fault."

"You said you're on psychobiotics?" the other FBI guy asked. "Is that like psychedelics?"

"It's like yogurt," Damon said.

"You have the personal data of millions of Americans. We need access to that data."

"I can't just give you that. I'm doing my best to disable the network. I know it's a compromise. I put in a patch to stop it."

"You need to hand the whole thing over to the government."

"And we all know how well that works out."

"Mr. Indigo, this is a national emergency."

"I realize that, but I can't just—"

I gave up eavesdropping and, beer in hand, realized I needed to hit the head. I went down the three steps from the kitchen to the main living area and crossed over to the hallway. I pushed open the door to the bathroom, but it was already occupied. The guy in the T-shirt and jeans, the special ops guy, was sitting on the edge of the bathtub with a black case open on his knees. I caught sight of steel syringes and a row of stoppered bottles.

He looked up at me and said, "Can you give me a minute, please?" He stood, leaned over, and swung the door closed.

I waited for a moment before deciding I did not need to go that bad. I returned to the couch to check on Lauren and Olivia. Chuck was back with his beer, sitting on the couch, staring at the blank TV screen.

"You guys want to talk to Susie again?" I asked.

There was a landline phone on one table beside the couch.

"Sure," Lauren said. "Let's ring them."

A voice called out from the kitchen area, "We're going live on the freighter in two minutes. Senator, you want to patch it through to the screen in the living room?"

"We'll just keep it on the one in here," I heard the senator say.

The guy in jeans and a T-shirt had come out of the bathroom, and he beckoned Senator Seymour to join him at the dining room table. I had just picked up the phone when the senator waved at me. I glanced at Lauren—she shrugged and indicated for me to give her the phone. I walked over to join the senator and the T-shirt guy.

"Name's Archer," the man said, extending his hand. "Walsh Archer."

I shook his hand. He seemed to know who I was. He was built like a refrigerator, big and wide with square shoulders and gave off the impression of keeping things cool.

"Sorry for giving your friend a hard time there," Archer said.

"Just doing your job," I said without enthusiasm.

Walsh Archer sounded like about as fake a name as someone could come up with.

The senator opened the folder and spread the contents out on the table. "We are looking at the papers we retrieved from the truck when you smashed into that house in Virginia Beach."

Archer said, "A whole list of Americans, some names of towns. We're trying to track down the people now. We've gotten in touch with most of them, but so far, we can't find connections between them. We don't know why they're on this list."

"Why would they have printed out a paper list?" I asked.

"They weren't expecting anybody to get into that safe house," the senator said.

"The bigger question is," Archer said, "why did they target you, Mr. Mitchell? To get to Senator Seymour? What makes him such a special target?"

"Five minutes to the freighter video feed," a voice cried out from the kitchen area.

"Mike," the senator said, "come join us?"

"Sure, but we're talking to Susie first."

Behind me, I heard the TV turn back on. The Fox news anchor detailed another list of satellites destroyed in the past hours. An image returned to the screen, mostly blank, of Moscow with its lights out. Chuck shrugged—he couldn't help it, he needed the news feed—with the TV remote in hand.

Lauren dialed the cottage number.

Enlarged prints now occupied most of the surface area of the dining table. Enhanced reproductions of the soggy papers that had flown when the truck had crashed the party at the terrorist safe house. I scanned the incomplete and smudged-out names on the list. They were doing number crunching to figure out how they were connected, and whether these individuals were participants in terrorist activities, or targets, or something else entirely. One place name popped out. We had almost driven through the place on our way here a week ago.

Pleasant Shade, Tennessee. The date beside it was September 9th. That was ten days ago.

I asked, "Did anybody talk to people in Pleasant Shade?"

Chapter 3

D ad," Ellarose squealed into the receiver on her end, "check your phone."

Lauren had dialed Susie and Ellarose on the landline.

The growing cacophony of the chopper from the kitchen made it difficult to hear Chuck's daughter over the speakerphone. Glasses clinked and feet shuffled as the Secret Service and others assembled to watch the show. I almost asked them to turn it down but decided I would go up to watch.

Like watching one of those drone strikes on the internet, except this was in real time. This was about to happen "live" and had the feeling of a movie premiere. My stomach twinged at the realization that real people might die as we munched popcorn and cheered. Were they the same ones that had attacked us?

Nobody really knew.

The fiber optic internet connection to the cottage was still working, so when Susie connected her phone to the wireless up there, she could send pictures to us here. Between the rolling blackouts sweeping back and forth through Virginia and the rest of the country and the patchwork of communications, it was a minor miracle we could talk with her and the kids.

Chuck picked his phone up awkwardly with his right hand— his left in a sling—and clicked an email. He showed everyone. It was Ellarose, holding a fish as big as her arm and grinning a toothy smile into the camera.

"It's a brown trout," Ellarose said over the speakerphone.

"That's my girl." Chuck beamed.

"Susie," I said. "We'll be coming up tomorrow. Oscar is on his way, maybe with my brother? They haven't gotten there yet?"

Susie replied, "Nobody up here but the two security contractors the senator sent. That and some muskrat and eagles. You guys will love it up here. We've been having fun. Seriously, Mike, you'll love it."

I wasn't so sure.

The memories of that place lingered.

My wife, though, insisted that we needed to get past it, that it was a beautiful spot, and we needed to come to terms with some of the ghosts from our past. Time up in the mountains would do us some good, she had told me the night before when we were trying to go to sleep. She and Susie were ganging up on me.

"Did you talk to Ken or Joe?" I asked.

"Yesterday," Susie replied.

"My brother Terry is always late," I said.

"You tell the elder Mitchell when you see him," Chuck said, "that he still owes me fifty bucks from our last arm wrestle. You tell him."

"Susie?" It sounded like the line had gone dead.

We waited a beat, then another. Chuck looked at me. I looked at him.

"Susie?" Chuck said.

Gone.

We tried calling back, but the line was busy. Maybe she was trying to call us. We waited a few minutes and tried again. Same result. We tried the meshnet app, the new one Damon had asked us to install. But the call didn't go through. Might be that there weren't enough connections up there and the internet wasn't connected again. Chuck sent her an email and asked her to call us when she got it.

"We could drive up tonight," Damon said as he walked over. "It's only an hour. I want to get back up that way myself."

"Not a bad idea," I said. "We could go now."

Damon flopped onto the couch and sighed.

"You still thinking about that Paulina girl?" I said, smiling.

We had met her at Farmer Joe's place in Kentucky, and the two had become an item. He had called her once over the meshnet and had huddled in a corner like a teenager and stayed clear of the rest of us so we couldn't hear him talking.

"We're talking." He grinned sheepishly. "But I've got other stuff that's more important right now I need to deal with." He glanced at the FBI agents still at the table in the kitchen.

The noise of the choppers in the background was getting louder and louder. Commands barked over a loudspeaker, telling whoever was on the boat to shut off the engines.

Damon continued, "I've been asking people to uninstall and reinstall the new app from the University of Washington. The FBI and government want me to give them access to everything."

"Can't argue with The Man," Chuck said, "Who was that Chinese guy they showed you?"

Damon ignored the question and said, "It's me giving the government the personal data of millions of people who trusted *me*. I'm not sure it's legal."

Chuck said, "Not like they don't have everything anyway."

"But it's exactly what I've been trying to stop. I'm part of an MIT and University of Washington project where we're building an open-source social media platform for people to keep track of their friends. Like a wiki social. No profits. No big corporations and no government. Something that's not evil."

"Heard that before," Chuck said.

"Don't remind me."

I sat with Damon on the couch. "You need to be practical. Terek and his sister targeted us. They infiltrated America, starting with you. I know you had the best intentions, but this *is* a national security issue. You have to let this go, do what they ask."

"Hey," Chuck said, "can we watch the live video of the SEAL team on the big screen?"

This was like the World Series and Super Bowl wrapped into one for him. I wasn't as enthusiastic, but still curious.

Lauren was on one end of the couch with Olivia in her arms. My little girl looked like she was asleep. My wife whispered to me, "I'll take her up to the bedroom with Luke. I don't want the kids seeing this. People they've met might get killed."

"That's a good idea," I whispered back.

She walked past us. Damon and Chuck stayed silent. When she was gone, Damon went to a corner and held up his phone to start recording a video telling people to uninstall his app and use the new government one on his website.

"Hey, Leo, can we get the video on the big screen?" Chuck called out.

"One second." The senator asked some questions, talked to a tech guy about security clearances.

I pulled my phone from my pocket and opened the new meshnet app. Found Joe's number. I called. I wasn't sure if I would get through, as that would require having a meshnet all the way from here to the farm in Kentucky, but the line rang.

A second later I heard that familiar drawl. "Mike," Farmer Joe said, "that you?"

"How are things over there?"

"Holding our own. Those fires came in from the west and we dug up a firewall to stop it. They kinda petered out. Big rainstorm swept over the top of the Shenandoah and this whole area. There's still fires burning up in the hills, but seems to be calming some."

"That's good to hear. Did my brother make it down?"

"He said he couldn't make it."

Didn't surprise me. Terry was never on time for anything. "Did Oscar leave yet?"

"Yesterday."

"What time?"

"About noon."

I checked my watch. That was twenty-seven hours ago. It was only a five- or six-hour drive up there, but who knew what they might've encountered? Fires. Roadblocks. It had taken us seven days to drive up from New Orleans the week before.

"Didn't they get up to the house yet?" Joe asked.

"I'm sure they'll be there soon."

"I'm not worried."

Damon was still recording the video on his phone. He stood next to the TV. Its screen blinked to life. The grainy image of a freighter appeared in the middle. The noise of the choppers was now almost deafening as the sound came on through multiple sets of speakers.

"Shut off your engines," we heard the pilot calling out on a loudspeaker. He was yelling instructions to the captain of the freighter.

"I gotta go," said Joe. "I can hear you're up to something. You keep in touch, tell me when they get there. If you can, I mean."

"Joe says that Oscar left yesterday at noon," I said to Chuck.

Chuck's eyes were glued to the big screen in front of us. The chopper closed in. The camera view of the ocean and ship filled the entire screen. People ran on the rooftops of the containers, some of them with what looked like guns in their hands. One of them fired. Return fire stuttered. In the distance, on the ocean's horizon, ships appeared all around the freighter.

Nowhere for it to go.

The senator came down from the kitchen to join us in the sitting area. He stood by the immense windows looking out over the Potomac. I got up to stand by him, my arms crossed.

"This will be over in a minute," the senator said.

A startling crack.

It wasn't from the TV.

The senator looked to his right. A bird had hit the glass. It squirmed around on the paving stones just below the window. A red-hot flash in the distance. Something else impacted the window. A bright light like a flashbulb lit up the room.

Chapter 4

Was that an explosion? Sounded more like a big firecracker. The last two days, since we'd routed the terrorist threat, people had been setting off fireworks all over the nation. A celebration of a victory that I didn't feel.

The glass of the windowpane hadn't shattered.

The Secret Service outside crouched in the wind and rain. One man inside pulled the senator behind him. Silence. Just the wind howling outside.

Maybe the flash was an electrical short?

And what was that on the grass? A bird?

One of the Secret Service carefully moved over to investigate the thing squirming in the dirt. He talked into his wrist mic. As he leaned closer, a red mist clouded his head. Something spattered against the window beside him.

The man slumped to the ground.

At the same instant, more thudding impacts hit the window right in front of where the senator stood, concurrent flashes and cracks that didn't shatter the glass but bent it inward, like a windshield hit by a fat rock thrown from an overpass. More red dots flashed by outside.

The lights went out. The TVs went off.

Silence.

The room pitched into near darkness. Then screaming. Stuttering gunfire.

I was already running before I realized my feet were moving, my sneakers squeaking against the marble floor of the dining area as I cleared the corner to the sweeping staircase up from the foyer.

"Luke," I yelled. "Lauren!"

Three more loping steps and I leapt up the staircase. Lauren was already at the first landing, half crouched with both kids under her arms. I scooped up Olivia, who wailed with fear.

"This way," the senator called out from downstairs. "We have a safe room in the basement."

Chuck was already on his way up the stairs to meet me. The stairway was in darkness. Emergency lights clicked on and lit up the corners and angles of the house in stark light. Damon nowhere to be seen.

Right behind my wife, I saw her mother, Susan. Her eyes were saucers even in the dim light. She had an Adidas tracksuit on, her hair a mess. She must have been sleeping or watching a movie with the children. She looked like she'd just woken up, but she was spry and quick for her age.

With one arm around my kids, I reached around Lauren to grab Susan's hand.

"Get downstairs, now!" The senator's voice thundered from just below us.

Beyond the walls, men shouted. Gunfire in short bursts.

Thudding pops like fireworks going off all around the house.

Urging Lauren and Susan and the kids ahead of me, with Chuck leading, we ran as fast as we could down the stairs. A wall of Secret Service men formed around the senator, but he shoved some of them back to pull Lauren and Susan into the middle of the knot.

"We're heading down to the basement," one of the Secret Service men said into his wrist mic.

I looked around for Damon. Couldn't find him. No time. Like a phalanx of Roman soldiers, we edged down the hallway.

"Did anyone get a look at who's attacking us?" Chuck asked.

Farther down the hallway, a spindly object hovered into view. Below the stuttering gunfire and screams, whatever it was buzzed with a high whine and wobbled in space at about head height. It looked like a giant hummingbird, with a glittering head atop a spiny metal neck six inches long. A single red LED at its center. It stopped for an instant, as if observing us.

Everyone in our group froze.

The spindly hummingbird tilted forward. The whine ratcheted up an octave. It shot straight at me. I lurched back. The Secret Service man ahead of me raised his gun and fired, then jumped and put his left hand out to block the thing as it shot straight at his face. His hand exploded in red mist and yellow flame. He screamed.

I fell backward. Another agent crashed down and sprawled on top of me. Lauren had hold of one of my hands. Olivia dangled around her neck. Lauren pulled Luke up, grabbed me under my armpit, yanked, and got me to my feet. Angry buzzing behind us. I looked back over my shoulder.

Another whirring killer hummingbird appeared in the room behind us.

"Back, back!" I screamed.

Three of the Secret Service were already down in their stance, weapons up and firing. Two more grabbed the senator and rushed him along the hallway toward us. My head down, I wrapped my arms around my family and spurred them back the way we had come, but there were already more of those swarming machines.

We were trapped.

Susan, Lauren's mother, was behind us and right in front of the senator.

"Mike," Lauren said, "get my mom. She can't—"

Susan did her best to run to us, but she fell over. Hard. Toppled awkwardly onto the marble floor.

I let go of Lauren, who now had both Luke and Olivia in her arms, her eyes desperate, and turned to go back to get Susan. She was struggling to her feet when she turned around. A high-pitched whine behind her. One of the bastard hummingbirds took a line straight at her.

Lauren's mother lifted both hands up, but the thing went between them. With a sickening thud, heart-rending spatter and flashing orange flame, it dove into her neck.

Lauren shrieked behind me, then let out a keening wailing moan.

More of the savage little machines flooded the hallway. I turned blindly, reached for my wife and kids. Someone grabbed and tugged me. Together with Lauren and the children, I fell backward, plunging spinning into open space.

Lauren yanked away from me.

My head crashed into an edge, sending a bolt of pain down my neck. My vision blurred. Olivia yelped. Somebody cursed. I gritted my teeth and strained, felt a heavy body tangle into me, spinning into space, a sharp corner biting into my back and arms. We skidded to a rolling stop. I smelled engine oil and rubber.

A door slammed behind us.

Chattering gunfire and yells echoed dully from beyond the walls.

"Mom!" Lauren screamed.

Olivia shivered and mewled. Somehow, I had cocooned her within my arms. "You okay?" I whispered.

She burst into a screeching wail.

My face was flat against the cool cement of the garage. I cooed gently to Olivia and propped myself up with one hand. Chuck was halfway up the four flights of stairs to the entrance to the house, his good arm—his right—wrapped around my wife's waist. She hammered on the door.

"Lauren, honey, she's gone," Chuck said into her ear.

"Mrs. Mitchell, you gotta stop making noise."

I turned to my right. The person I had fallen over was Archer, the special ops guy from the kitchen. He must've grabbed me. My instinct, now I knew my kids and wife were safe, was to scramble to my feet and get back to the door, back to Susan. Lauren's mother was still behind that door.

A strong arm held me back.

"Mrs. Mitchell," Archer repeated, louder and more insistent this time. "Mr. Mitchell. You gotta hold quiet. Everybody's gotta keep silent." He released me and held out both hands, fingers splayed, as if he were pushing something down.

My whole body shook.

"But... my..." Lauren's voice cracked. "My mother, she..."

One of the TVs had started playing loudly again in the kitchen. Had someone inside turned it on? We heard the clamor of the chopper, and one of the pilots yelling instructions to the people on the boat. Beyond that, the rhythmic chatter of gunfire from the outside had died down.

One gunshot echoed dully. A second later, another.

Then nothing.

Except the sound of the chopper on the TV in the kitchen.

"Ricky? Johnny?" Archer yelled out tentatively.

No reply from beyond the walls of the garage.

My brain circled back on itself and rechecked my family. Luke was right behind Lauren, holding onto her leg. I checked

Olivia again. She was shaking, but looked unhurt. She had stopped screaming, but now sobbed in my arms.

Damon was to my left, standing next to a black limousine. He had a backpack on. Archer stood in front of the senator, using himself as a shield. The man had a submachine gun in his right hand, a backpack on, and a tactical vest strapped around him.

Chuck was at the top of the stairs, beside Lauren.

"Make certain it's locked," Archer said.

"What do you think I'm doing?"

I said, "You think those things can open doors?"

"Grab those pallets"—Archer indicated along the back wall—"and stack them against it. Then take that metal shelving and pile it up. Make sure nothing gets through there. And somebody secure that outside entrance." He pointed to the only other door at the end of the garage.

"We need to get my mother," Lauren whimpered.

"Ma'am. We cannot do that. We cannot open that door." He gently but persistently tugged Lauren back.

I did a quick head count. Eight, including my kids. None of the Secret Service had made it in with us. "How many agents do we have outside? How many other people were in the house? I saw two gardeners out there, did anybody else see them?"

"We need to secure the perimeter," Archer said. "Make sure none of those garage doors can open." He pointed at me, then past me. "Mr. Mitchell, please, can you do that? And Chuck, move that workbench on the far wall against the exterior door."

My eyes followed where his jabbing finger had indicated.

There were three garage doors, all metal and all shut, but each of them attached to automated openers. There was only one car in the three bays, the limousine that Damon stood beside. I squeezed Olivia's hand, whispered to her to stay put, then ran to the first garage door, grabbed the manual handle, turned, and banged the lock into place.

I kept turning back to keep an eye on Olivia and Luke and Lauren.

Chuck gently eased my wife farther away from the door. I heard him telling her we would go out there if we could, that help was coming, that we needed to protect the kids. My wife whimpered her mother might need help. I'm sorry, I heard Chuck say.

He let go of her, double-checked she didn't bolt, then ran to the small door that led out into the garden. He yelled at me to help. By that time, I was at the last garage door, so I jumped over to help him haul the wooden workbench, filled with tools, partway across the door. I ran around the other side of it to push it fully in front of the entrance.

I went back to the garage bays and checked the locks again, then stopped to scan the room myself.

No windows.

The only entrance to the house was the one we'd come through. Sheet-metal door. One exit this end to the garden. Three metal garage doors. Twenty-foot ceilings.

"Can we get to the safe room in the basement?" I asked.

"No chance," Archer replied.

He had stacked more pallets against the interior door.

Luke was crying but did his best to keep one arm around his mother's waist.

Rain drummed against the roof over our heads. The noise of the chopper rumbled on the TV in the kitchen. It had to be connected to an emergency power source. Which could mean we weren't cut off entirely.

No other sounds from inside the house.

Except a low whirring buzz. No mistaking what that was. Those little killing machines.

After a beat I asked, "Is someone coming? Did we get an emergency call out?" That had to have happened, right?

"We need to keep moving." Archer stacked another pallet against the door.

Senator Seymour had his arm tight around my wife now, and Olivia and Luke hugged each other and grabbed onto the two adults' legs.

Damon wasn't helping stack anything against the door but was opening backpacks on the hood of the limousine. Chuck and Archer had grabbed each end of the ten-foot metal shelving unit by the wall and hefted it up, walked back a dozen paces, then turned sideways to let it slam against the pallets and door.

"Did we see who's attacking us?" I asked breathlessly.

"Pretty sure I've got a good idea who the assholes are," Chuck replied.

"All I saw were those miniature drones," Archer said.

He backed away from the door, submachine gun slung across his back, firearm in his right hand. He spoke into his wrist mic. "Richard?" He paused. "Agent Dumont?" He turned and continued whispering urgently into his mic trying to raise someone.

"There's gotta be a team controlling those things," Chuck said.

Damon said, "We fly drones over Afghanistan from trailers in Utah and Nevada. And they didn't look like they were under manual control."

"You know what those are?" Archer asked. He kept whispering into his wrist mic.

"Ornithopter bots," Damon said. "The way those are acting, those are fire and forget. Autonomous control, at least in close quarters."

"You sure?"

"As I can be."

"Enough to bet your life?" Archer holstered his handgun and checked the magazine on his submachine gun.

"But somebody's controlling them, right?" I asked.

Archer said, "I counted two dozen or more hovering outside the windows. As many buzzing inside before we locked ourselves in here."

"What are our options?"

"They're changing behavior," Damon said. "I think they went from personality kills to signature. Soon their behavior will probably change again. They seem to be swarming. The element of surprise is gone, so we have a few minutes to breathe before tactics change, but I agree with Archer. We need to get out of here, keep moving. Maybe we can use these?"

Damon held up his backpacks. He still had three drones left from our previous misadventures.

"Are they weaponized?" Archer squinted, his eyes scanning back and forth across the walls as he hunted for threats.

Damon shook his head. "Maybe I can lead some of them away. With three drones sent out in different directions, we could create some confusion."

Archer muttered into his wrist mic, paused, and then swore. "I can't get anyone on any channel. Whatever confusion you want to create, Damon, get it done soon. Can someone try their phone? Did anyone get a call out? 911? Anything?"

Senator Seymour had his phone in his hand. "I've been trying. The house's internet is down. And there's no connection to any outside meshnetworks, nothing to anyone."

"The rain is getting harder," Damon said. "That'll make it more difficult for those miniature drones to fly and process. They're small."

"Which makes me think something bigger is coming," Archer said.

"They can't have much battery power. Maybe single use? It's been at least ten minutes."

"That was just the first wave. We need to move."

"Out there?" Chuck pointed toward the garage doors. "As far as I can tell, everybody *out there* is dead."

"You got a better idea? One way or the other, worse is coming—"

"Or help is on the way," I said.

"You want to bet your family's life on that?"

Damon tossed me a backpack. He walked over to the first garage door, stopped at the bags of leaves, and picked one up. "I have an idea."

Chapter 5

Why don't we get in the limo?" Chuck said. "That thing's got bulletproof windows, right?"

The senator flicked his chin at a set of hooks by the stairway going up. "Keys are up there on the wall."

"Bingo." Chuck piled anything and everything he could find against the door leading out to the garden. He pulled out two fake Christmas trees and threw them on top of the growing mess.

Rain thumped on the roof of the garage.

My stomach in my throat, my heart hammering. Face covered in a slick sweat.

Luke pulled on my shirt and I bent over to take hold of him. He wrapped his arms around my neck, his legs wrapped around my waist. Lauren had Olivia tight to her, my little girl's face pressed into her neck. She was crying. They both were.

I realized I was as well.

My breaths came in catching sobs. My hands shook.

"I can't get anyone on the comms inside or outside the house," Archer said. "Whoever sent those drones has got to be waiting for us. On every road in and out. And in the surrounding forests."

"Do you *know* that, or do you *think* that?" I asked. Did he see something on a monitor or get word from the men out there?

Archer replied, "That's what I would do if I were them. This is a well-planned attack."

Damon opened the sack the gardeners had left in the garage, and multicolored oak and beech leaves spilled onto the cement. "We use these."

"Against what?" Archer asked.

"Against what's out there."

Archer said, "Explain." His eyes scanned back and forth across the three garage doors, up and down, his weapon ready. "They know we're trapped. Those things have to be relaying video back to whoever is operating them."

"Not necessarily," Damon said.

"We need to go back and get my mother," Lauren said between sobs. She gripped Olivia, the knuckles on my wife's hands white as her fingers clung to our daughter's blouse.

I stepped to her, put my right arm around her, wincing as I felt my injured ribs, and whispered, "We can't do that, honey." My voice tremored as I said it, realizing the finality and dreadful thing I was saying to my wife, the mother of my children, who had just lost hers.

"There might not be any human operators," Damon said. "Those things aren't exactly Predator drones. Miniature ornithopter slaughterbots, more like."

"I've never seen anything like them," Archer said.

"I've seen a lot of experimental—"

"These are more than experimental."

"Who has hardware like that?" Chuck asked.

"Anybody with enough cash," Damon said. "Never heard of someone using those operationally, but you should—"

"Whatever they are," I interrupted, "they're not going anywhere, and I think more just arrived." My arms a vise around Luke. He squirmed and I released pressure.

Like giant mosquitoes, the hum and buzz of the tiny killer machines grew just beyond the walls, the sound rising above the thrumming rain.

"Go on," Archer said to Damon. "You're the genius, right? You said they were changing behavior." He swept his weapon to follow a cascading clatter rolling down the roof.

We all held our breath. Had to be a branch?

Chuck peered through a gap in his barricade through the window of the exterior door, then quick-walked back to us around the limo. "I can see some hovering outside. They look like they're waiting."

Waiting? For what? I said, "Damon, you said something about signature versus personality?"

"When that first one hit the glass, it was clear it was heading straight at Senator Seymour. Then the second and third ones hit. Their image recognition system had to be keyed to him. The Secret Service agents were trying to fire at them, but when the controlling system realized it had failed with the initial attack, it switched to signature."

"Signature of what?"

"A personality attack is when a drone hunts for a specific person. Signature attack is when they look for an activity, not a specific person. The algorithm must have switched tactics."

"What other tactics might they have?"

"I'm afraid we're about to find out."

"We're sitting ducks," Chuck said. "We need to move." He stepped past Lauren and grabbed the limo keys from a set of hooks on the wall by the stairs.

"Hold on," Archer said. He held one hand out at Chuck. "Damon, you think this could help us somehow? That they're autonomous? What was your idea?"

"These things operate using image recognition. They're guided by AI, especially in swarms in tight quarters. Probably not human-operated. Maybe the fleet of them is being guided remotely, but not individually."

"You're telling me there's nobody out there?" Archer said.

42

"I'm saying a little camouflage might go a long way if we're going to go out there." He kicked the gold-and-red leaves across the cement floor. "This close to Washington? I don't think our attackers have any overflight capability. This is highly controlled airspace, even with what's going on."

"So, there's no Predator drone with Hellfire missiles hovering above us?" Chuck said, the keys in his hand.

"Only ours, if there are."

"The Chechen terrorists seemed pretty good at owning our assets last time," I pointed out.

"That was a sneak attack. A sucker punch. And they didn't own military assets, just some commercial ones. Big difference."

Archer said, "GPS and overwatch satellites might be out, but our military still has radar. The 1st Fighter Wing at Langley Air Force Base is right around the corner, and they scramble whole fighter wings when a flock of birds paints a blob on their screens."

Chuck nodded. "And there's gotta be an AWACS orbiting over Washington."

"English, please?" I said.

"He means," Archer said, "our military has aircraft up there watching. Even right now. Whoever is attacking us is keeping low to the ground. Small radar signatures."

"The whole military is still on DEFCON 2," Chuck said.

"And yet they just attacked us here," I said, my voice rising. "Again, and we were defended to the teeth."

Chuck said, "Only small drones? Is that what you're saying?" He walked around in circles, his mind obviously going in them as well. "What we need is a diversion, then get the hell out."

I said, "We cover ourselves with leaves? Walk out of here? Is that your plan, Damon?" It sounded idiotic and suicidal.

"You go out there first," Chuck said to Damon. "Proof of concept."

Damon ignored him. "Image recognition keyed to human forms and faces will be fooled by simple camouflage. Enough that they won't target lock. The rain will help. It's our best shot."

"I say our best shot is inside this bulletproof tank," Chuck said. He still had the limo door open.

I asked Damon, "But you just said they might change behavior?"

"They will. That much I'm certain of."

"You think we can fool them with leaves? Those things just killed an entire platoon's worth of Secret Service in minutes flat." I trusted Damon on technical stuff, but he was asking me to trust my entire family's life on his guess. "You said you've never seen anything like these?"

"Not operational, but—"

"Why don't we burn the damn house down? I've never liked it much, anyway," the senator said.

He was in a corner that held gardening equipment. Beside a big mower sat two red gas canisters. He picked one up and the liquid in it sloshed around. "Send out a smoke signal. Phone lines and the internet and meshnet might be down, but there's no way anybody out there is going to miss this house going up in flames. Even in this rain."

I said, "What if someone is still alive inside?" Even as extreme as this situation was, this seemed callous to throw out so suddenly. I glanced at Lauren. Her mother was on the other side of that door, but I was certain she hadn't survived.

"Nobody is responding," Archer said. "There were dozens of those things in there. Everybody inside is dead. I guarantee that."

"We're still alive," I pointed out. He could *guarantee* it?

"I'm calling out on all frequencies. No response."

"It's okay," Lauren said quietly. "We need to do whatever we have to, to save the kids." She gripped Olivia tight. "If there is anyone alive in there, they'd be able to get out—"

"Not if they're injured," Damon said quietly.

"Trust me, if anyone was alive, they would be responding," Archer repeated.

"And whoever comes, those drones will kill any first responders," Chuck said. "Or whoever's waiting for us will kill them on the way in. You think those Chechen terrorists aren't out there? That they're still on that ship?"

We hadn't seen the end of the show. The TV had gone silent now. Had the emergency power been cut as well? We had no idea if they found anyone on that freighter or not.

"One way or the other," Damon said. "The Chechens are definitely targeting Senator Seymour. This is the second attack on this house in almost as many days."

"They might not be targeting Senator Seymour," I mumbled.

"Why do you say that?" Archer said.

"I killed her brother."

Silence as the words sunk in.

Tears streamed down Lauren's face. "Was Terek really her brother?"

"That's what Russian intel confirmed," Archer replied.

Chuck stopped circling. "We need to move. Now." He walked to the limo and clicked the key in his hand. The lights blinked and the door locks clicked open. "I say we get everybody in this thing and drive hard and fast—"

"They scouted this place," Archer said. "They know the limo is in here."

"You don't know that."

"Aren't you a restaurant owner?"

"Yeah."

"So, not a tactical strategy expert. If there *is* anybody waiting, they're blocking the roads. Snipers in the trees. Someone or some*thing* is out there. We need to do what they won't expect. Senator, you sure you want to burn this place down?"

Chuck had the door of the limo open. "What about first responders?"

"If we draw the adversary away, make clear we're not inside, there wouldn't be any reason to continue the attack."

"Unless they just want to kill people. These are terrorists, right?"

"This isn't random. It's targeted. Like Damon said. And burning the house down would make a good diversion."

Lauren said, "This is a trap. We can't stay still." She turned to Damon. "What's your plan?"

Damon turned to Archer and Senator Seymour. "Is there anything sticky in here?"

Archer wiped a red spatter from his face. A deep cut across his forehead oozed. "Apart from my blood?"

Chapter 6

Luke hung in the air at the edge of the stairs leading up into the house. My son was in his sneakers and red shorts and the English rugby league T-shirt I gave him in the summer. The senator held him up by his waist, and they both hung onto the side of the steel cabinet that was leaning against the wooden pallets.

Archer had jammed one of the red gas canisters in the heart of the pile of wood. We soaked a rag in the gasoline and stuck this into the top of the container. He made sure it was half empty. An improvised explosive device, he explained, and splashed the rest of the fuel across the pallets.

The senator grunted as he tried to hold my son in place.

With one shaking hand, my little boy held the lighter closer to the rag. "When should I do it?"

"Don't do anything yet," I called back. "Luke! You hear me?"

"I hear you." His voice caught. He was as terrified as I was.

The limo's engine raced.

I glimpsed at the tachometer. In the red.

In the confines of the garage, it felt like we were toying with a caged rhinoceros. We had the two back wheels of the twenty-foot Escalade stretch limo jacked off the ground, and the monster swayed and vibrated as the twelve-cylinder engine roared.

Exhaust spewed from the dual tailpipes.

47

Chuck held my belt—in case this went sideways, and I got snagged in the limo if it fell off the jack—while I balanced headfirst through the open driver's-side door. My face right down, below the seat. I jammed a log from the woodpile against the accelerator, so the pedal hit the floor. "Pull me back," I yelled over the noise.

Archer was at the rear, hanging onto the fender with his weapon slung across his back. "We good?"

"Now, Luke!" Chuck screamed. "Luke, light it now!"

I took two steps toward my son, but Chuck held me back with his good hand. "Let him do it."

Luke clicked the lighter once, then twice. A small orange flame appeared. It leapt onto the rag stuffed into the gas canister. His eyes wide, my son looked back at us.

"Hurry, get back here," Chuck said to the senator.

He lowered Luke to the cement as the flame licked higher and engulfed the whole red canister. We waited for them to run to us, both crouching, and I grabbed Luke and lifted him from the ground as we cleared the other side of the limo at a sprint.

Archer was already by the garage door in front of the limo, next to the keypad.

I ripped up the edge of a gray tarp we had drizzled with contact cement we'd found on the workbench. Lauren crouched under the tarp with Olivia in her arms. Damon knelt beside her with his backpacks. The senator, Chuck, Luke, and I huddled beneath it with them and did our best to hide.

The tarp trapped the exhaust stink. Dark beneath the cover, except for the dim glow of Damon's phone. He had it in front of him, watching it intently.

Archer must have pushed the garage door opener, because I heard the clicking groan of the mechanism come to life over the roar of the limo's engine. The tarp lifted into the air as Archer pulled himself under. Through a gap between the edge of our cover and the cement, beyond the garage door as it pulled open, I glimpsed a hovering cloud of beady red dots.

"Get the edges down," Archer whispered urgently.

A gush of wet autumn air slid past my hands against the pavement. With Olivia wrapped around her neck, my wife had hold of a frayed brown rope with both hands.

The garage door whirred and clacked further open. The whine of the ornithopter bots grew louder, but now there was no wall between us. We had only the crinkled cover of the tarp to protect us.

"Now, do it now," Chuck said.

Lauren pulled on the brown rope.

Olivia squealed. I grabbed her from my wife and whispered, "Honey, quiet, quiet," as softly as I could and put my hand across her mouth.

"It won't—" Lauren hauled back on the rope again.

The limo's engine roared.

The cement beneath my sneakers vibrated through the soles and into my legs as I squatted and tensed, making myself ready to run. It seemed insane to sit still. I sensed the machines searching beyond the cover of the tarp, the unfeeling minds processing and assessing, the image of the open garage door imprinted in a million matrices and distilled down.

Her teeth bared, Lauren grimaced and yanked again.

"Pull, baby," I said, "you gotta—"

She tumbled back against Damon and knocked him to the pavement as she fell. A deafening squeal over the clattering of the jack skidding across the cement. The stink of burning rubber. The furiously spinning wheels bounced off the pavement once, twice. Flecks of shredded tire skittered under the tarp. The limo careened into the side of the garage door in a rending screech of metal.

Olivia's body tensed as if an electric current coursed through it. I felt her scream through my hand clamped over her mouth. "It's okay," I whispered, "quiet, baby, be quiet."

The squeal of the limo's tires receded as it pulled away and sped up. The suffocating stench of burning rubber made my eyes water and burned my throat. Through holes in the old tarp, orange flames flickered. A blast of heat and light flattened the tarp against us, and the plastic cover felt like it melted against my face.

"I'm away," Damon whispered.

Another screech of metal and distant roar as the limo hit the outer brick wall of the driveway. That was a hundred feet away. The noise of it receded as the car bounced and raced off, replaced by the crackling pop of burning wood. The flames had already spread across the ceiling of the garage.

"Stay still," Archer commanded. In the dim light and shifting shadows under the tarp, illuminated by the glow of the flames spreading above us, his hands and arms were dimly visible, the fingers spread wide. "Hold still. Damon, you see anything?"

"Three or four in pursuit, the rest went after the limo."

"Any signal?"

"Nothing so far."

"Is it still there?" Archer asked.

"Yeah, it's still there."

I released my hand from Olivia's mouth to let her breathe. She whimpered but didn't scream.

Luke was beside Damon, their faces lit by the glow of the screen. We had positioned one of Damon's drones by the edge of the garage door, so once the limo cleared it, he used his controller to fly the drone away. It gave us the only clear set of eyes outside.

That, and maybe the cell phone strapped to the bottom of it, might get us a line of communication out, if we could get it high enough. If someone else was close enough.

I leaned over to have a look. For an instant, a grainy image of the limo flashed on the screen as it raced up the road. The image wobbled. Damon urged his drone higher and away.

"Let's move," Archer whispered. "Follow my lead."

I handed Olivia back to Lauren, and with her and Luke and the senator in the middle, Chuck and Damon—who left the drone on automatic pilot as it climbed away—and I formed a perimeter as we began to crouch-walk out of the garage with the tarp covering us.

We had spread the leaves across it, and hopefully enough of them stuck. As many, Damon had decided, as needed to fool the image recognition. Break up any solid areas. Confuse the pattern detection systems.

It seemed a good plan five minutes ago, but as we cleared the edge of the house, I felt naked. Those things were out there, above us, hunting. Searching.

I tensed, expecting the buzzing whine of one of the little bastards diving at us.

"Dad, I'm scared," Luke whimpered. He held onto the hem of my T-shirt.

"Me too. Listen to Archer, okay?"

As one, we inched onto the asphalt of the driveway, then sideways onto the concrete walkway. Archer pulled the tarp forward. Away from the walkway. To the grass. Damon had said to avoid anything that would give high contrast. We needed to blend in. They trained these things to hunt for the outlines of people, for faces and arms and limbs. Don't present them a target, move slow, Damon had explained.

Fat drops of rain pelted the tarp pulled tight over us. They hammered down on it like it was a drum. Loud. We hadn't talked about that. Was it too noisy? Did these things listen?

"Keep moving," Archer said. He didn't bother to whisper.

He crab-walked sideways, quicker, but not too fast. I wanted to run, to sprint away as quick as I could, but I gripped the tarp and willed myself to keep pace with the others. We edged past the bushes by the side of the garage.

And found the first one.

Damon stepped carefully over the body of one of the Secret Service.

"Senator," Archer said, "retrieve the weapon."

Leo reached down and pulled the submachine gun from the fingers of the dead man. The grass was slick with blood.

"Luke," Damon said, "get the bits of the drone."

Scattered fragments of the bots that had killed the agent were in the grass. My son did his best to collect what he could as we frog-stepped past, putting the bits into the pockets of his shorts.

Step by careful step, we edged as one down the slippery grass slope. Through the dripping holes in the tarp, I saw flames leap into the dark sky from the front of the garage. Tiny red dots hovered high, but they didn't dart toward us.

Rain battered against the tarp.

The smell of cut grass and damp leaves and wet earth.

At the next dead body, the senator collected another gun, and then another. He had to hand one to Luke, which was terrifying. Seeing my eight-year-old gripping a submachine gun seemed wrong, no matter the circumstance, but Lauren and I didn't have an extra hand as we held up our sides of the tarp.

We edged down the incline.

Another noise rose above the drumming rain and the crackle and roar of the inferno engulfing the house—the growing rumble of the Potomac rapids.

The water.

It felt like spiders crawled up and down my arms and back as my hands shook and I tried to keep hold of the covering. Just three nights before, I had almost drowned in that white water, and now I was going back into it. There was still brown sludge from the Potomac swilling in the bottom of my lungs.

I couldn't swim, I had explained to Archer when he came up with the plan. We won't have to, he'd said. There's a boat. The Secret Service had moored one to a small dock they had secured in an eddy current by the bottom of the garden, just before the whitewater of the rapids in front of Turkey Island.

Damon had checked that the craft was still there, using visuals from the drone as he flew it up and away before we left the garage—hopefully taking a few of the nasty drone-bots in pursuit—otherwise we would have tried to quiet-walk away through the forest in the rain and dim light.

I almost wished the boat hadn't been there.

Not almost.

My legs burned from crouching. My hands trembled. My breath came in heaving gasps.

We reached the dock. Its wooden boards creaked beneath my feet. Water sloshed against the rocks by the water's edge.

The roar of the rapids grew.

Rain battered the tarp.

Distant flames disgorged into the sky over the house. We edged farther out and stepped across another dead body. The senator collected the weapon and fumbled for a magazine from the man's vest pocket.

"Everybody in." Archer knelt by the edge of the end of the dock, one hand on the gunwale, the other holding the tarp high.

The craft bobbed and heaved in the waves coming from the river. Damon hopped in first, holding the plastic high so Lauren could hold Olivia as she stepped over the watery gap and in. Luke, with two submachine guns under his left arm, hopped in next, followed by the senator with two more weapons. Chuck knelt by the back, holding up the cover with his right hand while he fumbled with his left to untie the rear rope from its cleat holding the boat in place.

My eyes following the water to the cresting white waves a hundred feet away. The tarp flapped in the wind, out of my grip, and I realized I was unprotected. I looked up.

Chuck reached out to grab me. "Mike, just keep calm, we're almost—"

I tried to jump into the back, but one foot caught the edge and slipped. I went down hard. My left arm grappled for the edge of the boat, for anything to hold on to, but it drifted away.

I fell face-first into the water.

My arms windmilled. I corkscrewed and squirmed, then gasped in a lungful of water. Panic flashed hot in my veins. I catapulted my legs down and suddenly shot out of the water to my waist. It wasn't even three feet deep.

"Mike!" Chuck yelled.

He was in the boat, which spun away from me into deeper water. Luke hung over the gunwale, reaching out.

I realized Archer was behind me, thrashing through the water. He shoved me forward. "Go, go, go," he yelled.

I did my best to push through the deepening water, trying to high-step forward. Strong hands grabbed my waist. Chuck leaned over the edge to me, our hands almost touching. Then Chuck and Luke grabbed me and pulled. I flopped over and into the boat.

A gray, lifeless face stared back at me.

The tarp slithered in the air past us to reveal gray clouds. Crimson dots danced in the wind and rain above us. I got up just in time to see Chuck falling over the edge, into the water.

The rapids thundered as our boat twisted and spun through the current into the maelstrom.

Chapter 7

Hold on," a voice yelled.

Leo, the senator, was at the controls.

We rocked back and forth in the waves. I slicked water from my face. Checked on Luke, who was doing the same to me. Two inert bodies laid at the bottom of the boat in a black pool of sloshing blood. Lauren was under cover of the hardtop at the front. She put Olivia beneath the dash of the controls, away from the open sky.

I looked up. Red dots raced through the rain.

"There!" Damon yelled.

The boat's engine thundered to life and we surged forward, brown water boiling in our wake. A squall of wind dragged a sheet of rain over the churning river. I followed Damon's outstretched hand and finger. Thrashing arms broke the surface. Chuck's face appeared for an instant. The water had already swept him fifty feet downriver. Archer was in the water behind him, taking powerful strokes toward my friend.

Boats. I hated boats. I hated the water even more. Gritting my teeth, I leaned over the edge toward the swirling brown and extended my hand. "Chuck, Archer, over here!"

Chuck still had hold of one end of the tarp, but we were heading in opposite directions. Leo angled the boat. The nose swept up high and around. I lost sight of them.

"Where are they?" Leo yelled.

"Stay there," I heard my wife say to Olivia.

"That way," I hollered to the senator.

I pointed past the bow to the right, toward an outcropping of rocks and bushes I'd last seen Chuck being swept toward. The water frothed and sprayed fifty feet away at the first set of five-foot standing waves as the river tilted downward into the seething rapids.

"Mike!" Lauren was behind me. "Get down. Get hold of something. And Luke, grab your father." She knelt on the deck and picked up one of the guns.

I grabbed a seat by the rear of the boat and crouched but kept my eyes ahead. I couldn't see any sign of Chuck. Again, I looked up and shielded my eyes from the rain, strained to see any scarlet dots against the scudding gray clouds.

"Everyone get a tight grip and stay low. We're going to shoot the rapids. I know this water. It's a short stretch." Leo brought the nose of the boat around again and headed straight at the foaming water rushing toward us.

"Are you sure we sh—"

The first crunching impact snapped my mouth closed halfway through the word. I had squatted for balance, but the floorboards rushed up and doubled me over. I slammed into the deck.

And went airborne the next instant.

Slow motion as the boat arced through the air. I still had hold of the seat with my left hand and hung tight as my body spun sideways in the air. Luke had wedged himself almost under the seat. A hand grabbed me from behind.

We hit the second wave.

I hammered back into the deck.

A mountain of water flooded over the bow and sluiced in a sheeting roar over the windshield and hardtop. Olivia screamed. Pain lanced in my right knee; my left shoulder felt like it dislocated as it wrenched behind me. The boat went into the air again, but not as high this time. It tilted sickeningly sideways.

Leo gunned the engine.

We lurched back upright and shot forward, skipping back into the air. I held onto a gunwale cleat and scanned the frothing whitecaps we sped through. A metallic tang in my mouth. I spat out a mouthful of blood. There. Was that a hand? "Leo, right there, they're —"

A hand yanked me over again as I tried to stand up.

"Mike, I said to get down!" my wife yelled.

She crouched above me as I tumbled to the deck. She swept back and forth with one of the Secret Service weapons in her hands, the butt of the rifle against her shoulder. The boat bucked and twisted through the waves, spray flying over us, but Lauren remained steady, her eyes scanning the sky behind us.

The first volley of gunfire was almost deafening.

My head was right beside her weapon. I put my hands to my ears. The muzzle flashed. She repositioned and fired again, this time lowering to one knee. She swore and let rip another burst. I followed the line of her gun to the flickering dot racing toward us. I tensed to jump up and wrap my body as a shield around her.

The red mote behind us flashed into an orange fireball that tumbled into frothing water in our wake.

"There's more coming," she yelled and pointed. "Mike, Damon, get guns and start firing."

Through the rain in the distance, flickers of scarlet.

A blast of air and something whirred skyward beside me. I thought it was one of the attacking drones but then recognized the heavier black bulk of one of Damon's rising into the air. Somehow, he launched it.

"I'll try to draw them away," Damon said.

I scrambled to find a gun on the deck. Found one and picked it up. "What do I do?"

"Mike, goddamn it." My wife put her weapon under her shoulder and took mine. She pulled back a handle on its side, then let go. The mechanism clicked into place. She flipped a switch on the side. "The safety is off. Just aim and pull the trigger, put the stock into your shoulder."

I swore that the first thing I would do after taking swimming lessons was go to a firing range. I said, "Damon, do you see them?"

We had cleared the big standing waves at the head of the rapids and shot down into the choppy water curving toward the right. The engine gunned high as the senator tried to put as much distance between us and the tiny killer drones as he could.

"Do you see Chuck?" I asked again.

Damon had a bird's-eye view from the camera on his drone. I held my weapon up and scanned the clouds for red dots, my finger trembling on the trigger. The boat sped into the calm waters at the bottom of the rapids. We just might outrun the little bastards.

"Damon, any sign of Chuck? Archer?"

"I don't trust that guy."

"Archer?"

"You think it was a coincidence he was the only government agent that survived the attack?" Damon was close enough to me that we didn't have to yell over the grinding of the engine. "He's not FBI. He's not Secret Service. Who the hell does he work for?"

I hadn't thought about it. Leo seemed fine with him, so I assumed Archer was part of the team. My mind flitted back to seeing him in the bathroom, a black pouch filled with needles and syringes open on his knees.

"Mike, twelve o'clock," Lauren said.

"I can't draw them away," Damon said. "They're not following my drone. They're coming. I'll bring it back around and try again."

A red dot wavered in the rain behind us. The wind rushed through my hair. We had to be doing thirty or forty miles per hour. How fast were these things?

The pinprick of light grew larger.

Faster than we were moving.

Our diversions and cover had been clever enough for us to escape the house, but now we were out in the open. And the machines knew where we were.

I raised my gun. Tried to aim it. Pulled the trigger.

The recoil spun my weapon tilting high into the air. Lauren's gun stuttered beside me.

"Go to the right!" Damon said. "Right. Right!"

Lauren fired again. I aimed and pulled the trigger, this time doing a better job of keeping the muzzle down. Another red dot appeared in the rain. The boat angled almost forty-five degrees to my left as Leo turned us.

"Do you see them?" I asked Damon. I held on to stop from toppling into Lauren.

He pointed almost at the bow. Just visible on the shore, a figure waved at us.

"Who is that?" Leo called out. "Secret Service?"

"No," Damon said. "But head over."

Lauren fired again in a staccato burst, then again. "Whatever you're doing, hurry," she yelled.

The boat slowed. The senator said, "Mike, you sure about this?"

I wiped away water dripping down my face. "Damon, who is that?"

"Trust me."

"Mike?" Leo called out again.

"Two more bogies," Lauren yelled. "Three. Four. Move this boat!"

She pulled the magazine from the submachine gun, tossed it to the deck, and reloaded. She knelt to a stable position, took aim, and fired in an unending stream, sweeping the weapon back and forth. I looked back at the red dots racing toward us and realized they were now hunting my wife. I held Luke behind me and clumsily raised my own weapon.

Chuck thrashed in the swirling brown water. He knew getting Mike anywhere near a boat was a bad idea and had planned ahead. Made sure he was in front of his friend, had hold of him when he got near the boat.

Mike had defied the odds and gone straight into the drink anyway.

A wave swept over Chuck and he gagged in a mouthful of water and spat it back out.

The tarp had swept away from the boat when he'd fallen in after hauling Mike out of the water. With only one good arm and one real hand, Chuck had to give it his all. Which was too much, as transferring momentum had sent him sprawling over the edge.

At least Chuck could swim.

With two arms.

He wasn't doing very well with just one. His left had been in the sling, which he'd taken off when they went down over the grass, but the arm was still useless. He took a bullet in the shoulder three days before. Not even three days ago. More like two and a half.

Chuck took in a deep lungful of air and held it. Better to float at the top than sink.

He used his good hand and arm to flutter the water and try to orient himself feet-first to the rapids. From his perspective in the water, the frothing waves looked ten feet high. He glimpsed the boat roaring into the waves and going airborne before he lost sight of them.

Rapids weren't a big deal.

The key was not getting caught in growlers. Those recirculating currents in the big standing waves. He just had to float down, keep his feet up and—

"Chuck!" someone yelled.

It was Archer. The man took powerful strokes like a water polo player, his head high in the water, his weapon still slung across his back. Chuck thought he had made it back into the boat. What was he doing here?

Chuck didn't need rescuing.

The river angled down. The current accelerated and sucked him over the first ledge into a big standing wave just as Archer reached him. The man grabbed the tarp floating in the water behind them. "Get under this," he yelled as he pulled the plastic cover over them both.

"I don't want to get—"

Chuck's mouth filled with water and he submerged. Kicking his feet and pushing water down with his right hand, he spun back up to the surface, but not into clear air. His face was pressed straight against the plastic tarp now pinning him below the surface.

He felt Archer's body roll over top of him. The man's thick arms and torso submerged Chuck again. The water roared in his ears, spinning and turning him as they dropped through the incline and into another surging wave.

Chuck grappled with Archer on top of him.

What the hell was this guy doing?

Trying to drown him?

Chapter 8

"M ike!" Leo screamed over the blazing submachine gun's stuttering fire.

The figure waved at us again from the shore. Red dots raced below the clouds.

"Just move!" I yelled back. "Head for whoever that is."

Was it a hiker? That didn't make sense. A passive observer would have heard all the gunfire, seen the flames. They wouldn't be waving at us to come to them. They would be running, if anything. Away from us. And if it were the attackers, they would be firing *at* us.

Wouldn't they?

The boat surged forward again. I stumbled as the deck tilted back. Luke had his hands over his ears. I shouldered my weapon, did my best to steady myself, and took aim. Pulled the trigger. Almost fell backward again.

We got lucky with the first one Lauren hit.

How she even managed that was a miracle.

I counted six. Seven. Maybe a dozen dots raced toward us. We needed a miracle now. Twelve more of them. At least.

"We're going to hit the shore hard," Leo yelled over the noise. "It's a muddy incline right ahead so we should slide up— but we'll stop fast. I'm going to get Olivia. Damon, help Luke get up on the side and jump when we hit. Mike. Lauren. You guys gear up to get clear as well."

Lauren released her trigger and stood.

She gripped my arm to steady herself. We both looked back at the red dots, then at the tree line racing toward us. Thirty feet from the shore, Leo pulled back on the throttle, let go of the wheel, and leaned over to get Olivia. He clambered to the side of the boat.

Damon had Luke in his arms.

"I love you," Lauren said. She hopped on the gunwale to her side.

I just had enough time to swing myself to the side when the bow catapulted up. I spun out and through the air, the weapon flying from my hands, my body cartwheeling into open space before impacting wet dirt and grass. The boat shot forward into the trees and bushes as I tumbled to a stop.

And sprang to my feet.

Leo had jumped early and landed in the water. He was just getting up. Olivia in his arms, wailing. Damon and Luke had leaped to my right and flew into bushes.

I didn't feel any pain.

Didn't feel anything at all.

I scanned for my weapon, then looked back at the red dots descending on us.

I had no gun. All I had was my body to protect my family. Where was Luke?

"Mike!" Lauren screamed in an agonizing wail.

The buzzing whine of the attacking drones grew to a crescendo.

A buzzing red dot fell from the sky, headed straight at Olivia and Leo. He did his best to lunge through the foot or two of water by the muddy water's edge, but he wasn't fast enough.

Chuck gagged up a mouthful of sludge. Now he knew how Mike had felt on the Mississippi when he fell in. Chuck sloshed on all fours through the water and mud by the edge of the river. Almost on all fours. His left arm was still mostly useless. His crawl was more of a three-ring circus act.

He spat up another gob of brown. "Were you trying to kill me?"

"Not very successfully," Archer replied.

The man was already out of the water and crouched behind a rock. After Chuck had almost drowned underneath it, the tarp had been sucked down the river. So much for camouflage. Chuck had struggled out of the main current by himself, but Archer grabbed to help him when they neared the sludgy bottom in the eddy current.

"Do you see them?"

"I don't see anything yet."

The river had dragged them a few hundred yards below the rapids. Chuck was certain he'd heard gunfire when he was rolling through the last of the waves, but then everything had gone silent. Which could be good. Maybe they got away.

But it could be bad.

Chuck heaved himself from the water, stumbled over jumbled rocks, and collapsed into cover between scraggly bushes. The rain had diminished from a downpour, but heavy raindrops still dotted the turgid waters of the Potomac. "Anything in the air?"

"Nothing I can see."

The steady, distant hiss of the rapids and birds singing in the canopy of oaks wasn't reassuring. The smell of a campfire drifted through the trees. Had the boat raced ahead of them? It couldn't be more than fifteen minutes down the Potomac to DC from here, maybe less aided by the strong current. That boat was small but looked fast.

The relative silence was unnerving.

That smell of smoke wasn't a campfire.

The house.

The fire.

No sound of sirens. No distant flashing lights through the trees. No helicopters on a rescue mission. No sounds of screaming jets.

The four hundred acres of Scott's Run Nature Preserve occupied this side of the Potomac just downriver from the senator's mansion.

Over the past few days, Chuck had come down here for walks through the trails. It was amazing this slice of nature was so close, next to the Capital Beltway. Yesterday, he had a packed lunch in the preserve at the site of Burling Cabin, a homestead from the old days.

All that remained now was the stone chimney and some foundation rocks, but Chuck heard that old man Burling used to come here well into his nineties, before he passed in 1966. Chuck loved that the old codger had refused to allow even one tree to be cut to bring in power or telephone lines. Old school. Just like Chuck.

He struggled to his knees. Scanned the trees for Archer, who had disappeared.

The man was like a cat. Somehow, when he got out of the water, he didn't seem wet, like the water knew better and slid off his hair and clothes before it got into trouble. Archer sprang up and into the underbrush the second they got here. Gave the impression that he would always land on his feet if knocked off a table.

Chuck, by contrast, felt like a wet sack of cardboard. He coughed up another mouthful of water. Searched his pockets and came up with a ballpoint pen as a weapon.

Not much of a prepper, he laughed grimly to himself. He gripped the pen in his fist. Better than nothing.

"Archer?" he whispered as loud as he thought prudent. Then louder, "Archer!"

"Keep quiet," came the hushed reply. The man materialized from the underbrush to crouch beside Chuck.

The light was dim, the rainclouds low and moving fast above the treetops, but the air had a crisp and almost electric overtone above the drifting smoke. On second thought, the smoke didn't smell like a campfire. It had the sickly sweet and acrid stench of burning plastic. Chuck searched between the leaves against the sky for any red spots.

"You got any more of those?" Chuck pointed at the carbine in Archer's hands.

The man shook his head slowly as he scanned back and forth with his weapon.

"What were you interrogating Damon about back there?"

"Just doing my job."

"Who was the Chinese guy you flashed a picture of?"

"His father."

"Damon's never met his father."

"Strange that a colonel of counterintelligence at the MSS has never contacted his son."

"MSS?"

"Chinese Ministry of State Security. Like the KGB on twenty-first-century steroids."

"You can't be serious."

"I read the report on you, advising Mr. Indigo not to lie to the state police about the terrorists at that checkpoint. He did anyway."

"He was trying to be nice."

"Uh-huh." Archer scanned the tree line. "I'm no drone expert, but what's one thing they all need to operate?"

"I didn't know we had to study for an exam."

"GPS. *Especially* autonomous ones. Bonus question: Do *we* have any GPS? And by we, I mean anyone in America?"

Chuck didn't have an answer for that. He didn't need to. Even the US military was flying blind, from what the senator had said.

Archer said after a pause, "Just keep down and keep quiet."

"What's in the backpack?"

"If I told you, I'd have to kill you." He flashed Chuck a smile. "Stay here. I'll be back in a minute. I think the boat hit the shore back there."

In two bounding but soundless steps the man disappeared again.

Chuck planted his right fist, the one with the pen in it, into the mud by his knees and leveraged himself into a squat. At least he was now on his feet.

That weapon in Archer's hands. Chuck recognized it. A Colt M4A1. A favorite of NATO special forces. Basically, a lighter and shorter variant of the M16. Not something you got off the shelf at Walmart.

He said he thought the boat landed upriver from them?

The birds singing and the pitter-patter of rain wormed nausea deep into the pit of Chuck's gut. His first thought was of Luke and Olivia. The children. The sick-gut sensation morphed into brimming anger. He gripped the pen tighter in his fist and got fully to his feet.

If the boat landed farther up from them, maybe his friends were already looking for Chuck. Which meant they might be risking their lives to find him—either that, or they were injured or worse and needed him back up there somewhere.

"Mike," Chuck whispered urgently. "Lauren," he said louder. "Archer?"

He scanned the river.

Nothing.

He knew these trails. Better than Archer, he wagered. He had an idea of the topography. Chuck took one step, and then another, and began a staggering run along a trail at the water's edge, his fist holding the pen out ahead and swinging for balance. Through the trees to his left, he spotted glittering orange. The growing inferno of the house flickered.

He skidded to a stumbling stop.

His blood felt like it drained from his spine and out through his feet. His stomach a bag of needles. He froze.

Behind him, he sensed that high-pitched whine, like a giant mosquito. A beat later, right ahead on the path, a beady scarlet eye blazed. A bug-drone beelined straight at him.

Chapter 9

Ellarose wondered what her dad was doing.

"Honey, sweetheart, why don't you go outside?" her mom said.

Even when her mom was being annoying, Ellarose still liked the sing-songy way she talked. She loved her mother's long honey-colored hair and freckles. One day she would be just like her.

"Just five more minutes?"

"Honey Rose, you know the rules. Thirty min—"

"I know, I know."

She was only allowed half an hour of video games a day, but Ellarose was *right* in the middle of a siege in *Call of Duty*. *Modern Warfare* was by far her favorite of the series, and she and her dad would play late at night sometimes. When her mom was asleep.

It was annoying that the internet had gone down earlier.

Ellarose couldn't connect with the rest of her squad, so she played solo this round. The phone had cut out during the call with her father. That was the landline, her mother had said. The generator had come on, because Ellarose heard the noise of the diesel in the basement. Vented, of course. Dad always said to make sure you vented a generator.

Another power cut.

She didn't get to see her father's face when he saw the picture of that trout she caught the day before. That was the main thing she was excited about when they called. Why no video chat? No internet, her mother had explained; it had shut off again. Not having the internet felt like one of Ellarose's arms had been cut off.

"Ellarose," her mother said.

Momma only used her full name when she was mad.

"Yes, Susan?"

"Ella—"

"Okay, okay." She leaned forward and turned off the PS4. The TV screen went blank. No cable television either. The satellites were all gone. Ellarose knew that much.

"Now, go on. It's a beautiful day." Her mother had Bonham in her arms.

Her little brother was being a *pain in the ass* today. That's what her dad would say. Her little brother was only four, still a baby, and Ellarose needed to be an adult and help out. She was seven. Almost seven. In two months, she would be. Her birthday was right before Thanksgiving.

"I'll go out to finish the bridge, okay?" That was her new project. A dam and bridge over the stream out by the driveway on the way in.

"And please, don't call me Susan," her mom said and turned away.

"I'm sorry, Momma. I'm being funny."

"Your dad teaches you to be funny too much."

Ellarose knew better than to poke the bear. She smiled and got up off the couch. That was another of her dad's ways of talking about her mom. The bear. Susie. That was what her mom liked to be called, but mostly she liked just being called mom.

But never Susan.

Everyone called her dad Chuck.

His name was Charles. She liked Charles better. Chucky was the name of the mean doll in a movie her cousin Luke got her to watch. Charles was the name of a prince, and she was his princess, he always said. Charles Mumford. That was her dad's full name. Like the band, he liked to joke, except it was Mumford and Son and Daughter.

Ellarose skipped to the door of the cabin and opened it, then pushed back the screen door. It was chilly outside, so she stopped and took her North Face from the hook. Only 4 p.m., but the sun set early behind the Blue Ridge mountaintops to the west of the cabin. In September it was still hot as heck back in Nashville, but up here in the mountains the leaves had already started to fall from the trees.

Every thousand feet of altitude, the temperature dropped four degrees, her dad had explained to her. The climate up there was like the northern states, so the trees were different than in Nashville, even the animals. Bobcats and black bears up here, he said.

The two black Escalades were still in the gravel driveway—one her family and the Mitchells had driven in from Farmer Joe's in Kentucky, and one the two men that were sent to help out came up here in. That's what her mom said. Help out. They had guns. They weren't helping clean, Ellarose knew.

"Thomas!" her mother yelled through the door. "Could you keep an eye on Ellarose?"

The black-clad man was at the end of the driveway. He waved and nodded and began walking back toward the house. Morty, the other one, wasn't anywhere to be seen. Ellarose liked talking to them.

They were cool. Like John Travolta in *Pulp Fiction* cool. She liked her movies. Was a movie buff, just like her dad.

She grabbed her walking stick from beside the door and skipped across the gravel, her mind still on that last campaign in *Call of Duty*. Was Urzikstan a real country? She liked to play on the

Hardened settings, which meant she died more but never got stuck.

Ellarose whistled out a birdsong, the trilling whistle of a grasshopper sparrow. She and her dad played games all the time, imitating the birds out here. They even used them when playing *Call of Duty*, using different bird calls to signal different moves.

She said hello to Thomas, who smiled and gave her a high-five, and she explained she was just going down to the stream. He nodded and said not to go too far.

At the end of the driveway, where the fir trees began, she took a right turn onto the path that led down to the stream. That's where she caught the trout the day before. Farther down from there was where Tony was buried. She was too young to remember all that, but her dad had told her Tony had saved their lives one day after the CyberStorm. He had died to save them, he said. She didn't like the idea of dying, but her dad said it was natural.

He said that death was a part of life.

Ellarose reached the stream and considered the rushing water. The branches she had put down the day before had been washed away already. Maybe she should put down a stone or two in the—

"Hey there," someone called out.

Ellarose thought it was Thomas, but that was a woman's voice.

"Hello?" She couldn't see anyone.

"Ellarose," said the voice. A woman appeared twenty feet back along the path. "How are you?"

It took her a second to recognize the lady, and Ellarose relaxed. Long black hair. Pretty face and brown eyes. It was Irena. She was the lady they drove up here with. She had volunteered to go down to the beach to help find Luke's mother. She was brave. And she loved dogs.

Ellarose liked Irena.

Then she got excited. "Did you drive up with my dad?"

Irena came closer. She smiled that beautiful smile that Ellarose loved so much. "No, I did not come here with your dad. Did anyone else come up?"

"Not so far."

"Do you know where your uncle Mike is?"

Ellarose frowned. Irena had a carbine strapped to a vest. Guns were the norm in her family, but that wasn't a hunting weapon. And then she thought, wait, wasn't Irena doing something bad? She and Terek had done something awful, but her mom said she would explain more later, when her dad got here tomorrow.

Something about Irena's smile changed as she neared, Ellarose thought. The grin became a smirk and reminded Ellarose of an animal she had seen at the zoo. What was it called? A hyena? Ellarose took a step back.

Irena swung the muzzle of the carbine around. "Ellarose, don't move."

Chapter 10

"**M**ike, do not move," my wife Lauren said.

Twenty red dots hung suspended in a cloud above us. Halted in space, as if God had pressed pause.

The boat engine whined to a stop behind us. After slamming into the mud-and-grass shoreline of the eddy pool below the rapids, the boat had rocketed through the bushes and small trees at the water's edge and slid fifty feet into the forest until jamming between larger trunks.

A kind of silence descended.

Just the hissing white noise of the rapids and pattering of rain against leaves overhead. And if I listened hard, the humming whir of the bug-drones' motors holding them preternaturally still in the gusting wind.

Those things weren't dead. God hadn't pressed pause on them.

They were resting.

Or something.

One of the vicious machines hovered a few feet above the senator, who cowered below it in the ankle-deep water sluicing past his feet. He wasn't cringing, I realized. He was bent over, cradling my little girl below him, his back to the drone-bot on its final attack.

"Uncle Leo," Lauren said, "come over this way. Slowly."

She had her weapon up and pointed directly at the bug-bot over the senator's head.

I said, "Damon, what the hell is going on?"

"I think they've been reset."

"Luke, you okay, buddy?"

"I'm fine, dad," my son said. "Are you?"

"I'm good."

That wasn't exactly the truth. My left leg almost buckled as the adrenaline spike subsided. Air came in and out of my lungs in heaving gasps. I trembled like one of the leaves rustling overhead. My eyes located the gun in the thick grass by the water's edge, but I wasn't sure if I should move. I stood stock-still, like I was caught in a game of Simon Says.

"Damon, what do you mean, reset?" I asked. "What happened to them?"

The senator stepped slowly and carefully through the mud and onto the grassy bank, still holding my sobbing daughter below him. He glanced above and behind at the red dot of the bug-bot that had stopped just short of him.

"I got it," Lauren said to him. "If it budges an inch, I'll kill it. Keep coming to me."

Damon said, "I'm not sure."

"But you said reset? Can we shoot them?"

"I wouldn't do anything to threaten them. Might switch back their programming. These things are in an automated kill mode, which seems to have been flipped off, but I'm sure they have a self-preservation routine."

"So no target practice?"

Those things were little kamikaze dive bombers. Hovering still like this, I could see what I thought had to be the explosive charges hanging below the spindly metal necks and beating wings. This close and holding motionless, even I might be able to pick off a few.

"I would not advise it," said a voice.

The accent was vaguely German, but clearly American.

Lauren swung her weapon around and scanned for the speaker.

"Damon," said the voice, "are these your friends?"

"Yeah, they are."

"Can you ask them to put down their weapons?"

"Damon," I said, "who is that?" I remained motionless.

"Ma'am, can you please not point that at me?"

Inching my head slowly to my left, I moved my eyes far enough to see a lanky, black-clad silhouette emerge from the bushes next to the boat. The light was dim, but I saw it was a man with blond hair. He had his hands up but held a square gray metal box in one of them.

"We need to hurry," the man said. "You can move. They won't target you if you don't threaten them. At least, until their signal is reset. I don't know how much time we have."

Lauren kept her weapon aimed at the man's chest. She raised her focus an inch when he emerged fully. He wore a ballistic vest. My wife had to be calculating that a head shot had a better chance of lethality.

"Did you stop those things?" she asked.

"I did," the man replied.

"You were the one waving at us?"

"I was."

"Are you controlling the drones?"

"Not exactly."

"Not exactly?"

"I mean, I'm not *in* control of them. I was only able to stop them."

"Damon, who is this guy?" I asked again. He looked very familiar, but I couldn't quite place him. Had we met before? At a meeting?

And why wasn't Damon answering me?

Lauren asked the man, "Is there anyone else with you?"

"There is nobody else with him," answered a gruff voice. "I scouted the perimeter and followed him in."

Lauren swung her weapon around at the new threat. Another silhouette emerged from the shadows. It was Archer, stepping forward without a sound, his weapon trained on the man.

I said, "Is Chuck with you?"

"He's fine. He's two hundred yards back, waiting for us. Mrs. Mitchell, can you aim somewhere else?"

My wife took her eye from sighting down the barrel, put it back in a moment of indecision, but then lowered her weapon. She slung the strap over her shoulder, then took two steps to her right and took Olivia from Leo. The senator was dripping wet.

"Archer," the senator said, "do we have any backup? Is there anyone—"

"I'm sure the cavalry is on the way." He sidestepped toward me without looking my way, his eyes and gun on the mystery man. "You okay, Mr. Mitchell?" He stole a quick glance at me, decided I didn't have any gaping wounds, and then advanced toward the senator.

Lauren asked the blond man, "If you're not controlling those things, then who is?"

The man answered, "I think we know the answer to that."

"You'll probably be less clever with both kneecaps gone," Archer said. "Try again. One kneecap per answer I don't like."

"The Chechens."

"You know this?"

"I surmise it."

"That's bordering on clever, my friend." Archer lowered his weapon to point at the man's legs. "You know where they are?"

"I have an idea. Close enough."

"To what?"

"To us. We need to move, Mr. Archer. Those drones are going to come back to life any moment."

Archer quick-checked the senator, then my wife and the kids. He gently separated Luke from Damon and whispered for him to go to his dad. Luke ran over and jumped into my arms. I almost fell backward.

Archer asked, "How much time do we have?"

"Seconds. I assure you, I have no desire to die here either." He kept his hands up.

"And how did you disable them?"

"With th—"

Footsteps thudded on the wet path behind me. One person? Two? More? Shielding Luke, I turned away and crouched. A man burst through the bushes.

"Mike, Lauren, holy God I'm happy to see you. Those things, the drones, they've been disabled. Maybe something scrambled them? Somebody's jamming them, I thin—"

Chuck windmilled to a stop.

"I thought I told you to wait," Archer said.

"Who is that?" Chuck blurted as he scanned the faces and pointed.

The mystery man held forward the gray metal box in one hand toward Archer. "As I prize my kneecaps, Mr. Archer, I will finish answering. This is an EMP device."

"Like a nuclear bomb?" Chuck said. "You can't be seri—"

"They also produce EMPs, but this one is more like a giant capacitor. Electromagnetic pulse. Not powerful enough to fry electronics, but ample to disrupt at short distances. I had to wait until all of the attacking drones were in a tight enough radius to—"

"So where are the Chechens?" Archer demanded. He moved his aim from the man's kneecaps to his face. "Only one try at answering the bonus question."

"That way," the man pointed back toward the growing conflagration of the house, now clearly visible between the trees. The rain had stopped.

"At the house?"

"My guess is in the mountains. I triangulated the control signal. We need to move from here." He checked his wristwatch. "It's been seventy-two seconds since I disabled them. Their diagnostics will reset any moment."

Chuck frowned. "What do you mean, in the mountains?"

"The frequency is VHF. Line of sight. To get a reliable signal here, they need to narrowcast from as high a point as possible. My guess is—"

"The mountaintops over Shenandoah?" Chuck's face went a pallid shade of sick.

"That's right. Whether you shoot me or not won't matter, as we will be dead in half a minute if we don't hurry. This device was a one-shot tool until we recharge it. I have a truck we can all fit in."

"There aren't any vehicles near us," Archer said. "I scouted the area. Didn't see anything."

"You wouldn't."

"You realize I don't need to kill you to hurt y—"

"Can we play biggest dick later?" Lauren hurried past Archer and shoved the muzzle of his weapon aside. "Where?" she asked the mystery man.

"This way." He pointed behind himself, past the boat.

Archer glanced up at the hovering red dots of the drones. He lowered his weapon and slung it over his back. "Let's move."

We didn't even know who this guy was, but we were going to follow him? Did everyone else know something I didn't? We'd just escaped from a trap; how did we know this wasn't another one? But there wasn't time to debate.

I followed Archer as he broke into a jog and motioned for the man to lead us. We hustled along a path toward the center of the nature preserve's forest. I held Luke in my already burning arms.

Damon jogged beside me.

"Who is that guy?" I asked him. "He clearly knows you, why didn't you—"

"Tyrell Jakob."

"Tyrell?"

"Jakob."

It took me a second to process.

Of course. That's who he was. I knew his face, but my stressed-out brain hadn't been able to dredge it up.

So, it wasn't God that had pressed pause on those drones, but someone close. The billionaire who owned—*had* owned, I corrected myself—the SatCom constellation and rocket facilities that the Chechen terrorists had hijacked. What on God's green Earth was he doing hiding in the bushes around the corner from Senator Seymour's house? Right when we were attacked? Had *he* sent in these killer drones?

Why would he do that?

We didn't have time to discuss options.

He said the Chechens were in the mountains behind us. How did he know? He *triangulated* a signal? Was that even a thing? It sounded like something a ship captain on a clipper might do.

But the look on Chuck's face when Tyrell had said those words had sent creeping fear jangling through my arm hairs and down into my fingertips and gut. Tyrell said those terrorists were in the *Shenandoah* mountains, at a high altitude.

And there was only one place that could mean.

Chapter 11

"Ellarose?" Susie called out through the kitchen window she'd just opened.

Fresh mountain air swept in. The dogwoods were blooming again, just like six years before.

Bonham wriggled from her grip and slithered between her arms to the floor. Arms windmilling and laughing, he ran as fast as he could away from her. Her four-year-old was being a rascal today, as he often did when daddy wasn't around. When he heard Chuck was coming home tomorrow, Bonham's energy levels went to full nuclear mode.

She couldn't wait for her husband to get back, either.

Susie looked again out the window of their log cabin and scanned for her daughter. Ellarose had to be down at the stream, building her bridge, which was fine, except she had been gone for an hour. It was getting dark. Cooling off.

The seasons came fast at this altitude.

Susie leaned farther out the window and looked left and right across the parking lot.

Odd. She hadn't seen Morty, the other security contractor, in at least an hour. She guessed Thomas was still down at the stream with Ellarose. That made some sense. That was about the last time Susie had seen either of them. Ellarose probably had both down there building her dam for her. Her daughter could charm the spots off a leopard, that's what Chuck always said.

She laughed at herself.

"Bon Bon, get down from there. Please."

If someone could tap this kid's source of power, bottle it up, the world wouldn't need fossil fuels anymore. Climate change solved if humans could figure out where Bonham got all his energy. She smiled. Her son was now climbing a set of wooden shelves built into the wall by the living room window. If he fell from that height, he might hurt himself.

"Bon—" she started to say again but stopped.

Within reason, Susie and Chuck let the kids make their own mistakes. Hurt yourself by sticking your fingers into a fire, and you won't do it again. More effective than nagging them to keep their hands away from flames their whole lives.

The main living area of the cabin was thirty feet across and open, the kitchen, living room, and dining room all one space. A twenty-foot cathedral ceiling arched overhead. The second-floor atrium had doors leading to the four bedrooms, with a stairway leading up and down into the basement, which was dug into the earth.

Huge front windows looked down from the four-thousand-plus feet of altitude here onto the plains of Virginia and DC sixty miles away. Rain clouds still sat heavy below them, but the sky at this height had been clear all day—except now a dark smudge appeared in the near distance.

The whole house was constructed with massive poplar logs, even the shed and outbuildings. Poplar was an underappreciated wood for building homes, Chuck liked to explain to anyone who visited. The tulip poplar here grew to two hundred feet, although it was more closely related to the magnolia than either the tulip or the poplar. It grew straight and almost knot-free, and was a joy to notch and hew, Chuck said.

Not just that, but its R-value for insulation was better than any other wood out there, and it had immense stopping power— that was the final point Chuck loved to tell people. The combination of the huge tulip poplar logs and the cement mortar that bound them could just about stop a tank shell, and easily absorb .50-caliber rounds.

His father had built the place with his grandfather, years before Chuck was born, and before they restricted construction in Shenandoah National Park. No other houses allowed now, which was why they'd snapped up the Baylors' place when it came up. Just two hundred yards through the woods, but getting that cabin together with this one turned their place from a cottage into a compound.

Chuck loved it.

And that this place was literally grandfathered to them.

Chuck had told her about the Burling Cabin Site in the nature preserve next to Senator Seymour's house. How old man Burling used to go there well into his nineties, and wouldn't let anyone cut down trees to put in telephone lines. That's what Chuck wanted to do with this place. Become an old man here.

It was their oasis.

Really more of a bunker.

Chuck's father and grandfather had built the place, but Chuck had rebuilt it from the inside out to be their bolt hole if— and when—civilization disintegrated out there. They didn't wear tinfoil hats or anything, and if she was being honest, she didn't think it would ever come to that. The cabin was more of a hobby. Just about every penny from their restaurant businesses went into this place.

But after what happened six years ago, their desire to be prepared had accelerated.

Other families went to Disney World, but the Mumfords did weapons training and close combat classes and wilderness survival camps on their holidays. In the last two years, they had done some massive construction work here instead of taking trips anywhere. She had married Chuck and everything that came with him—and she loved it, no regrets.

Susie had even done advanced tactical training last year at a boot camp.

It was a bit of a mystery how they'd become the fastest of friends with the Mitchells, who were so different from them. They were CNN people, whereas the Mumfords were Fox. It was that experience when they'd lived in the next apartment over in New York that had bonded them forever. Mike hated guns—Susie wasn't even sure if he could fire one—but Susie had convinced Lauren to take up weapons training.

They even did some hand-to-hand combat classes together. Girl stuff.

Bonham was now about seven feet up from the hardwood floor. He turned to grin at his mother. "I can climb all the way to the top," he proclaimed.

That was another two shelves he planned to scale. Susie decided it was time to intervene. "You fall from there, you'll probably break an arm, and don't scre—"

"Hey, what's that?" Bonham pointed with his left hand, his knees on the shelf below, his right hand the only one keeping a grip.

"Bonham, you keep hold." Susie broke into a jog across the dining area toward the living room.

"Is that a dog?"

"Bon Bon, what did I just tell you?"

Her boy put his left hand back up and steadied himself.

Susie reached out her hands and grabbed her son. He turned and let go to drop into her arms, his mischievousness suddenly gone. She turned in the direction he was looking, just in time to see an animal disappearing.

It was not like any creature she had ever seen before.

The light was dim, and the thing was a hundred or more feet away, but the bounding gait was beyond odd. Something unnatural about it, and the legs—they seemed straight, gray. The body oblong and black and squat. It bounded away like an awkward deer. Or a big dog. A *very* big dog.

A huge murmuration of starlings undulated in the distance over the trees. She'd never seen that up here before. Not this high.

Closer to the horizon, she could see that the dark smudge she'd noticed before wasn't rainclouds. The black smoke curled and billowed from a ridge in the foothills. How had a fire started now? It had just been raining down there.

That gave her a chill.

This place was a fortress, but fires were her nightmare.

No neighbors meant peace and quiet, but it also meant no neighbors. No help. No emergency services for miles—and anyway, right now emergency services had been crippled across the entire nation. No GPS. Not even any power in half the country. Nobody would come up here to dig fire breaks for just two houses.

She was on her own, but then that's what they designed the place for.

"Hello?"

Susie froze in place with Bonham in her arms.

Who was that? Thomas? The timbre of the voice was different, and she had told the two of them to come in whenever they wanted for coffee or the bathroom or whatever. It was someone outside, toward the driveway.

Someone she didn't know.

She reached for the inside pocket of her yoga pants for her keys and clicked a remote. All the locks in the house slid shut at once with a satisfying, coordinated chunking sound. She took a few steps through the living room and peered out the kitchen window.

A young man stood in the gravel driveway, about fifty feet up, behind the two Escalades and near the edge of the fir trees.

He hovered. Looked uncertain. Waved when he saw her.

Susie went to the front door, put Bonham down behind her, and opened it an inch after checking her three and six. "Can I help you?"

"Sorry to bother you, ma'am, but our car broke down on the 55." He hooked the thumb on his right hand and indicated back up the driveway. He was wearing only a Black Crowes concert T-shirt—despite the chill growing in the air and darkness descending—with jeans and Converse sneakers. His accent was southern. "No cars going up or down the road, not at this time. We waited an hour, then I walked. No gas stations—"

"There's one in Riverton. That's about six miles straight downhill. You can't miss it."

"Ma'am, six miles? That'll be twelve miles up and down this mountain. And the power is out everywhere. We drove up through Riverton on the way in. Not a light anywhere. My girlfriend is pregnant, ma'am. It's getting cold. Do you have a landline? Cell phones are not working, as I am sure you know. I could call a tow truck?"

"We have no working phones."

He scratched his left arm and shifted from one foot to the other, glancing away at the trees and then back at the gravel before returning to look at her. He had shaggy blond hair and a tattoo on his neck. "My name's Billy, ma'am. My girlfriend, Shonda, well, she's pregnant, like I said. Could we maybe come in? Warm up? I hate to ask, but we got nowhere else."

Susie leaned the door open an inch more. It was twilight already. Still no sign of the security contractors. They were somewhere with Ellarose.

Tattoo.

She squinted. When she talked to Lauren, her friend mentioned that one of the people—the *terrorists*—that had kidnapped her a week ago had a tattoo of a rose on his neck. But a lot of people had neck tattoos these days. The hair on the nape of hers prickled. Was that a rose?

Susie leaned another few inches out of the door, still in its protection, but enough that it seemed like she was being inviting.

"Yeah, sure. Okay," she said "But let me put on a jacket and get you a couple of coats. Then we'll get you in and warmed up, get you some food."

She beamed her best southern hospitality smile, then turned and half closed the inside door.

"Bonham," she said in her I-am-not-the-hell-kidding voice. "You go downstairs. Get into the secret room. Remember how we did in all the drills? You remember?"

Her boy's face went slack.

"I am being serious. This is not a drill. There are very bad people outside. You remember everything we said?"

He nodded.

"You leave that door open a crack down there. No way in or out except that hallway." That wasn't exactly true, but she couldn't make it complicated. "Anyone but me comes in that hallway, you shut that door and lock it. You hit the flares. You understand? Repeat to me what you understand."

"Go to the safe room. Anyone but you comes in the hallway, I shut the door. And then the flares." He still lisped his "f" sounds.

Susie's heart felt like it broke into a million pieces seeing the sudden fear in her boy's face, but pride swelled in her chest, too. He stood up straight and still, his eyes focused and steady on her, if tearing up more than a little. Hers too. She wiped them away.

88

"Go now," Susie said, "run, and don't open for anybody." She hesitated. "And if you have to, blow the whole thing. You remember?" She pulled her keys out and unclipped a red one and handed it to him.

"Now?"

"Run!"

Bonham took off and skidded to a stop on the hardwood floor in his socks, paused and looked at her as he grabbed the banister going down. She nodded and he nodded back before he padded cautiously down the stairs, the red key swinging in his hand. They always told him to be careful going down the polished wooden stairs in socks.

Susie had to go outside the house and find Ellarose.

Her hands shaking, she turned back to the young man in the driveway. He walked toward her. She waved through the glass exterior door, then came back inside around the main door to the jacket hooks.

She didn't take a coat, though.

She used her keys to unlock a bolt hole in the wall. Then hauled back on the top hook of the coat rack. A switch that released a hidden compartment behind it. The panel swung down and open. The jackets attached to the hooks flopped to the floor.

Behind the panel was an arsenal of weapons.

First, she needed protection.

As quick as she could, Susie slipped on a ballistic vest and chest plate, then a neck guard.

"I'll be out in a second, just hold on," she yelled as loud as she could while she put on the rest of the body armor. Shin guards. Upper and lower arm protectors.

They practiced this in drills.

After their friend Tony was killed here six years before, when they were attacked by raiders looking to steal their supplies, Chuck and Susie had sworn they would never be so unprepared again. Anybody ever came here again looking for trouble, the Mumfords would have some surprises waiting for them.

And Ellarose was out there.

Any fear Susie had was eclipsed by a blossoming momma-bear protective rage.

Letting out curses that would have made her pastor blush, she grabbed a belt of 37-millimeter smoke bombs, another of high-explosive ammo. The explosive rounds were illegal, but a few of the modified weapons up here stretched the limits of the law. She strapped them both to her waist. Then took one of the two modified SIG Sauer MCXs from the rack, attached a launcher, and stacked her vest with four sets of double-taped-together magazines.

She snapped one into her weapon. Banged it to make sure it was set. Paused and considered. Grabbed a Bowie knife from the wall.

"Okay," Susie said in a sing-songy voice as loud as she could, her back still to the door. "Sorry, I spilled my coffee. I'm almost there." She donned a Batlskin Viper armored helmet, pulled the mandible and nose guard into place, then snapped down the ballistic visor.

She closed the hidden closet back up. Pulled back the charging handle on the MCX and set the selector to live. Her heart hammering through her chest and up into her throat. She slowed her breathing and counted to ten under her breath.

Susie swung around the door and leveled her weapon.

Chapter 12

I hurried along the forest path. Tried to command my legs to run. The best I could manage was a stumbling jog. How long did Tyrell say it would take for the miniature drones to reactivate?

Being hunted by machines.

Death from the sky.

I'd had people point guns at me, even chase me with weapons. It was terrifying, but at least it had made a sort of sense—however misguided, I knew the people attacking me were trying to right some perceived wrong or some other twisted logic. It was within the scope of my emotional understanding.

But this.

I had never stared into the eyes of a machine hunting me.

But those weren't eyes. They were red LEDs. Maybe not even vision sensors. Running lights like on an airplane? My imagination turned them into eyes. A fantasy that made it seem like "they" were hunting us. Those things had no feelings, just algorithms. No rage. They even destroyed themselves to kill us.

Perfect machines for terrorists.

My body shook, wet and cooling down now, as the adrenaline drained from my bloodstream and created a void.

"Dad, you okay?" Luke jogged beside me, leaving me the main path while he dodged branches and bushes and gnarled tree roots to my right.

"Fine."

"Are you hurt?"

"I'm okay."

"Because you're covered in blood."

I checked myself in the gray light. My hands were caked with mud. My forearms smeared red. I swept my arms down my chest as we jogged and checked again for gaping wounds. "I think it's from those guys in the bottom of the boat," I replied after a second.

When Chuck had pulled me in, I'd slid over the gunwale face-first into the dead body of one of the Secret Service agents, half of whose head had been blown away.

"Good," Luke replied. "I mean, not good, but I mean—"

"I know what you mean."

I thought about pulling him up into my arms to carry him. A million times before, I'd picked him up when he was a baby— when he screamed, when he needed something. But my little guy wasn't a baby anymore.

How much time did we have? Where were we going? And why hadn't anyone come to help us yet? This guy Tyrell better have a good plan, or he wouldn't need to worry about those drones. I'd kill him myself.

And this could still be a trap.

Chuck and Damon jogged on the path right in front of me, Tyrell a few paces ahead of him. Archer had started out behind Tyrell, but the man seemed to melt into the shadows only to appear beside me, then behind, and then I thought I saw him up ahead somewhere. No idea where he was right now, but I sensed him hovering around us.

"I'm so sorry, Leo," I heard my wife say behind me.

She seemed more grounded than me, and yet she had just lost her mother. The senator, Leo, had just lost his sister, his only sibling. Susan Seymour had just been killed.

My God. Susan.

As much as she had frustrated me sometimes, as my mother-in-law, I had developed a soft spot for her, even more after her husband died. She was my kids' only remaining grandparent. I had come to love her, treasure her as part of my family. And now she was gone, just like that. An image of her blood spraying against the wall flashed in my mind. We hadn't been able to even go back and get her. Had she been alive and struggling?

I pushed that thought away.

No way she survived what I saw.

And then another thought. How many more of us would die before this was over?

Olivia was in Lauren's arms. My baby girl had just witnessed her grandmother being killed. Minutes before, they had been cuddling together on a couch, watching some Disney movie, and then these machines killed her. Appeared from nowhere.

Assassinated was a better word. Murdered. She didn't just die, like at an old age home of natural causes. Someone purposely ended her life in the most terrifying way I could imagine. And personal. Right in front of us.

And what did Tyrell have to do with it?

The senator had the same thought. "We're going to get some answers," he said gruffly. "Get it from the horse's mouth, and if anything he says doesn't match what we already found out..."

He mumbled an apology and pushed between me and Luke. The senator still had on his blue dress shirt and slacks and red tie and brown loafers, but was soaking wet head to foot and spattered with blood and mud.

I looked over my shoulder and saw that Archer was behind us. Bringing up the rear.

"Where are we going?" Chuck said from in front of me. "How did you get here?"

The senator stalked past him and Damon in a stiff run, one hand up in the air. "Mr. Jakob, I have some questions."

"Can it wait?" Tyrell replied.

"What happened in Mississippi?"

"Same thing as just happened here. Those little machines appeared and killed everyone at my SatCom headquarters."

"Not everyone," Chuck gasped as he ran. "You're here."

"That is true."

"So just everyone else."

"You escaped?" the senator said. "How? How did every single other person die and yet here you are?"

"You're going to find out in a minute. There are advantages to being a billionaire."

"Now is not the time for being evasive."

"Ask me anything."

"When was the attack on your HQ? What day? What time?"

"September 7th, mid-morning. I had everyone on deck, and I mean everybody. Every friend that I personally hired, everybody died..." Tyrell's voice caught.

"Why was *everyone* there?"

"Because I asked them. We'd been hacked."

"You never alerted the government."

Tyrell didn't reply.

"Fill in the timeline, Mr. Jakob," the senator said. "Late evening on September 4th, India launched their first anti-satellite attack from Satish Dhawan Space Centre on Sriharikota Island near Chennai."

"If you say so."

September 4th was exactly two weeks ago, when all this had started. It seemed like a parallel universe, when the world had been normal and we had been on that fishing trip in New Orleans

94

with Chuck and Damon. When the first anti-satellite launch was announced on the news.

The senator said, "GenCorp reported that day that you lost contact with some of your SatCom birds."

"It wasn't unusual that we had signal drop," Tyrell replied. "We are—we *were*—building out a constellation of tens of thousands of satellites, adding a hundred a day sometimes, and they communicated and coordinated with each other directly without needing to relay through base stations."

Listening to him, his satellites sounded a lot like those things that just attacked us.

"Our reports say you lost contact with eighteen?"

"At first, yeah. By September 5th it was ten times that."

"That was never reported."

"We didn't have time. Pakistan launched another anti-satellite weapon, and then another. We thought we were suffering from debris fallout, like everyone else. Our birds had automated collision avoidance. They might have been getting out of the way. We built them to be self-reliant, put a lot of AI into them."

"But you realized you had been hacked? When? The servers at your HQ were wiped clean."

"By September 6th, it became clear it wasn't just our AI going haywire. We figured someone had gotten into our servers. But remember, it was chaos. The Air Force lost a dozen GPS birds that day, and cascading debris fields hit fifty other satellites."

"That was the day the International Space Station was destroyed," I said.

"That's right," Tyrell replied. "Our phones were ringing off the hook, email servers jammed with requests. Every agency with a bird up there, every nation on the planet, was calling and trying to figure out where everyone else's equipment was."

"Even so, that is gross negligence, Mr. Jakob, even criminal that you did not alert—"

"I didn't know terrorists had hijacked my birds to use them as bombs to kill everything else up there. We just knew we had a hack. It happens sometimes. Hell, half the time it's you guys. At that point, I thought I'd been infiltrated by you."

"Us?"

"The American government. The NSA. You know how often I've found nuggets left behind by your government hackers in our systems. Little back doors? And if not you, then the 3PLA, IRGC..."

"3PLA?" I asked. I knew the IRGC was the Iranian Revolutionary Guard.

"The Third Department of the People's Liberation Army. The Chinese NSA. You're all like rats in the walls, everything I do—"

"I warn you, Mr. Jakob," the senator said, "we need answers."

We broke through into a clearing.

It was past 6 p.m., and the sun was setting somewhere behind the thick clouds overhead and the mountains to the west. Dismal light under the dense tree canopy. The air had that earthy, fresh scent after a rain. Drops filtered from the sky. The reek of burning plastic wafted past, reminding me that the house was still on fire somewhere behind us and to the right.

I looked up. Low clouds. Searched for red dots. Lumbered to a stop and held Luke and Lauren back behind me. I wasn't going into any open areas, and neither was my family.

To one side of the clearing was a crumbling chimney stack of old, mortared-together round stones. The ground was jumbled with rocks, which I realized formed a foundation. An old house. A wide double-tracked path led off the other side. Must have been the driveway.

"Why are we stopping?" I gasped it out, doubled over with my hands on my knees to catch my breath. For the millionth time, I promised myself I would hit the gym.

Tyrell said, "Before we get in my vehicle, I want to understand where we're going. Because I'm not going into DC. I have a house down the coast, not registered in my name, on a barrier island in South Ca—"

"I am not sure how you thought this was a negotiation, Tyrell." Archer materialized from the shadows to my right. He had his weapon up and trained on the billionaire's head.

"We're going to my cabin." Chuck had run ahead and now circled the stone chimney. "Why have we stopped here? This is old man Burling's place. I thought you had a vehicle? A Humvee?"

"Not a Humvee, but it's big enough for all of us," Tyrell replied.

"Where is it?"

"It's here."

"Where?"

The clearing was empty, save for the stone chimney.

Chuck said, "Is this some kind of game?"

"Tell me about your cabin, Mr. Mumford," Tyrell said. "Why are we going there? Where is it? What's there?"

Chuck yelled, "My goddamned children and wife!"

Tyrell shrank back. "I see."

"You ain't gonna see much in a second, after I blow a six-inch hole through your skull." Archer advanced past me and Lauren and Damon to stop three feet from Mr. Jakob.

Nonplussed, Tyrell said to Chuck, "I assume this cabin is in the Shenandoah mountains?"

"Five seconds, dickhead, until you're picking daisies in the Devil's asshole." Archer sighted down the barrel of his weapon.

"If you have no plan, we're outta here and leaving you behind to feed the trees. Tell me if I'm lying."

"To be honest, I really came here only to get Mr. Indigo," Tyrell said.

"Me?" Damon's eyes went wide.

"Two seconds." Archer put his finger next to the trigger.

Over the hushed rustle of leaves swaying in a breeze, a warbling sound. The buzz saw whine of mechanical insects cut between the trees. Not just one, but a whole chorus of them echoed.

Archer began to pull the trigger. "One."

Tyrell still had hold of the gray metal box in one hand, but with the other he held up what looked like car keys.

"Time's up, asshole," Archer said.

Red dots flashed between the tree trunks.

Chapter 13

Susie straight kicked the exterior glass door back.

It swung out hard, slammed against the outside wall of the log cabin then bounced back right into the muzzle of her rifle. The glass cracked but didn't break. She and Chuck had coated all the windows—the ones that weren't already done in ballistic sheets—in heavy plastic film. Made them shatterproof. One in a long list of ways they had hardened this place.

She used her left leg to hold the door open and edged forward. The guy in the Black Crowes T-shirt was gone from the driveway.

"Damn it," she muttered under her breath.

Had he seen her getting a gun? Had he guessed what she'd been doing?

Maybe she was too hopped up on all the stress. Seeing bogies in the shadows. He looked like a nice kid, to be honest. And it didn't take a genius to guess someone up here might be getting their gun out if you show up on their doorstep unannounced at nightfall. It made sense the guy had ducked for cover.

"Hello?" she called out. "I'm sorry if this looks crazy, but with all that's going on—those terrorists in the news? I'm a bit jumpy."

Perhaps that wasn't the right thing to say from a woman armed like she was stepping into the Second Battle of Fallujah. He probably didn't want to hear that she was feeling twitchy.

Where the hell were those security guys?

Even if they were off with Ellarose, they must have heard something by now.

She stepped through the doorway and checked left and right. Swept her weapon along the edge lines of the two Escalades, then along the rooftop of the workshop and to the sides of the old outhouse.

"My husband and his buddy are inside," she lied. "Got my kids in there, too. Like I said, we're awfully remote up here. Come out but keep your hands up. I'm happy to help if you need it."

She was starting to feel ridiculous. How long had it taken her to get suited up? It seemed like a split second, but it might have been a minute. Obviously too long. Maybe the kid had run, gone back the way he c—

A flash to her left. Her head snapped back. Hard.

A sharp crack followed by a pop an instant later. She staggered back as two more rounds punched her chest. Her feet were already moving, muscle memory more than brain instruction. A succession of loud claps and muzzle flashes. Impacts against the armor on her legs like hammer blows trying to knock her feet out from under her.

In four awkward, loping steps, she ran past the front of the house and launched herself to the grass by the side of the back deck like a runner heading home, her SIG Sauer rifle out ahead of her.

Susie skidded to a stop, almost on target to where she needed to be.

She quick-crawled on her stomach into cover of her hydrangea bushes and rock garden. Straight in front of her nose, a white plastic tag from the plant nursery explained these were the "tea of heaven" hydrangea, with pretty purple and white blooms.

She and Chuck had fought over picking these bushes. Stupid things people did sometimes. A sudden pang of regret. She shouldn't fight with him like that over dumb things.

Her breaths came in quick gulps.

With the back of her left hand she adjusted her helmet, but it wasn't the angle obscuring her view. The visor was fractured over her eye where that first round hit. It could have taken off the left side of her skull. And that was no .22 caliber. The sharp crack before the pop of the muzzle report had the distinctive supersonic shockwave of a high-velocity round, not the run-of-the-mill AR-15s she was used to. She'd never been downrange of a shot that close, but there was no mistaking it.

Powerful assault rifles.

And not just one.

She saw multiple muzzle flashes from the side of the old brick outhouse—now converted into an aviary—and the workshop farther back. If the two security guys had been off at the stream with Ellarose, no way they were now. Maybe she had help coming.

But she couldn't count on it.

Whoever was attacking, they weren't trying to injure her. They were aiming to kill. That was a head shot that had glanced off her visor, and at least two more straight in the chest, and a dozen or more shots that sprayed around her legs. She didn't feel anything. She was numb.

What the hell was going on?

No time to ruminate.

Susie needed a tactical plan. She should have told Bonham to hit the flares right away, but she hadn't been sure at the time. As a backup to the backups, there were flare rounds secured to the chimney. They had a deal with Sheriff Gupta—if anyone saw the flares, they would send up help. She should have told her son to hit the alarm, but then, that might have forced some action by the attackers before Susie could find Ellarose.

She still had no idea who or what these people were.

Her little boy was safe for now, so what she needed to do was find her Ellarose. Should she go back inside the house and take the tunnel to the Baylors' place? That was what they still called it, even though they owned it now.

But she didn't know what or who might be on the other side.

She checked her breathing. Her hands barely shook. She had always wondered how she would react under fire. Six years ago, she hadn't been ready, but now her mind was crystallized, clear, the colors on the leaves brighter somehow, her vision sharper.

A plan formed in her mind.

The mile-long driveway in from the main road led only here, but two hundred yards farther up it branched over to the Baylors' property. Two years ago, Chuck had rented a backhoe and dug a trench across the drive and through the trees to connect the two places, poured cement walls, and then covered the whole thing. Hidden the entrances into the basements on both ends. Covered and surfaced so nobody would guess anything was there.

That was their escape route. Chuck had purposely made it as a way to get out of the house from the basement after they'd been trapped there six years before.

Susie needed to find Ellarose and get her back in the house. The trail down to the stream was at the edge of the parking area, about a hundred feet north of where Susie was now. The ground sloped down and provided natural cover, although whoever was shooting at her had the high ground. There was no way anyone could approach from the west, across the craggy rocks and steep slopes, or from the south, which was equally difficult terrain.

So her attackers were probably in front of her.

The tunnel wasn't the only surprise she had for them.

Susie crawled on her stomach, keeping low behind her geraniums and rock garden, toward the control box she had plunged into cover to get to. She put her weapon down and flipped over the big flat rock at the end of the garden. Below it, a set of switches. She armed two of them. Chuck had wanted to install explosives, but Susie had reminded him the kids played back there. It would have to be good enough.

Susie flipped over one switch and then another, then pulled the rock back into place.

The wet of the cold ground seeped between the cracks in her armor.

She grabbed her weapon, adjusted the visor so the cracked left side didn't obscure her sight, and lifted her head a few inches. A series of popping hisses echoed off the granite mountainside hidden by the dense trees. Clouds of tear gas wafted into the air behind the workshop and outhouse, the fog of a dozen canisters of it clouding the air. Gagging and coughing echoed next.

Didn't think to wear masks, huh?

The smog of the tear gas thickened. A shadow emerged from the gloom, lurching at a half crouch across the grass behind the workshop toward the cover of firs. Susie took aim, held her breath, and felt the trigger pressure. Take your time, she said to herself. Focus.

One shot. Two. Both head shots.

The figure crumpled to the ground.

Susie swung her weapon back to the left. More hacking throat clearing and swearing, and not in English. What language was that? Chechen? Did they speak Russian?

She slipped a smoke bomb into the launching tube under her rifle's muzzle and popped it off at the outhouse, then in quick succession fired two more into the driveway. She waited for the hissing smoke to begin rising before she took off at a run, bent over, toward the path leading down to the stream.

She wanted to scream her daughter's name, but held her tongue.

That would tell her attackers that her little girl was somewhere outside, but then again, what would they guess Susie was out here for anyway? She had the element of surprise, and that was buying her precious seconds she couldn't waste. No way they expected this to be a siege, not like this, and not one where the prey burst forth and began attacking them.

They were regrouping, that much she was sure of, whoever *they* were.

And that gave her a slice of time.

A tiny advantage.

She had already dropped ten feet in height, giving her cover from the ridge. She followed the edge of the garden and bounded into the trees. The armor was awkward to run in. The trail down to the stream started from the driveway, but she could cut through the undergrowth and angle to it without going back up.

At a run, she dove straight into a blackberry bush.

Ellarose's favorite.

Through the gaps in the armor, the thorns ripped at her leggings and skin. She toppled headfirst, gasping, into the net of tiny blades. Swearing, Susie struggled to get back to her feet. The barbs shredded the back of her neck, the exposed skin on her wrists.

The branches clung to her.

Ripping and pulling, she tugged through, and then stopped cold.

Between the trunks and branches of the oak and birch, many of the leaves already stripped away by fall, she glimpsed khaki steel and black rubber. A Humvee. Military. Two of them. She pushed away a clump of blackberries. And what was that? Farther up the driveway? It looked like a semitrailer and more vehicles. Men were unloading crates.

This wasn't someone raiding her house for supplies.

A chill overcame the burning sizzle of the thorns in her neck and arms.

They wanted the house itself.

The house.

Bonham was alone inside.

After the tear gas and her brief counteroffensive, she was sure her attackers were taking stock and recalibrating their approach, but this wasn't one or two or even three people up here on a revenge mission. That's what she had figured. Maybe this was the Chechens returning to exact some payback for Mike and Chuck and Damon derailing their terror attack in space.

Mike had killed one of them.

More than one.

But this was a whole platoon. The attackers were surrounding the house.

Spinning and wrenching her arms, she broke free of the blackberries. She floundered onto the stream trail and kept low, her weapon up and sweeping back and forth.

"Ellarose," she hissed, as loud as she dared. "Honey, if you're here, come to me. We're going back to the house."

This wasn't over. She didn't care how many men were in those Humvees. She needed to get back inside. Once there, she could signal for help and escape through the tunnel.

Susie raised her voice a little more. "Ellarose!"

The trail opened into a clearing as it crossed the burbling stream coming down the mountain forest slope. A bridge of sticks and twigs was still there, with a wall of rocks spaced across the middle forming a dam that pooled the water to one side.

"Ellar—"

Susie stopped in the muddy grass. Drops of water dotted the rushing stream. And something else. Dark clouds swirled through the stream and collected in the pool.

Blood spatter against the rocks.

Red blood mixed with the cascading water.

Chapter 14

W ait!" Tyrell held the keychain, rabbit paw dangling, above his head.

A two-tone alarm signal beeped.

I cringed and waited for his skull to split open as Archer squeezed the trigger on his assault rifle. The muzzle near point-blank at Tyrell's forehead. The barrel of the weapon dipped.

"What in Jesus's..." Archer's voice trailed off.

I held Luke tight to me. His fingers dug into the skin under my sopping wet T-shirt. I had one arm out, holding Lauren back, my splayed fingers attempting to hide from Olivia whatever was about to happen.

Staring straight ahead at Tyrell, Archer's face went slack.

I had one eye on the man's trigger finger, now released, but most of my attention was on the flickering red dots approaching through the tree trunks.

Could those drone-bots navigate through a forest? My gut twisted. Seemed like exactly what they were good at.

But that expression on Archer's face. What had just happened? I blinked and looked away from the red dots and followed Archer's gaze.

The trees to my left shimmered.

A hole opened in the fabric of reality.

Branches and leaves seemed to suck from the ground into a vortex that reformed and solidified. The angular outlines of a squat enclosure scintillated into being. Brown-gray panels coagulated from nothing. A twenty-foot-plus hulking monster appeared from nowhere, cleaved from the air in Gollum-clay, as if transported through a wormhole and onto the damp carpet of leaves in the clearing.

Two gull-wing doors hissed open to reveal an interior of leather and glowing blue lights.

"We need to hurry." Tyrell still had his hands above his head.

The rabbit paw swayed.

"If you're going to point that thing, kid, you better use it." Archer's voice regained its hard edge.

He had his weapon down now, not pointing at Tyrell, but I sensed his body coiling up like a storm cloud about to unleash a bolt of lightning.

Damon stood with his legs apart and two arms raised in a vee directed straight at Archer. A handgun's barrel sighted at the man. I'd never seen Damon pick up a gun, never mind aim it at someone. He scowled. Damon's lip curled, and for a sickening moment I thought he was going to pull the trigger.

"What are you doing?" I asked him, fear and incomprehension making my voice rise. My eyes flitted back to the approaching red dots.

"Can't let him kill Tyrell."

"He's not going to."

"Not now."

Tyrell waved the rabbit's paw at us. "Everybody, please, in the truck. Mr. Indigo, I appreciate the show of support, but can we litigate this from a safer vantage point?"

Damon considered for a split second, then released and opened his arms wide, holding his hands away—one of them up with the gun, the other palm out in surrender. My brain was still attempting to process the materialization of this muscular—

truck?—in the middle of an empty forest clearing, but my mother had always said not to look a gift billionaire in the mouth.

"Damon, get in the"—I searched for a word but gave up—"just get in."

I hustled my wife, with Olivia white-faced and terrified in her arms, ahead of me forward and past Damon and Archer, who stood stock-still and glared at each other like they were playing chicken against the advancing drones. I took the submachine guns from Luke's arms, carefully making sure they didn't point at anyone, my mind coming to grips with letting my eight-year-old son handle deadly weapons.

The senator followed us.

The vehicle had three-row seating. I helped my wife into the middle one, then lifted in Luke and climbed in behind them. It had that new-car smell of polyester and polished cowhide.

My wet rear squeaked across the polished tan leather. I shivered. Hadn't realized how cold I was.

"Hurry, hurry, hurry," I urged the rest of them.

The inside was an open cockpit, rows of seating like a luxury SUV done in light and dark brown leather. A large flat-panel display occupied most of the center console between the driver and passenger seats in front of us. Double sets of moonroof panels revealed swaying tree branches and scudding clouds through their smoky glass.

Chuck climbed into the row of seats behind us, the senator beside him with two of the submachine guns he had collected from the Secret Service agents. Damon tried to get in next, but Archer ripped him backward and knocked my friend into the wet dirt.

"In the front, asshole." Archer clambered in beside Chuck.

"You swear a lot," Damon said as he got back to his feet. "You know that?"

The gull-wing door to our left hissed closed.

Through the large passenger-side window to our right, red dots emerged, bright in the tinted glass. The trees and branches remained dim, but the eyes of the advancing drones seemed magnified. They shifted back and forth with mechanical precision as they advanced through the trees right at us.

I asked, "Is this thing bombproof?"

"To some degree." Tyrell hefted Damon ahead of him, over the driver's seat to the passenger side. The door began to slide closed after he climbed in behind him.

Red dots to that side as well.

I assumed "some degree" meant these mechanical wasps couldn't penetrate this thing's defenses. Luke had his nose against the glass to his side and pointed. He recoiled. One of the drone-bots hovered not ten feet away, its LED lights pointed this way.

I asked, "Are you sure they can't see us?"

"Get this thing moving," Archer barked.

"Mr. Archer, while the metamaterial sheath covering us can bend ultraviolet through infrared, it cannot absorb outgoing sound waves, and I am quite sure the AI controlling those ornithopter drones—"

"Drive," Archer repeated, his voice lower but still menacing. "Slowly," he added.

"Selena," Tyrell whispered. "Please engage and route a course to—" He stopped.

Archer muttered, "What's wrong?"

"I am looking up Mr. Mumford's address, however, with network connectivity down, the stored internet database I have—"

"Just get us the hell moving."

I asked, "Are you sure we should be going to Chuck's?"

"We should be going anywhere but here," Chuck replied from behind me. Two more of the hovering drones had floated into the clearing. "This is covered with a metamaterial that bends light? I've seen that in my military magazines."

Tyrell said., "The sheath is also backed by a radar-absorbing coating over an OLED backstop."

"An invisibility cloak?" Luke said. "Like in Harry Potter?"

"Can we get moving?" The strain in Archer's voice growing even as he tried to maintain a forced whisper. "Any funny business up there, remember I got a gun pointed at your heads."

The barrel of a Glock appeared over the seat between Lauren and me.

"Is that necessary?" my wife asked.

"You know what's fun about the passenger seat?" Damon hissed from the front, turning to face Archer. "I got a set of controls for the doors. Just one button and I can let in one of those explosive insects to air your head out."

"Damon," my wife scolded.

"The window controls don't work right now," Tyrell said. "Selena is in stealth mode."

"Who's Selena?" I asked. "Your truck?"

"More than just the tr—"

"Are you men out of your minds?" Lauren kept her voice low, but the urgency in it carried. She held Olivia in her arms, my little girl's face pale. "Can we argue somewhere else?"

"Punch in Front Royal," Chuck said. "That's close enough."

"Selena," Tyrell said. "Engage a route to Front Royal, Virginia. Begin now. Evade targets."

"Yes, Mr. Jakob," replied a pleasant female voice. The calmest one in the truck.

The truck began to creep forward. Soundlessly.

Luke shuddered beside me, but still whispered, "This is so cool."

III

Three of the drone-bugs hovered outside his window, oblivious to us watching them from a dozen yards away. They must have heard us, or seen us, running through the trees to get here—but now we had effectively vanished.

I asked, "Lauren, can you make sure the safeties are on?" I indicated the weapons on the floor by our feet.

"Can you hold Olivia?"

I took my little girl while my wife checked the guns.

"You okay?" I whispered to my daughter. She quivered in my arms. I held her tighter.

She nodded and put her face into my chest. "Do we have an iPad?" she asked in a quavering voice.

"Not right now, honey."

What exactly were we doing?

I hadn't had any time to think about it in the last ten minutes, while we were under attack and in imminent danger of death. What *was* the next step? Chuck's cottage? I hated that place to begin with.

I needed time to think.

The immediate threat dissipated, the hovering drones outside the smoky glass became fascinating. Watching them, I saw they executed a coordinated grid search pattern as more of them moved to this area.

Our vehicle slid forward over the carpet of leaves on the forest floor. A branch snapped and one of the bots shifted to look our way.

"What happens if one of them bumps into us?" I asked. We might be invisible, but we still occupied a lot of space. This thing had to be more than ten feet across, eight feet high, and twenty long.

"We're not *exactly* invisible," Tyrell said, squashing my hopes. "Just tricky to get a good lock on. A human could see something was odd, if they knew what to look for."

"Still doesn't answer the question," Chuck said from the back.

"They would realize something was in their way. Collision detection. I imagine swarming activity might ensue, but Selena is monitoring the threat matrices. We could accelerate away. It would take their sensors and AI longer to recalibrate than for Selena to navigate a path to safety."

"Great," Chuck said. "We have one artificial intelligence hunting our asses, while another tries to evade and protect us."

Chapter 15

The truck picked up speed as we advanced up the winding path and left the drone-bots behind. A pressure lifted from my shoulders. An opening appeared up ahead, and seconds later we pulled onto the main road. The truck drove itself. Tyrell kept his hands off the wheel but punched some buttons on the main display.

"Hey, hey," Archer said. "Keep those hands off the controls. All fingers on the dash where I can see them, or I'll cut one off for each infraction."

The light was fading as the sun went down. From the road we clearly saw the glittering flames of the house, which was going up like a torch.

"Why no fire engines?" I asked. "What about the military? Someone must be seeing this. Radar? Alarms?"

There wasn't another car in sight up or down the road.

It felt deserted.

The population in this area of Virginia was spread out, but it wasn't empty. Large houses occupied wooded acre-sized lots. I had just been discharged from the hospital the day before, and the place had been crawling with police and EMTs, with a corridor full of FBI and CIA personnel on our floor, even after the senator left. Where were all of them now?

The truck accelerated.

"Stop the car," Chuck said. "Archer, get him to stop it."

Tyrell was already whispering to Selena. The truck slowed to a crawl, and then pulled over to stop on the shoulder. The flames from the house arced into the dark sky over the treetops in the distance to our right. Did Chuck want to go back for something?

"Did you forget something, Mr. Mumford?" Tyrell asked.

"This better be good," Archer mumbled.

"We need to think about this," Chuck replied.

I turned in my seat to face him. "Your kids and Susie are up there. If he's right—"

"And why are we trusting him?"

"He just saved our lives."

"Maybe. Maybe not."

"You are free to exit the vehicle, Mr. Mumford, although I would advise against it."

"And why's that?"

"Because I am sure *they* are watching."

"And who are *they*?"

"The same people who hijacked my satellites."

Chuck asked me, "Mike, what do you think?"

"I think I feel pretty safe inside this thing."

"Do you trust him?" He flicked his chin toward Tyrell.

"I just met him."

"I trust him," Lauren said.

That stopped us for a few beats.

Chuck exhaled and ran a hand through his hair. "You shouldn't be bringing *your* kids into whatever we're heading for. And Leo?" He turned to the senator. "You don't need to come. You should head back to Washington."

"Lauren," I said. "That's a good idea. You want to take the kids? Go with your uncle and Archer. It's ten minutes the opposite way down the road. We could dr—"

"If anyone goes back with the children, it's you," she replied. "You're not exactly tactically ready, Mike. You could barely even shoot that gun."

"You both go back," Chuck said. "You shouldn't split up, not again. We just spent all this time getting you guys back together. That's what I came here for. Mission accomplished. Go with Archer. I'll get Susie. Maybe nothing is happening at the cottage."

"I don't trust Archer," Damon said from the front. "How is he the only government guy that made it out of the house?"

"I'm not sure I like what you're implying," Archer replied.

"I'm not implying."

"We're not leaving you and Susie alone," I said. "I think this is Irena. I think she's after me for killing her brother. I think she's going to use you to get to me."

Chuck managed a grin. "Always gotta make everything about you, huh?"

Silence for a few beats. I checked up and down the road. Still no headlights. No streetlights blinking on as darkness descended. No house lights flickering through the trees. Should we go and knock on someone's door? And then what? Drag them into this mess? It made more sense to drive back into the McLean village center and find a police station, get some help.

"Those drones needed a GPS signal to operate," Archer said. "Whoever is—"

"Not necessarily from a satellite," Damon interrupted. "Could be a local signal generator up on a tower, even on the ground. Or maybe an inertial guidance system. But someone dropped those drones here. They can't fly far, being that small. Where were you just before you found us at the boat?"

"Searching the area and tracking Tyrell."

"So you say. Senator, do you know this guy? Who sent him?"

Leo was sandwiched between Archer and Chuck in the back. "The FBI liaison said that someone from JSOC"—he pronounced it jay-sock—"came to the door."

"Could be Chinese GPS," Chuck said. "Right? Don't the Chinese still have a working geopositioning system? BeiDou?"

"Are we really doing this again?" I said.

"They only have three satellites still operational," Damon pointed out. "Senator, wasn't that what you told us in the last report?"

"That's what they told us. They might have more birds working by now," Leo replied. "We're trying to get some parts of our GPS back u—"

A bright flash lit up the trees to our right, followed by a thudding concussion. A fireball roiled into the dark sky.

"Had to be the propane tank," the senator said after a pause. "We had a big one toward the front for the generator."

"That is definitely going to attract attention," I said. "Won't that show up on radar? Why don't we just sit still and wait for emergency services to show up? There's going to be police or somebody, even if all communications and power are down."

"Honey," Lauren whispered. "We cannot sit still. I think Tyrell is telling the truth. If Susie and the kids are in trouble—"

"Tyrell." I held one hand up to Lauren, apologizing for cutting her off. "You said you evaded the drone attack at your Mississippi headquarters somehow, then used your fancy truck to escape. But that was eleven days ago."

"That's correct, Mr. Mitchell."

"Fill me in on *exactly* what you've been doing the last week and a half. All your co-workers were killed, you miraculously escaped, and then terrorists spoofed communications to the government, pretending to be your friends. And don't tell me you didn't know this somehow—"

"I did know."

"But you didn't say anything? And you've got this magic carpet you could use to literally drive into the lobby of the Capitol Building undetected, and you didn't warn or contact anyone? You didn't even try?"

"I have exactly the same question," Archer said. He still had the Glock in his right hand, but pointed at the moonroof. His relaxed pose.

"You show up right when we're being attacked by super-sophisticated drones," Chuck added. "Which, excuse me for saying, seem like exactly the kinds of things you might have on hand."

"You said you were coming here to get Damon," I said.

Tyrell held up his hands and turned in his seat. "Are these questions or accusations or merely observations?"

"Just explain yourself, bawbag," Archer said.

"What's a bawbag?" Chuck frowned.

Tyrell said, "I tracked down Damon because he's the only one I trust. He back-hacked the"—he paused to choose a word—"*terrorists* and brought down my constellation of satellites."

"Which I think is part of some bigger plan," Damon said. "Otherwise, why would they still be here? Their game is up. Unless their game is *not* up."

Tyrell nodded. "Exactly, Mr. Indigo. What is the bigger plan? That is the real question. And, Mr. Mitchell, you asked already why no help seems to be coming? The senator's house just exploded, ten miles from DC, and yet no jets are scrambling overhead."

A question tickling the back of my mind bubbled up. "Earlier, when we talked about the first anti-satellite attack by India, you said, 'If you say so.'"

"Because India still denies the attack," Tyrell replied.

The senator said, "Our military chain of command confirmed the launches by India. Satellite photos. The works. Our own government independently verified it with allies."

"And I think that is exactly the problem," Tyrell replied. "And it's why I didn't contact anyone in the past eleven days. And why I think you might want to be cautious going back into DC. Why I went to ground, so to speak. Mr. Mitchell, why do you think these so-called terrorists have not yet left the country?"

"I'm guessing this is a rhetorical question?"

"Anyone here is free to answer."

"Mike, I got a bad feeling," Chuck said. "Whatever you're going to do, I need to get up to the cabin. Right. Now."

"Senator," Archer said. "Why don't we get going? I'll walk you back to Washington myself. It's ten miles. You can walk that?"

"You want to saunter past those killer drones?" Lauren said. "They were hunting for my uncle not even five minutes ago. My mother was just killed by them. They're still out there. Are you insane?"

"I'm going with Lauren," the senator replied to Archer. "She's my only remaining family. Her and the kids"—he looked at me—"and Mike."

"Jesus H. Christ," Archer muttered under his breath.

"Mr. Mitchell?" Tyrell waved a hand from the front. "You have not yet answered my question."

"You want to know what I think?" I paused to gather myself. "I think Irena is hunting for me, not the senator. I killed her brother. And I think they've got something else they're going to hit America with. Before he died, Terek said, 'This is just the beginning.' Of what, I don't know. Why don't you enlighten us as to why you've been hiding?"

"And it better be crystal clear," Archer said, "because if there's even one word I don't understand, I'm dumping you on the pavement and taking Selena for a joy ride."

"Mr. Mitchell, I have been avoiding all contact with anyone in government, and especially anyone in the secret parts of it"—Tyrell smiled at Archer, but not really a smile, more of a grimace—"because I do not believe this was an attack by terrorists. Not in the usual sense of the word."

"You want to call them freedom fighters?" Archer said.

"What I would call *them*, Mr. Archer, is our *own* government."

"Excuse me?"

"I believe these attacks have been perpetrated by someone inside the American ruling regime, and that's why I have not contacted anyone within or even remotely connected to it."

"Mike." Chuck squirmed in the back seat and looked forward through the windscreen toward the mountains. "We need to move. I got a really, really bad feeling."

Chapter 16

No, no, no!" Susie cried out as she sloshed through the cascading water streaming with blood.

A jumble of pallid skin and blond hair blocked the stream fifty feet toward the road, claret liquid gorging into the brook from a mass of twigs and leaves. Gray tendrils from her smoke bombs wafted through dripping yellow foliage lining the burbling stream. The bony trunks of stripped young birches wove into a swaying chapel over an inert body submerged in the water.

What had Ellarose put on when she went out? Her North Face? The black jacket? Please, God, no, please—

Her modified AR-15 held high, Susie dropped to her knees in the water and wrenched her half-shattered visor and nose guard up. She threw her weapon into the muddy bank and gently put her hands under the blond hair.

Something wasn't right.

The head was twice as big as her little girl's. The man had on a ballistic vest. His lips blue, skin paper-white.

It was Thomas.

The security guy who had arrived the day before. Susie had gotten him a coffee and a muffin this morning. They were probably still in his stomach. Maybe the muffin still in his pocket. He didn't like muffins, his partner had said with a smile, even after Thomas had taken the offering she had just baked. The man had lied and said he loved the carrot ones. Nice guy. He'd come up here to protect her family. Had shown her pictures of his wife and their little boy.

Susie had asked him to keep an eye on Ellarose. She paused and closed her eyes.

Pictured that little boy in the photo. Oh, God. She opened her eyes.

Another body was wedged under a fallen log twenty feet upstream.

Susie didn't need to go look. Dark skin. That was Morty. Mortimer, she said his full name silently. He also came here to protect her. She scanned the underbrush and stream up and down from her. No smaller lumps with blond hair appeared between the trees.

Nothing. She didn't see anything else. Didn't see her daughter's body anywhere.

Her heart began beating again.

She released the man's head gently back into the water.

A second ticked by. Another. She needed a tactical plan. Surrender?

Her attackers had made it clear that they weren't trying to take her hostage.

Surrender was not an option.

Time was ticking, seconds she couldn't get back. Susie knew these woods like she knew her own children's faces. Ellarose was good in the forest too, even better than Susie when it came to evasion. Like when they played hide-and-go-seek out here. She was smart. Like her dad. Crafty and suspicious. She wouldn't have gotten caught.

"Ellarose!" Susie called out. "If you can hear me, you stay where you are. Stay quiet, do *not* answer me. Stay away from anybody you see, anybody but me." She paused. "And go to Uncle Tony, you hear me? You meet me at Uncle Tony's in ten minutes."

If anyone was listening, they would think that meant the other cabin.

The brook chattered and bubbled in the silence.

Susie brought her visor and mandible and nose guard back down. Her own blood seeped into the stream from jagged wounds where the blackberry thorns had ripped through her yoga pants between gaps in her armor. That stuff could stop bullets, but apparently not brambles.

Her senses felt heightened. A red maple leaf floating by in the water seemed iridescent, even in the flat light. The ice-cold water stung her wounds, numbed her legs and feet.

She took hold of her weapon.

In a crouch, she headed into the long grass by the side of the creek. She broke into a jog, her head down but scanning through the trees. Following the slope down into a hollow that provided cover from the top of the ridge and parking lot, she could double back to the house. She had the keys to the security system in her pocket. The place was a fortress. Nobody was in there yet, that she was sure of.

Nobody except her little boy.

Scared and by himself. Alone and terrified.

There might be twenty or more of them and only one of her, but these assholes had just picked on the wrong family. You didn't attack her kids and get away with it. She picked up her pace and let the anger burn into her veins. She loaded an explosive grenade round into the launcher under her rifle.

Nobody messed with the Mumfords.

She and Chuck had planned for this, as crazy as it might have seemed to outsiders at the time. Paranoia sometimes paid off, like a stopped clock that was right twice a day, Chuck liked to joke. Today the clock wasn't broken. Right now, it was ringing loud and clear in Susie's ears.

Chapter 17

Twilight descended on Virginia as we swept along the darkened streets. No lights twinkled between branches. No other cars on the road.

A sullen silence had fallen over the interior of the truck after Tyrell re-engaged Selena and fed in the address to the cabin. It was an hour drive back along Interstate 66, the infernal road I had walked along six years ago, into DC and back, starving to death in a delusional waking nightmare of my own creation. Today started to take on that same deranged cinematic sensation, a tight hamster wheel of spiraling speculation.

Everyone was lost in their thoughts, taking a moment to gather themselves in this brief calm at the eye of the storm, the cabin quiet apart from the faint thrum of the vehicle's electric motors and the wide-tread tires against the pavement. It was capable of faster speed, Tyrell said, but Selena calculated the optimal velocity for its stealth mode.

No new-car smell anymore, the interior now reeked like a wet dog. Blood caked on my arms and face that I didn't bother to try and clean off. Olivia nestled in my arms. She was thirsty, she said, but Tyrell didn't have any water and refused to stop. Just fifty-two minutes to our destination, he added.

But what exactly were we heading into?

The rear half of the truck's occupants thought the forward compartment was the enemy, and the front felt the same about the back—with the middle seats occupied by Lauren and me somewhere in between. My wife and I had taken on the uncomfortable role of referees between the two emerging factions.

We headed to Chuck's cabin, using Tyrell's signal triangulation as a guide.

He had explained to Archer exactly how he deduced this, and the man seemed satisfied that it made sense. If he was telling the truth. In less than an hour we would find out—if we got there—and for Archer, this was the way to resolve the conundrum. No need for overthinking.

Just go straight into the teeth of it.

We had no idea of the size of the monster we were heading toward, but I got the feeling Archer had faced worse odds in worse places than Virginia. Probably in places whose names I couldn't pronounce without help.

Of course, neither did we have any way of knowing if this meant the signal was coming from Chuck's place, or from the terrorists who were there. Or even that it was them controlling the bug-drones that attacked us at Senator Seymour's.

What were the odds?

There were no coincidences, as Chuck liked to say.

We'd been at Chuck's cabin three days before, with two of the Chechens. It made a perfect mountaintop lair for conducting operations, which was why Chuck liked it so much himself. Isolated. Up high. And their base of operations by the water had been demolished. If the signal was really coming from Shenandoah Mountain, it seemed too much of a coincidence for it *not* to be related to Chuck's cabin.

Chuck nearly had to climb into our row of seats to explain to Tyrell that the coordinates to his cabin in the navigation system weren't right. He had purposely gone in and changed the location of his house in all the online databases—Google and so on, using Damon's help the year before—so that nobody could find the cabin, even if they entered the address.

He gave Tyrell the latitude and longitude, which Chuck of course knew by heart. Which brought up another question.

"How does Selena know where she's going without GPS?" I asked.

"Inertial tracking and visual cues," Tyrell explained. "Like most military positioning systems, if it loses GPS, it reverts to backups. First the European GNSS, Galileo. Then GLONASS. Any L1C international timing signals. Failing that, it takes the last known position and overlays inertial tracking and checks current imaging data with known databases."

"Like Google Street View?" Luke said.

"Exactly like that. You have a smart kid, Mr. Mitchell. Extra-large batteries. Selena has a range of over six-hundred miles."

"Or we could just take the wheel and drive," Chuck said. "Can we do that?"

"Manual override switch is here." Tyrell indicated a mechanical switch beside the flat-panel display. "Brakes and accelerator just like you'd be used to."

He seemed to be trying to earn our trust.

"But we have no internet," I said. "How do you get Street View? How is Selena getting her data?"

"Onboard storage of ten petabytes. We have half the internet copied in here with us. That's an exaggeration, but we store a lot of map data and personal information."

"Personal information?"

"Places. Faces."

"Peta-what?" Chuck said.

"That's a thousand terabytes, Uncle Chuck," Luke explained. "Do you have an iPad in here, Mr. Jakob?"

"I have something much better than that. Mr. Archer, can I engage the entertainment system? I would need to access the main display."

"Just don't do anything funny," came the gruff reply behind me. "I am watching."

"Would *Peppa Pig* classify as funny?"

"Now you're being clever again."

Olivia perked up in my arms. "*Peppa Pig?*"

"Mr. Mitchell," Archer whispered in a raspy voice.

I turned in my seat. Olivia was in the seat beside me, watching cartoons on a big display in the seatback. Luke was doing the same. Both wearing earbuds that Tyrell had handed back. Luke was playing Minecraft. The entertainment system had games, too.

"Did you say something?"

Archer leaned over the seat to get closer to me, his eyes on Damon. "When we get there, I advise that you and your family stay close to me."

What was I supposed to say? "I understand," I replied.

The man sat back, apparently satisfied I was on his side.

Forty-one minutes till we arrived at Chuck's cabin. My thoughts swirled around and around, my brain trying to plot a path through whatever was coming. What was true? What was real?

Someone in this truck was lying, one way or the other. That I was sure of.

But who? And why?

Archer had decided that his new mission was to protect Senator Seymour, after an entire platoon's-worth of Secret Service agents had been killed trying to do just that. The senator, for his part, adamantly insisted on staying close to Lauren and the children, so Archer had no choice but to come along. A secondary goal, if I was interpreting Archer's behavior with any accuracy—he didn't like to talk, but mostly stared ahead with a blank expression—was to help protect our group.

Of course, this analysis of Archer depended on your point of view.

He was the most unknown quantity of anyone in the truck.

Damon's revulsion toward Archer—I wouldn't call it hatred, because he hadn't known him long enough for that—was almost palpable. The air between them seemed charged with negative ions, like two magnets repelling each other. I hadn't witnessed Damon really dislike anyone in the six years I had known him, but then, I hadn't spent that much time with Damon in those years.

On the other hand, Archer had been grilling Damon back at the house, just before all this kicked off. It had gotten heated, and I had the sense Archer was digging under some corners of Damon's life that my friend preferred to stay dark.

And what was Archer doing in the bathroom when I walked in on him? He had syringes out, some kind of chemical kit. Was he about to do something to Damon?

Was he allowed to do that?

But then what were the rules when a massive terrorist attack was launched against your country? The normal codes of conduct went out the window, but should they? Did we have the right to do that?

And how well did I really know Damon?

Damon had been about to shoot Archer in the clearing in the forest. *Kill* him. To protect Tyrell. And Tyrell said he came here to find Damon. How well did they really know each other? Damon said he had met Tyrell twice before on trips to GenCorp. They seemed more friendly than mere business acquaintances. Would I threaten to kill a special ops soldier for someone I met on a business outing?

Then again, Tyrell wasn't your run-of-the-mill businessman. The guy was literally a rocket scientist.

I had to admit, his star power put me in a bit of a daze. He was a celebrity, like George Clooney famous, especially among anyone in tech. He built space stations, rockets for journeys to Mars, and half the equipment the internet ran on—not to mention military equipment like this invisible truck we were in. If you had asked me two weeks ago, I would have said that anything coming out of Tyrell Jakob's mouth was God's gospel.

He was the smartest person in any room, but now my entire family's survival depended on him. My children's lives. Was my judgment being clouded?

And the reason he refused to allow us to stop and talk to anyone? He thought the attack was coming from our own government.

If I believed he was the smartest guy inside this futuristic Humvee—then should I believe, as he did, that the terrorists weren't Chechens, but some faction of our own American government? He was convinced this was a false flag operation, that somehow Senator Seymour was a target, and that this was the beginning of a new civil war.

Which made things even worse than I could have imagined not three hours before.

Thirty-three minutes.

"Is it just me, or does this have the feeling of a funeral?" Chuck whispered to me.

"I'm not sure I like your metaphor."

"Then it feels like we got a Mexican standoff going on in here. Is that better? Is that politically correct to say anymore?"

"Can't we just call it a standoff?"

"A standoff is usually two opposing parties. The Mexican variant is between three."

"I think we have more than three opposing points of view in here," I replied. "More like an Irish standoff. Nobody has any idea of what's going on, and nobody trusts anyone."

"Isn't that just as racist?"

"Not if you're personally a member of the group you're making fun of." My family had roots in Ireland.

"Thanks for clearing up the rules. Lauren, what's the status?"

My wife was checking the guns we'd collected from the dead Secret Service agents on our escape. "We've got three working MP5 submachine guns and six full magazines, three half full. I mean, operational as far as I can tell without firing them. Two Glocks and six clips. Plus, Archer's weapon."

"And the Glock Damon has," I said.

"Yeah, and that."

"One of you should get that away from him," Archer suggested.

Nobody volunteered.

"Who gets the weapons when we get there?" Chuck asked.

"I think we keep these in our end of the truck," Archer replied. "Let the geek squad do backup."

"Speaking of that," Chuck whispered, then raised his voice, "Mr. Jakob, how's the top up of that EMP gadget you used back at the river?"

"About half charged, Mr. Mumford. That's about the best we can do. I can't afford to pull much more juice from Selena's batteries, not if we want to retreat afterward. Finding somewhere to plug the truck in might be tricky, but I will keep my eyes peeled."

"I noticed the boxes in the back." Behind Chuck's seat was access to the trunk. He had already opened the four crates back there and inspected them with Archer, but they couldn't make sense of what was in them.

"Nothing that blows up, Mr. Mumford."

"But stuff that could be useful?"

"If we had more time, perhaps. We might have enough when we get there."

"I doubt that. At least, I'm not waiting."

"So what's the idea when we arrive?" the senator asked.

"We need to do some reconnaissance," Archer replied.

I said, "This thing is invisible, right?"

"Sort of," Tyrell replied.

"I've got a plan," Chuck said. "If those Chechen bastards are there, Susie and I have some surprises they won't be expecting. I know them. We spent almost two weeks with them."

"With one of them," I said.

"The most important one. The leader."

"You think."

"Yeah, that's what I think, Mike. Jesus, are you with me or not?"

"Of course I am." Wasn't I?

I glanced up at Tyrell.

But maybe it wasn't the Chechens at all. Too many things were bothering me to concentrate.

If there were no coincidences, what about Tyrell Jakob showing up in the nick of time to rescue us? Did he even really save our lives? Would we have been able to outrun those bug-drones in the boat?

Maybe we hadn't even needed him.

If I hadn't told the senator to head for the shore, maybe right now we would have been in Washington, surrounded by a fresh detail of the Secret Service, checked into a comfortable hotel with crisp sheets and room service, talking to more FBI agents.

Or we might be all dead.

And maybe Tyrell was leading us straight into a trap. That was my biggest worry.

Tyrell was enigmatic. He used our surnames to address us, like we were about to go rowing in Cambridge. Chuck had started doing it now, too. It had a charming way of disarming, but why was Tyrell sweet-talking us?

Why did he need us at all?

Maybe the goal of whoever had attacked us wasn't to kill Senator Seymour, but to capture him. What was the bigger plan? Something was going on in a larger scope.

Or maybe they wanted me. Or someone else here?

Maybe they needed Damon, which Tyrell had even made clear from the start—that this was why he had come to the senator's house. The Chechens had needed Damon in the first attack, and maybe there was something they needed him for now. What was it that I wasn't seeing?

If any of these theories were true, we were now willingly heading—I caught sight of Olivia's cartoon—like Peppa and her whole family of pigs to the slaughterhouse.

I checked my watch. Twenty-two minutes till arrival.

"Mr. Jakob?" Chuck asked. "Do you think you could explain a bit more about your EMP tool? We might need to use it again."

Tyrell replied, "I am quite sure we will."

They began talking about technical specifications, but my mind wandered.

I was the one who had told the senator to head for the man waving at us when we were in the boat. I made the decision to head for Tyrell. Did I recognize him? Did that have something to do with it? I had pulled us on this path, and now we were being dragged back to the cabin, straight into the birthplace of the nightmares that had plagued my sleep for the past six years.

"Strap in," Chuck said to me. "We're almost there."

"Oh my God," Damon said, pointing out the window. "What is that?"

Chapter 18

Susie didn't have much time.

She checked her watch. 7:24 p.m. Six minutes to go.

Twilight faded into the edge of night as late-season crickets chirped in the long wet grass. Susie squeezed through a tunnel of rock to the outcropping between two mammoth fir trees that guarded the lower edge of their property. One step at a time, as quiet as an Iroquois on the hunt.

She knew each root and rock on these trails like familiar lullabies underfoot.

Muttering quiet curses, she scolded herself for not grabbing night vision goggles before she'd left the house. She might be able to navigate the woods here blindfolded, but she could guarantee her adversaries had their gear on. The failing light would soon make her infrared signature an easy target soon.

On the other hand, she might not have night vision gear, but *they* would—which was her ticket to getting back into the house. Jujutsu was her favorite martial art. Use the enemy's advantage to their disadvantage.

Men tended to be big and strong, which meant heavy and clumsy.

But *why* hadn't she grabbed an extra layer or two of fleece? They'd been right there on the wall. At the time, she had been so focused on weapons she hadn't thought of the longer game, what would happen if she got stuck outside. The cold. The dark. To be honest, part of her had thought the person at the door really was just a kid who needed help.

Susie grabbed the first rung of the wooden ladder up into the blind.

Under the armor she had strapped on, she only had a long-sleeved cotton shirt and yoga pants and sneakers—her standard cottage outfit, now soaked toe to tip. The temperature plummeted on the mountain the moment the sun went down behind the ridge. The first star of the night appeared in the indigo sky.

Not a star, she reminded herself. Venus rose over the scimitar of a crescent moon.

Her teeth chattered.

She clenched her jaw. Stars broke through the deepening purple-black sky. She scanned the grass and dark underbrush below the sagging lower branches of the fir trees. Strained to listen over the forced attempt to suppress her own breathing. The chirps of a snowy tree cricket pierced the air as she held still. She counted: one, two. That was it. Only two chirps in about fifteen seconds. That meant it was forty-two Fahrenheit.

She had to hurry. Only three minutes to go.

Ellarose was out there somewhere too, and her daughter didn't have much fat on her bones. Chuck always said that it was good to have a reserve lard tank, but Susie thought that was mostly an excuse for his belly. He said she would stop laughing if she ended up in a frozen lake. Ellarose had probably taken her North Face jacket, but Susie doubted she'd grabbed a hat or gloves.

Ellarose got cold very easily.

Another rung on the ladder, and then another.

Susie's weapon was slung over her back as she climbed. The attackers hadn't found this hunting blind. It was well hidden in these fir trees, and it wasn't really for hunting. More of a treehouse for the kids to watch deer and elk that passed through the property.

She hadn't heard any alarms go off.

That meant the house was still secure. The power was still on. The generator was in one corner of the cement foundation and vented outside, which made it impossible to cut off without entering the house itself.

If no alarms had gone off, it meant nobody had broken through a window or set off any of the interior motion detectors. Susie had set the system to secure as she ran out of the house, after she was sure Bonham had gotten himself down into the safe room. Her son was still okay. She was positive that nobody had gotten in there yet.

The game now was to lure the prey in. Get as many of them as close as possible.

First, Susie had to get back inside herself.

She was the bait.

Slowly, slowly, she raised her head into the treehouse. Nothing. Nobody there. A small exhale of relief and she climbed in, got to her knees, then retrieved her weapon and unclipped the cover from the sight. Checked her watch.

One minute to go.

She slipped onto her belly and sighted along her barrel, staring through a gap in the blind. The grass and trees around the house looked empty. No movement that she could detect. No lights but the ones that should be there. Except.

What were those red lights hovering in the deep indigo sky?

Red dots in the distance. Not just one or two, but a whole cloud of them. Airplanes? Was the Air Force conducting an operation? Helicopters? Maybe if she set off the house flares, they would bring whoever it was over here.

No time to think about that.

She unclipped the 37-millimeter smoke bombs and explosive ammo and laid them out on the wooden deck. Loaded one of the explosive rounds into the launcher.

The glowing hands on her watch read 7:29 p.m. With one hand cupped to block the light, Susie took out her cell phone and turned it on. Her eyes had adjusted to the darkness. She needed to reset the dilation of her pupils. The bright blue light of the screen blinded her for a second. She checked the bars. This close, the phone had reconnected to the house's Wi-Fi. Maybe it would give her a chance.

Damn it.

Still no outgoing internet, but she could text Bonham. She considered doing it, but the time to tap in a message would eat up precious seconds, and what would she say?

She turned the phone off but kept it out.

Right on cue, the exterior lights of the cabin clicked on. Bright floodlights lit up the log walls of the house, the brick walls of the outhouse, all sides of the workshop and outbuildings. The grounds lit up like daylight.

She scanned back and forth.

To the left, just past the jungle gym, she detected motion. The bright lights had to be a surprise, but she knew exactly when they would turn on. Her attackers, trying to encircle the house, must have on their night vision gear, she wagered. Any grunts or movement in her field of view would expose them.

Off to the right, in a stand of ferns, she heard a quiet curse. Farther along the side of the house, past the back deck, slight movement in the hydrangeas.

Susie clicked her phone back on, accessed the house lighting through an app, and shut off the lights. The scene ahead of her dropped back into blackness a second later. She pocketed her phone. Even in the darkness, she knew exactly where she was aiming. She knew every patch of switchgrass and milkweed and goldenrod.

A hollow thump and flash as the 37-millimeter launcher released the first explosive round. In quick succession, she reloaded, aimed, and fired another to the far side of the house. The first round found its target and detonated. Incoming muzzle fire lit up from her left and right. She loaded a smoke bomb and fired one, reloaded and fired off another.

That was enough. She needed to get out of here. She got to her feet. Stepped forward.

Dropped into empty space.

She held her weapon up and to her chest, squeezed her arms tight to her body and straightened her legs. She'd seen Chuck do this a hundred times, but had been too chicken to try it herself. Until now. He said you needed the same tucked-in body shape the SEALs had when they jumped out of helicopters into the water, except she wasn't going to hit anything liquid.

Her back and head slammed back as she hit, then pressed down as her body shot forward. Chuck had installed a children's slide. She needed to get this dismount exactly right. An instant later she went airborne. Susie leaned her body up and put her left foot forward.

It jammed into the dirt.

Off-balance, she stumbled forward and managed to get her right foot out in time to catch herself and propel forward into a run. Bullets snapped into the tree branches twenty feet overhead, the cracks of the shots echoing off the cliffs to the north of the house.

Smoke billowed into the air from the hissing casings she had launched. She ran into the cover of it. Scanned back and forth, leading with her AR-15's barrel. Muzzle flashes indicated they were still firing at the hunting blind, now fifty feet behind and twenty feet over her head. She sprinted forward to the sunken garden path that led around the back to the patio doors.

That first explosive round had found its target. She was sure she glimpsed the shadow of a body cartwheeling away from its blast. She didn't bother to watch the second one hit. What she needed more than anything was ten seconds of confusion. Their night vision goggles were off by now, their retinas still overexposed. Their fire and attention directed somewhere she wasn't.

She plunged into the billowing cloud from one of her smoke bombs. This path brought her between the hiding spots of the attackers she had seen from the blind. If she cut between them and to the house, she could unlock the exterior doors with the fob in her pocket. Once locked behind her, the ballistic glass and plastic coatings would make it tough for them to get inside. All she needed was ten-second head start.

She just needed enough time to get downstairs and into the safe room with Bonham.

From there, she could use the webcams to watch them breach the exterior and enter the house. She would wait, make sure as many were inside as she could.

And then blow the hallway.

Chuck had installed explosive devices in the downstairs corridor.

The basement was off-limits, nobody ever went down there except with mom or dad. Susie had argued with Chuck, said it was dangerous, but this had been at the height of his paranoid phase last year, when he'd dug the tunnel from the Baylor cottage to theirs. When he was in one of those moods, she had to let him have his way.

Now, she could kiss him.

Through the smoke, she could see the patio door.

Someone yelled off to her left. They were moving to flank the tree blind. She kept low and felt for the key fob in her pocket. Stepping quietly, she reached the edge of the deck. She pressed the fob and unlocked the house doors.

The gunfire around her stopped. Voices went quiet.

A loud ringing punctuated the moment of silence. Susie was one step up toward the patio.

She froze in a sickening realization the noise was coming from her own phone. It rang again. It had to be Bonham. "Damn, it, not now."

She got to the top of the stairs and reached for the door. She scanned to the right, looked at the workshop and thought she saw something shimmer. Was there something in the driveway?

A man stood to the side of the workshop and stared into the middle of the driveway as well, staring at empty space. What was he doing? Why wasn't he keeping in cover? What was he looking at?

Her left hand snapped back as if jerked by a string. Her head whipped sideways.

Two deafening cracks.

Susie staggered and ducked.

A man fired again at her from ten feet away, advancing steadily along the flagstone path from the garage. Her AR-15 tumbled from her right hand. She swung around and grappled for it.

The man reached the bottom of the patio stairs. Still five feet below her, but he had to be at least six-three and two hundred pounds. Dressed in full body armor. And coming at her fast.

She didn't have time to retrieve her weapon.

Time slowed down.

Size didn't matter.

Technique and surprise were everything. Focus, she said to herself. Be in the moment. Unstable and already spinning from the impact of the rounds, Susie ignored her weapon now sailing away. She bent her legs and used her momentum to come around fully, and kept her eyes on the man.

At a jog, he bounded up two steps at a time. His weapon pointed at her. He fired again, a glancing round that Susie barely felt.

She launched herself straight at him.

He didn't expect it. He fired point-blank at her midsection.

This time, she felt the gut shot. Agony mushroomed in her abdomen. The armor wasn't designed to stop high-velocity rounds at this range, but she had no choice. With her left hand she dug her nails under his neck guard and ricocheted off his shoulder. She fell into open space behind him.

Dropped five feet toward the garden, her body accelerating.

She used both of their bodies' opposite momentums to yank on his neck. Her left shoulder ripped agonizingly as it dislodged—he was twice her weight—but he jerked back. They pirouetted in the air for a long beat before slamming into the wet flagstones in a mess of arms and legs.

The man was built like an ox.

He bounced off the ground and was already halfway back to his feet. But one thing jujutsu had taught Susie. A good grip was worth more than all the muscle in the world. Lancing pain screamed through her shoulder, but she kept her fingers locked on his neck guard, her legs now wrapped around his torso. He lifted her from the ground as he rose. His weapon up and forward, but this was close contact fighting now.

Susie had the Bowie knife in her right hand.

With everything she had, she jammed her right toward her left. The blade hit something solid. The man recoiled. She kept her grip, her body going airborne, and shoved the blade again. This time the man crumpled, and they fell back into the dirt.

With one final grunting, screaming effort, she heaved the blade home.

Soft gurgling noises.

Hot blood spilled over her hands.

The man convulsed in the grass, his hands grappling at his neck. She disentangled herself. Gasped and made it to the first step, struggled up three more, then stepped onto the deck. The door just inches away from her outstretched fingers.

Her face crunched sideways into the patio door. Like someone had hit her with a two-hundred-pound sledgehammer. Her ribs caved in, the wind knocked out of her in a sucking blow. She fell to the deck face-first and gasped for air.

She turned her head, screamed, and got to one elbow.

Her mind tried to make sense of the information coming from her eyes. What was in front of her? A giant machine-dog, pogoing from one leg to another. Six feet long with cylindrical robotic legs that it bounced back and forth on as it toppled back from her and regained its own balance in a jerky mechanical flail. It reared to attack her again, but then stopped.

The pause gave her the split second she needed to get back to the door.

In Susie's peripheral vision, a dot raced toward her.

She struggled to one knee, slammed back the patio door, and was just running in when the flash-bang of a grenade shot her forward onto the hardwood floor. She didn't feel anything, couldn't hear anything. The world went into a blank high-pitched whine. In a haze, she turned, grabbed the door, and slid it closed just as the huge mechanical dog crashed into it again.

Bullets punched at the ballistic glass. Crisscrossed and dotted and dented it, but the glass held. For now. It wouldn't for much longer under this onslaught.

The room seemed to spin.

She was next to the shelves Bonham had climbed up a few hours ago. She put a hand to the back of her head. It came back covered in blood and burnt black skin. Her stomach seared with pain. She wanted to retch. Another spray of bullets thudded into the plexiglass. One of them punched through. She ducked.

A red dot flashed past and then into the kitchen window. Another detonation. A splash of orange flame sheeted across the glass.

Those red dots in the sky were kamikaze drones, Susie realized.

"Momma? Where's Ellarose?" Bonham stood at the top of the stairs. His knuckles white as he gripped the banister. "I'm sorry, I know you said—"

"Come. Come help me." Susie struggled to her feet but almost fell back. "Ella's outside, we're going to get her." She stumbled toward the stairs.

Bonham ran over in his stocking feet and took one of her hands. The four-year-old did his best to provide some support to his mother.

He didn't cry, didn't shrink away.

They reached the steps and she stumbled and fell down half of them. Behind them, upstairs, concussions rocked the log walls. Battering against the windows. Susie dragged herself along the twenty-foot hallway and into the safe room. A grim thrill of excitement as she shoved the door closed with her right shoulder, then slumped into a chair by the bank of monitors.

Her chest armor had cracked. Blood spilled from her midsection, dribbled down her legs, and pooled on the parquet floor by her feet.

Footsteps over their heads.

The attackers had breached the outside door and windows. Yelling and someone barking a command. Not in

English. A group of men appeared on the kitchen monitor. A ghostly white face came into view on the hallway monitor. The man peered around the corner and ducked back.

"That's it," Susie grunted. "Come see us. Come have a look. Come see what I've got for you."

This space wasn't exactly a panic room. It was more of a honey trap.

Chuck hated the idea of being cornered somewhere, especially up here, where there was little chance of help. Which was why he'd dug the tunnel from here to the Baylor house. It was hidden, no way you would see the wooden entrance built into the paneling if you didn't know it was there. The concealed egress point was five feet behind Susie, behind the metal shelving stacked with sacks of rice.

That was Chuck's big plan.

If anyone attacked this place again, and they got trapped in the basement like they did last time—draw them in, blow up the basement, then escape out the back tunnel.

It was a good plan. "Chuck, honey, if you can hear me, I love you," she whispered.

It had been twenty minutes since she'd called out to Ellarose in the forest, telling her to meet them at Uncle Tony's.

Her little girl was waiting for her.

Susie took the red arming key from Bonham, inserted it into the lock, and turned it. More faces appeared around the corner in the hallway. Two men edged their way in and called out. Now four people were in the hallway outside her door. Three more arrived.

Susie's finger hovered over the detonation button.

A loud ringing echoed. It was Susie's phone. It buzzed and vibrated in her pocket. She looked over at Bonham. "Are you calling Momma again? You shouldn't have called me before, I said to st—"

He shook his head. "I don't have my phone. It broke, remember?" He had an old one they'd given him, not connected to the cell service, but that he could use to connect to the Wi-Fi. He had dropped it in the toilet two days before and it had stopped working.

Susie's phone rang again, even louder, it seemed. Insistent. It couldn't be a coincidence.

Who was calling her now? And *how* were they calling her? There was no outside connection to the cell network, no internet connection.

The men outside in the hallway had something in their hands. Something bigger than a gun. Was that a rocket-propelled grenade launcher?

Chapter 19

O h my God..." I stared slack-jawed out the window. Lauren leaned over Olivia to look out. "My God," she whispered.

The truck swept past huge metal towers supporting high-voltage electrical wires strung across this section of Interstate 66. The twilight sky was indigo toward the east, faintly orange to the west where the sun had gone down over the Shenandoah, but we could clearly see them.

Hundreds of birds sat on the electrical wires high overhead.

Except they weren't birds.

If we hadn't had such an intimate experience with the vicious killing machines, we might not have even noticed them. The grouping looked like a gathering of crows. A dozen of them took to the air as we passed underneath. They didn't fly in formation. Not like airplanes. They undulated together like a flock of sparrows, like a school of fish. Not mechanical-looking, but natural, biological.

"They can't see us," I said. "Right?"

"Probably not," Tyrell replied. "The truck's surface bends infrared through ultraviolet wavelengths around us. The panels are flat and radar-wavelength absorbing. Standard stealth stuff. Backed by the organic light-emitting diode displays, in optical terms the effect is like an octopus changing its skin as it swims past a coral reef."

I craned my neck and pressed my face against the glass. Luke, sitting beside me and watching a video with earbuds in, protested and tried to push me away. I ignored him and kept my eye on the rolling wave of drone-birds in the night sky.

They didn't follow us.

"Powering themselves up," Damon said quietly from the front.

I said, "Excuse me?"

"The drones we just saw. They were recharging on the power lines. We've done designs like that. Uses induction from magnetic fields around the electrical lines, saps a little power out to recharge their batteries."

"You said those things were small. That they couldn't travel far."

"I was wrong."

Chuck said, "I think that's about the first time I've heard you say that."

"I'm glad you're enjoying it."

"Can't say that I am," Chuck replied.

"Can't say I'm surprised," Damon said.

I peeled my eyes away from the window. "Not surprised at seeing a flock of killer drones flying over Virginia?"

"You know how long we've had killer drones flying in other people's skies?"

"This ain't exactly Yemen," Chuck said.

"Tell that to the Yemeni women and children. We've been doing this to everyone else on the planet for twenty years."

"This ain't the best time to be moralizing," Chuck said grimly.

"I'm just saying it doesn't surprise me that it's finally happened here."

I said, "This isn't the same."

"As what? Killing Americans with drones?" Tyrell said from the front. "Who do you think was the first one to do that?" When nobody replied, he answered himself, "In 2011, our American government assassinated Anwar al-Awlaki, a US citizen born in New Mexico. Not in a war zone. No trial by jury. No assumption of innocence. Death by drone."

"He was a terrorist," someone said quietly.

It was Archer. He didn't lean forward to engage in the conversation but kept still in the back-left seat. He watched everyone else carefully.

"That was an extrajudicial execution," Damon said. "No due process. He was an imam right here in Virginia, did you know that? He served as a chaplain at George Washington University. The FBI investigated him, but didn't find enough evidence for a criminal prosecution. So we assassinated him instead."

"And two of the hijackers of American Airlines Flight 77 that crashed into the Pentagon on 9/11," Archer said, almost whispering. "They attended his services when he was imam here. Can you add that part to your bleeding-heart story?"

"So, if two white nationalists blow up a building, do we go and arrest the pastor of the church they attended in Savannah?"

Chuck said, "If the pastor told them to do it, yeah, we do."

"And we have a trial, right? Present evidence?"

Archer said, "The Fort Hood shooter. Al-Awlaki exchanged at least two dozen emails with him. And the guy that tried to bring down Northwest Airlines 253 with that underwear bomb. Remember him? And the Times Square bomber. The list goes on and on. Al-Awlaki was the Bin Laden of the internet. He deserved what he got."

"Where was he killed?" I asked.

"Yemen."

"Isn't that a war zone?" Chuck said. "Virginia isn't a war zone. This is terrorism, pure and simple." He repeated, "This is *not* an active war zone."

Damon said, "Neither are most of the places we carry out assassinations using drones."

"Now hold on, son," the senator said from behind me. "We are not assassinating anyone. Every drone strike is a legally sanctioned—"

"By who, exactly, Senator Seymour?" Tyrell said from the front. He turned to face us. "By you? Or perhaps by your niece?"

"Pardon me?" I said. "Why are you dragging my wife into this?"

"Isn't that what you were doing in China?" Tyrell asked Lauren. "What you were just in Hong Kong for?"

The way he said it, I had the sinking feeling he knew more than I did. I turned to my wife. "What's he talking about? I thought you were at a conference on international relations."

"I was," Lauren replied.

"Then what does he mean?" I made sure the kids had their earbuds in.

Lauren stared at her feet.

Archer leaned forward, his Glock back in his hand. "Mr. Jakob, what exactly *are* you getting at?"

"I apologize," Tyrell replied, "but I did do my homework on Damon's friends, especially after you all became front-page news. Mrs. Mitchell *does* work for you, Senator, does she not? In the drone program?"

"Lauren?" I repeated. "*What* is he talking about?"

"I do some work, sometimes," she said, still not looking at me. "Evaluating the legality of certain targeted kill lists. Particular targets. It's part-time work the Department of Justice sends to our firm."

"Why didn't you tell me?" My mind raced. Her sudden rise to making partner at her firm. The international meetings and travel. She was connected to—*related* to—one of the highest-ranking members of Congress.

"It's classified, Michael," my wife whispered back. "It's not the sort of thing I could bring up over cornflakes."

"Damon, did you know this?" I turned to the front.

"I had no idea."

I wasn't sure I believed him. Then I had another thought. I asked my wife, "Did those Chechen terrorists kidnap you because you authorized killing someone?" It had seemed too random that she had been taken hostage by them, when maybe it wasn't accidental at all. No coincidences, right?

"I don't know. I have no idea."

"Lauren, honey, you're going to have to do better than that."

Tyrell said, "Terrorist Tuesdays, isn't that what you call them, Senator?"

"Pardon me?" The senator's voice gained a harder edge.

"Like Taco Tuesdays, except instead of sharing tortillas, you get together with all the branches of government and decide who you want to kill this week."

"I'm not sure I like your tone, Mr. Jakob."

Archer leaned forward with the Glock. "Whose side are you on, Tyrell?"

"Does questioning our government automatically make me an enemy?"

"Wait," I said, raising my hands to defuse the situation. I checked the kids again and made sure they couldn't hear us. "Keep calm, please. I want to hear this. It might be important." I turned to Chuck. "Maybe we can understand what's going on better." I finished by staring at my wife, who avoided my gaze.

"Senator Seymour," Tyrell said. "You are chairperson of the Armed Services Committee, correct?"

"That is a matter of public record. Yes, I am."

"With Congressional oversight of the drone program?"

The senator didn't reply but nodded.

"Which is a bit of a misnomer," Tyrell said. "As oversight is a bit lax." He turned to me. "Did you know that the US military flies targeted killing operations for the CIA? All over the world? Each Tuesday, the various branches of government get together and submit a list of who they would like killed—based on who might be against American interests."

"We didn't start this," Chuck said. "The assholes who flew two planes into the World Trade Center are where you should be laying blame. Are you saying this is payback? Blowback?"

"An eye for an eye," Tyrell said. "Isn't that what the Bible teaches?"

"Leave my faith out of this."

"I'll tear out both eyes of whoever is behind this when we find them," Archer said. "Problem solved."

"Amen to that, brother," Chuck muttered.

Tyrell said, "Between the CIA and JSOC, we've basically got two shrouded, private armies that are carrying out daily assassinations using drones all over the world."

"That's not exactly how I would assess it," the senator said quietly.

"How would you assess it?"

"Those are justified, targeted killings. That's what I believe."

"And *I* believe we should change the middle word in CIA from intelligence to murder," Tyrell said. "That would better reflect its mission these days. Didn't the US make it illegal to assassinate people on foreign soil? President Gerald Ford passed that law in 1976. And it's *still* the law. So, what happened?"

Nobody answered.

"Lawyers are what happened," Tyrell answered himself again. "They don't even call it a kill list anymore. I believe it's called a disposition matrix, isn't it?" He turned to the senator again.

"This is why I said it didn't surprise me," Damon said quietly from the front. "We create a targeted kill list of anyone we judge to be against American interests—"

"It isn't like that," Archer said.

"And now, it seems that someone has created their *own* targeted kill list of Americans," Tyrell said. "That's what that ledger of names has to be."

Archer asked, "What ledger?"

"Damon mentioned it to me. Remember, Mr. Archer, the list you asked him about? The ones they collected from the house on the water. The list of names of American citizens?"

"You know this for a fact? And that was classified."

"I'm guessing."

"You sound like you know a lot more than you're letting on."

"Just because I can understand the enemy's motivation, Mr. Archer, does not mean I *am* the enemy."

"Damon," Chuck said. "You're sounding like you're against all this, but aren't you the one designing drones for our military? Aren't you *and* Mr. Jakob here both sucking on the teat of Uncle Sam?"

"I don't build drones that kill people."

"Really? Because only people kill people? Sounds like something I would say."

"And we're not the only ones with drone programs," Damon said. "Twenty years ago, maybe. Ten years ago, fifty countries had their own drone research. Now every country on the planet does. Even corporations have their own. Turkey was the first to add a machine gun to one, and those fly in automated formations. Even has the capability to kill autonomously."

"You think these are Turkish drones?" I said.

"These are Chinese drones," Damon replied.

Silence descended as we all digested this information. Just the thrum of the tires against the pavement, and the quiet squeaks of *Peppa Pig* through Olivia's earbuds. Lately she had said she was too old for *Peppa*, but she seemed to find it comforting now. Me too.

Archer said from the back, "You know this for a fact?"

"I know they were manufactured in China."

"Almost everything is manufactured in China," Chuck said. "Hell, I bet half of the Predator fleet is made there."

"They most certainly are not," the senator said.

"You know this how?" Archer asked.

Damon said, "Luke collected fragments of the drones that attacked us back at the house. Bits and pieces scattered across the lawn. I've been reconstructing them, looking at the chips and circuits. These are definitely Chinese drones."

"So this is an attack by the Chinese?" Chuck said.

"Please, let's not go down that road again," I said.

"Someone is doing this," Chuck pointed out.

Up ahead, through the windshield, I made out a flickering light. For the last forty minutes, as night descended, we'd wound silently up Interstate 66 in near darkness. No headlights coming or going. We had our running lights off, kept the interior almost dark except for dim blue reading lights.

When we'd passed the city of Front Royal, it had been almost totally dark. No lights, except for a few emergency ones in parking lots. Riverton was the same. Complete power blackout across the entire area. I hadn't seen any bright lights in almost an hour, and we were now climbing upward into the mountains.

I hadn't expected to see any lights at all.

"Look at that." I pointed.

Excitement rose in my throat. Maybe it was the police? A town with power? The suffocating blackness enveloping us gave me the feeling that we were alone, abandoned. The light ahead had a surprising effect. The others in the truck felt it too.

Except.

It wasn't a streetlight.

The truck accelerated up the incline and swept around a switchback in the road. The flickering light grew in intensity. Orange flames leapt into the deep purple sky under roiling clouds of black smoke. As we climbed closer, the churning blaze stretched into the distance along a ridge line.

Hadn't it just rained here? How was such a fire possible?

The answer slipped into view. A five-foot-wide platform suspended on six rotors hovered near the top of the tree canopy. It spit a gorging river of flame from a device suspended below it. Our truck swept along the hairpin and turned back, close enough to hear the roar of the flamethrower below the drone.

Smaller drones hovered nearby, their tiny red dots visible against the inky darkness.

A flotilla in the sky.

If the machines had sensed us coming, they would have hidden, I realized. They didn't know we were here. They didn't try to hide.

This answered a two-week-old mystery—where had all the fires come from? The ones across the Appalachians? They'd seemed to spring up everywhere. My mind retreated to a map I had seen of the fires, back when they'd been reporting them on TV. I reminded myself that had only been this morning. The locations of the fires seemed random at the time, but I added the ridge of new blazes here to that image in my mind.

It wasn't random. Someone was connecting the dots. Fiery flaming dots.

"Twenty minutes," Chuck said. "We're going to be at the cabin in twenty."

"They're cutting off Washington," I said. "The machines are cutting off DC."

Chapter 20

Susie extricated the phone from her pocket and looked at the number on the screen.

Irena.

The call was coming from Irena. Or Amina. Whatever her name really was.

One of the Chechen terrorists that Susie had invited into her home less than a week ago, before she knew who or what they were. They had fooled her and her friends. Susie had given Irena the Wi-Fi password, of course. They had been her guests.

Never invite a vampire in, wasn't that the rule? Except you didn't always know who the bloodsuckers were.

With one shaking finger she slid the answer button over. "Hello?"

"Susie," answered the familiar voice. "Whatever you are about to do, I suggest you stop."

A prickling heat crept down Susie's spine at the sound of Irena's lilting foreign-but-distinctly-Boston accent. Dread slithered into the pit of her gut, but not for herself. This woman Irena had played with her children just days ago, and shared warmth under a blanket on the couch when they ate popcorn and watched movies. How could she do this? Raging momma-bear anger eclipsed any fear for herself.

"You tried to kill me."

"We saw you had full body armor. We were trying to disable you before you hurt yourself, or anyone else. Which we failed at. You killed two of my men."

"What do you want?"

"Same thing as you."

"I don't think so."

"You don't want your children to survive the night?"

Susie's chest heaved in and out. Pain like fire burned through her torso.

Irena said, "You have a beautiful little boy."

A video chat request popped up on the phone.

Susie's finger hovered near the detonation button. She needed help. She couldn't trust anything this woman told her. Then again, she needed to get as much information as she could.

Susie accepted the video call.

But it wasn't Irena's who appeared on the screen. Ellarose's tear-streaked pale moon of a face materialized on the screen, her blond hair in a bob. Susie eyed the detonation button, looked back at Ellarose's eyes, closed her own.

Tick-tock. Tick-tock.

She tried to budge in her seat, adjust her position to lessen the pain, but her feet slipped away from under her in the blood now leaking from the pool below her to the door. Pain lanced like hot needles stuck into her spine. No way was she doing a Usain Bolt out the back tunnel with Bonham in her arms.

She studied her little boy. His lower lip trembled. Face white.

In the darkness of the forest behind Irena, over Ellarose's sobbing, Susie heard an owl calling out. Was that a barn owl? There was one out by the workshop most nights.

She stepped on a pedal by the floor.

"You want to watch another *Peppa Pig*?" Lauren asked Olivia.

"Yes, please."

My daughter smiled at my wife and then at me in that earnest way that melted my heart. Terrifying and confusing things had happened today, but to her, they had been erased into the past. She didn't understand. All she comprehended was that we were in a nice warm car with *Peppa Pig* episodes playing, mom to one side and dad to the other. She was hungry, but we said we couldn't stop yet.

Peppa Pig videos solved most big-world problems. Luke, on the other hand, had progressed to playing *Fortnite*.

"Fifteen minutes," Chuck said from behind me.

My stomach lurched each time he gave another countdown marker.

Going to his cabin in Shenandoah made me feel ill even in the best of circumstances. We still had no idea what we might be facing. We might show up and Susie would be making dinner. That's what I hoped. A nice cold beer and a laugh and some chicken wings, and we could hide up in the hills until whatever was happening was fixed by someone else.

Fat chance of that, a voice said in the back of my head.

Luke switched to watching *The Lego Batman Movie* on the display in front of him. He leaned against me. I put an arm around him.

Behind us, Chuck explained the layout of the cottage, all the modifications he and Susie had made, including the tear gas and explosives outside the safe room in the basement.

I didn't need to listen.

I had spent two months starving to death in that cabin. I knew every inch of it all too well.

"Mr. Jakob, I gotta ask." I leaned forward over the seat back in front of me to get closer to the man. "You must have kids, right?" Nobody would load all these videos into their entertainment system without them. Right?

"Two boys," Tyrell responded. "Want to see?"

I nodded.

Tyrell said, "Mr. Archer, can I access the display to show—"

"Keep an eye on him, Mitchell," Archer gruffly interrupted from behind me.

A few keystrokes and the image of two young boys appeared on the screen. "Ensign is six, Olympus seven," Tyrell said.

They stood on their own in the picture, a view of white-capped mountains in the distance behind them. No other humans in view. Neither of the kids smiled.

"You didn't go to them when this happened?" I asked. It would be my first reaction. Get to my family.

"And drag them into it?"

I looked at Luke. What I would give to *not* have him here with me, but then, where would he be? "I understand."

"Humans are capable of terrible things."

"I suppose humans are behind the machines," I said.

"Maybe not," Damon said. He was in the front, and back in his safe space. On his laptop, analyzing something. "The machines might be operating entirely independently. Now they've been let loose, those things could roam the entire United States, killing indiscriminately. Maybe the machines even launched themselves."

"Like Skynet?"

"Maybe. What about that artificial intelligence that got loose in that hedge fund in Connecticut a few years ago? Nobody even knew all the people in the organization were all gone. The machine operated as a legal person, an incorporated entity operating entirely by itself making trades and mimicking people for months before the authorities realized it and shut the thing down."

"Can we at least stick to human bad guys? We know humans are involved in this. They kidnapped my wife."

"Might have been humans hired by machines."

"You're kidding, right?"

"I'm just saying."

Tyrell said, "It was Sun Tzu who said not to use flames in battle unless you are fireproof yourself. Letting artificial intelligence loose in weapons systems is something I have long campaigned against."

The truck hummed along in silence for a few seconds.

I asked Damon, "What are you doing?"

"Analyzing the signal spectrum I picked up when we passed that flock of drone-birds and the flamethrowers. They operate off UWB, ultra-wideband, as I figured they might. 2.4 GHz is too crowded and doesn't penetrate water or rain or leafy environments well. Optimal antenna length is about a quarter to half of wavelength—"

"Smart," Tyrell interrupted. "Drones that small, the antennas need to be tiny as well. A quarter wavelength of 10 GHz is what? About—"

"Eight millimeters," Damon answered. "Which would fit the size of those devices. Low power. Short distance." He pointed at his laptop screen. "See? The signal is jumping around in predetermined sequences. To most outside observers it would look like a bit of RF noise. The VHF signals you picked up are for intermittent long-range communications to larger drones, I would guess. Maybe ones on the ground. They must operate as a pack."

I asked, "How does this help us?"

Damon shrugged. "Now that I can see where they're communicating, maybe we can jam them. Hack their network if I can decrypt and understand the protocols."

The flames receded in the rearview mirror.

I leaned closer to Tyrell. "You think it's someone inside our own government carrying out these attacks. Isn't that what you said? If that's a targeted kill list, you think it's a list of US citizens to kill, made up by Americans?"

"As Mr. Indigo pointed out, it would not be the first time the American ruling class has decided to assassinate its own citizens without trial, for political purposes."

"I wouldn't call terrorism a political opinion."

"What would you call it?"

"So, these aren't really Chechen terrorists?"

"Might be. Or they could be guns for hire. Maybe both."

"Mercenaries?"

"Don't tell me you don't think half of America wants to kill the other half."

"That's a double negative."

"You get my meaning. I believe this presages a second civil war, of sorts. Or, perhaps, might avoid one. The whole idea of a targeted kill list is that, in theory, it averts the indiscriminate killings of full-blown war."

"Who inside our government?" The more I listened to him, the more he seemed unbalanced. Weren't genius and madness two sides of the same banknote?

Then again, half the time Chuck had most of these same types of conspiracy ideas. That a "deep state" was acting within our government for its own purposes. Whatever Tyrell was thinking, I seemed to have gained some of his trust. Or maybe that's what he wanted me to think.

I probed further. "Do you have an idea? Of whom, exactly?"

"The same people carrying out these types of precision attacks on foreign soil, except they have now turned our own country into the battlefield."

"You need to be careful what you say, Tyrell," Archer said from the back.

"Indeed I do. I do." He lowered his voice to a whisper and beckoned me closer. "Think about it. Degrading our own military, shutting off communications and power. Isolating the population, and then assassinating the people who might oppose your rise to power. How is it that the mighty American military has let this happen on their own soil, unless they are *letting* it happen?"

I asked again, "Any idea who that someone would be?"

"Who would benefit the most?" Tyrell replied. "Who is the last man standing, so to speak? Who, despite their protests, is the one that ends up in power? Imagine how this plays out. Massive terror attack rocks the nation. Then terrorists are killed, mission accomplished. Sound familiar? Who will be the king left on top of the hill when the dust settles?"

He looked at the third-row seating, right at Senator Seymour.

I glanced behind me, then back at Tyrell. "Did you come to find Leo on purpose?"

Before he could answer, Chuck asked, "How does this EMP thing function?" He held up the gray metallic box. "We got about five minutes till we get there. How does it work? You're saying this *isn't* a miniature nuclear bomb? Because that could be handy."

"It's not the EMP you get from nuclear devices, which have three components," Tyrell replied. "E2 effects are due to scattered gamma radiation, which that gray box cannot reproduce, nor the E3 components which can last for minutes and are similar in effect to a solar geomagnetic storm—which is why low-yield nuclear weapons high over North America might be the best option for taking out the electrical infrastructure."

Chuck said, "Might be? I've heard—"

"And so has everyone else in the sixty years since the Starfish Prime test. Yes, that nuclear blast over the Johnston Atoll took out streetlights seven hundred miles away in Oahu, but most military equipment—-and even civilian infrastructure—has now been upgraded to handle E2 and E3 pulses, and even E1 fast-pulse effects."

"So this box can't do E2 and E3," Chuck said. "What's left? The E1? Fast pulse?"

Tyrell nodded. "Nuclear devices produce fast-pulse effects that trigger the Compton Effect, in which gamma radiation transfers its energy to electrons in the stratosphere that then travel downward at relativistic speeds, and depend on the shape of the Earth's magnetic field—"

"Can you spare us the physics lesson?" Archer complained.

"In practical terms, that's a single-shot, ultra-high-storage capacitor. Push the button and it discharges—a by-product being a short-duration but high-intensity magnetic field, enough to scramble the volatile random access memory of unshielded computing devices with an effective range that falls off with the square—"

"Please?" Archer asked.

"Fifty feet, maybe a hundred. Small flying drones need to be light and don't have much shielding. A word of warning—I wouldn't discharge it if someone nearby has a pacemaker or other medical implant."

The truck slowed.

"This is it," Chuck said.

We pulled off the Interstate and stopped to turn left onto a smaller road heading south along the ridge line. A crescent moon hung high in the sky, offering the only illumination beyond the steely pinpoints of the stars. We had the interior lights low. Most of the interior illumination came from the video screens the two children watched. Tyrell said the inside lights wouldn't be visible to anyone outside.

Of course, we kept the headlights off.

Selena navigated in the dark. A heads-up display on the windscreen showed a vector line drawing of the road and the destination of the truck's navigation system.

"What is our plan, Mr. Archer?" Tyrell asked from the front.

"Whoever sent those drones to attack us, even if they had people on the ground, it was less than an hour ago. Gotta be unclear exactly what happened back there, assuming whoever sent the attack isn't sitting in this car." He kept his eyes straight ahead on Tyrell.

"I think we need to assume that," I said.

"We still have the element of surprise," Archer continued. "We go in and do reconnaissance. This might all be bull. We are only here because Tyrell said he triangulated a control signal up near—"

"The second set of drones we encountered was getting a transmission from this direction as well," Damon said. "The encrypted signal is hopping frequencies, but the signature is consistent and growing in power as we get closer."

Archer replied, "I'm going to take that with a heap of salt."

Chuck said, "The Baylor house is two hundred yards from mine, along the same dirt path in, but that driveway branches off just before you can see it from my place. We go in, see if anyone is at the Baylor place, then Archer and I access the tunnel while you guys creep in back along the driveway."

Archer said to Lauren, "I don't like people who point guns at me," while he kept his eyes on Damon, then added, "And we're up here to collect your friends. We do reconnaissance, get them safe and clear this cabin. If there's nobody up here, Tyrell is wrong, and we go back to Washington."

"I am not going to DC," Tyrell said calmly.

"Which is why you are not getting a gun. You can get out here, if you wish. Stay at Mr. Mumford's cabin for a few days while we sort things out. It's heavily defended, from what he's explained."

"This is my vehicle."

"Which I am commandeering in the name of the United States Armed Services Committee. We have the chairman sitting right with us." He tapped the senator's shoulder. "Wasn't this truck built and paid for using Uncle Sam's dime? And we have the guns—might makes right, at least for now."

Tyrell's mouth opened, then closed before he said, "I still protest."

"Which you can do all you want."

The truck slowed and turned.

Tar black outside the windows in the shadow of the high treetops. Ghostly lines painted on the front windshield's heads-up faded away as the navigation system's data exhausted known paths. It had been heading for the latitude and longitude coordinates Chuck had given us, but was now using radar, Tyrell explained. The wheels rumbled over gravel and dirt.

Selena slowed to a crawl to reduce noise.

I peered out.

The outline of fir trees painted a jagged black edge to the emerging carpet of stars, clear and bright at this altitude. To the south, straight ahead, the sky was black. Had to be clouds. Flickering lights danced around from the kid's videos. I better turn them off soon, explain to them they needed to be quiet.

Archer lowered his voice. "Lauren, you take one of the submachine guns and stay with the senator and the kids. And keep an eye on those two." He indicated Tyrell and Damon.

"Mike, you get the second carbine. Your wife will explain again how to use it."

Was he trying to be funny? Or practical? "Okay." I grabbed the gun.

"Once Chuck and I go into the Baylor place, you guys go back along the main driveway and pull up to the front. If it looks good, you go ring the doorbell. We still don't—"

A flash lit up the tree line, followed an instant later by a thudding detonation. The forest ahead of us seemed to light up like daylight. The staccato stutter of automatic weapons fire. We all looked up.

Everyone except Chuck.

Before we could stop him, the gull-wing door beside him slid open a foot. He ducked and darted out of it, then took off at a run into the black night, his dangling prosthetic hand attempting to hold his phone for illumination, his right hand gripping a submachine gun.

Chapter 21

"Chuck, get in the goddamn truck," I whisper-yelled as loud as I dared.

Tyrell switched to manual and guided the vehicle next to him as he ran.

Archer jumped over the senator in the middle seat, leaned out the door and snagged my friend by his shirt collar. Hauled him, legs still pumping, back into the left side of the truck, then grabbed the gull-wing door and pulled it closed. The truck didn't slow.

The bright lights around Chuck's cabin had just gone out, dousing the area in darkness. Another flash and a crunching detonation ahead of us.

And something else.

Smudges of light through the trees to the left. We coasted toward the turnoff to the Baylor house, and passed the bullet-riddled remains of a Mini. It had to be the one Oscar had brought up. He must have never made it to the house. Didn't look like he could have survived the vicious attack.

"My wife and kids are up there," Chuck gasped. "I gotta get—"

"Shut up." Archer clamped a hand over my friend's mouth.

Floodlights on tripods lit up the gravel path. A semitruck with two containers was stopped halfway down the driveway. No markings. "That's the same one I saw at the beach," I said.

Archer said, "You're sure?"

"I think so."

"I'm sure," Lauren said.

Two Humvees were parked beyond it.

Already three men in ballistic vests, weapons up and pointed this way, hustled along the gravel drive toward us. Red dots appeared against the star field in the sky. Drones approached at high speed.

"Go, go, go," Archer whispered.

The truck accelerated slightly. Wind swayed the treetops. The dark edges of the canopy flickered the stars and drone dots in the distance. We passed the Baylor driveway. The men's heads didn't follow our path but remained fixed on the dark dirt road behind us.

"Sorry," Chuck said as Archer released his fingers from his face. "I wasn't thinking."

"I know what you were thinking. I can't blame you. Anyway, it was a good diversion." Archer's head tracked back, his gaze now fixed through the rear window. "We didn't break cover for more than a few seconds. They have no idea what just happened. Might have been a deer for all they know."

Chuck slithered upright. The senator shifted in the seat to his right.

Burst of automatic weapon fire ahead of us.

A rattling barrage began.

In the dim light, I could make out the edges of the gravel road opening up into the clearing of the cabin's parking area. The bright lights of a few seconds ago, now gone dark, had to be the exterior floodlights of the cabin. Muzzle flashes lit up the semidarkness in the woods to the north.

But they weren't firing at the house.

Their target seemed to be the hunting blind that Chuck had built for the kids in the fir trees to the south of the house.

We'd gone up there on our brief stop. Red dots hovered in the distance, then grew in intensity. Getting closer.

Twenty feet to our right, a man crouched by the cover of the workshop, the back of his torso and head lit up by a solar pathway lamp. A body lay face down in the dirt by his feet.

The crouched man didn't see or sense us approaching but kept his attention forward.

The house became obscured.

"Those are 37-millimeter smoke bombs," Chuck said after a moment. "Susie must be trying to get inside."

"Or she's *already* inside and someone is trying to get close," Lauren said. "You can't know those are your smoke bombs."

"Then why would they be firing at the blind?"

"Can Ellarose fire a gun?" Lauren asked.

"She can."

"Maybe she's—"

"Stay still." Archer had his thick left arm locked around Chuck's neck, his right holding my friend's weapon pinned to the leather seat. "We need to get some situational awareness."

Chuck grunted, "I need to get to my wife. My kids."

"We don't even know where they are."

The interior lights had all been turned off. The kids' screens now dark. Lauren had Olivia back in her lap. My eyes adjusted to the darkness.

Luke peered over the seatback in front of him and pointed. "There's Aunt Susie!"

About a hundred feet south of our position, she looked straight at us as she sprinted the last ten feet to the deck through the wafting fog of the smoke bombs. Did she see us?

Luke squealed, "Look out!"

Chuck grunted and squirmed to get free, but Archer squeezed the lock-grip around his neck, the man's bicep bulging as Chuck's eyes did the same. He gurgled what was surely intended to be a roaring, cursing howl, his face going beet red.

Susie reached the patio door on the deck, but a man advanced along the garden path to her left and fired straight at her. The rounds nailed her, snapping her arms and legs like she was a toy doll. She spun around. Lauren put one hand over her mouth to stifle a scream.

"She's got armor on," Archer said.

The man surged up the stairs at her, the muzzle of his weapon flashing, the cracks echoing. Susie spun around, launched herself straight at him, and yanked back on his neck. A steel blade flashed in her hand.

"That's...my...girl," Chuck gasped.

Nobody breathed for two beats. Susie reappeared and staggered up the stairs. We exhaled together. Olivia sobbed. Lauren shushed her, said to keep quiet.

I said, "What in God's name—"

An animal burst from the trees to our left. In three awkward-but-graceful leaping bounds it crossed the hundred feet to the deck. Sailed into the air over the railing. The black-bodied beast slammed into Susie just as she opened the glass patio door. She bounced hard off the door and disappeared from view.

"That's a robotic carrier," Tyrell said, pointing to the deck.

"I'm in," Damon almost screamed from the front.

I said, "In what?"

"Their network. I got control of that thing as it passed by us. Not control, exactly, but I'm accessing its internal systems."

"What thing?"

"That robotic carrier. It had an open near-field communication channel. It looked like a troop support model. Sloppy, but I guess they didn't expect anyone to be this close. Not someone with a signal sniffer, anyway."

Ahead of me, Damon's fingers worked furiously across his laptop's keyboard. I looked back at the house. The robot-animal hesitated on the deck. Susie got to her feet and grabbed the door again.

"That's it," I said, "just get in—"

A red dot flitted in from the left. Susie's head disappeared in a flash of orange flame.

"No!" Chuck's body writhed as he tried to escape Archer's grip.

I said, "She's up. She's okay. I can see her inside."

On her knees, Susie slid the door closed behind her. But slowly. She looked hurt. Bad.

A spray of white dots appeared in the glass behind her as she disappeared. The glass clouded up with the impact of dozens of rounds. The echoes of the shots almost deafening. How many attackers were hiding in the bushes and trees around us? I counted three, four muzzle flashes. Maybe more.

"Did you say you got into their network?" Archer said over the noise at Damon.

"I have access to that robotic carrier."

"Now they know we're here. I did not give you permission t—"

"I don't think we need to worry about them knowing we're here because of our network access," Lauren interrupted. She pointed to her right and moved Olivia to her left.

Archer cursed.

The attacker who had been crouching by the workshop stood not more than two feet from Lauren. He had his weapon in his right hand and reached out with his left. Fingers outstretched, he hesitantly placed his hand flat against the window, right by my wife's head.

Even in the fading light and with his face guard and visor down, I saw his frown of confusion. He pulled his hand back and shouldered his weapon. Pointed it straight at Lauren and Olivia. I cringed, expecting him to pull his trigger, then flopped my body to the right to try and cover my wife.

Instead of firing, he prodded forward with the muzzle.

Archer barked, "Why aren't we moving?"

"Because there are targets coming from behind us," Tyrell replied.

The senator said from the seat behind me, "Is that who I think it is?"

I didn't have time to turn and see what he was talking about.

The man to Lauren's left knocked the glass with the tip of his barrel. His look of confusion changed, his expression hardened. He swung forward with the weapon again, but the truck was already accelerating backward and to the right. His gun swung into open space, just missing the front side window where Damon was still focused on his laptop screen, unaware of the man swinging a rifle barrel almost at his head.

Cool air washed over my left hand as I extricated myself from my wife's lap. Chuck was upright in the seat behind me, rubbing his neck, but where was Archer? Another draft of cold air. The left side gull-wing door was a few inches open.

I turned in my seat.

Chuck pointed to the front.

The man in the ballistic vest and armor was prodding the open air in front of the truck. He began swinging his weapon, then lifted his wrist to his mouth and started speaking. A dark shape materialized behind him. One hand darted, viper-like, around the man's neck. Archer pulled a steel wire tight into the unfortunate's windpipe and hauled him back, dragging the man into the shadows of the tall grass by the side of the drive.

Just in time.

Six more men marched in quick time past us. The barrage of gunfire died down. The truck edged to a stop on the gravel. Echoing cracks of gunfire went silent. Crickets chirped. The six men walked on the left side of the gravel drive and didn't seem to notice us. They were fixated on the house. Except it wasn't six men.

One of them was blond.

A very small one.

"Ellarose," I whispered.

Right behind her, holding the back of her neck, was a familiar face. The men had flashlights on their vests, and in the reflected light I saw her clearly.

Irena.

She fast marched Ellarose toward the house, flanked by four guards. Irena had her phone out and looked like she was calling someone.

"Chuck," I whispered. "Chuck, did you see—"

A trilling wail echoed in the night air. So close I thought an owl had flown into the truck. I looked into the rear row, but only the senator remained back there. The leather bucket seats beside him were empty. The gull-wing door to that side open a foot.

Where was Chuck?

"Oh, no," Lauren whispered. She pointed.

Chapter 22

I'm coming out," Susie said into the phone. "Do not shoot."
In the phone's display, tears streamed down
Ellarose's face, but her daughter seemed to be beckoning to
her.

Irena said, "A little courtesy can go a long way. *Of course*
we will not shoot. This is a ceasefire."

"This is an invasion."

"This is no invasion, Susan. Your own American
misadventures have proven that invasions of an uncooperative
indigenous population will always result in failure. Despite my
comrades regarding you to be soft as a nation, I believe the
average American would be *very* uncooperative. You have more
guns per capita in Virginia than Yemen."

"You're a terrorist."

"We can debate that when you come out." The woman's
voice echoed in the hallway. She was now in the upstairs living
room. Susie recognized the wood paneling in the image on the
screen.

Susie stepped on the pedal by the floor again. Nothing
happened. She should have heard the flares strapped by the
chimney going off, seen their flickering red-and-blue lights
illuminating the treetops in the exterior camera displays.

"Please come out, hands up," Irena said. "One of my men
disabled your warning device. Chuck explained the flares when we

were here. He told me a few things about this house. He is immensely proud of it."

Susie bowed her head and closed her eyes. Chuck, you *idiot*. A pretty girl shows up at the house and you can't keep your mouth shut, can you? What else did he tell her? Part of her interior emotional wall crumbled.

"Please," Irena said, "I do not want to hurt your children."

Groaning, Susie got up from her chair, her feet slipping in her own blood. As terrified as he was, Bonham did his best to help her. She was scared too, but making no decision was also deciding. She had to do something, and this was the last gambit she could use to try and protect her children. Sacrifice herself. Susie opened the locks on the safe room door, strained to hold her hands up. Two men in ballistic vests, face shields, and visors, their weapons pointed at her, directed Susie between them. They forced her along the corridor and up the stairs.

Amina—who Susie had met as Irena—was in the dining room. She had Ellarose by the scruff of her North Face jacket. She let the little girl go, and Ellarose ran over to Susie and Bonham. Susie knelt, groaning in pain again, and wrapped her arms around her two little ones. They said they loved each other. Tears flowed down their cheeks.

Amina turned and said something to one of her men. He nodded and ran back out the patio door.

In addition to Amina, there were now seven men in the kitchen and dining room, all dressed in the same nondescript black armor and face masks and visors, each with a submachine gun and backpack. Two of the men were already unpacking a crate. One of the large dog-bots ambled over the patio and back down into the garden. It had just carried the crate up. Red dots hovered in the black sky.

"Please, sit on the couch," Amina said to Susie. "I have a medic coming. I can see you are badly hurt. We are not animals."

"I would prefer to stand."

Susie was still crouched with her arms around her children. Ellarose grabbed her mother's neck and whispered as low as she could, said that she had something she needed to tell her. Susie said she knew, she loved them too. She said she needed them to be a big boy and girl, and that she was going to find out what these people wanted.

"That is the right question," Amina said. "What is it that we want?"

"You want to destroy lives."

"You think I am thousands of miles from my home for no reason?"

"No reason could justify this."

"Susan, I want to save lives. Let me find the right language that you will understand as an American. This is an incursion. Maybe a police action? Did you know that I was a policewoman, once upon a time, before my mother and father were killed?"

"Whatever happened to you," Susie said, "does not justify this."

"You do not even know what *this* is. It's not personal. At least, it wasn't—until your friend Mike killed Pyotr. He didn't need to do that." Amina took a deep breath and looked at the floor. "Do you know that America has eight hundred military bases on foreign soil? In almost a hundred foreign countries?"

"What does that have to do with anything?"

"It has to do with *everything*. By comparison, Britain, France, Russia, and China—the next largest military powers in the world—*combined* have fewer than thirty bases in foreign countries. Compared to America's *eight hundred*. Even at the height of their power, the world-spanning British Empire, which was the largest the world had ever seen, only had two dozen foreign military bases. America has now garrisoned the entire planet Earth on a scale never before seen in history."

"Excuse me if I'm not in the mood for a history lesson."

"What we are doing now will serve as its own history lesson. We are using your own weapons against you. You kill us with drones, we return the favor. Your own medicine."

"I just want my kids safe and away from you. Tell me what you want."

"Seymour."

"Lauren's uncle?"

"Senator Seymour, the chairman of the Armed Services Committee, with oversight of the drone program—the greatest terrorist on the planet. He kills hundreds of people a year in foreign countries, even his own citizens, without accusation, trial, evidence, or jury. You think this does not inspire terror around the world? Is this not terrorism? To borrow your language, in this operation, he is our Ace of Spades. And you think your friend Lauren Mitchell is so innocent?"

"What does Lauren have to do with it?"

"Ask her yourself. Your husband is on his way here with them. Soon this will all be over, and we will be gone into the night."

"I just want my kids out of here."

Susie stood upright, wincing in agonizing pain, but didn't want to give Amina the satisfaction of seeing her stay down. She grimaced a smile and shook her head when Amina again offered the couch. Ellarose pulled at her arm and insisted she needed to tell her something.

Amina said, "You Americans are using your worldwide garrisons to assassinate anyone you like. Death by committee. Drone strike from the sky." She held up a finger. "This person is against American interests? No problem. Gone." She retracted the finger. "How is this possible?" The finger extended again and pointed to the ceiling. "Eyes in the sky."

A man carrying a knapsack appeared through the door. Susie assumed it was the medic. She shook her head, I'm fine. But she wasn't. She felt lightheaded, the room wavering in her vision. She gripped her two children to make sure she stayed upright. Ellarose tugged at her again.

"Now," Amina said, "we poke the bully in the eye. Both eyes. Blind him. Take away all the satellites. Take away the GPS."

"Isn't that done? Why are you still here?"

"You think we are able to do this all on our own? Infiltrate your country like this? We have brothers and sisters all over the planet who have been under your thumb for years, under your robot eyes and killing fingers. What do you think I am still doing here? *How* do you still think I am here?"

The two women stared at each other for a moment, Amina smiling, Susie scowling.

Ellarose tugged and tugged on Susie's blood-soaked yoga pants. Susie relented and leaned down. Her daughter whispered in her ear. Susie nodded and told her, okay, okay.

"You will be pleased to hear that our mission is almost complete. In one or two days, we do need to disappear," Amina said. "The last thing we need to take from the bully is your money. Might makes right, but might comes from money in this world. We are waiting for your friends to arrive, which should be soon. As I said, this has become"—she paused to find the right word—"personal."

"Can we go to the bathroom?" Susie said. "The kids have to go, and I do too. Ellarose is desperate. I know, I know, no funny business. Send two or three guys in with us, have them sweep it. I'm not going to do anything stupid."

Amina's mouth opened and then closed. She said nothing.

"You want us to go right here on the floor? It's your choice. Aren't you making this your command post?" Susie said. "They're scared. You know what that does to a kid's stomach?"

Amina said something in a foreign language to the two men nearest her. They nodded, walked toward Susie and the kids, and began leading them to the upstairs bathroom.

Susie shuffled along behind her children, doing her best to look beaten and frail, which wasn't far from the truth. But Ellarose didn't need to go to the bathroom. What she'd whispered into Susie's ear was that daddy was already here. He was outside, right behind her, when she was brought in. That he was invisible somehow, the men didn't know he was here.

Was her daughter making it up? Susie made sure not to let her facial expression change as Ellarose repeated it again in a low whisper, right into her ear.

Invisible?

The barn owl, Ellarose said. When she and Chuck played *Call of Duty* missions and they wanted to exchange signals over headphones that only they would understand—that not even other teammates would get—they had a system of bird calls they would use to coordinate. Sparrow trilling meant to attack. The barn owl was a signal to hide. Whatever Chuck was about to do, they had to hide. The only place she could think of was the bathroom.

But how much had Chuck told Amina about this place?

And how could he have gotten here this fast? She had talked to him barely even an hour ago. These attackers had been here for less than that. How was it possible? Did she really trust Ellarose? Her daughter had a way of playing make-believe sometimes. A pattering noise came from the rooftop, but it was only the rain. Fat drops began falling on the deck outside.

In the distance, the call of a barn owl.

Amina began speaking in excited, hushed tones in a foreign language. Something was happening. They had found something. Or *someone.*

Susie hustled forward into the bathroom.

Chapter 23

I watched Amina, flanked by four large men in black armor and face masks, force-march Ellarose to the patio doors of the house. To our right, Archer had slipped a steel wire around the neck of the man who had pressed a hand against the invisible window and discovered us. He'd dragged the man off into the blackness of the tall grass and bushes behind the workshop.

Archer returned a moment later, just as Amina walked past the truck, which provided him cover. Instead of coming back to us, Archer took up position exactly where the man he just took out had been. Archer had on the man's vest and armor and helmet. He nodded at Amina as she walked by with the other men.

With mounting, desperate fear, I was afraid Chuck was about to single-handedly try to take out the four men who were with Amina. As tough as he might be, he only had one good arm, and these were professionals. After the bullet he'd taken a few days before, he could barely use his left arm with the prosthetic. Chuck appeared in the underbrush to our left, the glow of his face just visible in the light of the crescent moon.

He didn't shoot his submachine gun, though.

He cupped his hand around his mouth and mimicked a bird call.

"Is that an owl?" I whispered.

One of the men with Amina turned in Chuck's direction. The man clicked on a flashlight and played it along the bushes. Amina said something to him and he turned the light off and rejoined the group.

"I'm going out there to help him," Lauren whispered to me.

I held her in place. "You are not. I'll go."

"I'm the better shot," my wife said.

"Exactly. You stay here in the truck. Three of these are full." I dropped one of my submachine gun's magazines on the seat. I had a new one loaded in my weapon. Two half-empty ones on the seat on the other side of her. "You keep the children safe. Anything happens, you take off. Stay with the senator, he's your only family now."

Lauren squeezed my hand. "You're my family, Mike."

I kissed her, lingered for an instant, then leaned over and gave Olivia a little peck.

"I'm coming too," Luke declared.

"Whatever you're doing," Damon said from the front, "do it now. Amina has gone inside. Chuck looks like he might be about to dive right into the house."

"You stay here, protect mom," I said to Luke. "And if those drones get too close, you push the button on this." I gave him the EMP device, now almost fully charged. "You got that?"

He nodded.

"Damon, Tyrell, are you guys really inside their network?"

I readied myself by the left side door, gripped the submachine gun, and made sure the safety was off. Out the back window of the truck, faint glows came from the men back by the Baylor driveway, still searching for whatever had made the brief commotion there a few minutes ago.

We were surrounded. And about to attack.

"We're working on it," Damon replied.

"You can jam their drones?"

"Might be able to do more than that."

I gripped my weapon and closed my eyes. Opened them and looked at my family. I had to go. Susie and her kids were our family too.

"Oh, no," Tyrell said quietly from the front.

"What?"

A faint drumming began on the rooftop of the truck.

"It's raining."

"Is that bad?"

"You'll understand in a moment."

"Mike, go," Lauren whispered urgently.

I took a deep breath, hit the door button, and slid down and out into the cool night air. The door only opened a foot. I used an elbow to quietly close it behind me. Took two crouch steps backward away from it into the bushes by the side of the gravel road. I looked at the spot I had just emerged from.

Nothing.

The light was dim, almost dark, yet I saw trees and bushes on the other side of the road, exactly where the truck was. Knowing it was there, that I was seeing an optical illusion, I could see the bending of light, as if I was looking into a carnival mirror. The trees and bushes wobbled and warped. A black line focused and quivered in the middle, where nothing should be.

"Amazing, huh?" Chuck whispered from behind me.

A wet splotch hit my face. And then another. The treetops chattered with a squall of rain. Right in front of us, the illusion was shattered. The outline of the truck's roof became clearly visible as the rain hammered down on it, the sides now black with rivulets of water.

"Fun while it lasted," Chuck said.

The truck reversed past us and to the side in the cover of trees. So much for invisibility.

"We better hurry." Bent over, Chuck hustled across the gravel to Archer, who was still pretending to be the man he'd just killed. I followed.

"What was with the bird calls?" Archer asked.

Chuck explained how he used them in *Call of Duty* with his daughter. He told her to hide when she got inside, Chuck said. Through the rain, the red dots hovered in the distance.

"They've already seen us," Archer said. "Your heat signatures. Whatever overflight capability they have, they've detected us by now. Maybe they're trying to figure it out, but we have seconds till we have someone—or more likely, some*thing*—here."

"What's a bawbag?" Chuck asked.

"Excuse me?"

"In the car, you said bawbag. Where does that come from?"

"I spent time with a Scottish SAS unit in North Africa. A bawbag is slang for scrotum. A stupid person. What's the plan, Chuck? I'm giving you this one. I'll help you get your kids out, but after this, you owe me. You understand? You. Owe. Me."

Rain dripped down Chuck's face. "I understand."

"You have a plan?" Archer looked back at the house and then at the sky.

"Chuck always has a plan," I said.

Rain battered against the wooden roof. It was more of a barn. I knew Susie used it as a glassblowing workshop; that and pottery. There was a kiln in the opposite corner. The main area was open, forty feet long by thirty wide with a cement floor and cathedral ceiling twenty feet overhead. A collection of junk by the wall toward the house—old toys, rakes, a rusted antique tractor. It smelled of manure, but not from animals living here. Chuck had piled it along the south wall. For planting, he had explained when we came a few days before. A single emergency light shone near the exit door toward the main house.

"Just get in there with your hands," Chuck said. "Pretend you're diving in."

I hated manure in the best of circumstances. A lifelong urban dweller, my nose crinkled and throat gagged every time we swept by a farm on the highway and I smelled the stuff. Now he wanted me to dive into it headfirst?

"I only got one good hand," Chuck said. He was on his knees, submachine gun slung across his back, and wiping away as much manure he could with the forearm of his right hand. "Mike, stop being such a city pansy. Get in there, boy."

Taking a deep breath, I waded into the middle of the pile of manure, dropped into it up to my chest, and began a front stroke through it.

"That's it, Mike. Get some."

"I think I'm going to throw up."

"It's basically just mulched-up hay."

"And the dump I took this morning *used* to be a ham sandwich." I gagged.

"Mike, we gotta—"

"I got it."

My fingers felt a handle. With every bit of strength I could muster, I pushed back the cow dung. I took hold of the handle with both hands, bent down with my legs, and hauled up.

"Attaboy," Chuck said and joined to help me.

A yawning black hole opened in the cement floor. Chuck flopped onto his stomach in the manure and dangled his legs over the edge, then slid back and disappeared.

I checked the counter on my phone. Sixty-two seconds elapsed. Fifty-eight to go. My heart in my throat, I slipped on the

185

manure to my rear, then dropped through the black hole. Chuck caught me.

A string of lights blinked on.

Small LEDs lined the two rough concrete walls of the seven-foot-high concrete tunnel.

"Nothing." Chuck froze and listened. "If they knew about this, they would be shooting at us by now."

He grabbed an aluminum ladder from the wall, extended it, and propped it up to the opening overhead. Checked it once and then twice, looked at the counter on his own phone, then hustled ahead of me.

Fifty feet farther on, the tunnel ended in another door.

Chuck unlocked it with keys he took from his pocket, then gently, gently opened the door inward. I kept my gun up and pointed over his shoulder. Voices echoed from inside, but the safe room was dark and empty.

He motioned for me to come forward. I strained to lift the metal shelves, loaded with bags of rice, away from the door. Just needed enough for us to squeeze through. Chuck stepped through first, tiptoeing into the middle of the room. The light grew brighter as we neared the entrance to the safe room, the door wide open.

Chuck stopped and looked down.

I followed his eyes.

Blood covered the floor by the entrance. Bloody footsteps led away down the hallway.

The voice became louder. I recognized the accent. That was Irena—or Amina, I corrected myself—the Chechen terrorist. Susie was explaining to her that the kids had to pee.

I checked my phone.

Eight seconds.

We padded soundlessly down the hallway, Chuck ahead of me, his weapon up. We were quiet, but somebody had to smell our stench. So much for stealth. I caught sight of Bonham and Ellarose's little legs as the first explosion lit up the room above us.

Archer had begun his bombardment.

He had a dozen grenades and two slabs of C-4 in his backpack, he had explained outside. He could light up the front of the house, mount an assault that would get their attention, and then hightail it back into the woods. We had to pick him up a hundred yards past the Baylor turnoff, he said, and he made Chuck promise. On the lives of his children. I would never leave any man behind, Chuck had replied.

Another explosion rocked the cabin. The voices upstairs went from talking to yelling. Chuck made a hand motion. I assumed he wanted me to go up the stairs first. Great. I got onto the first step.

A bloodcurdling screech.

Susie's scream.

Chuck bounded up the stairs past me. I cursed and jumped up after him. Susie appeared from the upstairs bathroom; her legs locked around a man's waist. She stabbed him in the neck with something, over and over and over. I reached the edge of the floor, leveled my weapon through the gap in the guard rail, took a split second to look, and then pulled the trigger.

The recoil knocked me back.

But my guess had been correct.

Everybody up there had their attention on the explosive light show Archer had started at the back-patio doors. I sprayed the room with a stuttering hail of fire. Chuck roared and darted into the bathroom. Gunshots behind me. Susie was on the floor on top of the man she had been attacking. Figures darted in my field of vision to my left. I pulled the trigger again and showered rounds back and forth across the cabin's interior.

Someone clapped me on the back.

"Go, go, go," Chuck said.

A small body was gripped to his chest with his right hand. A blond head bobbed lifelessly in his arms. Susie passed by me, hobbling and dragging herself as fast as she could, with Bonham in tow behind her. I pulled the trigger and scattered another ten rounds. Incoming fire blasted the wood and walls around me into a furious cloud of splinters and chips.

I turned and hopped down the stairs, landed and sprinted down the hallway. Grabbed the door of the safe room as I heard footsteps behind me. I slammed the door shut.

Looked at the control panel.

Pulled the switch.

Chapter 24

A thudding detonation almost blew the door off its hinges. Even protected behind the door, the concussion's shockwave popped my ears. A loud whining blocked out everything else. My brain lost coherence. I blinked. Dust billowed from the air gaps around the door. What was I doing here again? I had a vicious-looking weapon with a curved magazine in my right hand. The buzzing whine edged away.

Looked down.

I stood in a pool of blood.

Probably Susie's.

Susie.

I turned to the metal rack by the back wall. A gaping opening behind it, dimly lit with a string of LEDs along the tunnel wall. Screaming. Was that Chuck? Susie? A man's voice cursing and howling, but not in English. The screaming came from the outside of the door, half caved in beside me.

A voice in my head. In Chuck's southern twang it said, "Get in the game, Mike."

I blinked again. Wiped my face with the back of my left hand. Slipped in the blood. Checked the submachine gun in my right hand and stumbled toward the metal shelves.

A hollow thud on the half-wrecked entrance door. Someone was throwing their shoulder into it from the other side. I squeezed past the metal shelves loaded with rice and into the tunnel. I stopped, my entire body shaking, and took the time to concentrate and close the tunnel door behind me. Locked it. That would take them at least a few seconds to figure out.

Fifty feet ahead of me, Chuck struggled up the aluminum ladder.

A blond rag doll in one arm.

Not a doll. That was Ellarose. Her head seemingly unconnected to her body. Cheeks spattered in mud. Not mud, I realized. Blood covered her face.

"Help me!" Chuck screamed.

I stumbled forward and broke into a run. Slung the gun strap over my shoulder and head and jumped onto the lowest rung of the ladder. The buzzing in my ears subsided enough that I could hear Susie's sobbing wails just above us as she squatted in the manure with her arm around Bonham. She did her best to reach down to grab Ellarose's flopping arms, but she was obviously badly hurt herself. Susie's blond hair matted to her face. A dark smudge around her midsection.

"I got her, I got her," I whispered to Chuck.

I was up beside him on the ladder, and took Ellarose's body from him. She was always tiny, but now she felt like she was made of glass and twigs, the angles of her arms and head not making sense. Moaning, Chuck let her slip into my arms and used his good hand to pull himself up the ladder. I held Ellarose and climbed up behind him.

The door to the tunnel, fifty feet down, thudded as someone crashed into the other side of it.

"Hurry," I didn't have to say but did.

Slipping on the manure, I got to my feet at the top of the ladder and ran as gently as I could while cradling Ellarose. Chuck had his weapon out and scanned the edges of the back door of the workshop. Stuttering gunfire and crunching explosions resounded inside the cavernous barn structure and echoed off the rock walls outside.

We ran out into the rain. I slipped and slid in the mud.

"Over here," Lauren yelled.

The truck was a hundred feet up the drive, the back-left gull-wing door fully open. Lauren on one knee, her weapon up and scanning back and forth around us. She raised her weapon and fired, then fired again.

I turned.

Angry scarlet pinpoints raced down through the drizzle.

I picked up my pace.

The muzzle of Lauren's weapon flamed as she swept it back and forth, firing constantly. I didn't look behind me, but I felt the heat of the little red dots homing in. Heard their terrible high-pitched whine growing over the fading buzz in my ears.

"Dad!" a small voice screamed.

Luke jumped from the back seat of the truck and ran past Lauren. She tried to grab him, but she was busy aiming upward. Luke slithered past her and ran out into the open.

The front door of the truck swung open.

"Dad! Get down!" Luke screamed again. He had the gray box outstretched in his hands.

I knew they were coming. I could feel them. I threw myself face-first into the muddy gravel slurry, curled my body around Ellarose, inert in my arms, and landed half on my back. As I spun in the air, a bright red dot appeared just inches from me. The fans of its blades blowing cool night air into my face.

It hovered but didn't move.

A dozen red dots now motionless in space around us. Using my feet, I scrambled back far enough that I could get up to my knees.

Twenty feet closer to the truck, Luke held up the gray box. He had pushed the button. Delivered an EMP pulse around us, but more red dots raced in the distance. Someone was behind Luke and wrapped their arms around him. Tyrell picked Luke up, shielded my son with his body, and began turning to get back to the truck.

"Watch out!" Lauren screamed.

Two shots rang out.

Spray shot sideways from Tyrell's head and he slumped into the dirt.

Right behind him in the truck, the senator had a Glock up. He'd just shot Tyrell. In the head. Lauren raised her weapon and pointed it at me. I cringed. She fired, but the shot skimmed past me. I turned. A man in a black ballistic vest crumpled to the ground.

Stumbling, I closed the last twenty feet.

Luke had extricated himself from Tyrell's body.

I paused the briefest of instants and considered trying to grab and drag Tyrell, but blood poured from his head into the leaves and grass. It was either try and save him, someone looked already dead, or make sure my son got to safety. With my left foot I kicked Tyrell, but he didn't flinch or budge. I felt more than saw the buzzing machines in my peripheral vision. Keep moving, said a voice in my head.

I grabbed my son with my left hand as I kept a grip on Ellarose's body with my right.

Chuck was already in the driver's seat of the truck.

Damon was in the passenger seat, his face pale, staring at Tyrell's body. He jumped forward as if he was going to try and get out, but then stayed still. Gunshots cracked from all directions around us. Another thumping detonation lit up the trees to our right. I collapsed into the truck's third row, doing my best to protect Ellarose's body.

The tires spun against the gravel, the truck accelerating as the two gull-wing doors began to close. Bullets ricocheted and thudded into the windows and walls of the vehicle. Ahead of us, on the dark road, three men ran toward the house. Chuck skidded toward the center of the road and straight into two of them, who flew into the air. The truck thudded up and down as we drove over one.

We sped past the driveway to the Baylor house.

Chuck jammed the brakes on.

"What are you doing?" Damon said.

Chuck didn't reply, but didn't move either.

"Chuck!" Lauren screamed.

In the dark, they might not be able to see the truck, but with the rain still hammering down, they saw something. Bullets impacted into the glass at the rear.

"There," Chuck said and pointed.

A light flicked in the bushes. He stepped on the accelerator and pushed a button on the driver's side. Damon's door began to swing open.

"What are you doing?" Damon yelled.

For an instant I thought Chuck was going to shove Damon into the trees.

But Chuck said, "Grab him. Get Archer into the truck."

The flickering light gained some intensity.

Archer's face appeared through the bushes. "Help me," he grunted.

"You have got to be kidding," Damon said to Chuck. "Leave him here."

"It's either you or him." Chuck grimaced and took out his Glock. Pointed it at Damon. "Now help him in."

Gunshots cracked and echoed.

Swearing, Damon tossed down his laptop and jumped out of his side to help Archer, except the man didn't exactly need help. At least, not for himself.

Archer smiled grimly and pulled a body by the scruff of its neck, like he was dragging a sack of turnips, from the bushes. A man in black ballistic vest. One of the terrorists.

"I got one of them," Archer said. "Now make some room in the back."

Chapter 25

S he's alive!" Susie squealed from the middle seats.
Chuck smacked the steering wheel in joy and
glanced behind him.

"Keep your eyes forward," I said. "I'll check her."

The nose of the truck almost swerved past the faint lines of the road's edge painted on the windscreen's heads-up display. Keeping his eyes on the road didn't mean actually seeing it. It was black as soot beyond the windows. We had the headlights off, interior lights dimmed. Chuck knew every logging road and ATV trail around his cabin. We pulled onto the main road a mile down his driveway, but then turned off almost as quick.

Slowed to a quiet crawl.

We had a head start, and our attackers chased, but the truck was still a difficult mark to track. Even the drones overhead lost the target after a mile of us weaving in the dark. The metamaterial covering bent even the heat signature, Tyrell had said. The truck had taken a lot of rounds, the windows dotted and crazed and cracked, but it held. Damon said the tires were self-healing.

Tyrell.

The image of the man's skull bleeding over the leaves still fresh in my mind.

I was wedged between Chuck in the driver's seat and Damon in the passenger one. I turned my body and got up onto my knees to get a look in the middle seat behind me.

"Don't let him get your carbine," Chuck said.

I still had the submachine gun in my right hand.

"I already have a gun, asshole," Damon replied, not looking up, his eyes focused back on his laptop screen, his face illuminated by its glow.

"Where was she hit?" I asked Susie as I leaned over into the middle row.

"I don't think she was," Lauren said.

My wife had Ellarose's shirt up and was inspecting her pallid skin. Susie had her daughter pulled into her arms toward the left side of the middle row of seats. Luke looked up at me from the foot well, seated on the floor with his arms around Bonham. The EMP device on the floor beside them. Smart kid. Tough. Olivia was on the seat between Lauren and Susie. We kept the kids in the middle of the truck, protected by the adult bodies around them, as much security as that was.

"Momma?" Ellarose's eyes fluttered.

"Baby, just stay still." Susie smiled hopefully and looked at me. "She tried to protect Bonham. When Chuck came up the stairs, I attacked one of the men with a nail file. The other one tried to take Bonham, but Ellarose wrapped her body around her brother. I don't know what happened after that."

"We got out," I said. "That's what happened."

"Are you hurt anywhere?" Lauren whispered to Ellarose.

"I feel dizzy," the little girl replied.

"But no sharp pains?"

She shook her head.

Archer had his face pressed against the glass in the back seat, the senator looking out the window from his side. They had manhandled the terrorist Archer had captured over into the trunk area and pinned his unconscious body between the crates back there. Archer used straps to wrap his hands and feet. The man hadn't made a sound since we dragged him in.

"I think we lost them," Archer grunted.

He winced.

The man was hurt. Badly, I suspected, but he didn't give up much.

"I don't see anything either," the senator said.

By now, just about everyone in the truck was hurt. Half of us were bleeding.

And one of us was dead.

Damon slapped his laptop closed. He turned to the senator. "Why did you shoot Tyrell?"

"I didn't shoot him," Leo replied.

I didn't say anything. The senator did shoot Tyrell, as far as I could tell, and I had been looking almost directly at Leo when he'd pulled the trigger and Tyrell's head had spattered open. Not more than twenty feet away from me, but it had been dark. And confusing. And I had no idea if the senator knew how to shoot. He might be about as good as I was, which was terrible.

"Maybe it was a mistake," Chuck said.

"I was aiming at the guy behind Mike," the senator said. "You saw him. There was one coming right behind—"

"I saw the guy," I said. "Susie, how badly are you hurt?"

"She's not good," Lauren replied. "She's lost a lot of blood."

"I'm okay," Susie said.

"No, you're not," my wife said. She leaned closer to Ellarose and began whispering with her, asking how she was doing.

Archer said from the back, "Where are we going?"

"Right now, I'm just putting as much distance between us and those assholes as possible," Chuck replied.

"Which way, though?"

"West, as best as I can manage through these trails. I'm trying to weave and keep from a straight line, but mostly west and over the top of the ridge. I figure they'll be expecting us to head back into Washington. I'm not going that way."

"If they have scouts, they'll be at the ridgeline."

"But we've already seen those flame-throwing drones to the east. They have to have support personnel, right?"

"There's nothing to the west," Archer said. "Just forests and small towns."

"The heartland of America is not nothing. And open space is kinda what I'm going for. Hey, hey, what the hell is going on?"

The truck slowed.

"Don't stop," Archer growled from the back.

"I'm not the one stopping."

"Tactical defense systems detect no external threat," said a sing-songy female voice. It was Selena. "Emergency manual override now deactivated. Please use authorization Tyrell Jakob to reactivate."

"Great."

Chuck flipped the manual override switch once, then twice again. Then cursed.

The truck had stopped. Black outside the windows. No idea where we were, except somewhere farther up the mountain.

"You know where we are?" I asked Chuck hopefully.

"Sort of."

"We need to get to a hospital," Lauren said.

"Out here? We're fifty miles from the nearest vet," Chuck said, now pounding the main display with one finger. The entertainment system came on and asked if we wanted to play songs about animals or soldiers. He swore and told it where to put a song.

"Charles Mumford," Susie said from the middle seats. "We will have none of that language in front of the children."

"Sorry," he mumbled. "Damon, can you figure this out?"

"Now you want my help? Maybe point a gun at me, that might get me motivated."

"Did someone maybe cut one of Tyrell's fingers off?" Chuck turned in the seat. "Maybe grab an eyeball? We need t—"

"You're kidding, right?" Susie said.

"Mostly." Chuck leaned back and sighed. "Damon, I apologize about the gun. You looked like you needed extra motivation."

"Remind me not to hire you as a coach." Damon plugged his laptop into one of the USB slots of the truck. "Maybe I can get into Selena's systems."

"I'll get out and look around," Chuck said.

"Do not exit the vehicle," Archer said from the back. "The truck is providing infrared shielding. Someone is watching from up top. We get out, we are done."

"Great," Chuck grumbled. He turned in his seat and lowered his voice, "Susie, baby, can I do anything? How bad are you hurt?"

"Not bad."

Even I could see she was lying. We needed to move. We were trapped.

"I can't believe he shot Tyrell Jakob," Damon muttered. "It's like you just assassinated Michelangelo. Do you know that? Do you know what that g—"

"I didn't shoot him," the senator said again.

Archer said, "Did anyone check to see if he was dead?"

"He looked dead," I said.

"How many dead people have you seen?" Archer asked.

"Lately? More than I've wanted. He wasn't responsive. I didn't have much time."

"Did anyone else get a look?"

The others mumbled they were too busy trying to stay alive or something to that effect.

"So, we don't really know," Archer said. "I think he was trying to get us to go to that cabin. I think he and Damon were dragging us to that place."

"Screw you," Damon muttered.

"Mike, you're sure he went out to protect your son?"

"It seemed that way."

"Didn't you say Luke was about to press that EMP button?"

"That's right."

"Maybe Tyrell was trying to stop him."

"Are you being serious?" Damon said quietly. "Tyrell and I accessed their network; we were busting our asses to try and divert those drones."

"You did a great job," Lauren whispered.

Archer said, "Tell me again how you and Tyrell magically access the terrorist network?"

"I'm back in," Damon said quietly. "Please reactivate."

"Back in what?"

"Selena."

"Authorization Damon Indigo confirmed," came a sing-songy voice over the speakers.

The steering wheel and cockpit display in front of the driver's seat lit back up.

"Nice work, buddy," Chuck said.

"You can stick that where the sun doesn't shine. Anyway, I didn't do anything."

"Meaning what exactly?"

"I just logged in and found that Tyrell had given me access to all his systems. I didn't even need a password. Didn't need to hack it. Just biometrics to my voice."

"He just gave you access, then ran away?"

"He didn't run away. He was shot."

"I need to pee," Luke said.

"You're going to have to wait," I whispered to him.

"How long?"

"I don't know." I had to pee as well. We couldn't even get out of the truck. Maybe we could open the door a few inches.

"I need to pee too," Olivia said.

"We need to wait."

"Can I play some *Fortnite*?"

"I'm scared," Bonham said. He had his arms around Luke, and my son had his arms around him as well.

"I'm scared too," I whispered back. I nodded to indicate to Olivia she could use the entertainment system, whatever she wanted.

"Again, we don't even really know if he's dead," Archer said from the back. "We might have just delivered Tyrell to his friends. Another part of his plan."

"We got away," I said. "Pretty sure that was not in anyone's plan."

"It was in mine," my wife said.

Damon said, "Speaking of not knowing, did anyone check that buddy's new friend is really tied up?"

"What's that supposed to mean?" Archer growled.

"I mean, what if that terrorist guy back there is just playing dead? Maybe you're the rat here. Maybe you just brought one of your friends into the truck."

"For what exactly?"

"That's my question."

"Can we start heading to a hospital?" Lauren interjected. "Or at least find a doctor? Susie is really h—"

Another voice interrupted her.

"Fires have swept across the Shenandoah Valley this evening," said a deep voice. A very familiar voice with a faintly southern accent.

Chuck sat upright. "Hey, isn't that Fox News?"

The main display in the center console lit up. The rugged good looks of the main Fox anchor filled most of the screen. "Reports are coming in that it appears to be arson. A team of firefighters managed to get into the foothills and report back that an accelerant similar to gasoline had been detected, but as yet, no further contact."

"Are we connected to a network?" I asked.

"This is material we downloaded from the terrorist's network when we connected. Tyrell got into a media server and grabbed as much as he could from the past twenty-four hours."

The screens in the backs of the seats lit up all around the truck. The main display in front of me changed from the news anchor to a list of HTML files.

"Click on them to read the story or watch the video," Damon said.

"Why would the terrorists download news clips?"

"I bet to see what impact their handiwork is having," Chuck said.

"But Tyrell got us these?" Archer said. "How much can we trust what we're looking at?"

"You think he faked them?" Damon asked.

"I do not think anything was outside the realm of possibility with that guy. Including him not being dead. I have a feeling we will be seeing him again."

"Look at this," Chuck said.

A *Washington Post* story. "Martial Law Declared." The entire United States had been placed under martial law as of 4 p.m. today.

I checked my watch. That wasn't even six hours ago. What had happened in that time? I kept reading.

Reports of drone attacks all over the country, from Oregon to California and Minnesota to Florida. And not just in America, but in Moscow and all the European capitals.

The Stafford Act had been invoked and the National Guard brought in across the nation, but as of 7 p.m. Congress had been locked down under an emergency order as it tried to give powers to the president to bring in the military on domestic soil.

"Are you guys reading this?" I said. "The *Washington Post* article?"

The Fox News anchor appeared on my screen, replacing the newspaper story. "China is now backing up India's claim that the initial round of anti-satellite launches did not originate in India, but provides no other explanation. China has used the opportunity to invade Taiwan, cutting off all communications to the island nation and surrounding it with its navy."

"I told you," Chuck said. "The Chinese still have their BeiDou geopositioning satellite system up there working. Russians are blind, same as Europeans. The Chinese are taking advantage."

"They're not the only ones," Lauren said.

The image on the screen was replaced with a large CNN logo. A flash alert. Even Chuck didn't laugh at the CNN flash alert. Not this time.

"It is difficult to piece together information," the news anchor said, a very worried-looking blond woman with her hair done up. She seemed on the verge of tears. "Iran has attacked Saudi Arabia, although this is unverified, and Syria is now fighting with Israel. But we are getting reports, verified by multiple new sources in Europe over shortwave communication, from MTI in Hungary...Russian tanks have rolled over borders..."

"This happened today?" Chuck said incredulously. "All at the same time?"

"So far, NATO has declined to invoke Article 5 of the collective defense treaty, but at the moment, it is not clear that NATO really exists. NATO Cyber Defence headquarters in Tallinn were occupied by Russian forces pushing into the Baltic countries last week—"

"See," Chuck said, "I told you."

"Be quiet," Lauren said.

"And the American NSA—National Security Agency—and CIA and FBI together are now saying that the rolling blackouts across America are not just the product of misfired timing signals from the loss of GPS satellites, but are the results of a coordinated cyberattack against the infrastructure of America. Communications have been blacked out across much of the country, emergency services crippled. The same reports are coming in from Europe and Russia. There is worry of dam failures, nuclear power plant meltdowns—"

"Holy God," Chuck said, "look at this."

He took control of the screens and punched up another news story on Fox.

The news anchor changed back to the blond-haired guy. Now he seemed on the verge of tears as well. "With financial markets closed around the world, China has announced that it is unpegging its currency from the American greenback and calling in its loans. Even with markets closed, this has sent the aftermarkets into total chaos. The value of the US dollar has plummeted, and US Treasury bonds have been degraded to junk status. All shipments of goods into the United States have stopped—"

"Can I switch to a *New York Times* article?"

It was a story about Secretary of State Timothy Chen, a man who had just been appointed by the president a few weeks before. The story detailed his birth in San Francisco just days after his mother arrived in America from a small village outside of

Beijing. It detailed his inexperience in global affairs, and his mother's links to the Chinese Politburo through an uncle who had risen through the ranks over the years. Many of these connections to the political apparatus in China apparently hadn't been properly vetted before Chen was appointed.

Another article talked about a conspiracy theory from Xenon, the mysterious source who claimed to be a senior figure in the administration, which claimed that the attacks on the United States were not from outside, but from a deep state takeover. China was also claiming that the American NSA was to blame for the satellite attacks, not China, using their own covert military satellite network. Russia claimed that the cyberattacks crippling its infrastructure originated in America as well.

I muttered, "What in heck's name is going on?"

A tingling fear raised the hairs on the backs of my arms, still matted down in blood and caked with dust from the explosion in the basement. It felt like the floor of the truck yawned open and we'd begun falling down through a rabbit hole. The entire planet was tipping into global conflict, the exact thing I thought we had averted just days before.

"China says a dozen shipping containers of its Chengdu mini-dragon drones were stolen last month, and that these are the ones appearing in Europe and America." Chuck brought up an image. "Those are the same ones. Those little bastards on the electrical wires."

"Look," Lauren said, "there's a video on Uncle Leo."

She clicked it and brought it up on all the monitors. The Fox News anchor returned and said, "Senator Seymour, president pro tempore of the Senate, is now reported missing as well. Emergency services were called to his house this afternoon only to find that the entire structure had burned to the ground in what is assumed to be another drone attack. The US Air Force has begun sending out RC-130 reconnaissance aircraft across America and anti-drone platoons have been deployed—"

"My God," Archer said.

He changed our viewpoint back to a CNN news story, the most recent, from just an hour ago. "I repeat," said the blond anchor, now with tears streaking down her face, "both the president and vice president have been killed, along with several leading members of Congress, including the Speaker of the House. With Senator Seymour missing and presumed dead, the line of succession falls to Secretary of State Timothy Chen, but senators are refusing to accept—"

"Oh my God," I said and turned in my seat.

I looked at Uncle Leo. "You're now the president of the United States."

Chapter 26

Silence in the truck for long seconds.

Chuck broke the ice. "He's not exactly president yet. Someone's trying to steal it from him. Or the other way around."

"And what way around would that be?" the senator said. "I would appreciate it if you would talk *to* me, son, not about me."

"Leo, with all respect, he's right. You're not president until you're sworn in," Damon added. "But let's not start layering on conspiracy theories alread—"

"You don't think there is conspiracy here?" Chuck interrupted.

"None of this might be true," Archer said from the back. "The terrorists might have dumped all this information on us on purpose."

"To make us think what?" Damon asked.

"I don't trust the source."

Damon said, "You think they have the anchors for Fox and CNN holed up in a cabin somewhere, and are recording fake episodes of ne—"

"I think your friend Tyrell could fake just about anything, video or digital, including his own death. He's been a vocal critic of the American government the last ten years and growing in power."

"*Half* of America has been a vocal critic of the United States government *every* year for as long as I've been alive. What does that prove?"

"Not like him," Archer said. "Leader of a Libertarian cult—"

"It's a political party," Damon said.

"It's a cult. I've seen the dossier on Tyrell."

Damon said, "Dossier? Like a McCarthy-style red scare file? You want to know where the conspiracy theorists are? Go look in a mirror in the J. Edgar Hoover Building."

Ignoring him, Archer said, "Whatever you want to call it, Tyrell and his billionaire Silicon Valley buddies have been pushing an agenda to overthrow the American government the past five years."

"You mean vote out?" Damon sighed long and hard. "Citizens are allowed to create political action committees."

"I'm not talking PACs. And I wouldn't call controlling misinformation flow on the world's networks 'voting.'"

"The guy's not dead ten minutes, saved your life already today, saved Luke's life, and you're already denigrating him? He wants to *reform* the American system of government. Go to direct democracy, eliminate the layers of inefficiency. A technocratic solution. Does it seem to you like our government is working lately?"

"Now just hold on," the senator said from beside Archer. "You might not like the way our government works, but it *is* working. And it's working for you."

"Sorry," Damon said sheepishly. "I didn't mean to—"

"I think you did, actually, son. You're implying that I might have something to do with this. And I can assure you, I do not."

Damon didn't reply but nodded his head in silence.

"You said *wants*," Archer said.

"Pardon me?"

"Not *wanted*, as in past tense. Even you don't think Tyrell is dead."

"You just don't give up, do you?"

"Kinda my thing."

"Boys, boys, can we keep it civil?" Lauren said quietly.

"I think he's Xenon," Archer said. "I think Tyrell is the one flooding the social media networks and meshnetworks with false information, claiming the terrorist attack is a false flag operation run by our own government. He's the head conspirator."

"He's dead," Damon said. "You can stop worrying."

"I did see him get shot," I said.

Or did I? It was dark, and it happened so fast. Was he attempting to stop my son from pressing the EMP button? Or was he trying to shield Luke with his body?

"We've seen these drones in action," Lauren said, her voice rising. "One of them killed my mother. A whole swarm of them."

The interior of the truck went quiet at that statement. For the first time, I noticed how much I stank of the manure I swam in.

Lauren continued, her voice lowering, "This isn't make-believe."

I said, "We're trapped inside an invisible truck, in the dead of the night, in the middle of nowhere—with the president of the United States in the back seat. My sense of disbelief is—"

"Nobody is making up these news stories we just saw," my wife said. "It's real. It's happening today, right now. Damon already said these were Chinese drones. The attackers are recording all these shows and articles as a highlight reel. Probably going to use them to attract more converts."

"And why let us have them?" Archer said. "Why did they give us the videos?"

"They didn't *let* us. Tyrell took them. Hacked in."

"Seems a little too easy."

Damon said, "Next time I'll let you do the hacking. See if you think it's so simple."

"Enough," Lauren said. "Susie is badly hurt and needs a doctor. She's pale and cold. At minimum, she needs a lot of water, probably some blood. Archer, you're hurt too, I can see you shaking. And Ellarose has a serious concussion, maybe worse. We need to get to a doctor, or better yet a hospital. At least get some supplies, antibiotics, bandages, some food."

"They'll be gone in two days," Susie said quietly. "The terrorists. That's what she told me."

I said, "So, we just have to hide for two days?"

"She said something else," Susie said quietly. Her voice was reedy and thin. "When I was inside with her. She said they had brothers and sisters all over the world."

"Makes sense," Chuck said. "Boko Haram, Hezbollah, ISIS, Al-Qaeda. There are Muslim terrorist groups everywhere in the world. Doesn't surprise me that they finally coordinated on something."

"Not that. She said, don't you wonder how it's possible she was still here? Something to that effect."

"Meaning what?"

"Like she had some inside protection. Within America."

"The government?" Lauren said. "I wouldn't trust anything she said."

"And she said something about you," Susie said.

"Me?"

"Were you working on the US drone program, Lauren?"

Chapter 27

This side of the mountains had the feeling of a ghost state. Throughout the night, we tried to keep off main roads, staying on trails and logging roads, trading speed for stealth as we crept over the top of the Shenandoah range and down the other side, tracking mile by mile away from DC.

Archer muttered in the back the whole time, saying we were making a mistake and should be trying to go the other way. We had taken a vote, and the majority decided this was the safest plan.

We found a small bridge that crossed the North Fork of the Shenandoah River, then headed south and west, taking a chance on a small road underpass to cross Interstate 81 that ran all the way up and down the East Coast of America. From there we edged into the sparsely populated backroads of West Virginia and the Monongahela Forest.

We passed through the villages of Cootes Store and Fulks Run.

No streetlights, no lights over highway intersections. The local police stations closed. Stores along the main street had their windows boarded over. Occasionally the glimmer of an electric light and hum of a diesel generator, more often the flickering of candles through windows.

Selena displayed a ghostly image in 3D of the roads and buildings around us as we navigated in the dark. Once, a car passed us, its headlights glaring, but we pulled to the side. Whoever was in it didn't see us.

We stopped at a gas station.

Not to get fuel, but for food and water.

Chuck broke the window to get in, but the shelves inside had already been stripped bare, except for a few bags of chips and bottles of water. Almost as important, we found some T-shirts for Chuck and I to change into, so we could get rid of the manure-stained ones we had on.

The truck had taken dozens of rounds that punctured the metamaterial exterior and damaged the OLED beneath it. The windows were cracked in places. It wasn't really invisible anymore; not as stealthy as it had been. With sunrise coming in a few hours, we needed to get off the roads and into cover.

We needed somewhere to hide, and we needed help.

The forest around the house was slowly reclaiming the land.

The old homestead looked like it had been built a hundred years before, the beams and boards probably hewn from the trees that had been removed to make the two-hundred-foot clearing. Vines engulfed the left side of the structure, their tendrils crawling onto the front and roof. Moss and lichen ate into the edges of the plank siding; most of the paint had peeled away.

The air was humid enough that a fog drifted between the dense foliage and canopy surrounding us. Cool but not quite cold. An old banana-seat bike from the seventies rusted to one side of the deck. Frogs chirped as the last dregs of the night slipped away. Between leaves of the canopy overhead, the sky began to turn purple as the sun rose over the Appalachian range to the east.

We parked the truck a few hundred feet up the road and walked down the driveway to the house. There were two rusting old Chevies in the driveway and we saw lights in the windows. We walked in slowly, hands up in case the occupants felt threatened, making sure they could see we didn't have any weapons.

We knocked on the door, but after five minutes, nobody answered.

"Hello?" I said in a louder voice. "Please, we need help. We have someone who is hurt."

I leaned over a sagging bench to the left side of the front door to tap on the window.

"We're going to need to talk about this," I said to my wife under my breath. "I need to know about the work you were doing with Leo."

"Can we do this later?" She knocked on the door again and said in a loud voice, "I saw you looking out the window. Please, we need help."

The curtain in front of me edged back a few inches, pulled back by the double-barrel of a shotgun. A twangy Southern female voice said from inside, "Y'all just get going, you hear me? We don't want no trouble."

"We don't either," Lauren said, raising her hands.

"Then why you wearing face masks like bandits? You got a virus or something?"

"We're not sick." Lauren looked up, made sure she was well covered under the awning from any view to the sky, then pulled down the cloth she had over her nose. "We are being careful. You heard about the drones? Killing people?"

Damon made us wear coverings over our faces and mismatched clothing, changing what we had been wearing before and turning things inside out. He said we needed to be careful and not give anything that pattern-matching AI might be able to recognize, especially making sure to hide our faces.

Drones were able to do facial recognition from miles away, Damon said. And we wouldn't be able to see or hear the drones in the sky. They would be too far away for us to see, but their cameras and imaging technology would see us. We needed to stay as hidden as possible, stay below the trees.

The old woman inside the house replied, "We heard. We had that meshnet thing on our phones before. Now we're disconnected. And we're being careful too. They said there are terrorists everywhere across America. That you won't know who they are. They said the government is overthrown."

Lauren said, "Do I look like a terrorist?" She had pulled her face covering off entirely and let the woman inside have a good look at her.

"You don't look like family. Now get going."

Damon joined us on the balcony. "Please, we need somewhere to hide. We have Senator Seymour with us, he's the president of the United States and—"

"Damon," Lauren said. "Don't—"

"And we got the Queen of England in here having tea with us," answered the woman behind the woman.

After a pause a man's voice added, "And if you did have Seymour there with you, I would put a bullet clean through his head myself. Now you get going."

"This isn't going to work," I said. "We better get back."

The sky was getting brighter.

Lauren pleaded with the couple inside the house for another minute, but we had to give up. It was already the third house we had tried. We could maybe break into somewhere abandoned, but what we needed was a doctor, people with supplies. We needed a community to help us, but nobody knew us out here.

We walked back up the driveway.

"I was worried about this," Damon said. "People connected into the meshnet like everyone else, but then we started telling them to disconnect, that it was compromised and that they needed to use the government one. That's become the topic of a whole conspiracy rant itself. Nobody knows who to trust."

"How much further can we go?" I asked.

The truck's batteries were down to fifty percent. We hadn't seen as much as a streetlight all night.

Damon replied, "Another two hundred miles till we need to get plugged in."

That was the problem with electric vehicles. There were gas stations everywhere, and even if they were closed, we might have been able to get some pumps working. But with the power grids down, we were far down the Shenandoah without a paddle.

"Keep under cover of the trees," Damon said as he walked ahead.

Lauren waited until he was out of earshot. "Susie has lost a lot of blood. We need to get somewhere with a hospital soon. I think we need to go back to Washington. We can just about make it. We don't know anyone anywhere else."

"You heard Susie," I said. "The terrorists called Leo the Ace of Spades. No way they're going to let us slip past them back into DC. He's their number one target."

"We might have to risk it."

I said, "I'm more worried about what's going on inside our truck. Chuck pointing a gun at Damon? I am not sure we can control Archer for much longer."

"The bark is worse than the bite."

"Excuse me?"

"A dog doesn't bite when it's barking. The arguing isn't dangerous, it's just everyone warning the others, expressing themselves. It's when they go quiet you need to be careful."

"Point taken."

My wife looked like she wanted to add something. I asked, "What?"

"Something else Susie said. You were right, Mike. Those terrorists are coming after you. Personally. That's what Susie told me."

"There they are," Chuck said and pointed out the window. "Doesn't look like they had much luck."

Damon walked ahead of Lauren and Mike, the three of them keeping to the dark edge of the forest to the right of the driveway. His friends kept glancing up at the brightening sky.

Three of the kids were asleep in the middle row. The senator—president?—had climbed over the divider to sit with his niece, Olivia, who squealed when Lauren said she was going to leave the car. He was asleep now as well, snoring with his arm around the little girl.

Ellarose was awake. Susie wouldn't let her go to sleep. She had earbuds in and watched a video, nodding off every now and then. Susie would nudge her awake. She didn't want her little girl going to sleep so soon after the concussion that had knocked her unconscious.

"You realize we have the commander-in-chief of the United States in this vehicle," Archer said from the back.

Chuck was in the driver's seat just in case they needed to leave in a hurry. "Now you believe those stories we downloaded?" He kept his eyes on his friends.

"Your wife needs a transfusion."

"I'm fine," Susie whispered.

Chuck tried to keep his eyes forward, but he had to turn and glance back at his wife. She was pallid. Her lips bluish in the dim light. Her voice getting weaker.

She had managed to drink two of the bottles of water they had found at the gas station, while the rest of them shared one, but she needed more. She might have an infection. She had a deep wound from a round passing through the armor on the left side of her abdomen. They had staunched the worst of the bleeding, but she needed a doctor.

Chuck turned back to watching his friends. "We're going to get you to a hospital. Soon."

"You heard your wife," Archer said. "The terrorists called Seymour the Ace of Spades. He's their number one target. We need to get him back to DC as soon as possible and get your wife some help. There's only one way out of this."

"I can't just drive off."

"I'm not telling you to leave anyone, and nobody needs to get hurt. I'm saying we take control. And that starts with this vehicle. I need you to get Damon to give you authorization over Selena and the truck's systems."

Outside the windows, Chuck saw Damon point up at the sky. Mike and Lauren began quick stepping along the edge of the bushes.

Archer said, "I saved your family's lives. You owe me. Do you love your country?"

"Don't be an asshole," Chuck shot back, but then in a lower voice, "Susie, what do you think? Do we need to get you to a doctor right away?"

"I say we stick together," she whispered. "I'll be fine."

Chuck bowed his head. She was getting weaker by the minute.

"I'm with you," Chuck said quietly to Archer.

"Charles Mumford," Susie coughed. "Don't you—"

"Honey, we need to get you to a doctor. We won't hurt anyone."

Archer said, "Just follow my lead. Do everything I say."

The passenger-side door opened.

Damon said, "Is everything okay?"

Chuck grinned. "We are all good."

"Because those things are in the sky. Drones are following us somehow. We need to hide. I doubt they've been able to get a visual fix, not yet, even with the truck's shielding damaged. They might be tracking us electronically. Some signal we're emitting?"

"Would getting underground help?" Chuck said.

"Underground?"

"And I mean, literally."

Chapter 28

Wow," I said.

Lauren added, "Incredible."

Fantastical structures loomed from the roof of the cavern, dripping stone sculptures reflected in the water below. Stalagmites reached up from the floor, their tips almost reaching some of the weeping rocks above them.

Our voices echoed.

Seneca Caverns. I'd heard of the place, had seen the billboards when I had driven down Interstate 81 on my way up and down the backbone of America for one reason or another over the years, but I'd never taken the time to have a look.

Turned out, it was worth the visit.

Chuck reasoned there wouldn't be much in the way of a tourist trade right now, and last time he was there they had installed a new entrance to the caverns, a paved gradual incline looping around, all the way down into the bowels of the Earth. With the sky getting brighter, we drove a few miles down along US-33 and then pulled through the parking lot and drove the truck into the cavern. We parked at the end of the sloping entrance and got out on foot.

Fifty feet of bedrock overhead to block any electronic signal from leaking out.

Only one way in or out, which was both comforting and terrifying. The thought of being buried alive was a close second on my list of worst ways to go, right after being eaten by a shark.

We drove the truck in as far as we could, with Chuck walking ahead of us, removing the crowd-control stanchions and ropes both to be polite and so we wouldn't damage the truck by rolling over them. We parked the truck as far in as we could get in the first cavern, then turned on the headlights to illuminate the space.

Weird long shadows lit up the voluminous space, the stalactites and stalagmites like the teeth of some monster whose mouth and gullet we had walked straight into.

When we stopped, I opened the gull-wing door beside me and got out.

I took a moment to inspect the vehicle. I still couldn't get used to it. Even pockmarked with bullet holes, if I stood back ten feet from the truck, it blended into the background just like an octopus on a coral reef. Knowing it was there, I saw the outlines and the curvy mirror bending of light of the objects behind it, but it was still amazing.

"I'm going to spend a few minutes looking at Susie's wounds," Chuck said as he got out.

"The senator and I will set up a forward perimeter at the entrance," Archer said. "Why don't you three go and scout deeper into the cave, make sure we don't have any stragglers on our rear? I would really hate to get a surprise from behind."

"I bet you would," Damon whispered beside me, low enough that Archer couldn't hear.

I rolled my eyes at him. In a loud voice I replied to Archer, "Okay, good plan," and then to my wife, "Are you okay with leaving the kids with Susie and Chuck for a few minutes?"

She nodded as she checked her submachine gun.

"Oh, one thing," Chuck said. "Before you go." He turned to Damon. "Could you authorize me for control of Selena? To get authorization for Tyrell's systems?"

Damon was putting his laptop into its bag in the front seat. He stood up and leaned on the truck. "You want what?"

"I want you to tell Selena to authorize me to take control of her. Of Tyrell's systems."

"Why?"

"Are you kidding me? What happens if something happens to you? You get shot—"

"By who?" Damon frowned.

"Not by one of us, you idiot. Come on, I'm being serious. You could get lost, have a heart attack, I don't know. But if we lose you, the rest of us are screwed. We're sitting ducks."

Damon scratched the back of his head.

"Son," the senator said, "we do need backup in case something happens to you."

"He *is* the president of the United States," Archer said.

"You don't trust me?" Chuck said. "Fine, give the authorization to Mike."

"I trust you, Chuck," Damon said finally. "Selena, please give emergency override authorization to Charles Mumford"—he looked at me—"and Michael Mitchell."

She responded in the affirmative.

"Thanks, Damon," Chuck said and ducked back inside to find the first aid kit. "Oh." His head reappeared. "If you find any scraps of wood in the walkways, loose stuff, could you bring it back? I think I'm going to start a fire."

It was damp and cold this deep inside the caves.

We left two of the submachine guns with Chuck and the senator, with Lauren taking one with us. Damon had his handgun, and I felt like I needed something too. Nobody seemed to think I needed a weapon except me, but Archer relented and gave me one of the Glocks. He said we should try to wash more of the stink of the manure off, for everyone's benefit.

Lauren played point guard and went ahead, following the marked path that led deeper into the caverns. She used Luke's baseball cap and a strip of a torn T-shirt to fashion a head mount for her cell phone and shone its flashlight ahead of us.

Damon and I followed.

"Did you read that article I showed you?" Damon whispered.

I nodded.

A story in the *New York Times* about Senator Seymour's connections to GenCorp, about billions of nearly untraceable funds that had gone into black ops programs from the Armed Services Committee with almost no oversight. There were rumblings of an investigation, rumors it could topple Senator Seymour in a corruption scandal.

"There was something going on between Tyrell and Seymour," Damon said quietly, his eyes casting forward to check that Lauren was out of earshot.

"They worked together," I said.

"If working together means funding covert armies, then yeah. Did you read the other articles?"

I nodded again. I had.

These were articles from sources like the *Gateway Pundit* and *One America News*, right-wing news outlets I rarely paid any attention to. The stories were about Tyrell and GenCorp and an underground left-wing movement called the Jakobites made up of his followers. Extreme militants, the stories said, that had launched a coup against the American government.

On the other hand, the left-wing news outlets had stories that ran counter to this, talking about a right-wing plot that had taken over the government and used covert CIA resources to launch a false flag terrorist attack and take control of the country.

"Tyrell said this was the start of a new civil war," Damon said. "That we had to pick sides."

"I'm not sure he was stable," I said.

"But you saw Uncle Leo shoot Tyrell, right? He shot him in cold blood."

"He was trying to hit the guy behind me."

"How well do you know Uncle Leo?" Damon asked.

"If you're asking if I think he would sacrifice my kids and Lauren for some nefarious plot—"

"You're telling me you didn't think twice about leaving the truck behind with your kids in it just now? After I gave them the access codes to Selena?"

I stopped walking. He was right. There was a twinge inside me, the slightest of hesitations. I kept walking. "This is insane. Leo has nothing to do with this."

"Why did those terrorists keep coming back to his house, then?"

"He is one of the highest-ranking politicians in the country. He's a target."

"And why was Tyrell waiting there, too?"

"I think that's more a question for you."

"And the president and vice president and Speaker were just assassinated. This is the biggest moment in America's history. Chuck's right. There is a conspiracy going on, and Leo is at the center of it. Those are highly sophisticated Chinese drones. You know how long it would take to get trained up on using those? The kind of technical expertise? There are only a few pla—"

"What are you guys talking about?" Lauren asked.

She had stopped in the shadows up ahead to let us walk to within a few feet of her.

"Nothing," Damon said in a loud voice, and then whispered to me, "You should ask your wife about her involvement."

"I'm not deaf," my wife said. "If you've got something to say, I'm listening."

Damon replied, "I'm just trying to figure this out. I'm going back to the truck." He knelt to pull some wooden boards from a walkway. "Chuck said he wanted to start a fire."

"Uh-huh." The butt of Lauren's submachine gun rested on her hip.

I shone my phone's flashlight back and forth.

We waited for Damon to disappear into the darkness away from us.

Long shadows crept and jumped from the dripping stone fangs hanging from the cave's ceiling. "I don't think there's anyone else back here."

"Me either."

"I think Archer was just trying to get us away for a minute." The worm that Damon had planted began gnawing into the pit of my stomach. "We should get back."

"What are you worried about?"

I turned and began quick walking back along the path. Damon had already disappeared into the next cavern.

"What am I worried about?" I laughed. "We're trapped hundreds of feet underground in a cave with killer drones and Chechen terrorists trying to murder us while America disintegrates in a civil conflict and the third world war erupts."

"You shouldn't read all those left-wing articles—"

"It's not the articles, Lauren." I quickened my pace, partly because I was worried about what Damon had said, but mostly because I wanted to put some distance between me and my wife. "It's you."

"Pardon me?"

"This has a lot of the same feeling as six years ago. In the CyberStorm. When you were about to take that job in Boston, have an abortion, and leave me."

"Are you insane? I'm not pregnant."

"But you are hiding things from me, and you're doing it for your career."

"Could you stop running away and talk to me?"

My pulse hammered in my chest, a pain rising, but not a physical one. An ache deep inside. I stopped and turned. "You lied to me. You told me you were going to China for an international relations conference."

"I was. Mostly."

I noticed my wife kept the muzzle of her submachine gun pointed toward but still slightly away from me. "But you were working on the drone program with Leo? You were vetting and authorizing the targeted kill lists around the world?"

"I was."

"So you lied."

"I omitted the truth. There is a difference."

"Same difference as six years ago."

"There is a difference," she insisted again.

"Yeah, this time you put the lives of our children in danger." The question I had lingering in the back of my mind finally formed. "Did you authorize the targeted killing of any Chechens? Anyone in the Islamic Brigade?"

Silence. Just the echo of the stalactites' tears dripping into the water around us.

The lack of response was all the answer I needed. "Are you pointing that gun at me for a reason?"

"Mike," my wife said softly, lowering the weapon. "I'm s—"

"Guys!" Damon's voice echoed from the next cavern.

Lights and shadows played along the ceiling.

My mouth was still open and halfway to spitting out another accusation. "What?" I said instead, and turned back to the walkway to the front.

"I'm picking up a signal inside the cavern."

"We'll finish this later," I said to my wife, then turned to jog along the path.

Whatever Damon was excited about, it seemed important. I rounded the bend through a narrow section and into the first cavern. Smoke drifted along the ceiling. Chuck had managed to light a small fire by the water next to the truck and kneeled beside it, fanning the flames.

Archer and the senator were nowhere to be seen. I assumed they were farther up the entranceway, setting up whatever defenses the special ops soldier decided might be most effective. None of which I sincerely hoped would be necessary.

The pit-of-the-stomach nausea returned as I realized we were trapped underground. Maybe this place wasn't such a good idea.

Damon walked in circles by the entrance tunnel, then turned back toward the truck, only visible as its four gull-wing doors were wide open. The kids were inside with Susie, all of them in the middle row watching videos on the seatback screens.

"I think I know how the drones have been tracking us," Damon said, his laptop up and ahead of him like he was conjuring water with it. "The truck should be invisible. I shut down all her systems just now to make sure I was right. I had to make sure she wasn't leaking any RF."

"RF?" I asked as I approached.

Lauren was right behind me.

"Radio frequency." Damon walked to the rear of the truck and clicked a button on his laptop. The back gate swung open. "Damn it, I was so stupid."

"What were you stupid about?" I was ten feet away now.

Chuck knelt by the fire, his submachine gun on the rock next to him.

Four crates were stacked in the back of the truck, with the semi-conscious Chechen tied up in the back between them. Damon leaned his laptop right next to the Chechen's chest.

"It's how those drones knew not to home in on their own team," Damon said. "Their body armor has a transmitter in it. I just set up a signal sniffer on my laptop. The transmitter signal hops frequencies, so it's hard to pin down. Since we're underground, all other electromagnetic signals are being blocked, so I've been able to isolate the pattern. This guy's armor is sending out a signal clear as day."

That made sense. I hadn't thought about it.

All of the terrorists we'd encountered were dressed head-to-foot in black, even their faces covered by visors and shields. How would the drones know not to home in on them? Of course— they had to have transmitters.

"The signal is weak, so they can't pick it up too well from a distance," Damon said. "But that's how they must be managing to follow us." He turned. "And I'm getting another signal, coming from the back corner of the cave."

We turned and peered into a dark corner.

A figure emerged. It was Archer.

The signal was coming from Archer. He had on the chest armor of the terrorist he had taken in the firefight. I had assumed it was because he was trying to blend in with them. Amina had walked by when we'd been shielded inside the truck, but she had nodded at Archer as she passed. Again, I had assumed because she'd thought he was one of her men.

But then again.

Maybe he was.

That churning sensation of vertigo in my stomach convulsed into a creeping snake of terror that slipped up my spine.

Damon held up his laptop, pointed it at Archer as if the machine would provide some magical protection. Like he was casting a spell. The special ops soldier grabbed the computer and tossed it into the open back of the truck, then grabbed Damon by the neck.

Almost lifted him from the ground.

"Enough of this crap," Archer mumbled.

The senator appeared from the shadows behind Archer, a submachine gun in his hands. He pointed it at us and scanned back and forth.

Damon gagged and gurgled as his feet left the stone.

"Mumford," Archer said. "Take their weapons."

I had my Glock in my hand, and Lauren was behind me with her weapon pointed forward. Chuck got up from kneeling by the fire with his weapon in his right hand, propped up by his left prosthetic one.

His submachine gun pointed at me.

"Chuck?" I said weakly.

His eyes downcast, Chuck blinked and raised his weapon.

"Mumford," Archer repeated. "Get their weapons."

"You better do as they say," the senator said from behind them. "We need to go to Washington, right now, and we cannot wait. Some things are more important." He raised his submachine gun and pointed it at us.

Lauren sobbed. "Uncle Leo? More important? Than family?"

Chapter 29

Chuck took a deep breath and shouldered his weapon. He kept it pointed straight at me. I lifted my Glock, but wasn't sure who to point it at.

"You assholes," Damon gurgled.

"Mumford," Archer commanded again. "Get their goddamned weapons."

"Lauren?" I said.

My wife crouched behind me. "I got your back, Mike, no matter what."

I glanced at her. Was she pointing that weapon at me? No.

"Mom, why are you aiming a gun at Uncle Leo?" Luke had stepped out of the truck.

Olivia was beside him and held his hand. "Momma?"

"Get back inside, baby," Lauren said. "Please, honey, get back inside the truck. Luke, get your sister back inside."

"Dad?" Luke said. "What do you want me to do?"

"Get Olivia in the truck," I replied in an unsteady voice. Wasn't a good time to contradict my wife.

I pointed my gun at Archer.

"You want to do this in front of your kids, Mitchell?" Archer growled. "Want them to see their dad be killed in front of them?" His left hand still levitated Damon from the ground, while his right swung the submachine gun around to point at my chest.

I realized I was practically naked.

Just wearing a T-shirt.

No ballistic vest.

One of the high-velocity rounds would go straight into me and explode like a hand grenade. I looked at Luke, my hand shaking. Tears in his eyes. I shook my head, don't come to me. Go back inside, I indicated with a flick of my chin.

"Chuck?" I said.

Was my friend really doing this?

"Damn it." Chuck groaned and swung his weapon around and pointed it at Senator Seymour. "Drop it," he said.

"Mumford, what are you doing?" Archer yelled. "You owe me your family's lives."

"Which you have a chit to call in for, but not right now. This is wrong."

"As wrong as me blowing a hole through your best friend? And what? You're going to shoot the president of the United States?"

"I was thinking more of a kneecap or something. And he's not president yet."

The senator grimaced but kept his weapon up.

"That's treason, Mumford," Archer growled.

"I have a feeling that word is going to be thrown around a lot in the next few days."

"You know what the punishment is for treason?"

"You know what the punishment is for being an asshole?" Damon managed to gasp.

"Drop it," said another voice.

It was Susie. Her voice thready and weak, but resolute and determined. She was on the ground, on her stomach, on the other side of the truck. She had a pistol pointed at Archer.

Lauren had her weapon aimed at Archer now as well. "I believe that is four versus two, if we could consider this a vote."

The sun rose toward midday in a clear blue sky.

I was in the middle seat again with Luke, who was watching a video with his little sister. They had their arms around each other. Bonham and Ellarose sat beside them, with earbuds in and watching the same movie. Lauren was in the third row behind me with Susie, and Chuck and Damon were in the front.

"Chuck." I leaned over the seat divider.

"Uh-huh."

"You know we just kidnapped the president of the United States?"

Silence for a few seconds. "History is written by the victors. Today it might be called kidnapping. Tomorrow it might be called 'rescued.'"

"More like treason or sedition."

"I never really understood that word, sedition. We just need to make sure we win, Mike. Keep everyone safe."

"You sure you should keep Archer tied up?" Waves of uncertainty cascaded through my mind the farther we ventured from DC, the depth and intensity of them increasing with the distance.

"Damon laced him up, not me, so ask him if he wants to untie the guy. And he's more of a mercenary than someone working for Uncle Sam, if I had to guess."

The senator had been the first one to blink in the game of Russian chicken we had back in the caverns. He told Archer to lower his weapon, that while he needed to get to Washington, this wasn't the right way to do it. He was wrong, he told Lauren, and tried to apologize.

My wife ignored her uncle, took his weapon, and told him to get in the back.

Archer, though. Damon reasoned we couldn't just let him sit in the truck with us. The man was literally a killing machine and might take us all out with his bare hands if we gave him the chance. Damon took a special relish in tying him up, making sure the bindings were just tight enough not to cut off circulation, and then knotting a torn T-shirt around his mouth.

"We are going to need to untie him at some point," I said.

Chuck replied, "Might be easier to let the two in the back kill each other, unless they're both on the same side. A lot of unknowns here. That's what we're going to whittle down over the next day. Make sure we're doing the right thing. And right now, that means getting to a hospital somewhere we trust the people. I need to get my wife and daughter some medical attention."

"I assume we're not taking a circular route to Washington?"

"Correct, Boy Wonder."

Chuck still hadn't told us where he was driving. Once we got loaded into the truck, he took off and said he knew exactly where he was going. Didn't need to engage the geopositioning system, said he didn't trust it. Said it would become obvious, but he didn't know who might be listening if he explained. He didn't say *who* exactly might be listening.

He just said to trust him, which was a stretch given that he'd just tried to carjack me.

"The terrorists said they needed to be gone in two days," Chuck said. "Isn't that right, Susie?" He turned and looked into the back.

"That's right, honey." Susie was in the middle seats with Lauren, her head in her friend's lap. The kids were back to watching videos. Susie was pale, her lips turning faintly blue.

"And Charles, darling," she said, her voice barely more than a whisper.

"Yes, my honeysuckle?"

"If you ever tell a pretty girl about the defenses around our family home again, I will castrate you myself, do you understand?" She was still mad about Chuck telling Amina about the flares attached to the chimney at the cottage.

"Yes, honey," Chuck replied sheepishly to his wife, and then to me in a lower voice, "that was one of the most stupid things I ever did."

"I can vouch that's not true," I replied with a grin.

Chuck laughed at that. He lowered his voice more and said, "Seriously, though. If your Uncle Leo is the good guy, then we're just keeping him safe for a day until the bad guys clear out. We're not kidnapping the president of the United States, we're safekeeping him. I think Amina and her crew were waiting for us on all the passes back to Washington."

"So, we're not going back to DC?" When Chuck shook his head once more, I asked in a whisper, "And if Senator Seymour *is* the bad guy?"

He whispered back, "You really think your Uncle Leo is the villain in all this?"

I didn't answer. That depended on your point of view. Targeted kill lists. Oversight of the international drone program, dealing out death across the planet. A lot of people might see someone like that as being worse than a villain. And now that broad brushstroke was also painted across my wife.

"You saw it in the newscasts," Chuck said, raising his voice. "Our military has been called in domestically. They're sweeping the nation, getting rid of whatever scourge got in here. If there's funny business going on, we've got to wait it out. Wait for the good guys."

Waiting for the good guys was what almost got us killed six years before.

"And where exactly are we going to wait it out?"

The cabin in the Shenandoah obviously wasn't an option anymore.

"This is your idea, Mike. You didn't hand over your gun when your Uncle Leo demanded it. I was going with your gut. You didn't want to go to DC, so my loyalty went with you. Now you gotta trust me a little."

"So now this is my fault?"

"Gotta be somebody's." He smiled a goofy grin at me and stomped down on the accelerator.

We sped down a country lane, heading deep into West Virginia.

I said the obvious, "You know we're being tracked by enemy drones in the sky? And we're driving through them in broad daylight?" I was hoping he had some clever plan he could explain, more to help my nerves than anything else.

"Which is why I've got my foot as far down on the gas as I can."

Not quite as clever as I had hoped for.

"There's a good chance they won't detect us," Damon said.

We had taken the armor chest plates, where the transmitters seemed to be, and bent around them a box of thin metal plates we'd found in the gift shop. Damon said this would act as a Faraday cage and capture any electromagnetic signals, if we could wrap them all the way around and make sure they were grounded. I said we should just leave them in the cave, but Damon pointed out that we might be able to use them later. Or find a way to mimic the signal. Either way, better to bring them with us.

I asked Damon why the metamaterial coating, which bent optical radiation around us, didn't work to block the outgoing radio frequency transmitters, and he said the wavelengths were wrong. Too long, he said.

I said to Chuck, "You've got a plan, right?"

He smiled. "Does the pope do his business in the woods?"

"I assume you mean preaching?"

The senator was in the back seat with Damon. He had given up his gun and said he would do whatever Lauren wanted— and he had instructed Archer to give up his gun—but made it clear he believed the right course of action was to go back into Washington.

On that topic, we agreed to disagree.

He was still trying to convince Lauren to turn the truck around.

"You can't believe I had anything to do with this," I heard the senator say in a low voice.

He sat beside my wife. I turned slightly to listen.

"Didn't you always tell me family first?" Lauren had Susie in her arms. "Did you work with Tyrell? You never told me that."

"Those things killed my sister, your *mother*," the senator said.

"I know," Lauren replied quietly. "You still haven't answered the question."

"I didn't know about any transmitters in the armor," Archer garble-yelled from the back. "That was stupid, I admit that, but Tyrell is still alive, you idiots. You're walking into his trap."

"Please be quiet." Lauren said it softly and smiled at Susie. "Or I will have Damon stick one of Luke's socks in your mouth."

Susie tried to return the grin, but only managed a grimace.

The sun arced high overhead in the clear September sky, then began its gradual descent to the west. The lower we dropped in the Appalachian foothills, the more the trees turned from orange and gold and yellow back to green, as if we went back in time the farther we traveled down. Chuck turned us slightly north, and the green forests became interspersed with fire-blackened swaths of scorched earth and scrub.

After five hours of driving, Selena's batteries were down to less than five percent. I would have been worried, but it became obvious where we were headed.

Chuck craned forward in the driver's seat to get a better look out the windshield. "Has anyone else noticed that the electrical wires strung from the poles seem to be cut down or ripped out every few miles?"

"Might have been a storm or those fires?"

"No fires up this way."

"Then maybe the drones? They attach their feet to them. Maybe they cut them, too."

"Only seen them on high-voltage lines," Damon said from the passenger seat.

"Does that mean they wouldn't use local lines?"

"Wouldn't be as efficient."

"So it might be them doing this?"

"Might be."

"I've been getting sporadic connections to the meshnet," Damon said.

"You haven't been sending out any messages?" I said.

"Of course not."

"What about the truck? Is it sending out"—I searched for the right word—"any pings or anything? This thing isn't talking to anyone, is it?"

"I turned off all her comms."

"You trust him?" Archer gag-yelled from the back.

"Yes," I replied, turning to investigate the back. "We do."

I could see that the terrorist was now awake. He had propped himself up on one side, against the crate. Archer leaned himself up on the other side and kept his eyes on him, four crates stacked two high between them.

"He's not wrong," Chuck said to me, glancing at Damon. "I mean Archer isn't wrong. Tyrell was involved in all this. His satellites wiped out everything up there. He and the senator had to have something going on."

Damon rolled his eyes but didn't look up from his laptop.

The awkward sensation of being a referee had returned, of being a nexus that two sparring sides trusted as a go-between. Problem was, one of the sides wasn't being honest, and I had no idea which. Just because one side had to be wrong didn't mean the other one had to be right. They both could be wrong.

I was still looking at Archer, who stared back at me with wide eyes, the look asking me what I was going to do. "Maybe we should untie him," I said and looked back to the road.

"He did just try to blow a hole in you," Damon pointed out.

"Yeah, but he also let you tie him up."

"We had four guns pointed at him."

The more I thought about it, the more I realized Archer *had* let us tie him up. He could have probably fought his way out of the jam that Chuck had gotten him into. If he really wanted to take Senator Seymour to Washington, we would all be lying in a heap back in the cave.

Archer had listened to Senator Seymour in the end. He hadn't hurt us.

I said, "I don't think that mattered."

"He's the only one who's an outsider," Damon said.

Chuck replied, "You were once an outsider to us."

Damon didn't say anything to that, but opened an image on his laptop. "The American military is now at DEFCON 1. There's talk in a *New York Times* article of a limited nuclear strike against China. The Chinese have mobilized their nuclear attack subs, and Russia has warned the United States against it. The Russians are demanding peace negotiations."

Up ahead, a familiar figure loomed into view, walking along the side of the road.

The man was stooped over and moving slowly. Burned forests swept up into the West Virginia foothills past the flattened rows of corn.

"Stop the truck," I said.

"That's Farmer Joe," Luke said, standing in his seat and pointing forward.

If I was my son's superhero, then Joe was his hero. The Robin to my Batman, although I really felt it was the other way around. Joe was a certifiable warrior. He'd fought with the 101st Airborne, the Screaming Eagles, back in Vietnam. When we were here the week before, Joe had told us some harrowing stories of his fighting days.

"Stop the truck," I said to Chuck. "Park it over there. Behind those trees to the side. Go slow, keep quiet."

They hadn't seen us yet. Of course. We were in an invisible spaceship. Two men walked together with Joe. Wasn't sure who they were yet. Was it possible someone got here ahead of us? Irena and Terek had been there just a week before, same as us. Were they force-marching Joe ahead of them? The men didn't look threatening.

But it was always better to be on the safe side.

Which was just the advice Farmer Joe had given me a few days before.

Chapter 30

Afraid we would be seeing you again," Farmer Joe said. The man spoke with a wry smile that said he couldn't be happier, though. He strode purposefully if slowly along the hardscrabble edge of the field. The sun low in the sky behind him.

The air was still heavy with the stench of burn, but already regaining the earthy smell of the farmland and the clear air of the Virginia mountains behind us. I recognized the two men walking with Joe. Percy and Rick, one the owner of the gas station in town, the other the manager of the diner across the street from it.

My level of stress edged down to a low simmer.

Joe held out his hand. "Is Oscar—"

"We had some trouble."

Joe's head dropped an inch, but he kept his hand up. "I was afraid of that, too." The lines in his weathered face deepened.

Luke was ahead of me. He didn't run straight into Joe and wrap his arms around him, as I feared for an instant, but stopped short and held out his hand. Joe smiled and redirected his own into my son's.

Why did I fear Luke running into him? I wasn't sure of Joe's reaction if my son suddenly wrapped his arms in a hug around his body. My son thought of him as a real-life action hero, but I wasn't sure the old man returned the affection.

That, and Joe suddenly looked frail.

He shook my hand next.

"We need a doctor," I said. "We need help. Susie's hurt really bad, and Ellarose..."

I turned and indicated behind me. Lauren came out of the scrub on the opposite side, Susie's arm around her neck.

"Where did you just come from?" Percy asked. "Did you walk here? I didn't see any cars up on the road ahead."

He and Rick had rifles slung over their shoulders and followed five paces behind Joe. All three had recognized me the moment I had appeared on the far side of the street and waved, even if they'd been somewhat confused. The last time I saw Percy, he was hugging and thanking me for helping save the town. That was just a few days ago. He'd nodded a greeting, but now barely cracked a smile.

"That's not important," Joe said. "Get on the horn and get some help out here, fast. Get that medic." He pointed at a fallen tree in the shade. "Lauren, you get Susie sat down over there. Percy, Rick, you help them. Get them some water."

"Luke," I said. "Go help your mother."

Joe waited for Luke, Rick, and Percy to cross to them before asking, "Now tell me, what happened to Oscar?" He turned his back to the others and held a hand up as he looked into the sun.

I turned with him. "They ambushed him."

Joe turned and inspected more of the blue sky. "By 'they' I assume you mean the same people you brought here? The terrorists?"

"I'm sorry. We found the car up at the cabin, but we didn't find his body. We didn't have time. Maybe he's alive."

"But probably not. And son, never be sorry. Just do your level best."

What was he looking for? I followed his eyes as he scanned the heavens. He took another few steps away from the others. Unsteady steps. He held a hand out, warning me not to try and help him.

"Who else do you have in that vehicle up there?" Joe asked.

I hesitated.

"My eyes are still sharp, young man. That shimmering in the road up there," Joe said, "some kind of fancy camouflage?"

I paused again, but this time from amazement. "How did you know?"

"I might be old, but I still read. A metamaterial coating? I've seen it in videos."

I felt like I was the only one who thought the technology was bordering on magic.

Joe heaved in a wheezing deep breath.

I checked behind me. Percy and Rick helped my wife and Susie to the fallen tree and were asking them questions and talking into a phone. A distant whine began in the distance toward the farmhouse. I could just make out the barn and top of the church next to Joe's place across the flattened cornfields to my left.

Joe gasped in another breath.

"You okay?" I asked.

"The old ticker. Had a bit of an episode two days ago. Think my pacemaker needs a tune-up. Hard to get in touch with hospital people, as I'm sure you're aware. My diabetes meds have run out, too. In a bit of frail shape, but I'm fine."

"Sorry, I didn't kn—"

"You didn't answer my question, son."

My mind backtracked. "Question?"

"Who's in your fancy truck? Wouldn't happen to be Senator Seymour, would it?" Joe stepped away from the others. He scanned the blue sky to his right. Avoided looking at me.

Joe said quietly, "I am putting two and two together." He began slowly pacing back and forth. "People don't usually show up in a hundred-million-dollar piece of newfangled military hardware without someone important inside. You were just at his house, right? He is your wife's uncle?"

"Right." An admission of him being correct on all counts.

"I assume you do not have the cavalry coming? Seeing as you are showing up here asking my ragtag for help? And seeing as you about single-handedly saved our town a few days ago, seems I'm not in a position to refuse you."

"Chuck was the one that drove here," I said.

"You don't want our help?"

"Susie is hurt bad. Lost a lot of blood. My wife and kids, the senator, we're being chased—"

"Some of the boys will be a mite suspicious of Senator Seymour," Joe said. "We need to be careful how we do this." He wiped a calloused hand through his white hair and stopped pacing back and forth.

"Careful? I'm not sure I understand."

"We haven't had much contact with the outside world in a few weeks now. No TV. No internet. Now not even any power. Just KLMB radio that's still broadcasting from Portsmouth, two towns over. That and some ham radio operators, and the meshnet that your friend Damon installed here."

"Damon's in the car, too," I said.

"And which we were then instructed to uninstall from our phones," Joe continued, still scanning the sky, "and install a new government version. Which made people suspicious."

"Of what?"

He laughed. "Suspicious of everything. We are at war, young man. We get little bits of information—about the terrorist attacks all over the country. The drone attacks." He scanned the sky to my left. "About the president being killed."

"You heard about that?" We had only just found out ourselves.

"And the conspiracy theories. About Senator Seymour being the leader of a deep state attack against our own government."

He stopped looking at the sky and turned his gaze to me. I said, "You don't believe that, do you?"

"Hard to know what to believe. Three days ago, the feds were here, taking that Range Rover you left behind. The one owned by your terrorist friends. Last time you showed up here, your best friends were the very same people that have wreaked havoc on our nation. You are not the best judge of character, young man."

"They fooled us, Joe. I don't know what to say."

"Fool me once..." Joe started walking again.

The whine from the direction of the farmhouse grew louder. A motorcycle and driver sped along a dirt road toward us and kicked up a plume of dust.

Joe said, "So the president is really dead?"

"I don't know, to be honest. We accessed some news articles and videos from Fox and CNN. That's what they are reporting. Joe, you can't seriously think that Senator Seymour has anything to do with this?"

"I do not know the man from a hole in my stone wall," Joe replied. "Do you?"

This time, he didn't fidget or look away past me. His eyes locked with mine. He seemed to be searching, but this time inside of me, not through the sky overhead. I didn't look away.

I held his gaze.

What did I believe?

That was a loaded question to ask, even to myself. I had been wrong before, more than once, even when my gut screamed at me that I was right. I hadn't been able to see things right before my own eyes. I had made mistakes that almost cost my family their lives.

Joe said, "You gotta trust your gut, son."

"That's what I'm worried about."

"And that's what learning from our mistakes is for."

"Seymour has nothing to do with this," I replied. "You think he'd be out here if he did?"

"I'm asking you."

"That's what I think. I think they're trying to make us think he does."

"And who is 'they'?"

"I..." Now that was a good question. "The Chechens," I replied after a pause. "Islamic terrorists. We heard reports they've hit targets all over the world."

"You really think that?"

"Who else?"

"I think we are fighting an enemy who creates deception at all levels," Joe said. He turned and began walking back toward the others. "That attacks when it seems unable. That is active when it appears inactive. When they are near, seem as if they are far away."

"Excuse me?"

"Sun Tzu, son."

"So, you believe me?"

He was the second person in as many days who had quoted Sun Tzu to me. Tyrell had said something similar the day before. I followed Joe. The rumble of the motorcycle rose in pitch as it approached, now coming up the paved road leading down from here to the Ohio River.

"That man in your vehicle might just be the commander-in-chief of the country I have sworn to defend with my life. And we are now at war, make no mistake about it, and this is war being waged on our own soil. Our own wives and children are now in danger." He quickened his pace. "You go and get the senator. I'll tell Percy and Rick and the boys to dispel this nonsense. We got more important things to fight than each other."

"We have other people in the truck," I said.

"I don't doubt it."

"We got one of them."

That stopped Joe in his tracks. "One of who?"

"We captured one of the terrorists, up at Chuck's cabin. Well, *we* didn't. It was Archer." I paused. He was also tied up in the back. How was I going to explain that?

I realized I didn't need to sugarcoat anything when it came to Joe. Explain it in no-nonsense terms, and Joe would cut away the chaff. A sense of relief swept over me. Joe would know how to make sense of all this nonsense, would be able to get us all in line. I hadn't had time to think in the past twenty-four hours. My brain was scrambled goose eggs.

The motorcycle roared the last fifty feet toward us and squealed to a stop. A pickup truck followed a half mile behind and cleared the dirt path from the farm to pull onto the paved road. The young man on the motorcycle pulled up his visor.

He said. "Who needs the medical help?"

Joe pointed up the road. Lauren and Susie were partly hidden by the overhanging branches by the fallen tree. Charred branches hung high over their heads and into the burnt hills in the distance behind them.

"Name's Travis," the young man said and held out his hand.

"Mike." We shook.

He disembarked from the bike and held the two handlebar grips to maneuver to the side of the road. "I should make it clear that I'm not a doctor."

I inspected his motorcycle. A Yamaha YZ. Trail bike. I used to ride dirt bikes when I was a kid. Lauren made me stop riding motorcycles when we met. Said they were death traps. Right now they seemed about as safe as anything.

Luke took hold of my hand. I had almost forgotten he was with us. He had been listening to Joe and me talking. "I like the bike," he said.

"Thanks," Travis replied. His bike had a large set of saddlebags, one each side, and he had an overstuffed backpack on, almost splitting at the seams.

"If you're not a doctor," Luke said. "How are you going to help Aunt Susie?"

"Your Aunt Susie is hurt?" Travis said. "She's the one in the middle?"

He squinted and pointed with his right hand while he kept the left guiding the bike.

Luke nodded.

The pickup truck was halfway up the paved road toward us. Someone waved out of the driver's-side window. Were they waving or shaking a fist?

"I was a medic in the army," Travis said to Luke, then looked at me. "And an electrical technician. Jack of all trades, really. Had to be, out where we were stationed."

"I didn't serve." I thought he was looking at me to ask if I'd been in the army.

But he wasn't looking at me, he was looking past me. He frowned and turned his attention back to Susie up ahead. "I know who you are, sir," he said. "Everyone in town does."

"Luke, why don't you go up and get everyone else out of the vehicle?" Joe said to my son. "If that's okay with your dad."

"Yeah, that's a good idea."

Travis pulled out the kickstand and parked his bike. He slung his backpack off and opened it on the seat.

I started to ask, "Where did you s—"

"Mike," someone called out in the distance.

I turned. It was Ken, the head of the Vanceburg Rifles, who we had met the week before. He was the one driving the pickup truck. Another man was in the bed of the truck, his head just up over the cab. Two men, actually, in the back, and one in the passenger seat. Two rifle muzzles pointed high from the back. My stomach twisted. Ken waved again.

Ken and Oscar had been best friends.

Luke scampered up the road and pointed to show them where our truck was parked. Travis was on his way to Susie, twenty feet from Joe and me, when I heard the noise.

He heard it too. Turned and squinted into the setting sun.

"Mike!" Lauren called out.

"Incoming!" Travis yelled.

Chapter 31

The hairs on my neck prickled at the thin whining of the drones. Not quite the buzzing electric motor of quadcopters, more of a fluttering-whirring-hiss. Nothing else sounded quite like them, and their insistent and growing trilling over the sound of the wind brought on nausea and vertigo. I almost vomited.

"Mike!" someone yelled from my right.

It was Damon. He ran toward me from the just-opened gull-wing door of the truck. Two hundred feet away. Luke was on his way over to him, but paused and looked back at me.

Chuck was out of the vehicle as well, Ellarose in his arms.

"Get back inside!" I yelled and waved.

Damon had his laptop in his hands. "I'm getting a signal, there's a control signal coming in. They're sending drones—"

"We know. Get back in the truck!"

He pulled his gaze from his laptop screen and looked up at me. I pointed toward the sun. He stumbled and almost tripped up on himself—Damon was never the most athletically gifted—but he reversed course, hesitated, waited for Luke, and then they crouched and ran back to safety together.

My head swiveled to my left.

To Lauren.

She was already hauling Susie over the top of a fallen tree. My wife had her submachine gun in her right arm, up and high.

Dots in the sky over the trees behind her. A cloud of them.

I patted my chest and waist. I'd left the Glock in the car. I hadn't wanted to step out of the car armed. Too late now.

"Mike, get down!" Travis yelled.

I was standing still, right in the middle of the paved road. Time seemed to slow down. I watched Travis's arm waving at me to move to one side. Overhead, the drones to my left were at least a few hundred yards away, the ones behind Lauren even farther.

How long would it take those machines to cover the distance? Twenty? Thirty seconds till they reached me? How far could I run in that time?

I was no sprinter.

"Mike!" I heard Chuck yell. "We'll come to you. Get into cover."

I was in the middle of the road, the chipped yellow divider paint stripe under my sneakers. The kids were safe. Luke had made it into the truck. Olivia was there too. Ellarose and Bonham. The super-truck would provide protection from these things. Right?

To my left was ten feet of hardtop, then twenty feet of hardscrabble gravel and dirt that ended at a wood-post fence of chicken wire that extended around Joe's farm. Flattened corn stalks beyond that, which provided no cover. To my right, five feet away Travis crouched behind his motorcycle, maybe forty feet to Lauren and the fallen tree, and fifty feet up the road to the pickup.

My feet felt frozen to the pavement.

Screaming and yelling.

Rick and Percy stood over the fallen tree where Lauren and Susie were. The two men now had on silvery ponchos, both of their backpacks on the ground, open with black ropes spilling out. Their weapons were out and up, following the drone formations in the sky.

My brain finally kicked into action.

"Lauren," I yelled. "Chuck is bringing the truck to us. Stay down."

"You get down, you idiot," she yelled.

I remembered that Joe was beside me. He seemed like he could barely walk a minute ago. I turned to grab and help him into the cover of the motorcycle, but he shrugged me off.

"Get into cover, son," he said calmly. "I got this."

Two. No, five. Maybe a dozen little dots raced toward us from the west. More of them hovered in the distance and seemed to spread out in a circle around us a few hundred feet up. I stepped backward and away from Joe, checking once over my shoulder at Lauren. I crouched under cover of the motorcycle beside Travis.

"Put this on," he said.

One of the silver ponchos Rick and Percy were wearing.

"Space blankets from the camping store," Travis explained. "It helps confuse their image recognition software. Don't know where the hell these little bastards came from. Must have followed you in."

I put on the poncho as I knelt. "You cut the power lines?"

He nodded and put on a tinfoil hat. "Don't laugh, it helps." He handed me one, which I tried to stick on my head by crinkling the foil around my ears.

I said, "You guys have fought these before?"

"You know how to use one of these?" Travis handed me a sawed-off shotgun. Two barrels.

The humming-fluttering whine grew louder. A terrific blast, then the clicking chunk of Joe pumping the action on his shotgun.

"Sort of," I said. "We tried shooting these things, it's way more diff—"

Another roar from Joe's shotgun. "Got one," he exclaimed triumphantly.

While Travis and I cowered, Joe stood straight and trained his weapon on the incoming swarm of drones. He seemed to be enjoying himself.

"It's a shotgun. Pull back the safety here." Travis indicated a nub on the top. "Then pull the trigger. We filled the cartridges with birdshot. About four-hundred pellets per shell. Sprays wide in kind of a fan pattern, much easier to hit them than with bullets. You only use this when one gets within five feet, you understand? And don't hit one of us, for Pete's sake. Probably wouldn't kill but definitely not nice."

I nodded and took the gun. The whining of the drones grew louder. Joe pumped and fired again, then cursed. Travis pulled another sawed-off shotgun from one of the saddlebags on his bike. He had a pump-action gun as well, but he laid both guns on the pavement and slung his backpack off. He peeked over the top of the bike's seat.

Joe pumped and shot once more, and this time whooped in glee. He pumped again.

The whining grated into my ears.

"Chuck is coming to get us in the truck," I said to Travis.

"Truck?" He peered over the seat again and grabbed something in his open backpack.

"It's armored enough to protect against these things."

"Didn't a guy run out and say he had a signal on these things?"

I nodded.

"That was Damon Indigo, right?"

Again, I nodded.

"Hot damn. Damon Indigo. Right here." He rose into a crouch. "We need to get to the pickup first." He glanced up. "And why the heck are these things spreading out like that? I've never seen them do that before."

While a dozen or so dove toward us, the rest had spread into a wide circle hundreds of yards across and more than fifty feet up, above the tree canopy.

From the corner of my eye, a flickering light and more shotgun blasts. A hot-orange flash as one of the drones exploded, then a squeal of pain. I saw my wife roll behind the tree on her back and fire upward and blast another drone.

Travis jumped into the air beside me. He left both shotguns on the ground.

Joe fired, pumped, and then swore. "I'm empty," he yelled.

"What are you doing?" I asked Travis.

He ran straight at the swarm of approaching drones to our left. They zigged and weaved as they zeroed in on him. He had no gun, no weapon. Travis twisted back and then threw his left arm high, his right following it, launching something up.

A spiraling net twenty feet across materialized in the air in front of him.

Spinning and spinning, it expanded.

Lauren squinted into the setting sun. She had one arm around Susie. "There's a doctor," she said to her friend. "He just got here on a motorcycle. You're going to be okay."

Susie nodded and tried to smile, but she was barely conscious. Lauren did her best to wrap up the wound in the side of her gut, but every time her friend moved, more blood oozed out.

"Just hold on—"

What was that? In the sky?

"Mike!" Lauren yelled, just at the same moment as the doctor on the bike screamed, "Incoming!"

Her husband started running toward Luke, but her son was already most of the way to the truck. Could she make it to the truck? Too far.

Lauren stood up and grabbed Susie, hauled her back over the fallen tree into cover. Her friend hit the dirt on the other side with a sickening thud and screamed in pain.

"Susie?" Lauren said. "Suse?" But she was unconscious.

Blood seeped into the dirt under her.

Percy and Rick, the two men who had come to help them, were already up and standing in a protective stance around the two women. The men had put on silver ponchos, which was odd, but Lauren figured it was camouflage against the drones. They had obviously encountered them before.

Which was good.

Through the burnt tree branches to the east, a swarm of tiny drones dropped in altitude, sped into the cover of the canopy, and veered toward them.

"Cover me," Percy said to Rick.

Percy dropped his pump-action on the ground and kicked it over to Lauren, then bent and fished something from his backpack.

Two drones dodged and weaved through the tree trunks not even fifty feet away.

Lauren tossed her submachine gun into the dirt and picked up the shotgun. These guys had fought these things before. They had to have shot cartridges in these things.

"What are you doing?" Lauren asked Percy, who stood in front of her holding what looked like a mess of string. "Get out of the way."

She raised the shotgun.

Percy hesitated, but as three of the weaving drones came within twenty feet and darted at him, he hauled back and threw a net whirling into the air. It expanded and enveloped the three approaching drones.

But then one twisting edge caught a branch.

The net collapsed.

Two drones sped around it. Lauren aimed around Percy and pulled the trigger. One of the little bastards exploded in a yellow ball of flame. Rick fired twice from her left.

But the drone darted into Percy.

He screamed, his hands out, trying to bat it away. An orange fireball engulfed his head. His body flopped to the dirt.

Another swarm of dots slalomed through the trees farther out.

"We've got to move," Lauren yelled.

She grabbed Susie's inert body and began dragging her through the dirt, a streak of blood left across the leaves and mud as she pulled.

Chapter 32

"Get down!" I yelled.

Travis's spinning net caught four of the drones speeding toward Joe.

One of them darted around it to the right, but Joe tossed aside his pump-action gun and swung up his sawed-off, leveled it from his waist as the drone sped straight at him. The drone exploded in flaming fragments that showered over us and clattered to the pavement.

"Want more?" Joe laughed a throaty growl. "Come on, I got lots."

Where he looked frail a few minutes ago, now he looked fearsome.

"We need to move," I heard Lauren yell out behind me.

I turned to see her dragging Susie's body. Her friend's head lolled from one side to the other. At a crouch, I ran the thirty feet across the pavement to the edge of the dirt and leaned in to grab Susie's collar. Rick followed behind us, his gun up and scanning the tree line. He fired his shotgun and pumped and fired again and again. Flaming yellow fireballs lit up the air as he hit the drones.

No sign of Percy.

And where the hell was Chuck? Where was the super-truck?

Lauren and I pulled Susie together, and we almost managed to run back to the rear of the pickup truck. Travis and

Joe were already there. I nodded at Ken, who had disembarked with the three other guys. Two of them to each side of the truck, all of them in silver ponchos and tinfoil hats, with sawed-off shotguns strapped to their thighs and pump-action guns in their hands.

Hundreds of drones circled in the sky, making a ring with us in its center. The first salvo of drones had apparently been sent in. They were testing our defenses.

"What happened to Percy?" Travis said breathlessly. He tore back a tarp covering whatever was in the bed of the pickup.

Rick shook his head. "He didn't make it."

I closed my eyes. Percy. Rosy cheeks. Had hugged me when we left here not even a week ago. Thanked me for saving his town. He owned the diner. Now he was dead, after protecting my wife.

I opened my eyes. "What is all this?"

Car batteries littered the bed of the truck, connected by protruding wires. Travis clicked an electronic device on the back gate. Switches and dials covered the device's surface. A squiggly green line glowed to life on its screen.

"It's a jerry-rigged jammer," Travis explained. "Those things communicate on low power signals. Any way to get your friend Damon up here?"

I glanced over the side of the pickup. It was an invisible truck, but now that I'd gotten used to the camouflage, I could see the way it patterned the background, like an octopus sitting on a seafloor. "They're not moving," I said.

Travis squinted into the sky. "Why are they circling like that?"

I held up a hand to guard against the sun. "We have an EMP device."

"Did you say electromagnetic pulse device?"

"In the truck. Disables them up to a hundred feet away."

"We had EM drone guns in Syria." He twiddled the dials on his device. The green squiggle on the screen wobbled.

"Where did you say you served?"

"Echo company. 160th Special Operations Aviation Regiment. Syria. Iraq. We were usually were the ones with the fancy drone equipment and the towelheads were the ones improvising." He considered for a second. "No offense intended if anyone here is Muslim."

Joe and Travis and Ken formed a protective shell around us.

"How's Susie?" I said to my wife.

Lauren knelt beside her friend. "Not good. She's bleeding internally, I think."

"If we can jam the external control frequency," Travis said, still fiddling with the equipment, "it at least removes the human operator."

"Does that stop them?"

"They're mostly autonomous. But it does make them dumber. And removes eyes on us."

"Eyes?"

"Stops whoever is spying on us from getting a look. Just wiggle this dial back and forth and try and get the waveforms to match up." He took a second to illustrate. "I'm going to see about Susie here—"

"Incoming!" Joe said.

The circling drones split off from their circling orbit into a tightening spiral. A dozen angled inward and toward us.

"Where the hell is Chuck?" I looked up the road past the pickup. A door opened on our invisible truck. Someone got out and ran toward us.

"Luke," I yelled, "go back!"

Luke was halfway to the truck when he heard someone yell behind him. It was so cool to see Joe again. Joe was just about his favorite person in the world, after his dad, of course. And maybe Uncle Chuck. So maybe his third favorite person in the world. Oh, and mom was pretty awesome too. So, fourth.

Someone yelled again.

Then his dad *screamed*.

Luke looked back and felt his stomach fall through his knees. Drones darted through the sky. He heard their flittering whine over the rustling of the burnt leaves in the wind.

He stumbled to a stop.

Uncle Chuck was ahead of him, with the truck door open, urging him forward.

Luke almost stopped to go back to his dad and Joe, but he had a better idea. He ran forward and jumped into the middle seat.

"Stay here," Uncle Chuck said. "Take care of your little sister."

Olivia was still watching *Peppa Pig*.

"Mike!" Luke heard Uncle Chuck yelling through the open driver's-side door. "We'll come to you. Get some cover!"

Instead of staying next to his little sister, Luke jumped over the divider into the back with Uncle Leo. "You okay?" Leo said.

"I'm fine." Luke reached into the foot well in the back, grabbed the gray box of the EMP device and grabbed the power cord. They said that they couldn't plug it in because it would take too much power, but this was an emergency, right?

He plugged it in.

"Let me go." Archer grunt-talked around the T-shirt tied between his teeth. "I need to get out there." He kicked one of the crates in the back.

Luke didn't turn around and didn't respond. His mother had told him not to. He heard the other bad man back there, the terrorist, kick the crate back. Uncle Leo was holding a submachine gun, guarding the both of them.

Uncle Chuck was in the front, talking to Ellarose and telling her to keep hold of her little brother. He flicked a switch on the front dashboard.

"What the hell?" He flicked the switch again and again then slapped the steering wheel. "Damn it, we're out of power."

Gunshots cracked in the distance. One and then two. Luke jumped in his seat and pressed his face against the window. His dad needed him. He looked down at the EMP device. More gunshots. Someone screamed. A man's voice.

Chuck said bad words from the front. "Luke, did you do something?"

"I didn't do anything," Luke lied.

Uncle Chuck flicked the switch again and again and let out more words that mom said were very bad.

More gunshots.

Luke heard Uncle Leo whisper, "If I untie you, you won't hurt anyone?"

"Only the right people," Archer growl-whispered back.

The senator continued talking to Archer in the back. Uncle Leo glanced at Luke, then at Chuck, then back at Luke. He held a finger over his lips. Luke nodded. He would keep quiet. He wouldn't say anything. Luke liked Archer, and he didn't see why he had to be tied up.

Uncle Chuck said more bad words from the front of the truck. Uncle Leo leaned over the divider into the trunk area and whispered to Archer.

Out the window, the circling drones broke from their pattern and began to spiral in.

Toward his mother and father.

Chuck said not to leave his sister alone, but she was fine watching *Peppa Pig*.

His dad needed him. Luke had saved his dad's life at the cabin. He'd saved his life at the waterfalls. Now he would save everyone. Luke reached down and unplugged the EMP, made sure Uncle Leo wasn't looking his way.

Luke clicked the door handle.

And slipped out.

The drones fell from the sky in a spiral, zoomed right toward his mother and father.

Luke ran to them as fast as his legs would pump.

"Go back!" I screamed at the top of my lungs.

My son held the gray EMP box out ahead of himself with both arms and ran as fast as he could toward us. Two hundred feet of distance, maybe less. I peered up at the drones streaming in a dozen spiraling arms toward us. Some of them split off.

They saw my son.

Someone appeared behind Luke. The bulk of him unmistakable. It was Archer. How had he gotten loose? The blood drained from my face. Had he killed Chuck? Was that why the truck wasn't moving to us? Was Luke running toward me, or was he running away from Archer?

"What's wrong?" Lauren said from below me.

"It's Luke, I..." I wasn't sure what to say.

Should I tell Luke to go back, or to run faster?

The circling drones angled in. The men around us tensed and began tracking their targets with their weapons.

"This is going to be ugly," Ken muttered from my left.

Luke ran and ran. He was fast for an eight-year-old, but not as quick as an adult. Archer gained on him from behind, his submachine gun bouncing on his back.

Twenty drones dropped from the sky, heading right at Luke.

He was halfway to us, out in the open. No cover.

"Damn it." I pushed past Rick and began running down the side of the pickup, past the motorcycle.

What was Luke doing? Trying to save us? Or trying to run away from Archer? The asshole was gaining on my son with every step. Had that EMP thing even been charged? Wasn't Selena too low on juice to fill it up?

No time to think.

Just act.

Run faster, you asshole, I said to myself. My legs pumped, my feet pounded the pavement. I cleared the motorcycle. A hundred feet to Luke. Get to the goddamn gym when this is over, for once, won't you? From the corner of my eye, someone else was already running toward Luke.

It was Joe.

The old man had surprising speed. As he ran, he leveled his shotgun and took aim at the leading edge of the drone swarm descending toward Luke.

Archer stopped running and took a knee. He swung out his weapon from behind his back.

And pointed it straight at me.

Thirty feet to Luke. I could make out his blue eyes and his gap-toothed grin. Was he smiling? Or grimacing in terror? My son stumbled to a stop and lifted the EMP device. He held one finger up to press the button. I watched Joe side-stepping toward my son, the warrior's weapon high and tracking.

Joe.

Joe's heart. The pacemaker.

"Luke," I screamed, "don't push—"

Muzzle flash from straight behind Luke, and a split second later, the crack of the shot.

The spiraling drones dropping toward us stopped. Hung suspended in space. Again. Luke smiled proudly, his finger on the button of the EMP.

Joe collapsed to the pavement.

I threw down the sawed-off shotgun. It clattered on the road. Dropped to my knees and picked up Joe and turned him to face me. His body convulsed, eyes glazed, but he recognized me and smiled. "Never finished that chat, did we?"

"Tell me later," I said softly.

Travis ran over, his medical kit in one hand.

"We don't see the world as it is, Mike," Joe whispered as he urged me closer, "we see the world as *we* are. You tell the boys tha..."

His eyes rolled back. Body went limp.

The mass of drones, beyond the frozen ones, circled high in the blue Kentucky sky like vultures.

Chapter 33

I killed Joe," my son cried out between sobs. I held him as tight as I could to my chest, tried to squeeze out all of the grief and pull it into me, but couldn't. I was crying, too. Joe had died, taken his last breath, right there in my arms in the middle of the road. His pacemaker had stopped, but that shouldn't have been enough to kill him. It was the stress, the exertion, his diabetes, a lot of things had gone wrong at the wrong time.

Travis had tried to revive him, but it was no use.

Luke cried great heaving wails, snot and spit mixing as he wiped his face.

We were back in the barn, the same place that Oscar and Joe had taken us a week before when the Vanceburg Rifles militia had taken us captive. Except now, both Oscar and Joe were dead. In the time between, we had become heroes and saved the town, but now we'd once again become unwanted outsiders. Not just unwanted but reviled by some here. Six of the Vanceburg Rifles stood guard in the center aisle between the stalls.

Our side of the family wasn't wanted inside the main house.

Lauren and Senator Seymour and Olivia were in the next stall over from Luke and me. My son wanted some privacy to cry, and I understood that, but I still didn't want him to be alone. Susie had been taken into the main farmhouse and Travis was doing his best to patch up her wounds. Chuck and his kids were in there too.

"It wasn't just the EMP," I whispered. "Joe had a lot of bad things happening in his body. He had a heart attack two days before. It was just his time. You saved our lives."

"Ken said I didn't. He said they could have handled it. He said I killed Joe."

"He was mad. He didn't mean it."

"Yes, he did."

My son was right.

Ken had meant what he'd said, but then I was also right. Ken was mad and angry and hurt as hell, and people feeling like that said things they might regret later. Not just Joe had died, but Ken had found out his best friend Oscar was dead as well, after leaving two days before, also to help us. Percy, another good friend of his, died out there today as well. I couldn't blame Ken.

But then, who could I blame?

When Luke had set off the EMP device, all the incoming drones had halted in place. Gone into reset mode, Travis said, just like they used to do to enemy drones in Syria. Frozen in place and hovering, Lauren and the boys had picked off the drones one by one with the shotguns. The drones farther out, in circles at a distance greater than the EMP had effect, then filed off and disappeared over the hills and left us alone.

With Joe dead in the middle of the street.

Damon watched the retreating drones and said that they were out of power and needed to recharge. Travis had a different opinion. These were scouts, he said, and they had found us and done recon and tested the target.

They would be back, and in force, Travis had said.

"Try and get some sleep," I said to Luke, wrapping him in a blanket. He pulled it around himself and nodded, sniffling and shaking.

I sighed, ran a hand through his hair, and got up from the bench. A candle burned in the corner of the room on the cement floor. Blackout curtains hung over the window and metal bars. Nice woodwork, I thought to myself, looking at the sloping roof. Joe had built this place for his wife, he had told me, for horses that they never got around to owning.

Now both of them were gone.

"This is an embarrassment," Archer hissed from outside my stall.

The man stalked back and forth down the center of the barn. He had his backpack on, his sidearm and rifle slung over his shoulder. The Vanceburg boys had tried to tell him he needed to give them the weapons, but after a tense standoff, let him keep them. Six of the militia stood guard in the middle of the barn, two of them inspecting our vehicle.

We had towed the truck, Selena, into the structure to get it out of the way. It was now just an expensive paperweight. They had generators, but it would probably take a week for a small diesel engine to repower the massive batteries. She still could be useful, Damon and Travis had both said.

The terrorist Archer had captured was in the stall at the end. We had tied him up, but the Vanceburg boys did one better and chained him to a wall. The man watched us but never said a word. He sat still and stared at a wall, seemed to be meditating. Two of the Rifles kept watch over him.

I checked on Luke again, asked him if he wanted an iPad or some water or something to eat. He pulled the blankets tighter and shook his head. I went to the next stall over.

"Lauren," I said quietly, "I think I'm going to go to the farmhouse. Do you want anything? Do you want to come in?"

"I'm staying here," my wife replied. "And could you get that out of here? It's scaring our daughter to death."

She had her arm around Olivia. In the opposite corner of the stall was a scarecrow, a remarkably lifelike one dressed in dungarees and a white shirt and with shoes on. I said I would take care of it.

Senator Seymour had his arm around my wife and my daughter, the three of them propped up on a bench in the stall next to Luke's. Ken and Ricky didn't want Seymour coming into the farmhouse. Security risk, they said.

"You okay?" I said to Senator Seymour.

"Not exactly the InterContinental, but it'll do." He smiled.

He still had on the same blue shirt and red tie that he'd had on when we'd left his house. We were all in the same clothes, spattered in blood and mud, coated in dried sweat. I still reeked of manure. I suggested we go in for a shower—cold water only, as the power was off—but Ken said that wasn't possible. He'd offered us a tin washbasin. Lauren and Leo had politely declined.

I said, "I'm going to go in and talk to Chuck, okay?"

"You do what you have to," my wife said and closed her eyes.

I dragged the scarecrow out and asked one of the Vanceburg Rifle guys if they could put it somewhere, a place where my daughter wouldn't see it. One of them said it would fit in the shed out back. I left the scarecrow in their care and walked to the back, nodding to the Vanceburg Rifle men doing guard duty. I stopped at the last stall, where Archer was eyeing the terrorist chained to the wall.

"I think it's time to get some answers from our friend," Archer said. "If you think he's one of my men, wait until you see me peel away a few layers of his skin. I speak two or three languages from this asshole's neighborhood. Not fluent, but well enough."

Archer terrified me, the way his eyes seemed to glow with intensity in the candlelight.

"Don't do anything in here," I whispered. "My wife and kids, please..."

"I'll take him to the shed on the other side," Archer replied. "There's a big cast iron bathtub in there I can use. I need to get some tools first."

I didn't ask what those might be, or what the bathtub was for.

Talking to Archer made my skin crawl, but I shared his frustration. Half of the people here thought that *we* were the enemy.

And they might not be wrong.

I left the barn and ventured into the cool night air. Looked up at the stars and the sliver of the crescent of the moon rising over the black mountains to the east. The smell of scorched earth wafted on the breeze. Almost black outside. I had walked the pathways of the farm many times when we were here a few days before. A diesel generator grumbled in the farmhouse, vented in the basement, but they put up blinds over the windows.

I made my way carefully to the veranda in the darkness.

A hundred feet to my left, candles flickered. Two people paid their respects. Ken had laid out Joe's body on a wooden table, put candles in jars to mark the spot, and had one of the Rifles stand guard to make sure no scavengers picked at the corpse. People came in from the town in ones and twos to pay their respects.

And *only* in ones and twos.

Travis said that funerals made for great targeting opportunities for drones. He said they used funerals all the time to target terrorists in Iraq and Syria, as people tended to congregate and high-value targets couldn't keep away.

Now *we* were the targets. Scurrying around in the Kentucky farmland, our bodies the glowing heat signatures to the eyes above. Travis said to keep the table with Joe's body at least two hundred feet from the barn and the main house, just in case it got hit with a missile strike from a drone.

I looked up. Who knew what was circling and watching up there?

I quickened my pace.

"Close the damn door," Ken said.

I had opened it a few inches and squeezed through. I closed it behind me.

Nine people sat around the oak table in the kitchen of Joe's farmhouse. A single incandescent bulb, dimmed, illuminated the center of the deer antler chandelier over the table.

Ken was closest to me on the right, scowling, with Chuck sitting between him and Rick farther down. Past them were Steve and Brandee, the two hikers my son and I had rescued from the fire the week before. They waved at me, Bonham and Ellarose on their knees. Travis sat at the other end of the table.

A crackling fire burned in the kitchen hearth just beside and behind him.

Damon sat at the table to my left, his laptop out, of course. I had no idea what network he might be connecting to. It was more his security blanket than anything else, I suspected. Paulina, all freckles and blond hair, who had kissed Damon on the dock when we left here a few days ago, sat right next to him. Practically on top of him. That made me smile.

"Nothing funny here, Mitchell," Ken said.

"No, I know."

"What's the goddamn grin for?"

"Sorry, I just..." I began to sit down in an empty seat.

"Not there, dammit," Ken growled. "That's Joe's spot, at the head of the table. That chair will forever remain empty. Can you not sit in his seat while the man is out there"—he pointed at the window—"being laid to rest?"

I took the place next to it. "I didn't realize. Can I take this one?"

He didn't reply. Looked away from me. Chuck didn't even meet my eyes. What had they been talking about? I had left them alone for an hour, which now seemed like it had been too long a time to let things fester.

I sat.

The fire crackled in the silence.

"Maybe we'll take the kids upstairs," Brandee said. She had straight brown hair and clear eyes and balanced Ellarose on her knee.

Ellarose had recovered quickly from the concussion, but we didn't want her going to sleep. Not that anyone would get much this night.

Steve, Brandee's boyfriend, said, "Yeah, why don't we do that? Go and see how your mommy is doing?" He said it both to us and to Bonham, who was on his lap.

Bonham nodded. "Yeah, let's go see Mom."

Travis had managed to set up a blood transfusion. Rick had the same blood type, which Travis had asked again and again just to make sure. He gave Susie some antibiotics and saline on a drip. He had set up a field hospital in a spare bedroom upstairs. I had a sinking feeling more of us might be needing his expertise soon.

Damon waited for them to leave the room before saying, "All the incoming connections to the meshnetwork have been cut off. Even radio signals are being flushed."

"KLMB, from two towns over in Portsmouth," Rick said, "can't get reception anymore."

"Means someone is purposely jamming it," Travis said.

Ken said, "Or someone destroyed Portsmouth."

"What we did hear, before KLMB went out," Rick said, "was a report that Senator Seymour has ties to the Chinese through GenCorp and Tyrell Jakob. The US government is looking for him, and not in a good way."

"Those are conspiracy rants," Damon said. "What I got on mainstream media was that our military has stamped out the drone attacks in Washington. The fires have been extinguished. There's talk of a military strike against China unless the leadership is removed. Of course, their Politburo is refusing."

"How do they know it's China?" I said.

Nobody answered.

"They're sure it's not Chechen terrorists?"

Damon said, "They're saying China supplied the weapons. China isn't denying the drones are theirs. Our government's hands are tied, anyway, without a commander-in-chief."

I said, "They haven't sworn in Secretary of State Timothy Chen yet?"

"Who is a puppet of the Chinese Politburo himself!" Rick slammed the table. "That man wasn't even elected to Congress. Nobody ever voted for him. He's an underling of Seymour, out there in the barn. It's not just China, it's our own government that's letting this happen. Cleaning house because they can't win an election."

"Hey, hey, come on," I said quietly.

"Come on?" Ken said, getting up from his seat. "First you bring terrorists here, last week, telling us they were your friends."

"They fooled us."

"You are saying you are easily fooled," Rick said to me, pointing a finger. "You just remember that."

"Then right after you leave," Ken said, "the feds show up, helicopters and Humvees and FBI and CIA and who the hell else knows what. They take that truck you came here in, they rip our town apart, look up and inside all our assholes and accuse us of things, and then leave."

"I am sorry about that," I said.

"You're always sorry, Mitchell. Now Joe is dead, Oscar is dead—"

"Percy is dead," Rick said, tears coming to his eyes.

Ken looked straight at me. "Why did you come back here, Mitchell?"

"Because we needed your help. And it was Chuck's idea."

"I think Chuck's on our side in this."

What did that mean? My friend kept his eyes averted. "Chuck, what are they talking about?"

"The last messages we got from Xenon—"

"That's their conspiracy theory message board," Damon cut in.

"A high-ranking member of the American military," Rick continued, ignoring him, "said that Senator Seymour wasn't dead. And he was right, because now, magically, here he is. Xenon also said that Seymour had a big secret contract with Tyrell Jakob, that the Jakobites were taking over the country. They're the ones that used his satellites to wreck our military over our heads. Again, connected to China, who are the only ones with their GPS and military still intact. Why do you think their drones are working?"

"This stuff is garbage," Damon muttered.

"And Mr. Indigo here," Rick said, jabbing a finger at Damon, "has a father who is a senior member of the Chinese State Security Ministry. Is that right, or am I just conspiracizing again?"

Damon's head bowed. He ran a hand through his matted black hair. "That's not a lie, no."

271

That was news to me. "Damon, that's true? You always told me—"

"I never met him, I swear."

"So he says." Rick was up from his chair. "They're also saying Tyrell and the Jakobites have put control of GenCorp into Damon's hands. Tyrell isn't dead, he's working with your friends, Mitchell."

"That's not true."

"I think it is," Damon said quietly.

"You're working with Tyrell? He's not dead?"

"I think Tyrell might have named me as a beneficiary for his corporate shares. I have no idea why. We had been working closely together on some projects, but I'm as surprised as anyone else."

"You see?" Rick slapped the table. "He's not even denying it."

Damon closed his laptop. "I need some sleep. I'm going to bed."

"Not in this house you're not," Ken said.

"Then I'm going outside."

"Stay, please," I said. "We need to talk this out."

"Nothing to talk out, Mitchell," Rick said, his voice rising. "We are cut off. Radios jammed, not even any shortwave. No networks. No power. No routes in or out, we tried. One way or the other, the assholes out there want your Senator Seymour. Maybe it's terrorists, maybe it's our own government, the CIA or something. They want to grab him and put him into power and kill all of us so there is no evidence of what happened, or they want to kill him to get rid of him."

Ken stood beside him and said, "Either way, before dawn, all of us, and all of our families, are going to be dead unless we get rid of you. And it's your fault, Mitchell."

Chapter 34

C an we calm down?" Travis said from the end of the table. "I think we need a little time to separate fact from fiction."

"You don't think we're about to be attacked?" Rick said.

"I agree with you on that."

Rick and Ken leaned into the table and glowered at me; their faces lit by the flickering light of the fire. Chuck sat between them but didn't hold the two back. He kept his eyes from meeting mine. The three of them looked like they were about to jump across the table.

Travis, on the other hand, looked as cool as a Kentucky spring. He had to be about twenty-three or so, with close-cropped brown hair, a muscular build, and a no-nonsense long-sleeved T-shirt with the arms rolled up, his two hands together in a steeple where he rested his chin, elbows on the table. His pale blue eyes looked in my direction, but not exactly at me—they seemed to stare straight through me, at some point a million miles away.

"They killed my fiancée, Jolene," Travis said. "Way back two weeks ago. In another universe before all this started. That wasn't Mr. Mitchell's fault. This isn't on him, it's on whoever is attacking us."

"That's what I'm saying," Rick mumbled.

"Please, sit down," Travis asked politely, "and let me tell you what I know."

Ken said, "What could you possibly know?"

"I've been fighting with and against drones for five years, out in sand holes that don't even have names, that's what I know. Afghanistan. Syria. Yemen. Echo Company of Second Battalion, the Gray Eagles of Special Operations Aviation Regiment."

Chuck said, "You're a Night Stalker? You served with SOAR?"

He nodded.

"Night Stalkers are the ones that flew SEAL Team 6 into the Bin Laden raid," Chuck said to me. "These are the guys who can fly any hardware anywhere in the world. You got your wings? You a pilot?"

"I got wings, but I'm more of a drone jockey. Gray Eagles. We've done more killing in the name of Uncle Sam than anyone else in the past decade. That's how I stayed alive the last two weeks. How do you think I know what I know?"

Rick eyed him, then everyone sat back down quietly.

Ken said, "You never—"

"You never asked, and it's not something I talk about. Not with anyone. Not usually, but these are about as unusual as circumstances get, I figure. And I appreciate you and yours taking me in for the past week, but you need to listen to me now."

The fire popped and spit an ember onto the table. I swept it away onto the ceramic floor.

"That, today, was a scouting group," Travis said. "No doubt about that. And I've scanned all the radio frequencies. Someone is jamming us, Rick and Damon are right about that. The signal jam is coming from south and east and west all at the same time. Surrounded. We can't send out a call, can't hear anything from AM to FM to shortwave. I can't even launch one of the commercial drones from the hobby store. The RF control won't work. We're blind and cut off, and there's only one reason someone does that."

I said, "We're about to be attacked?"

"They're doing recon right now, as we speak. Only reason they haven't come in faster is they're forming a plan, sizing us up."

Rick asked, "You ever see things like these before? These little drones?"

"The little killers? Heck, we have a tiny bastard called the Switchblade we've had for more than ten years. Fits in a backpack. Add C-4 and a detonator kit, same thing. We've been popping off bad guys with mini drones for years. But these ones, they're smarter. More AI wired in. They can operate autonomously."

"So they don't need human operators?"

"Maybe not quite that. I talked to Susie, talked to your crew." Travis flicked his chin in my direction. "Those flamethrowers you saw? They had to have human operators nearby, either that, or satellite hookup, which isn't out of the question, even with what's happened. Even if they did talk to satellites, they would need human tenders on the ground, like sheep herders. That's a lot of what we did. Get the drones up, let the pilots in Nevada fly 'em around and get the kills, then bring the drones down and service them."

"The terrorists are using our own tech against us?" Ken said.

"This *is* Chinese tech," Damon said. "We might have started using drones, but every country on the planet has their own now."

"We gotta stop calling them terrorists," Travis said. "Because whoever is running this, they are *not* terrorists, not in your typical sense."

I said, "Meaning what?"

"You said there were Humvees? A few semis? Up at the cabin? And down at the water where you rescued your wife?"

"That's right."

"I'm guessing we're talking platoon strength, maybe twenty to thirty special ops guys in three or four squads, with a tech team backing them up. If they're planning what we had cooking for our guys, maybe each squad has one of those big-dog bots in support. A couple of the flamethrowers. And those nasty little bastard drones? No idea how many of those they have. Must have slipped in a few shipping containers of them, let them loose. Operate them semiautonomously, one human operator per swarm, something like that."

"Which means satellite uplink?" Damon asked.

"Maybe they kept hold of a few of those GenCorp birds." Travis rubbed his face in his hands. "This crew is running an operation in the way that American special ops want to be working, but we're talking five years out. Even we're not there yet. A small ground crew supported by mobile ground and air platforms, semiautonomous, using local resources. Each human becomes like their own platoon using drone support."

He got up from the table and began pacing. "When we fought terrorists, they had their own drones, too, and they fought back something fierce, but it was sporadic. Low tech. Commercial stuff like you could get off Amazon, modified by hand. See, these guys are more like rebels, not terrorists. Rebels control their own territory and can hide from security forces. These guys needed time and space to conduct training exercises and had to stay *hidden*. Nobody saw or heard anything about this crew before this. How's that possible?"

"That sounds like Chechens," I said, except it was more of a question.

"Except Chechen terrorists don't really control their own territory. And this is sophisticated stuff. You don't just start using AI-powered distributed robotics together with ground troops and have it all just work. I mean, this is beautiful from a certain point of view."

I didn't share his enthusiasm.

"Commercial drones have ranges of one to ten kilometers. These haver capabilities are way beyond that. Definitely military hardware. Has to be state sponsored."

I asked, "If it's state sponsored, which state?"

"Chinese have the best tech these days," Damon said.

"But they don't have top-tier special ops," Travis replied. "Tech is one thing. Human capital is another. Not like our Delta Force or SEAL Team 6, or BOAT or MARSOC teams—they have nothing on that level. Their squads aren't trained for unconventional warfare or foreign internal operations."

"But it is their hardware," I said. "Maybe these are mercenaries?"

"Stealing high tech drone hardware is easier than grabbing nukes," Damon said. "And maybe just as deadly."

Travis nodded, but then shook his head. "They didn't steal this tech. This is a proxy war we're fighting. Somebody is backing them on purpose. Question is, how did they get in under the wire? How did they sneak in under our noses?"

Damon said, "All the confusion that's been going on? You should have seen the shipping ports when we left New Orleans."

"What's the point of all this?" Ken said. "Talking about it? Ain't gonna to solve nothing."

"The point of this is exactly the point," I said. "We need to understand."

"What we need is some kind of plan."

"We do have one advantage," Travis said, sitting down. "We know they need to be out of here, and soon."

"Out of here?"

"Of America. They aren't invading. This is a smash and grab. They caught us with our pants down, but only for a second. There's something about Seymour and your gang that's critical to their operation, but I think they were supposed to have egressed already."

Travis looked at Chuck and me. "You guys threw a monkey wrench into their plans, I'd wager, but this crew needs to disappear back into the night. And soon."

"How is this helping?" Ken said.

"What I'm saying is we just gotta survive one more day."

Ken said, "Surviving isn't winning. Just surviving means we *let* them win. We need to find a way to stop them getting what they want." He looked at me and Damon. "Whoever 'they' really are."

Chapter 35

Can you believe those guys?" Damon said. "'Just surviving means we let them win.'"

He mimicked Ken's voice as he said it.

I would take simple survival at this point, too. My family was here. My kids. But then, so were Rick's and Ken's. I said, "A lot of their friends died today."

That earned Damon's silence for a few seconds.

About a football field separated the barn and the farmhouse. Just being outside felt unsafe, the open sky a naked invitation to whatever might be lurking up there in the dark. We walked quickly, just one cell phone's flashlight lit and pointed at the ground.

"Shouldn't leave Chuck in a room full of conspiracy wingnuts," Damon said quietly. He had an armful of blankets for Lauren and Luke and Olivia.

"They're not nuts. They're scared, trying to make sense of this." I was too. I hadn't had time to think. Just staying alive had ruled the past twenty-four hours. "You never told me about your dad." It wasn't an accusation.

"News to me, too. And I'm being honest. I never met the guy. They think Seymour staged all this. You know that?"

"His sister died, my wife's mother. You think he faked that?"

"I'm just saying what they're saying in there. Her death might have been an accident, that's what they're saying. That he needed to make it look convincing he was attacked."

It had certainly felt convincing at the time. The terror on Seymour's face hadn't been faked, of that I was sure.

We passed the huge structure a few hundred feet away that housed the corn heads and tractors. The metal roof and massive machines were just visible, their eight-foot-high front-end blades gleaming in the dim light of the crescent moon. "That was good work," I said, pointing.

Damon had rewired two of them to use as drones to flatten the cornfields and create a fire break and save the town the week before. He nodded his agreement.

"Why don't I give you two a minute alone?" Senator Seymour said.

He had been in the middle of telling Olivia a story.

"How about you go out with Uncle Leo?" my wife said to our daughter.

The three of them were still cuddled on the bench in the same stall as when I left. Seymour got to his feet and picked up Olivia. I gave her a kiss and thanked him as he left, heard him saying maybe they could get enough battery power in Selena to play some *Fortnite*.

"I brought more blankets." I held them up. It was getting cold outside.

I heard Damon talking to Luke in the next stall.

"How's Susie?" my wife asked.

"Getting better. Travis is a good medic. He got supplies from the pharmacy in town."

"Sit down with me," my wife asked. More commanded.

I did as I was told and let out a sigh of relief as I felt her arms around me. I leaned my head back against her, felt her warm breath against my cheek, the heat of her body near mine.

She kissed me.

"I'm sorry," she said. "I should have told y—"

"No, I'm the sorry one. And don't worry, I understand. It was just a surprise."

"You think my involvement in the drone program has anything to do with all this?"

"That's the problem. I haven't had any time to think at all."

"Don't try too hard."

"What's that supposed to mean?"

She laughed lightly to make sure I knew she was joking. "You're funny, though."

"Oh yeah?" I had never thought of myself as being good with a laugh.

"Looking, I mean."

"Ha-ha."

She kissed me again. "You're all thumbs with a gun, and you'd struggle to fight your way out of a paper bag—"

"Did I do something to insult you?"

"Let me finish. But you're brave, Michael. You'll risk your life for a stranger, and for your family? You'd walk through an inferno for us. That's what I love about you. You see the way your son looks at you? You're his hero, and mine."

She hugged me tight.

"But your superpower? You know what that is?" my wife asked.

"Making waffles on Sundays?"

"People trust you, Mr. Michael Mitchell. You go ask anyone, and they'll say they trust you. And that's about the biggest thing there is in this world."

"They're going to attack us," I said quietly. "That's what Travis is saying. They've cut us off and isolated the farm. Radio frequencies are jammed. The second we stepped out of that truck today, they knew exactly where we were. They want your uncle, maybe me, too. Maybe all of us. And I can't get the people in the farmhouse to rally. Everyone is pointing fingers."

"And that's a problem of what?"

I exhaled. "Trust."

"So, then go and do your job, Mr. Mitchell. I trust you. Get us out of this."

Great. No pressure.

The senator appeared in the doorway of the stall. "The pig show is playing in the truck. Travis got it working. Olivia didn't want *Fortnite*. No more fighting, she said."

"He's here?" I thought Travis was still in the farmhouse.

"Can I speak to you a minute?" the senator asked me.

My wife kissed me once more for good luck, as she'd say, and I got up to join Leo. He took me off to one side.

"What they're saying is nonsense, Mike," Leo whispered urgently. "I had nothing to do with these attacks. You think I would plot to assassinate the president of the United States? It's total lunacy. And my sister?" Tears welled up in his eyes.

"I don't believe it, sir."

But was I totally convinced? Politicians had always been a slippery sort for me and became slimier the higher they jumped the Washington fish ladder to the top. But this was my wife's uncle.

"One thing I will admit," he said. "I did have an exceptionally large contract with GenCorp. Billions. It was off the books. Part of what they're saying is true. Wasn't entirely legal, but then, that's how we do things sometimes in Washington. But I didn't shoot Tyrell. I was trying to protect you."

"I understand, sir."

His politician's bright smile returned. "Thank you, son. Remember, we're family."

He had his suit jacket back on, more than slightly soiled, but no tie. His blue shirt was a mess of blood and mud. Lauren and the kids had changed into clothes Rick found, and he offered Seymour a change of clothes too, but he refused and said he was fine.

I checked on Luke in the next stall, but he was sleeping. On the ground, in the dirt, was the EMP device, the top caved in. Luke must have smashed it. I exhaled. Damn it, Luke, you shouldn't have done that. Still, I wasn't going to wake him.

I'd lost track of Damon.

Then I heard him, talking to Travis on the far side of the truck parked in the middle of the barn. Two of the gull-wing doors were open, with Olivia inside, her face lit up by a screen.

"We live in a post-heroic society," I heard Damon say to Travis. "We're risk averse. Used to be, heroes like you would go off and line up toe to toe in a field and hack each other to pieces. Now we fight from the comfort of a Barcalounger in a trailer in Nevada."

"Ain't quite that simple," Travis replied. "And it ain't an easy job, killing people on a screen. Gives you nightmares, I can tell you that."

"If you do a survey," Damon said, "and you ask everyone in a country if they would prefer to send in drones or robots to fight a war, instead of their own sons or daughters, guess what people choose?"

"Easy. We're already sending in the drones."

"And in countries with falling populations, like most western countries now? Sacrificing young people becomes unacceptable. So what do the politicians do?"

"You ask a lot of rhetorical questions, don't you?"

"But put the shoe on the other foot, and ask someone if they would prefer to be attacked by a human soldier or a machine? Nobody wants to be attacked by a robot dealing impersonal death from the sky. Maybe it's the machines that have finally taken over. Maybe this isn't even terrorists or China."

"You mean like Skynet?"

Both laughed nervously.

Travis said in a low voice, "Makes sense though, that it might have been someone inside our own government. Half of Congress has been looking for any excuse to attack China for years. They think the other half are turncoats. Might be that coup everybody's been talking about."

"Like the Night of the Long Knives in Germany, when the Nazis took over," Damon said. "In two days, in the 1930s, they killed about a thousand people across Germany, from high-ranking officials, even the top political leaders, all the way down to locals. Consolidated their power. And from the sound of it, right now it might be happening all over the world."

"Like targeted killing? Everywhere?" Travis said. "I heard you guys found a list."

"When the American government killed al-Awlaki, the first US citizen to be killed by a drone without trial or jury, they didn't stop there. The US government killed his fourteen-year-old son a few weeks later, and then his four-year-old daughter a few weeks after that."

"Those were accidents."

"Sure, like the ones the Mafia does to make a statement. Don't mess with us. Now either someone else is doing it to us, or we've expanded the program onto ourselves."

Travis said, "You really think it's the Chinese?"

"They just pulled the greenback as their currency peg. That's financial Armageddon, which might be the biggest crime of all for Americans. And these are their drones. And they're backing up India against our military, saying those first anti-satellite attacks didn't come from them."

"But China hasn't attacked anyone in fifty years. And they don't have the ability to project power. They couldn't even invade Canada."

They both laughed at that.

I pulled around their side of the truck and waved. They both looked embarrassed as they realized I had been listening. "Sorry for eavesdropping," I said, "but Travis, what town did you say you were from?"

"Pleasant Shade, Tennessee. Those drones wiped out just about everybody in my town."

"And that was two weeks ago? Just when the anti-satellite attacks started?" Why would someone take out a town in the middle of nowhere?

Travis said, glancing over at the stall where my wife and the senator were, "With all respect, sir, even if Senator Seymour was leading an overthrow of our government, that's way above my paygrade. You just tell me what you need me to do."

"You seriously think Senator Seymour's plan might have been to end up here? With us? If he was planning this?"

"One thing I can tell you, sir, is that everybody has a great battle plan when they start. And exactly five seconds after the attack starts, all that goes out the window. I listened to what happened to you, and it seems like you threw a big wrench in someone's plans. I could make up a million reasons why Seymour ended up here, for good or bad."

"What are you saying?"

"I'm saying it don't matter a hoot. What we need now is a battle plan ourselves. That's what I'm out here doing with Damon."

"I'm listening."

"They got eyes on us, that much I'm sure of, but they can't have more than about twenty commandos. We got more bodies than that here in the Vanceburg Rifles, and we got guns and ammunition and these boys know the land. Which is why they probably haven't attacked us yet."

"But they don't have much time before they need to leave, that's what you're thinking?"

Travis nodded. "They're in a hurry. So, what can we do? We need to make your Seymour bait, I'm sorry to say. We need to draw them in."

"The attackers might be only twenty people," I said. "But they have an army of drones, and we're cut off from any outside help."

"Which is where Damon"—Travis clapped him on the back—"and I come in. We can use Selena here, so we need to set up as many generators as we can."

"You want to drive it out?"

"We want to take it apart. This metamaterial coating?" He pulled off a strip that had been punctured by bullets. "It's almost paper thin. Makes much better camouflage than our dollar store space blanket ponchos."

"They're jamming us," Damon said, "but we can jam them too. Maybe even hack them. Selena has a sophisticated digital system for it, but we build a bigger antenna around the barn, amp up the power through a few dozen generators. Get a signal boost. Maybe we spoof their GNSS signals to the drones, maybe copy the emitter signals we got in that armor we stole."

"And those corn heads?" Travis said. "The GPS tractors in the barn?"

From the corner of my eye, I saw Archer walk into the barn. He must have gone into the farmhouse, because he had returned with a glittering collection of knives held to his chest.

I left Travis and Damon to keep talking. "What are you doing?" I whispered urgently at Archer.

"What we should have done already. Get some information from this asshole. Find out if they are who they say they are. Who sent them?"

I kept pace with him as he strode quickly down the barn toward the stall that held the terrorist captive. Six of the Vanceburg Rifles stood guard, and while none of them exactly trusted Archer, all of them gave the man a wide berth.

"I thought torture didn't work," I said.

"It's going to work tonight, that I promise you. I'm going to filet this bastard."

"You can't do it here. My kids."

He stopped outside the stall. "We'll drag him into the shed. Like I said before, use that cast iron tub to threaten drowning him. Water board. Whatever it takes."

"He'll just tell you whatever you want to hear. You won't get the real answers."

"You got a better idea? We are out of time."

"Trust," I said without really thinking it out.

"You what now?"

An idea bubbled up. "Trust," I said again. "That's the most important thing." I called out to Travis, "You have sedatives in your medical kit?"

"Yeah, why, you need some?"

"Amphetamines? Speed? Anything like that?"

He nodded that he thought he could find some.

To Archer I said, "And you still have those drugs and syringes you were going to use on Damon, back at the Seymour residence?"

He nodded. Then said, "That isn't going to work on someone hardened like this."

"If we do it right, it could," I said. "I'm going inside. I need to convince Rick to let me use Joe's room to get the prisoner comfortable, get the guy a shower and clean clothes."

I left a confused Archer in my wake as I ran back outside and into the darkness.

Chapter 36

"Is he awake?" said a gruff voice in the dark.

"You need to speak only Russian," I whispered back to Archer.

"He's stirring," Travis replied in a low voice.

"Turn up the lights," I said. "Just enough to barely see. Light a few candles. He needs to see enough that he's in a nice place, but not enough to understand where that might be."

Travis asked, "Do you want me to give him another shot of amphetamine?"

"I don't want to wake him up too much."

On the bed was a collection of other syringes. Back at the barn, we had crushed up a few Xanax and put them into his water when he asked for it. He had been complaining of thirst and drank the whole glass down. Twenty minutes later his head was lolling.

When he was semiconscious, Archer had injected him with sodium thiopental—from his stash back at the senator's house—which Travis explained was a barbiturate. One of the classic "truth" drugs, an adjunct to hypnosis therapy and an anesthetic. We didn't want to force it out, I said, we wanted to *trust* it out.

We took the man upstairs into the house, and three of us struggled to maneuver his naked body while we gave him a warm bath. We didn't want to attempt a cold shower, as it might wake him up. We needed his nervous system as relaxed as possible.

Clean clothes. Deodorant. Even some aftershave from Joe's cabinet. I had Archer get cleaned up as well and tidied myself. I wanted everything perfect.

We found one of Joe's old army dress uniforms in the closet. He had been a big man, and the clothes fit Archer, more or less. We removed any of the recognizable US insignias from it, and I apologized aloud when I took off Joe's 101st Airborne Screaming Eagles patch. We searched through Joe's closet for caps and boots. Army clothes were similar the world over, and Archer knew what he was looking for.

We put fresh sheets onto the bed, the big four-poster in Joe's open bedroom on the top floor. We removed any pictures that might have given away anything American, but then, pictures of fields and mountains were something on any wall anywhere in the world.

"You need to get out," I said to Travis.

"His eyes are moving under the lids," Travis replied. "He must be dreaming."

"Perfect, we'll wake him up with a loud noise." Whenever I was awakened from a dream into the waking world, I was disoriented for a while. Which was exactly what we wanted.

"You sure Archer should be questioning him?" Travis said. "Are there Black men in Chechnya?"

"I'm not sure if I should be insulted," Archer replied. "If this doesn't work, Mitchell—"

"I know, I know. You're taking him to the shed. No more English," I said. "Stick to Russian."

Archer spoke it fluently, he had told us, and some local dialects haltingly. It would have to be good enough.

"His eyes are fluttering," Travis said.

"Get out, get out," I told him.

I eased back into the shadows by the dresser. "Remember the plan," I whispered to Archer. "Tell him the operation was a success, that he damaged his eyes, that's why the lights are low. Tell him he was rescued, that the leader—"

"*Molchi*," Archer said.

"What?"

"Means shut up in Russian."

I held up my phone. Low-light video processing. One of the new models. I set the video to record, then held it up in front of me and pulled some curtains around to hide myself in the corner of the room. "Okay, I got a good view," I whispered. "I'm ready, you can—"

Archer clapped his hands together. Loud.

The candlelight guttered. The man's eyes opened. He was on his back, nestled in the middle of the large, overstuffed bed. Archer leaned over the bed and put one hand on the man's tenderly.

"*Dobro pozhalovat' domoy, soldat*," Archer said.

The man blinked once and then twice and turned his head. His eyes were glassy and red. "*Gde ya?*" he mumbled.

We figured that if they were supposed to be Chechen, then they had to speak Russian. Archer also spoke a little Chinese. Said he would adapt. That this was what he did for a living, fitting in anywhere in the world.

"*Ty doma*," Archer replied.

I kept filming. Long shadows flickered in the darkened room as Archer spun our story.

"So are you with me?" I asked Archer.

It was almost midnight. Eight hours till sunrise.

"This is one big clusterf—"

"Everything you just told me is true?" I asked. He had translated the whole of his conversation with the captive upstairs. I had replayed it and written down everything he told me.

"Because I can probably get Damon to do a translation through Selena."

"Why would I lie to you?"

"I don't want to speculate."

"Look, Mike,"—I think it was about the first time he used my first name—"we need to get out of here alive. I'm in this fight, for you and your family." He held my gaze.

"Should I go and get someone?" Travis asked.

"Everyone," I replied. "And get them into the kitchen, as fast as possible."

Rick and Ken sat on the same side of the kitchen table as before, this time with Chuck to one side of them. Damon and Travis and Archer sat on the other. Lauren came in from the barn for this and sat at the other end of the table. She stoked the fire and got the embers back into roaring flames with new logs over them.

I stood at the head of the table, but didn't sit in Joe's seat, just held onto the back of it.

Damon didn't attend, but not just because he couldn't stand half of the people around the table. He was busy outside, programming Selena, and working on the farm equipment.

Ken said, "This better be good, Mitchell. I was packing up my kids. We don't know how much time we have left to get out of here."

"I doubt they'll let you out," I said. "They don't know what you know."

"And who is 'they'?"

"That's what I am about to tell you."

"And why should I trust you?"

I leaned on Joe's chair. "Do you trust me? That's a good question."

Ken took a deep breath. Grudgingly he replied, "I trust you, Mike. Yeah, I do."

"Now what are we here for?" Rick asked. "And why the heck did you take that prisoner upstairs? I swear, Mike, if you weren't who you are—"

"Travis, tell them what we need," I said.

"We need anyone in town who can stitch or sew or tie knots to start making nets. As big as possible. Go get rope anywhere you can find it. Use fishing line if we need to."

"You gotta be kidding me," Rick muttered.

"We need to send someone around to collect up all the generators in town, bring them here, then round up everyone who doesn't want to fight and put them with all the children in the basement of the church. Figure out how we can defend it."

Ken crossed his arms and sat back in his chair.

"Damon and I are setting up our own signal jammer in Selena. We're stripping down that truck to make some camouflage. We need to round up all the guns and ammunit—"

Rick snorted. "You want us to stay and fight? For what?"

Archer leaned over the table. "Because it's our best shot at keeping most of us alive."

"With all due respect." Ken opened his arms. "I got a lot of faith in our Vanceburg Rifles, but most of them are shopkeepers and accountants. I was in the Rangers, but I doubt half of them could shoot a Coke can off a fence from thirty feet away."

Rick said, "Three of my friends are already dead. Percy and Joe yesterday. Oscar, up in the mountains. Rest their souls. This is your fight. They want Seymour and y'all, not us, and that's just the sad truth." He eased back from the table. "I'm not risking my neck for a politician."

"And what?" Ken said. "You expect a couple of good ol' boys to be able to fight back against an enemy that has"—he waved a hand over his head—"wiped out satellites and spaceships? That has evaded the entire United States military? Taken out the combined armed forces of half of the world's nations? Armed with high-tech wizardry? Seriously?"

The fire crackled and popped in the silence.

"You think that's what Joe would say?" I said to Ken.

"You leave Joe out of this."

"You know what his dying words to me were?"

"Don't use him in this."

"He said, we don't see the world as it is, but we see the world as *we are*. Those were his last words."

Respectful silence this time.

"And what does that have to do with anything?" Rick said quietly.

"If we are divided ourselves, then we will see our nation as divided. That's what he was saying. But if we are united inside, we will see the country as united around us."

"Those are pretty wor—"

"You are letting *them* get inside your head, believing all these stories. Who do you think is planting them? Conspiracies about this and that. Even if they come from us and not them. Even if we're the ones making them up. Those stories make an enemy of your neighbor, the guy right down the street? Those aren't your enemies. I am not your enemy, Rick."

He exhaled long and hard. "I know that, Mike."

"Do you? We are all fellow Americans. All of us, and we gotta ignore everything that tries to divide us and realize that we are *all* together. And right now, America is under attack. Heck, the entire world is. But from inside our borders, for just about the first time."

"Not the first time," Ken said. "We've had civil war before."

"But this isn't civil war, Ken."

294

I left a moment for those words to sink in.

"You said you trust me?" I waited and looked at each person in turn. Each one nodded. "And do you like ghost stories?"

I didn't wait for an answer. "Because I'm going to tell you one that will raise your hackles. Lauren, turn on the TV."

At the far end of the kitchen was a flat panel display we had hooked up to my phone. She turned it on and began playing the video we'd just recorded upstairs.

Chapter 37

W e're getting variations in the sig—" Damon's voice crackled over the walkie-talkie. "They're coming. We think they're coming."

His voice was barely audible over the white noise jamming up the radio's frequencies. Travis had set up a directional dish to increase the signal from the barn to the church, about three hundred yards down the main road of Vanceburg from Joe's farmhouse. Even with the boost, we could barely hear what they were saying.

Six a.m. and the sun colored the eastern sky over the West Virginia mountains. The white church's interior was lit by candles, their glittering flames providing the only illumination as we worked through the night. The church had a poured cement basement that the town had gotten together to build as a storm shelter a few years before, after a string of tornadoes had ripped apart Maysville, just down the Ohio.

I knelt to look my son in the eye. "You take care of your little sister," I said to Luke. For the first time since we had escaped from the senator's house, he was crying.

"I don't like this," he said.

"Me either." I tried to smile. "I'll see you soon."

He scrunched up his face and threw his arms around me. I hugged him back, then hugged Olivia, who was crying too.

"I'll keep them safe," Lauren said, her submachine gun slung over one shoulder.

Only one and a half magazines left for it. There was a collection of other weapons and ammunition just inside the door.

"I know." I stood to embrace her, took a moment to press my face into her neck.

"We need to go." Chuck pulled on my arm gently.

I had just watched him say goodbye to Susie. We had moved her over here and into the basement, with about forty other townsfolk and kids. Half of the residents didn't want anything to do with us and stayed in their own houses. I couldn't blame them. We told them to get under the stairs, find what weapons they could, and stay hidden.

Bonham and Ellarose were downstairs now too. Ellarose hadn't wanted to let go of Chuck, but he had explained that he couldn't ask these people to do something he wasn't willing to do himself. She hadn't understood, or didn't want to.

We had to go anyway.

My wife squeezed me tight. "Get going," she whispered.

I nodded, released her, and looked into her green eyes. "I love you."

"I love you, too." She took Luke's shoulder and nudged him backward. "Come on, guys, we need to get you inside."

I took one last look, and then turned into the darkness.

"Careful, that last step's a big one," Chuck said.

When they'd raised the church to put in the storm shelter, they hadn't quite gotten the levels right. I hopped onto the walkway and joined him. I tried to think of something clever or funny to say, but my mood wasn't up to it.

Travis's dirt bike was parked by the curb. I swung my leg over the seat and waited for Chuck to get settled behind me.

"You all set?"

"That was a good speech in the farmhouse, Mitchell," Chuck said. "You have a bright future as a speechwriter in DC, if I had to wager."

"You trying to be funny?"

"Does the p—"

"Don't answer that."

I pulled on my helmet, kicked down the starter, revved the throttle, and then looked up into the brightening sky.

Chuck was still on the curb beside me.

"What? Get on. We gotta get over there."

"If either of us don't get out of this—"

"Stop that."

"I'm serious." Chuck said, and he rarely was.

I looked at him from my seated position and revved the throttle once more.

"I love you, brother," he said. "Been a full-on bromance since the day I saw your face across the hall from my apartment in New York."

"Didn't you accuse me of stealing your newspaper?"

The noise of the generators near deafening. Thirty-four of them roared and whined in the confines of the barn. The doors of the truck were open, its panels pulled apart, cables snaking in and out like umbilical cords stretching up into the rafters, wires of all colors webbed across the cathedral ceiling of the barn.

Travis saw Chuck and me come in the door and extricated himself from the passenger side of the truck. "Selena is a beautiful piece of equipment. Next-gen stuff. Can't wait to see her progeny out on the battlefield."

"Probably not with tan crocodile leather seats," Chuck said.

Travis glanced back. "Is that croco—"

"He's kidding." I slapped the top of the passenger compartment.

Damon was in the driver's seat and had his nose in a laptop. Not just one laptop, but four connected together around him. Paulina was in the seat behind him, wiring another laptop up as Damon explained what needed to be done. Since we'd arrived, the two of them had been inseparable.

The three of them, really. Damon and Travis, the tech duo, and Paulina, the tech backup with a semiautomatic slung over one shoulder.

"We're getting enough raw power out to do some of our own radio jamming," Travis explained. "Selena is listening to their chatter out there. FHSS—frequency-hopping spread spectrum, and DSSS—direct-sequence spread spectrum. Before the shooting starts, it's always a war of the air waves."

They had ripped the truck apart and scavenged it for parts.

"You think they're coming in?" I said.

"The signal bursts we can decipher are getting closer. Sun will be up in an hour. They need to be out of here and finish what they need to do before clear daylight. Our own military has gotta be watching every inch of the continental US by now. Whatever is about to go down will definitely get the attention of our Homeland Security and military."

"Then shouldn't we just wait?" I said. "Set off a bomb? Wait for the good guys?"

Again, this plan came down to me. Again, it had been me, in the middle of the night, convincing everyone else to trust me. No matter how many times it happened, and how each time I swore I wouldn't do it again, there I was. Do you trust me? Great.

In the light of day, my nerves always got the better of me. Leaving my family behind. It felt like going up in a plane to go skydiving, but then when you get to that open door with the ground thousands of feet below, it suddenly seems like insanity. The other times I'd done this, it was mostly just me that was put in harm's way. Today, a lot of people might die, one way or the other.

"Our attackers are monitoring any radio chatter," Travis explained. "If they'd gotten wind that any US military or support was coming this way, they would have moved in by now. We have a good plan, Mr. Mitchell."

That was right. It wasn't just my plan.

Travis had been the one to come up with the actual order of events for the fight. Then again, hadn't Travis just explained to me the day before that any battle plan went out the window the second the fight started? My stomach knotted into a pretzel that made me feel like I needed to pee and vomit at the same time.

"We have some surprises for them," Damon said as he got out of the truck. "We got stuff coming they won't see."

"We stick to the plan, Mitchell," Archer said. He was cutting out the last panel from the truck. "Mumford, you're with me."

Chuck said, "Are you kidding? I'm going out with Ken."

"You got that bum left arm. I'm the best babysitter. Your wife made me promise."

"You can't be serious."

Archer smiled and said, "Does the pope p—"

"Don't even do that."

The two of them began organizing gear, ammunition belts and guns and grenades that had been rounded up from the basements and gun vaults and shops around town. They strapped on chest plates and ballistic vests. I heard Chuck say to Archer, aren't grenades illegal? They both laughed and began stuffing them into their pockets.

The senator was waiting for me. He had finally changed his shirt and suit and now had on jeans and a sweater with a tuque over his normally finely coiffed hair. A sidearm in a leather holster hung at his side.

"You're not getting a weapon?" Leo asked.

"Of course he is." Chuck strapped a holster around my shoulder and waist. "Nine-millimeter Glock, I loaded it with hollow points myself. Good enough for the Marines, good enough for Mike Mitchell."

"Safety?" I said.

"Technically, it's got three. Trigger, firing pin, and drop— but as far as you're concerned, just get it out and pull the trigger. No safety. Hollow points for stopping-power at short distances. Fifteen rounds." He slipped two grenades into the front pocket of my hoodie. "For good luck."

"I don't know how t—"

"You don't watch movies?" He got one out of his pocket to illustrate. "Pull the pin out, but keep hold of the spoon. Once you let go, a couple of seconds and *boom*. Easy as apple pie. Exploding apple pie, but you get me. Make sure you get them at least fifty feet away from you, or find some cover."

"Signals are getting louder," Damon yelled from inside the truck.

"We gotta move." Archer grabbed Chuck's shoulder.

My friend gave me one last smile, mouthed, *love you buddy*, and then joined the special ops soldier.

"Okay, Leo," I said to the senator, "let's go get ready."

Ours was a special mission.

We were the football.

Chapter 38

Chuck said, "You stink, you know that?"

"You don't smell like roses either, Mumford," Archer replied.

Chuck tried to keep step with the big lunk of meat behind him. It was like playing that game where you stepped on someone else's feet when they were dancing. No, not that. Like the potato sack game where you both needed to jump at the same time. Their legs were lashed together, their backs to each other. He felt like he was dancing with a two-hundred-fifty-pound hippo linebacker.

Step by step, they edged farther out into the cornfield, taking as much care as possible not to disturb the stalks and flattened corn underfoot. They needed to be as quiet as possible.

To the east, the rising sun, still obscured, lit up the craggy tops of the Virginian Appalachians in a blue-white line. To the west, the sky was purple and littered with dots of clouds. The air smelled of corn husks and dust, with an undertone of the burnt forests that rose into the foothills across the road a hundred yards away.

To the north, the field sloped away to the Ohio River. A single road cut along the edge of the river, passing beside the farm and into the town of Vanceburg. The farmhouse, painted white, seemed to glow in the dim light. The steeple of the church just visible over the oaks farther down the road. It was quiet. No birds chirping at the sunrise. Silence.

"This doesn't feel right," Chuck said.

He felt exposed. There was zero cover. All of the crops flattened when they ran over them with the corn heads the week before. Chuck and Archer stood straight up, erect, in the middle of the open field.

Except they weren't quite visible.

He hoped.

Travis and Damon had cut away Selena's skin. The metamaterial coating was paper thin, and it didn't care what it was being wrapped around. The material bent light around it, so they took a strip of it just high enough to cover two people and bent it into a cylinder. The effect was nowhere near perfect, but it deflected infrared and heat signatures, and in the dim light, nobody would notice them—probably.

Archer said, "Keep moving. We need to get as far from the barn as we can. Make sure you don't step on any lumps."

"Lumps?"

"Anyone hiding under the corn."

"I know. I'm trying, but—"

"Keep quiet," Archer whispered.

"I talk when I'm nervous."

"Look," Archer said.

Fifty feet toward the forest, to Chuck's right and Archer's left, a sheaf of gray corn husks shifted in the dim light. Rose up a few feet, moved ten feet forward, and dropped again.

Archer pointed but remained quiet. Chuck nodded.

The first sign of their attackers. Travis has been right. The young soldier had designed much of the battle plan together with Archer.

Draw them in. Pick them off.

Chuck and Archer remained motionless as the lump of corn husks advanced past them. More were visible now they knew what to look for. Chuck counted seven or eight slowly crossing the field.

A low whine in the distance.

Two and then three large drones appeared, quadcopter types. They came in low from the burnt forests to the east. The drooping muzzles of their flamethrowers were visible beneath. They glided over the road in, then across the cornfield toward the barn.

Chuck figured their plan was to light up the barn and farmhouse, maybe even the church, and then pick off people as they tried to escape the flames. He watched as the flamethrower drones approached the barn.

"Just a little closer," Chuck whispered under his breath.

Four hollow thuds, then four more. From the top of the barn, a flickering appeared against the purple sky. One of the flamethrower drones stopped near the edge of the structure and spat out an orange lick of flames. It took a split second for the roar of it to reach Chuck, about the same time as the net launched from the top of the structure sailed down and snared the drone.

It crashed to the ground, still spurting flames, and ignited into a fireball.

The next drone became ensnared but was only partly caught and stayed airborne. It veered to the right into a copse of birch trees. The third drone accelerated away to the left, out of the way of a net that landed harmlessly in the dirt.

The lump of corn husk closest to Chuck broke cover. Chuck made out a tattoo on the man's neck. A rose. Susie said the guy who came to the house had a rose tattoo.

Chuck's whole life, he had imagined a moment where it might come down to him defending his family and his country against invaders. Did he have it in him? He took a deep breath. The moment of truth had arrived.

Archer said, "Get free and target at will."

Chuck knelt, cut the cords that connected him and Archer, then put the blade away. He used his left hand to prop up the submachine gun in his right, lowered the muzzle through a crack in the metamaterial sheath around them.

A sizzling roar erupted. A bright flash sliced down through the purple sky.

The barn exploded in a heaving gob of blazing orange, a billowing sheet of flames blowing out the base of the structure. The glowing conflagration expanded, shredding the timber in an expanding, glowing ball. The shockwave knocked Chuck backward, the heat and fury blistering and ripping away the paper-thin metamaterial sheath around him.

Chapter 39

W here did you come from?" Lauren muttered.

The ghostly green outline of a human form edged along a wall in the inky shadow to the west of the small house across the street. That side was where the Ohio River began, not forty feet from the edge of the main street.

How did this attacker get into position? Lauren hadn't seen anyone come along the road from the east or west.

The sky was coloring, but still black as tar beneath the trees and houses across from the church. She had on night vision goggles scavenged from the gun store in town. The church had been raised so that the new storm shelter could be poured in cement beneath it, but they'd miscalculated a bit and left an edge of cement. She lodged herself under the front balcony, protected by the lip of concrete.

The man edging through the shadows paused and looked her way. They must have come up through the water. Didn't matter.

Lauren sighted along her scope.

Took aim.

She jolted down. Released the trigger without firing. Stuttering incoming gunfire erupted to her right. Chips of wood splintered from the balcony above her.

A strange loping creature bounded into view.

Lauren took a second to process what she was looking at. It had to be one of the dog-bots that Susie encountered at the cabin. A gun mounted on its top unleashed a fiery torrent of rounds at the church.

Lauren ducked again. Shrapnel sprayed.

The dog-bot bounded down the middle of the street and swiveled to unleash another burst.

"Now, do it now!" Lauren yelled.

A tennis-net-like web jerked up across its path, the wires supporting the net sagging from trees to either side. The dog-bot skidded and slid but became ensnared. The wires dropped. The machine flailed, hopelessly entangled, and fell to its side.

Another of the gun-wielding dog-bots came down the road from the other side, but held back and fired from a distance. An explosion lit up the twilight sky to Lauren's right; the blast hot on her cheek an instant before the shockwave blew her hair back. A firestorm roiled into the sky from behind the farmhouse, shattered beams of the barn cartwheeling in slow motion.

Lauren gasped, "Oh, no."

A white-hot needle appeared in the purple sky as another missile flashed toward the ground.

The searing fireball engulfing the barn burned Chuck's face and hands. He staggered back; mouth agape as he watched the splintering remains churn into the air.

Chuck was stunned, but Archer sprang forward. The man used the shattering detonation to begin methodically scanning and targeting the attackers that had moved past them. In a low crouch, he stepped forward and then sidestepped, his weapon up and firing in controlled bursts.

A second missile blazed down from the sky. It knifed through the roof of Joe's farmhouse. The ground floor splintered and spat outward before a thundering ball of flame engulfed the upper floors and the entire house disintegrated in the expanding conflagration. The thudding concussion of the explosion hit a split second after another blast of heat.

Chuck fell back but went to one knee and brought up his weapon.

Archer was twenty feet ahead of him and took aim at the rose-tattoo guy. A burst of two rounds knocked him down. Archer kept moving and found his next target. Splinters of wood and shattered fragments of the barn and farmhouse rained down onto the field. Ken and Rick were a hundred feet farther to his right and had broken cover and begun firing.

Chuck was about to get up from his crouch, but the crumpled body of the tattoo-guy shifted. The man rolled to his side. He had to be wearing armor. Archer was already ten feet past him. From a prone position, the tattoo-guy lifted his weapon and took aim and trained it on Archer.

Chuck raised his rifle, took careful aim right at the rose tattoo on the man's neck. The guy must have sensed it because he turned and swung his weapon.

Too late.

Chuck squeezed his trigger. Two shots. Right into the neck tattoo. The man slumped into the corn. Sighting down his rifle, Chuck got up and walked in measured steps toward the man and kicked his weapon away. The guy was gagging, his hands to his neck. Chuck aimed and fired two more times.

Corn husks at Chuck's feet erupted in spraying bits. Inbound fire from the left.

He took off at a run toward Archer but stumbled to a stop.

"Sweet Jesus," Chuck whispered.

Churning through the roiling flames of the burning barn, a swarm of tiny drones blew through the smoke, churning it in their wake. An undulating wave of dots stretched up and away into the purple sky. Rounds impacted the corn husks around him. Chuck sprinted for the church, but one of the flamethrower drones had survived and spat flaming liquid across the grass to his right.

Someone screamed and ran, arms high and flailing in flames. Had to be one of Ken's men stationed beside the barn.

"Motherf..." Chuck pivoted to the right. Leaned into the turn and pounded his legs as fast as he could. Incoming fire zipped and sprayed dirt into his face and arms from the corn rows.

Where was that coming from? Seemed to be coming from all sides. The flames of the barn burned hot on Chuck's face as he ran toward its right edge.

With their signal jamming equipment destroyed, the little drones had nothing to stop them—and there were hundreds of them up there.

He looked again.

Not hundreds.

Thousands.

Lauren swung her weapon back around. Bright light blinded. Her night vision was overloaded by the searing explosions. She pulled off the goggles. Maybe worse. Now just blackness before her eyes as her retinas tried to adjust.

She could barely make out the rooftop of the house against the lightening sky, so she trained her weapon down the edge and to where she thought it met the ground.

Muzzle flashes lit up the blue blackness.

Left and right. Center.

She unloaded a burst at the spot she thought she'd last seen the man hiding beside the house, then rolled to her left under the balcony. A hailstorm of incoming rounds impacted and sprayed wood splinters. She had on a visor, but shards of wood bit into her cheeks.

On all fours, she scrambled under the deck toward the side entrance that opened on a set of stairs to the basement. Two of the local teachers, Rhonda and Belle, fired over the concrete edges of the stairs, taking aim at the muzzle flashes that lit up the dark shadows under a stand of small fir trees by the edge of the property a hundred and fifty feet away, halfway back toward the seething flames now engulfing Joe's farmhouse.

Lauren scrambled on her elbows and knees to the stairs.

"Friendly coming in," she screamed.

Rhonda grabbed Lauren by her shirt collar and hauled her into the protection of the stairwell. Lauren tumble-rolled in. The concrete stairs bit into her forearms and knees. Her submachine gun clattered against the cement.

She needed to reload. Got back up into a crouch on the stairs. Tasted blood in her mouth.

"Maybe three or four to the front," she said to Rhonda, who nodded she understood.

Lauren took stock of the purple-blue sky and braced for the sight of a searing white flame of a missile raining down. Her kids were in here with more than forty others huddled together. She squinted and tried to find the dot of a bulkier drone against the sky, used the back of her hand to clear away the wood fragments from her visor.

Her vision seemed to shimmer.

But it wasn't her eyes.

The sky swarmed with dots of tiny drones. Flickering clouds of them against the deep blue sky. Cold dread iced down her spine. It was too many. Too much.

"Two targets, right under the small firs," Rhonda said and pointed.

Lauren blinked and snapped her attention back to the fight. "Another there?" She pointed to the right of the spot Rhonda indicated.

The woman nodded.

Lauren asked, "Any sign of Chuck or the others?"

"Saw muzzle flashes way out in the field after the first explosion," Belle said, her eyes forward as she fired a controlled burst into the base of the fir trees. A return stutter of rounds spat concrete fragments into the air before them.

"But nobody got back here?"

Belle looked back at Lauren for an instant, locked eyes, shook her head. The woman had dark skin but looked pale, like all of the blood had drained from her face.

"Keep looking," Lauren said. "Get them some cover." She slipped down the stairs, keeping her head low, and opened the door.

The basement of the church was a wasps' nest of activity. The small windows blacked out. Hay stuffed over them to dampen noise. They hadn't put all the generators in the barn. They kept half here in the backroom, vented with the windows open. Only started them up once the first shots were fired.

Damon waved at Lauren. "You okay?"

"Two of them under the small fir trees to the north of the farmhouse, two more under the one just south. And one guy to the west side of the house, another one to—"

"I got them," Travis said.

He was at the foldout next to Damon. Two rows of tables, all with monitors set up on them. Damon had the young people from the town manning the controls, with Luke helping. Everyone in the town who was good at video games, Travis had said the night before, could assist with their makeshift drone program—it had worked for the US Air Force, so it would work for Vanceburg.

Travis said the attackers had to have some heavier hardware in their arsenal, something they hadn't brought out yet. The attacker's recon must have indicated that the townspeople weren't running away. That they were armed and standing their ground. Travis reasoned they needed some juicy bait to draw in the attackers, so they wired up Selena and used her advanced signal processing to begin counter-jamming the radio waves the attackers flooded into the valley.

They sacrificed the truck.

Travis and Damon and everyone else had cleared out of the barn under cover of darkness and run back to the church. This was the real control center.

"Damon, one more missile strike and we're all dead," Lauren said nervously. "I'm not sure this storm shelter can take it." The roof was poured with a foot of rebar-reinforced concrete, but it was a storm bunker, not a nuclear fallout shelter.

Luke remained focused on his screens, his hand on a stripped-down game controller.

"There's two targets under the trees right out front?" Damon said to Lauren.

"That's right."

"Tell me if I hit the mark," he said and indicated the door.

Lauren retreated, opened it an inch, and peered out. The sky brightening to azure. Shadows appearing in the distance. Shapes of trees materialized from the dark.

A growling hum and the ground began to vibrate.

The churning roar grew louder.

Screams and curses from the front of the church.

A giant machine churned up the street from east to west, a dark figure running ahead of it. The man turned and fired back into the drone tractor. The bullets had no effect on the hulking machine as it bore down on him.

Straight in front of Lauren, a massive corn head tractor crashed into and over the small fir trees. The farmhouse flamed into the sky behind it. Yelping screams as the gnashing blades on the twenty-foot intake churned up the hapless victims. The two men under the next set of trees broke cover just as the next corn head slammed into those pines.

Rhonda and Belle took aim and unleashed controlled bursts of fire.

Chapter 40

Lauren watched Luke, wedged between Travis and Damon, his face bathed in the light of the displays arranged in a semi-circle on the tables around them.

"Didn't expect coming up against drone-tanks with razor teeth, did they?" Damon's mouth twisted in a grim smile lit by the glow of monitors.

Beside him, also fixated on the screens, Travis said, "Taking off the speed limiters worked. We're hitting maybe twenty miles an hour. They can't outrun us."

Lauren said to her son, "Those are humans on those screens. This isn't a game."

Luke glanced up and nodded that he understood, but he still looked excited. She didn't have the time to process it right now. She tucked her feelings away and refocused.

"Are you still getting a signal?" Lauren asked Damon.

That had been the biggest worry in trying to reconfigure the corn heads as giant remote-controlled toys. When they fought off the fires the week before, Damon had rewired two of the hulking machines to cut fire breaks, so copying what worked before had been straightforward for the other four. The bigger problem was overcoming the signal jamming.

The attackers had to leave gaps in their wide spectrum jamming in the 10 GHz ultra-wideband range for their own drones, Travis had explained. Problem was that Damon didn't have hardware that could communicate in that range.

The solution was brute force.

They had a team of people raid the hardware store the night before, grab every bit of wire and cabling they could find—anything that would conduct electricity—and use it first to create another antenna around the church, and then to lay wires out into the next street and across the field into Joe's farm, where Travis set up remote antenna and meshnet nodes. He said they only needed to defend and be able to operate within a short distance of a few blocks.

Lauren crossed to behind Damon and watched one of the screens. An image of the road ahead appeared in pixelated color. The picture froze and didn't update quickly, but the feed was working.

Damon scavenged a geopositioning emitter from Selena and set up a local GPS from the attic of a house across the street. A map app was open on one of his laptops, showing the positions of the six attacking machines.

"We got them scrambling," Damon said excitedly.

Lauren looked up at the cement ceiling. They might have the attackers scattered on the ground, but in the air? How long would it take their adversaries to figure out the command post had moved to the church? She unclipped the magazine from her submachine gun and clipped in another. Her last one. They needed to conserve ammo from this point on.

"Move the big one left," crackled a gruff voice over a walkie-talkie.

"Is that Archer?" Lauren asked.

Travis had his walkie-talkie in one hand and mumbled a reply, then nodded to Lauren. "They're guiding us from position. Just like we did in Syria and Iraq, but we're the low-tech guys this time."

"That's it, more left," Archer yelled into the walkie-talkie.

He held it to his ear to try and listen above the noise but couldn't make out any reply. It didn't matter. Damon and Travis were doing a surprisingly good job of sheep dogging.

Two corn heads rumbled across the field, and another one of the attackers had to break cover and run for it before he was turned into maize mulch. Archer was on his stomach, Chuck twenty feet to his right, and Rick and Ken a hundred and fifty yards past them toward the north and the Ohio River. They both fired on a figure running ahead of them.

The man fell into the corn husks.

But then got back up.

These bastards had heavy armor on. Hard targets. A second later, the corn head rolled over the man, probably removing the threat of him ever getting up again. Archer heard Chuck calling in commands over his walkie-talkie as he tried to figure out where the rest of the attackers were hiding in the cornfields.

On top of everything else, Archer had to babysit Mumford. He had to admire his enthusiasm, but with one arm gimp and the other a prosthetic—and beaten-up as he was—the guy wasn't exactly battle ready.

Then again, that's what soldiers did. Stayed in the fight.

Overhead, masses of the tiny drones buzzed. The sky an azure blue.

Archer suspected the little drones were hanging back as the attackers weren't sure about the EMP device. Except Luke had destroyed it in a fit of rage after killing Joe with it.

Losing the EMP was a serious setback.

The Mitchell kid should have restrained himself. It wouldn't take the attackers long to figure out they didn't have the tool at their disposal. On the other hand, it had been Luke's idea to use the corn heads as tanks.

Archer had sharpened the circular intake blades on the machines. He wasn't much good at technical stuff, but sharpening blades? That was right in his wheelhouse.

He scanned the fields.

Glanced at the circling drones overhead. To his right, Chuck cursed into his walkie-talkie as he tried to get the operators to circle back.

An ear-splitting roar. A flash lit up the field.

Another missile tore down from the sky, an instant later detonating in the cornfield a hundred yards straight ahead. The explosion lifted a mound of dry earth and just about flipped the corn head on its side. The blast of heat and concussion wave of straw and dirt scoured past Archer and he put his head down. The machine plummeted back to earth and began circling. They hadn't destroyed it, but it was disabled.

Another missile speared down on a spurt of white flame past the farmhouse and church.

His team wasn't going to have those farm tanks operating for much longer. Archer glanced up at the massing cloud of tiny drones. By now the attackers had to know their EMP was disabled. They didn't have much time until those little bastards got into the fight.

When that happened, this was going to be over fast.

Chapter 41

Archer scanned the cornfield to his left and right.

"Stay here," he said to Chuck.

Archer could just make out long black hair on a target fifty yards in front of him. He was surprised she'd come in so close on a raid, but he didn't know how desperate they were or how many operators were in the unit. The target was watching ahead, didn't see Archer behind her. He coughed to get her attention, sprinted on a path that would take him ten feet to her left.

Made like he didn't see her hidden under the corn husks, like he was watching the corn head circling in the flames from the missile strike.

At the last moment, he dropped.

She fired over the top of him, the flash and suction of the bullet passing so close he felt it on his cheek. Archer hit the deck at a roll, once over, twice. He dropped his rifle in the dirt before he ducked and had his knife out in his right hand.

Dug the blade straight into the neck below the face guard.

It had to be Amina, the leader. Long black hair. The target was slender, couldn't be more than one-twenty pounds. No match for Archer's two-twenty. She clawed at the knife lodged in the side of her neck, gagging and gurgling. Reached for her waist, searching for a weapon.

Archer rolled again and pressed his full weight over her and pinned her arms. Seemed too easy, but then, that was often the way it ended.

"Your left!" Chuck screamed.

Archer reacted without thinking. A scarlet dot flashed down. He dodged right, rolling over Amina. The machine exploded in a crunching thud into the dirt two feet past him, spraying corn husks and pebbles into his face. Archer continued the roll up onto his feet. More red dots danced closer in his peripheral vision.

"Run!" Archer yelled, already pumping his legs.

Between the surging flames of the barn and farmhouse was a stand of silver birches, about a hundred yards away. He took off at a sprint and grabbed Chuck's collar as he passed, jerking him into motion. In college, Archer had been a running back, used to do fifty yards in five-five. He wasn't going to be able to manage that, but he needed every split second he could muster.

Rick and Ken ahead of them.

Another corn-head tank, two hundred yards distant at the edge of the flaming barn, turned and began moving toward them. Travis and Damon must have seen them running and were trying to send cover, but it was too far away.

Archer felt the beady machine eyes following him but didn't look back.

He and Chuck made the first of the birch saplings as the whining drones grew louder over the strained heaving of his chest sucking in air. Chuck and Archer split off from each other and hit the dirt, then grabbed cords hidden in the earth and heaved. A darting swarm of bots flew into a net that fell from between the trees, trapping their fluttering wings like fish in a gill net.

More swooped in behind them even as they tried to alter course.

"Keep going," Archer urged.

The mass of enmeshed bug-bots exploded in a roaring bloom of yellow-orange flame.

Ken and Rick pulled up the nets on the opposite side of the stand of trees, but the obstacles wouldn't keep the machines back for long. The net behind them was already flaming and disintegrating.

They needed a passageway past the farmhouse to the church. A quick escape.

Flickering dots raced through the treetops. Most of the miniature drones in the circling cloud overhead were still holding back. Had to be waiting for someone to unleash the EMP, but the attackers would soon figure out Archer and his crew didn't have it.

Another flash lit up the trees to the left, followed a beat later by a thudding concussion and blast of heat. The steeple of the church, past the blazing farmhouse, splintered in a mushrooming orange fireball.

"No!" Chuck screamed.

Archer yelled, "Your right!"

Chuck was staring at the church, but flitting drones weaved through the tree trunks straight at him. At Archer's warning, Chuck glanced right, ducked to grab a cord to raise another net but slipped back in the dirt. Scrambled for his shotgun, but it skittered out of reach.

Archer jolted forward and pulled up his sawed-off shotgun.

The drone-bots swarmed into a tight circle around Chuck and cut Archer off.

Chuck feinted left, then ducked right and stumbled through the open shed door. One arm flailed to find the door to close it. A drone whipped in before he could. Reflected orange flames lit up the interior of the shed as it detonated within, an agonizing scream below the hollow thud of the blast.

Before Archer could react, four more of the machines lanced through the open door. A succession of thumping detonations. Flames spurted through the open door and gaps between boards of the shed like a blowtorch.

Archer kept low and crossed the last twenty feet of open space to the church basement at a run. He waved, hoping the women pointing guns at him saw he was a friendly. Last thing he needed was a bullet from one of his own.

"Where's Chuck?" Lauren asked the second he was within earshot. Spattered blood and cuts crisscrossed her face. Her body covered in dirt and ash.

"Still out there," Archer grunted.

"I'm out of ammo. You got anything? Shotgun shells?"

He shook his head as he stumbled down the stairs and almost collapsed into the cement at the bottom. He had taken at least two, maybe three or four rounds—he hoped into his vest and armor. With all the adrenaline jacked through his system, the pain was blotted out.

Usually he fed off it, let the hurt and confusion fuel his anger and sharpen focus, but the gas tank was sucking fumes. He hadn't slept in days, had no time to recover from previous injuries, and had barely eaten in longer than he could remember.

He was playing hurt. His hands shaking. Vision swimming. Stomach convulsed to retch, but he gritted his teeth and held it back.

This had the feeling of a CIA counter-insurgency operation he ran in Donetsk, Ukraine four years ago. That had taken two years off his life in convalescence. He swore he would never let himself get dragged into one of these messes again. Hadn't signed up for this, but what choice did he have?

"Help me up." He felt arms pulling him.

Archer watched the flames gorging in a conflagration from the roof of the church as he had run in. The missile hit the spire first, and wasn't a bunker buster, so the detonation had spared the lower levels of the full impact. That said, the church's exterior walls had shredded as if it was a sixty-foot white-paneled firecracker.

Flaming hunks of charred wood still rained down around the stairwell.

Even if there weren't another missile strike, he realized this place might become an inferno within minutes. They might have to evacuate, but where to?

Archer limped into the middle of the control room with the help of one of the women; he thought her name was Rhonda? He thanked her. Scanned the room. Maybe forty or fifty terrified people crouched under cover of whatever they could find, half of them kids, the other half elderly. Travis and Damon were in the middle of the fifty-foot-square room surrounded by monitors and cables.

The ceiling of the storm shelter held against the first strike. The cement overhead was cracked, fragments falling from it, but still intact. One more hit and this place would be a smoking pile of rubble.

"What do we have left?" Archer asked Travis.

"Three of the corn heads are KIA. I'm still chasing some of their guys but had to circle back as they're trying to lead us off. Maybe they're retreating?"

"They were testing our defenses. What about the main formation of drones circling at a few hundred feet?"

"Mostly staying at altitude." Travis checked a video feed. "Cancel that. Parts of the swarm are breaking off."

"Leaving?"

He checked video from other screens. "Hard to tell exactly but looks like they're lowering in altitude."

"Get everybody in," Archer said. "Get everyone left out there back here."

"Shouldn't we spread out?"

"Back to the church." Archer glanced at an elderly man and woman under a table by the back. "This will be our last stand. We need to concentrate firepower."

Archer slumped into a chair.

The attackers had to realize by now there was no clever plot to send up the EMP by drone into the cloud, or something else they weren't expecting. The corn heads rewired as remote-control tanks had been clever, as had the nets and signal jamming and using the metamaterial sheaths, but even with all that—this had always been a losing battle.

An Alamo.

Archer had known it even as he'd planned the defense. Their attackers had cut them off from the outside world, were professionals with far superior technology and numbers. At minimum they could wait it out, burn down the town and pick off anyone who tried to escape. Or rain down more missiles. Or just brute force attack with the cloud of miniature drones.

There was no escape from this. They were going to kill everyone in this town.

"Where's Chuck?" Susie limped over from beside Damon and faced Archer.

"He, ah—"

"What?"

Archer bowed his head. "We got separated."

Susie's eyes teared up. "Did you see...I mean..."

"I don't think he made it," Archer said in a flat voice.

"You know he didn't, or you *think*?"

"It's a mess out there."

"He'll be fine," Susie said. "He's always got a plan."

There wasn't time for this. Archer stood from his chair and addressed Damon. "Is Mike ready to go?"

"Tell me exactly what happened," Susie asked in a rising voice.

"Damon," Archer repeated, ignoring her, "is Mitchell ready? Answer me."

Ellarose began screaming, asking what happened to her dad. Luke jumped off his chair from between Damon and Travis and went to Ellarose.

"Ah, ah, yeah, I think so," Damon replied after a second. He checked one of his screens. "Should we tell him about Chuck?"

Archer shook his head. "No point. It's now or never. Everything is converg—"

Through the open door to the storm shelter, a ground-shaking rumble began and then mounted in intensity. The shuddering growl grew into a deafening roar.

"Get him going now!" Archer yelled. "*Right* now!"

Chapter 42

I waited.

And waited.

While everyone else took their stations and prepared, I sat on Travis's dirt bike at the curb in front of the farmhouse. The senator got behind me and helped balance the shield around us. I didn't keep the bike running. We needed to be as silent as possible.

Stay hidden.

We were the football, Archer had explained to me.

He used to play football back in college. Running back. He didn't say where he studied, but it was the closest thing I'd had to a real conversation with the guy. He said this was going to be a draw play, where the quarterback pulls the defense in.

That wasn't quite accurate.

I'd watched my fair share of football over beers at my local pub.

Travis and Rick and Archer had designed the battle plan the night before. We would offer up the barn as bait, make that the first target and draw out any heavy weaponry. With bitter satisfaction, I had watched the barn go up in a roiling inferno as a missile streaked down from some unseen drone high in the sky.

We hadn't seen anything like this in their capabilities, but Travis was sure they had to have something like a Predator lurking for when they might need it.

He was right.

Our only job—the senator and me—was to stay hidden. We used a roll of the metamaterial scavenged from the truck's windshield. It was riddled with bullet holes but did most of the job in the semidarkness. We taped it together into a cylinder around us, held another sheet over our heads. At least it would divert most of our heat signature from whoever was watching from above.

We sat still in the cold and dark as the sun came up over the mountains to the east.

One of the attacking terrorists crept by us not fifty feet away, but he didn't look our way. His eyes were focused on the corn heads ripping up the fences and trees in front of the church.

We sat still and shivered as Joe's farmhouse detonated in a bloom of flames, close enough that we felt it sear our faces as it burned. The senator almost crushed my ribs, his arms around me, when the church was hit. It looked like the missile impacted the spire first.

Lauren checked in with us a second later on the walkie-talkie. Said everybody was fine. I had a hard time believing that.

But again, this was my idea.

It might have been Archer and Travis's plan, but staying and fighting and finding a way to get Senator Seymour to Washington? That was all me.

Archer said that people only fought for things they believed in. He told me a story of a battle in the Ukraine, when the soldiers from the other side wandered in with a white flag. They didn't believe in whatever their politicians had told them, whatever cause they were supposed to be fighting for. Archer said you needed to feel it in your heart, right in your soul, if you were going to go all the way to the end.

He said my speech had been a good one, that I inspired the people around me, said they trusted me.

But was I right?

Six years ago, I was wrong.

So deluded that I almost killed my friends and family because of an idiotic idea I had fixed in my head. I had inspired them back then, too—into almost starving to death like some Japanese soldier on a far-off Philippine island I had read about, still fighting the Second World War twenty years after it was over.

He refused to give up, just like I refused to give up even when I was just as wrong.

And here I was again.

Did I really believe the story that man had given us on the bed the night before? I didn't speak Russian or whatever language Archer and the man began speaking. They'd laughed and they talked like old friends for nearly an hour, the man drugged up on so much Xanax and painkillers I could hardly believe he was conscious.

Archer said I did a good job, but then, what was Archer's job? What was the guy doing with us all this time? Archer said that I had to be the one on the bike, driving Senator Seymour into Washington, especially after I told him I used to have one when I was a kid.

He said that it couldn't be him. He was CIA, off the books, nobody would believe him if he brought a story in like we had to tell. It couldn't be Damon, there were too many connections to the Chinese. And Lauren was the better fighter. She needed to stay and protect the kids.

But was Tyrell really still alive? That question still circled in my mind.

I saw him die.

Right?

The farmhouse roared its flames into the azure sky. A surging cloud of drones circled. Screams of anguish. Stuttering automatic fire. Booming thuds of shotguns. The hissing slash of a missile as it flashed down and caught one of the corn heads three hundred yards away. The machine exploded in a crunching detonation of twisted metal.

Were we winning?

Someone ran past us, two hundred feet away, from the shadows of a stand of birches where a flotilla of drones had dodged in and exploded moments before. I swore it was Archer, but he didn't look our way. It was hard to see through the sheath around us.

"Mike, you okay?" the senator whispered to me.

My body trembled. Sitting here doing nothing bordered on insanity. My son. My daughter. My wife. They were all in the flaming wreckage of the church behind me, yet I was going to leave them.

For what?

For an idea? For my country? What did that even mean? In a rush of panic, I started to get off the bike. I needed to get back to them.

The walkie-talkie on the handlebars crackled to life. "Go, go, go," came Damon's voice.

A screeching roar split the morning air, the noise rising over the tops of the mountains in the distance.

I picked up the walkie-talkie. "Go?" I yelled into it as I thumbed the button.

"Go!" came the screaming reply.

The circling mass of drone-bots lowered and fragmented, the ones at the edges sluicing off into columns. The roar over the mountains grew in intensity.

The ground shook.

I grabbed the handlebars and kicked down on the starter. The senator wrapped his arms around my waist. I kicked the bike into gear and squealed the back tires as we accelerated away in a cloud of blue smoke and burning rubber.

Two darts shot through the blue sky and roared over us, barely skimming the tops of the biggest oaks. The sky erupted in a conflagration of flames and detonations, the heat singeing my exposed forearms and face.

"Those are our F-35s!" the senator screamed from behind me.

The fast-moving darts angled high in the sky and turned for another run. They used aerial incendiary bombs to light up the masses of drones now scattering.

The American Air Force had finally arrived.

I leaned down below the small windscreen to get aerodynamic and clicked up the gears. We accelerated past the cornfields, the wind ripping at my hair, leaving the burning wreckage of the farm behind us.

This was the last part of Archer's plan, that if we created enough noise, the big boys would come in. Wright-Patterson Air Force Base was two hundred miles to the northeast, the Kentucky Air National Guard in Louisville even closer. With everything going on, they would be flying patrols, on the highest level of alert. All we had to do, Archer had assured us, was last long enough in the fight for the good guys to get here.

And it had worked.

The draw play in football meant pulling the attackers in as far as you could, the quarterback weaving and dodging, and then letting the football go at the split second before the attackers took you down.

The jets screamed back overhead, letting loose another salvo of thudding bombs that blossomed into fireballs in the sky. They must have hunted these drones before.

I whooped and waved.

Lauren and the kids would be okay. The church had held against the onslaught. Damon had called me, right? They were still intact in the basement. I saw Archer running into the back, hadn't

I? We still had boots on the ground that could defend until the cavalry arrived.

What was the use of the attackers continuing their assault now?

At full throttle, we cleared the farm and continued up the incline of the foothills.

Here I was, taking the president of the United States back into Washington. We knew everything. We would be able to stop what was going on, I was sure of it. The senator knew what he was doing, he was going to be the commander-in-chief, for Pete's sake.

Up in the sky, the jets circled and banked again for another run.

"What?" I yelled.

The senator was trying to tell me something.

"I'm getting radio reception," he yelled over the noise of the engine. He had a set of earbuds in, connected to a pocket radio. We figured once we got out of the valley and the radio jamming stopped, we might be able to get some news.

"Chen has been sworn in as president," the senator yelled into my ear.

"We'll fix that, sir," I yelled back. "Soon as we get there."

At this speed, cutting through the roads, we would be in DC in four or five hours. Another voyage of mine into the nation's capital, except this time as a hero.

The senator yelled, "They're going to launch an attack against Ch—"

Water sprayed against the side of my head. I must have hit a puddle. I looked down and back but saw nothing. The senator's head slapped into my back.

"Hey, be careful," I said.

I turned in time to see Leo's body peel away from the back seat, his face a scarlet mess of skull fragments and brain. His body flopped and rolled onto the pavement in a spinning mess of skin and blood. Terror kept my eyes glued on his body even as I felt the handlebars vibrating out of control. The President of the United States was just killed, my daughter's uncle, Leo, my friend—

The bullet of the high-velocity round hit me before I heard the crack of the rifle shot. The front wheel of the bike spun in my hands.

I flew headlong into space. How fast was I going? Seventy miles an hour? Eighty?

The knobbled pavement rushed at my face.

Chapter 43

"Michael," said a voice.

I was drowning, the panic white hot in my veins. The blue water of the backyard swimming pool shimmered the outlines of the back of our house.

"Just keep moving," the voice said.

It was my father. He'd thrown me in the aboveground when I was barely two years old. I had swallowed a lungful of water and almost drowned. I felt the water filling my lungs again, my hands scrabbling against the pavement. The sky blue above me.

"You just keep moving," said the voice again, but this time it was a woman.

I recognized the accent.

Boston. But foreign.

I groaned.

Lifted my face from the dirt. I must have skidded two hundred feet across the roadway. The bike on its side a hundred feet behind me. Didn't feel anything, no sensation at all. Numb except for a burning in my face and knees.

Closed my eyes.

Ringing in my ears. An image in my mind of Leo's body cartwheeling over the pavement, spitting blood and bone at every impact.

I opened my eyes in time to see and feel a thundering blast overhead. Two darts shot by in the sky between the treetops. The

F-35s. Our jets. Strafing the valley, clearing it of the remnants of the attackers. Unless they were attacking us.

Had I miscalculated? Had I gotten it wrong again? I rolled over and stared up.

Tried to breathe.

"The senator is gone," said Irena's voice, still just a sound that carried on the wind. "There's nothing to fight for anymore."

I couldn't see her to my left or right.

"He was our Ace of Spades. Our mission is over. A success."

I rolled over again, farther away from the roadway and into the weeds on the side. Gravel stuck wetly to the blood smeared across and dripping from my face.

Fumbled with one hand and felt my nose—smashed to one side. I still had my front teeth, my fingers discovered. I stopped to blink, one eye and then the other. Both eyes working.

Groaning, I attempted to get to my knees.

"You never give up, do you?"

I stumbled forward into the bushes and small trees at the side of the road. The ground sloped downward toward the Ohio River, but we had come far enough on the bike that it had to be a mile or more to the water. No houses or towns this side of Vanceburg on Highway 9, not till Grayson, and that was another fifty miles through the forest.

Pain lanced in my right side. I dragged my left leg as I limped forward.

"The mission is over," the voice said, the sound getting closer.

"Is it Irena or Amina?" I coughed out. "What's your real name?"

"Does it matter?"

"You know everything about me."

"So fair is fair? You want to know about me?"

"Something like that."

I gritted my teeth and managed to break into a sort of jog. If I headed downhill, I would reach the river. There had to be cabins down there?

"It does not matter," came her voice, but now it seemed to be ahead of me.

I stopped.

Scanned the tree trunks and carpet of pine needles and moss underfoot.

"You did not need to kill him, though," she said.

Her voice changed. The American part of it seemed to disappear.

"Terek?" I said.

Where was she? I unholstered the Glock Chuck gave me.

No safety, right? I checked it, stumbled sideways, raised the weapon and scanned back and forth through the undergrowth.

"Whatever you want to call him, yes," her voice replied, still unembodied. The sound seemed to carry through the rustling trees. "He watched our mother die, burned alive in screaming pain from one of your bombs. Do you know that? You wanted to know something about me?"

"I'm sorry about Terek. I didn't want to hurt him." I scanned back and forth and tried to get a fix.

My arms felt like they were full of lead. My hands shook. I was too tired to fight back. I needed another plan.

"Our entire village was bombed, destroyed like—"

"You can stop the charade," I said. "And I'm lying. I'm glad I killed your brother. I enjoyed it. Little bastard."

I saw her shadow move in the trees to my left. Were those two people I saw out in the trees? More? I blinked and tried to clear my eyes.

Her voice changed again, now into something purely American. "Ah—no more secrets? Is that what you want? It doesn't matter, Mike. They will find Chinese drones scattered over that town and in DC, find the bodies of our soldiers that will be identified as Chechen freedom fighters. I will melt back into the background."

The shadows moved.

She appeared to my right.

I turned and pulled the trigger. Once. Twice. Again, and again.

Half of the shots didn't connect, but half of them did. Bounced off her armor.

"You'll need something with a little more penetrating power," she said and walked closer. She ducked behind a tree as I unloaded the last of my rounds.

I stumbled. My arms came down. Too tired to even hold them up.

She said, "We needed the illusion to be perfect, otherwise you might have sensed it. You didn't need to kill him, Michael. I would have left your family alive if you hadn't done that."

Was there someone else in the woods with us? My vision was blurry.

I raised my empty weapon. "Leave them alo—"

An arm wrapped itself around my neck. "Perhaps you will be payment enough."

She was incredibly strong, and maybe two or three inches taller than me. She pulled the gun from my hands and turned me around to face her, then pressed my back against a tree.

My feet dangled off the ground. My arms hung uselessly by my side.

I was spent.

Beyond exhausted.

I looked up into the blue sky. The tree above me had little acorns under its green leaves. An oak. Luke loved oak trees. Olivia liked the conker ones, what were they called? Chestnut? Lauren, she always liked maples. I didn't think I even had a favorite tree. Shame.

"I give you credit for persistence," Irena said.

I could just see her brown eyes behind the ballistic visor, her face obscured by the armor that her neck and the rest of her body was encased in. It was wrapped tight around her body, just a small gap under the armpits where the seals came together, and she lifted me up.

In her right hand, a cruel knife edge glinted in the morning sunshine.

She leaned into me. "Goodbye, Michael."

Small clinking noises punctuated the rustling leaves. I had pulled the pins from the grenades in my hoodie pockets, and now released the spoons. Just like Chuck told me. One, I counted. Nobody threatens my family. Two. I stuffed the grenades into the gap of her armor under the armpits.

Her eyes went wide.

Three.

I grappled to hold her tight and said, "Goodbye, asshole."

Fo—

Chapter 44

Lauren stretched her arms forward and yawned.

A warm breeze blew in from the rolling green fields, the air tinged with the sweetness of spring, the leaves on the trees bright green with new promise. Mountaintops rolled in the blue-shifted distance, and crickets chirped over the stirring of leaves in the treetops.

One of the horses whinnied in the barn. They must be hungry, Lauren figured, and was about to walk over to feed them when her son skidded onto the deck behind her.

"I'm going out," Luke said.

He slammed the screen door behind him as he came onto the porch.

"Just because you're ten doesn't mean you can come and go as you please," Lauren said.

"Mom, come on, where would I go?"

"I don't know."

"I'm going to see Ellarose."

Lauren smiled. "Ellarose, huh? You guys have been seeing a lot of each other lately."

"Mom. Please."

"I'm not saying anything. It's great you guys are hanging out."

It was before 9 a.m. She stooped to pick up her cup of coffee, her back still sore from the old injuries. She rubbed her left hand over her face and felt the scars, all healed, but still there, the bumps and calluses.

And some scars you couldn't see.

The ones on the inside. They were harder to heal. Might never heal. Lauren still had nightmares, and Luke woke up screaming as many nights as he didn't.

She had taken both of her kids to see a psychologist, which was helping, she thought. It was good that he and Ellarose were spending so much time together. Each might be the only person the other could really talk to.

She took the coffee and sighed, luxuriating in the warmth of it against her fingers.

"Hey, look at that!"

Luke hung off the front of the porch and pointed up into the blue sky. White streaks appeared, dozens of them, maybe hundreds. They looked like the contrails of jets, but they were higher. Much higher, Lauren knew. Debris being brought down out of orbit. It was an ongoing job that would still take many more years.

"That's your Uncle Damon looking out over you," she said. "Like an angel."

"Dad would have liked to see that, huh? That's a big one."

"He sure would have."

Luke watched his mother's face. "Why don't you come over to Auntie Susie's with me?"

A crowd of people had already gathered on the roadway in front of the house. Lauren sighed and took a sip of her coffee. She looked up and watched the spreading white fingers streaking across the upper atmosphere. "Okay, but we feed the horses first."

"You okay?" Susie said. "You want something stronger than coffee?"

The Mumford house was just a few streets down from her place, yet it provided much more privacy. She couldn't stand it, sometimes, but then again, what choice did she have?

Lauren still had her cup in her hand. "Maybe just a tipple."

"A little Kentucky moonshine is coming right up."

Ellarose and Luke had run out of the house and disappeared into the woods the second they got here. Olivia had attached herself to Bonham, of course, and the two of them were doing a puzzle on the dining room table. Her little girl had outgrown *Peppa Pig*, but her imitation of the British accent persisted. It was cute.

Susie reappeared with two jam-jar glasses and an unmarked bottle of clear liquid. She poured them a finger each and they cheered each other and took sips.

Lauren took a tiny sip and coughed, then put her glass down. "I better not."

"What's wrong?" Susie asked.

"That you're trying to poison me?"

"You know what I mean."

"I'm just away from the kids so much lately."

"I'm happy to babysit. Come on, that's not it."

Lauren took another sip and felt the bite of the moonshine. She grimaced.

"It's Mike's birthday coming up."

"Ah, of course."

"I never know what to do."

"It'll be okay. It just takes time."

They clinked their glasses again, but Lauren didn't drink. Susie poured more into her own glass, but when she lifted the bottle to her friend's, Lauren had her hand over top of it. "Really, I can't." She smiled.

Chapter 45

The swirling brown water bubbled and frothed and churned as it cascaded over the rocks.

I dove straight into the foaming whitewater, heard the roar of the rapids beneath the surface. I popped back to the top and let the creek carry me downstream as I laid flat on my back and took a deep lungful of air to float.

Why had I never learned to swim before?

"Dad!" Luke yelled.

I rotated upright to tread water. "You okay? What's wrong?" By habit, that was always the question when someone ran toward me in a panic.

My son appeared through the trees to the farm side of the creek, Ellarose smiling behind him. "Hi, Mr. Mitchell," she said, waving.

"Dad, did you see that big one come down?"

"Nope. I was swimming."

"You know how dumb it is to be proud of being able to swim when you're middle aged?" Chuck floated in an inner tube about fifty feet downstream of me, a beer in one hand. "You're getting soft, Mitchell."

"I've always been soft, Mumford," I laughed back.

After it was over, two years ago, the first thing I had done was learn to swim. Properly. The second was move out of the city.

I had had enough.

"Yeah," Luke continued, "it must have been a military satellite or something. You didn't see it through the trees? It was huge, like hundreds of fragments must have come down all at the same time. You could see the streaks of it reentering in broad daylight."

"That's your Uncle Damon at work," I said. "Probably wanted to give you a show."

Damon had taken over control of GenCorp when all the dust settled. He was leading an effort to remove all the junk from orbit. Despite all the conspiracy theories, it turned out that Tyrell Jakob had indeed been killed up at Chuck's cabin. The FBI had recovered his remains and tested the DNA. He was definitely killed that night.

The only thing he'd lied about was having two children.

He must have told me that to make me feel better, or not arouse suspicion about having *Peppa Pig* videos in Selena's memory banks. In the end, he had changed his will to leave his entire estate to Damon. Recorded the statement right there in the car just before he died, a digital copy of which had survived. It turned into one heck of an ugly fight with the diaspora of the Jakob family, but that's what he wanted.

Odd guy, but Damon was a bit odd himself. I guessed that Tyrell saw more of himself in Damon than the rest of his family.

We hadn't seen much of Damon lately, he'd been so busy with GenCorp. I didn't want anything to do with it, though. After all that mess, I just wanted a quiet place to raise my kids.

"Mom's kinda freaking out again," Luke said. He followed me down the bank of the river as the water pulled me along. "Your birthday and all, and she's going to be away."

That's right. My birthday was next week. I had almost forgotten. My dad had died on that date over twenty years ago. It always put me into a tailspin. Lauren was going to be away in Washington, so she wouldn't be able to be here.

"Don't worry, I got you guys here," I said.

Lauren's uncle, Senator Seymour, had died, killed by the assassin on the roadway as we'd tried to escape. In a groundswell of support immediately afterward, Lauren had been nominated to take his place. There had been a special by-election, and before we knew it, there was a Senator Mitchell in the house. We still needed a female president, my wife liked to say, and who was I to stand in the way?

The memory of the event was still fresh in my mind. Thinking about Senator Seymour made my stomach twist. "Maybe we should go in," I said to Chuck.

"But it's a beautiful day."

"I don't feel well."

Chuck's smile slid away. "No problem, let's go." He began paddling the inner tube to the shore. "We'll get things fixed up."

He always had a plan.

Back in the battle, what Archer had sworn he'd seen— Chuck's body, blown apart—hadn't been our friend. Just fragments of the scarecrow that the Vanceburg boys had put into the shed. Chuck had materialized at the church a few minutes after Archer had, stumbling down the church stairs and into Susie's arms.

Chuck always had a plan. Diving into the shed had been his last backup.

There was an old cast iron tub in there—as Archer had told us—and Chuck had gone in before the fight started and prepared it in case he needed a quick escape. He always had a plan.

The past two years had been more than a bit of a struggle for me. It took most of a year to recover from the grenade blast I survived at close quarters, even protected by Amina's armor. The wounds the experience had left in me went beyond the physical.

I still had nightmares.

Chuck was like a dandelion, however. He could thrive anywhere after going through just about anything. I was more of a hothouse flower.

Too much thinking, Chuck often told me with his grin.

For me, the events didn't just go away. The memories of being hunted by machines, of the red dots flitting through the trees, haunted my nights and my days. I had been in therapy along with the kids. It would take a while to get back to normal, for the night terrors to stop.

I pulled my T-shirt and Crocs on and joined Ellarose and Luke and Chuck for the walk back to the farmhouse. It was a ten-minute ramble down the hill into the outskirts of Vanceburg and back to Joe's place, as we still called it. We cleared the last of the trees, and the white farmhouse and church stood out in the fields and green shoots of corn below.

We'd rebuilt the place exactly as it had been.

After the farmhouse and church and barn had been destroyed, we'd come back in the weeks and months afterward and cleared the land and rebuilt everything exactly as it had been, down to the last sagging beam. In his will, Joe had given the land to the city of Vanceburg, as he had no family. The city, in turn, had offered it to us when we said we wanted to rebuild it. A way of erasing the insult to this land.

Everything now was exactly as it was before the Battle of Vanceburg, as we and the TV pundits had come to call it. The Vanceburg farmstead had withstood the final battle and turned the tide, had averted what could have become a global catastrophe from coming to pass.

I walked along the dirt path up from the creek into the forest. The trees had recovered quickly after the fires. Mostly just the leaves and branches had burned, leaving the trunks to regenerate. The greenery of the underbrush had returned within weeks.

"If Ella and Luke get together," Chuck whispered into my ear, making sure the kids couldn't hear us, "that would make us real brothers, wouldn't it?"

"I think grandfathers-in-law?"

"I don't like the sound of that."

Luke skipped up to join us. "What are you guys talking about?"

"Nothing."

Chuck dropped back and began explaining what each tree was to Ellarose, but she already knew each one. Maybe better than him by now. Our children were already surpassing us in some ways, and I hoped they always would.

We had failed in so many ways.

The original CyberStorm six years before turned out to have been a test run for the final events of what media pundits had started to call "World War C". The conspiracy theorists had been right—it hadn't been only an unlucky confluence of events.

Years later, after what happened here, the truth came out.

The seventy thousand people that had died in the CyberStorm had been part of a cyberweapons test that had been made to look like an accident—but wasn't.

Hundreds more had died in the targeted drone assassinations across America when the machines were unleashed from containers in New York and Seattle and New Orleans.

Under cover of the attack in orbit blamed on terrorists, dozens of shipping containers had made it through the ports that shouldn't have. They were unloaded and the drone-birds were unleashed across America, hunting out people based on facial recognition algorithms and last known locations from social media feeds.

But it wasn't Muslim terrorists in retaliation for America's own drone program. It wasn't an attack that was driven by America's own targeted kill lists all over the world.

That explanation was a deception, just as Joe had said it was. That was just something to fill the conspiracy websites. Blaming the attacks on Muslim terrorists was a fiction.

A way to divert attention away from the one person at the root of it all.

Or so they said.

A crowd of tourists blocked the roadway on the path back to the farm. Most of them looked American, but at least half looked Asian. There were some Indians in their colorful saris. This farm had become an international tourist destination, and probably would be for years.

And it wasn't the Indians who'd launched the first anti-satellite attacks, after all.

Chuck waved to Travis, who was leading the group.

"Please, leave some space," Travis said to his gaggle of well-wishers. "This is a real home. They live here."

Travis had started his own business, the Battle of Vanceburg Memorial Tours. Buses parked all along the main road beside the Ohio. Big business. Travis even got himself a new girlfriend.

"That's Mike Mitchell," I heard someone whisper in the crowd. "And Charles Mumford and his daughter," said someone else.

I held my hands to my face and rubbed the scars. I still wasn't comfortable with people taking pictures of me. The cell phones came out, the devices held aloft like fluttering flowers of technology soaking up the Kentucky sunshine. They parted like the Red Sea as we walked through, though, their deference and respect earning us a few feet of breathing room.

I noticed Ellarose and Luke holding hands and waving as they passed. I gave Chuck a nudge and wink.

"United," called out a voice farther down on the main road.

It was Rick, his fist up in the air. Chuck raised his fist. "United," he called back.

Chuck had become the second in charge of the Vanceburg Rifles, and it was like he had found his calling. Ken was still the leader. I had taken on more of the role of Joe, seeing as I was now living in his reconstructed house, but nobody could replace that guy. I did my best, as I always tried to do.

Joe was resting at peace now, in a plot next to his wife in the cemetery in the middle of town. Susie and the kids always made sure that a nice collection of flowers stayed blooming over them.

They'd found Oscar's body, too. Up near Chuck's cabin, where he had been ambushed trying to drive back Susie's Mini. They had buried him near Joe, with a big headstone. Hero of the Battle of Vanceburg. He would have liked that.

We walked through the rows of the cornfields, just planted, the green shoots poking up through the black earth. Horses neighed in the barn, a few hundred feet down from us. We'd done our best to rebuild it exactly as Joe had built it for his wife. She had always wanted horses in it, but had died before Joe could get her some. So, we rebuilt the barn and got Lauren and Ellarose and Olivia each their own horses—or pony, in Olivia's case.

My dream had always been to travel the world, but now it was to live in a small town.

In Kentucky.

"They want us to come over to your place," I said as I unstuck a
note from the front of the door. Just like my wife. No cell phone.
Message stuck on a door.

More country, she liked to say.

She wasn't wrong.

We walked along the porch and out onto the main road,
saying hello to everyone we saw. We passed the white church
right at the edge of the farm, rebuilt exactly as it used to be, even
with the storm shelter rebuilt and reinforced in the basement.

You never knew when you might need it.

My final dash up the road and into DC had been Archer's
idea. We hadn't seen the guy since all this happened, except for
one brief meeting at a Congressional inquiry. I figured Archer was
back out in the world, in some part of it I couldn't pronounce,
doing something I also wouldn't be sure of.

The draw play.

That had been Archer's plan.

Bring in all the attackers as close as possible, then send the
football—me and the senator—out up the field as fast and as far
as possible. Only trouble was that the enemy must have watched
the NFL, because they kept a safety in the backfield. Amina with a
sniper rifle at the ready.

She used it to put a high velocity round into the senator's
head. Would have done the same to me, except I went ass over
teakettle into the roadway.

Must have knocked me out, because by the time I came
to, she was right over me. I always knew it was personal, between
her and me, and when she trapped me, I made sure she knew it. I
needed to get her close.

At the end, she pinned me against a tree, but instead of blowing my brains out with a gun, she wanted to stick me with a knife. Gave me the opportunity to get out the grenades that Chuck had armed me with. Pulled out the pins and stuffed them into the gaps under the armpits of her armor.

She had exploded like a tomato sandwiched between two turtle shells in a microwave.

Her armor had saved my life.

But two fragmentation grenades from that close had ripped into the skin of my face and arms and hands. I did my best, bleeding badly, to stumble back to my bike. Got on it and raced, as best as I could, a few dozen miles up the road, maybe more. My memory of that part was foggy. I ran into a military unit dispatched and racing toward the farm the moment the battle had started.

I told them who I was, that I needed to see President Chen. Right away. And only him.

The plan hadn't been just Archer's. Travis had added to it. They knew that if we put up enough of a fight, forced our adversaries to bring in and use their big guns, then our own military would get wind of it.

Vanceburg was sandwiched between a half dozen US Air Force bases to the north and east and west. Once the radar and heat signatures got big enough, our boys came racing in. The F-35s took out most of the drones in the air, as they had been doing across the country. National Guard troops were rushed in on the ground.

We just had to fight back enough to raise a stink, and the cavalry would appear.

And it did.

Our attackers had to try and melt away back into the woodwork after that.

That was always their plan. Quick attack, sucker punch, fast and hard, and then disappear. And they might have gotten away with it.

Except for my recording.

Chapter 46

Chuck and Susie's house was five minutes down the road, just past Percy's Diner, which Chuck had now taken over. The diner had space out back with a terrace overlooking the Ohio River. Chuck had said he always wanted to live next to a pub.

His dream had come true.

Now he even owned one. He'd sold the businesses in Nashville and moved everything here.

We took our time on the walk over. I enjoyed the sounds of the town, the brief conversations, the cool, clear air coming down from the mountains. I heard a TV coming from someone's window. A spy show, someone confessing to something.

Which made me think.

Of that recording.

That dark room, Joe's old room, where we'd taken the captive, loaded up on Xanax and painkillers and sodium thiopental. We had put the man to sleep, given him a shower, gotten him clean. Woken him up suddenly with a shot of amphetamines and some loud noises.

The Achilles heel of the operation was making the attackers Chechen.

Which meant they had to speak Russian.

Archer told the man a story, all rested and patched up in the best bed in the house, explained to him that the operation was a success.

Travis had already convinced me that these "terrorists" had to be state sponsored, that they hadn't stolen the drones. They had been given them and had months or years to train with the equipment somewhere safe. Travis was sure these were not terrorists, not in the usual sense.

And Joe had said this was some great deception.

The drones that were being used against us were Chinese.

If this operation was funded by China, and they were trying to deceive us, then why use their own drones? And Travis had said that China didn't have the human expertise in special ops teams to do this. The only viable alternatives were the Iranians and the Russians, but these attackers didn't seem to speak any Iranian.

So, I guessed the only guess left.

I told Archer to spin a story that the attack had been successful, that the Russian special ops commandos had successfully used the Chinese drones and mounted the attack, and that they had gotten away with it. That the president of Russia was overjoyed with them, that his family had been given houses and riches.

The man was so happy, he gave us all the details. He was so high on Xanax and everything else we'd flooded his system with, that in his delirious dream state he gave us the names and locations and details of everything as it had happened, down to the last details.

Except that it hadn't been the president of Russia. It had been their prime minister.

He had been the one who had authorized the attack. Used a sophisticated branch of the FSB—like our own CIA—that had its own special ops drone program. Trained in secret for years together with their cyberattack branches of the military and even carried out the CyberStorm six years before.

During the attack, Russia had claimed its own GLONASS geopositioning birds were destroyed, but they weren't. They were fully operational, just switched to a new and hidden frequency. They claimed their military was blinded, but at the same time, rolled tanks across the borders into the Baltics and Ukraine and other old Soviet territories. Of course, by that time, the president of Russia had been informed, though he said he was kept locked away.

Before the attack, the Russians had goaded America into a confrontation with China, and stepped up anti-Chinese sentiment, hoping that America would attack China. Russia had hoped that the two great powers would fall at the same time.

All they needed to do was launch a cyberattack against GenCorp and use their satellites to take out everything in orbit, and then use the confusion to insert three special ops commando teams of thirty soldiers each supported by a small army of drones.

Two of the teams had disappeared successfully after their missions. It was only Irena's team, the one we became enmeshed with, that had failed in its mission of obfuscation and vanishing afterward, otherwise it would have all remained a deniable mystery.

That's all it took to launch World War C—three units of thirty commandos backed by a few shipping containers of drones armed with AI. The future of warfare had arrived, but we had managed to pull back from the brink. Barely.

The Russian prime minister had called it "Operation Star Rise," we later found out—when all the gory details came out in an international tribunal. By the time it became public knowledge, the prime minister of Russia had been executed by the president.

Russia claimed it was cleaning house. They apologized, disavowed everyone involved, killed them all maybe a little too quickly.

They were rogue agents, they said.

The most damning evidence was the targeted kill list, part of which we had found. Senator Seymour was the Ace of Spades because he was the single most ardent anti-Russian advocate in Congress. The drones sent all over America had been reprogrammed with the facial recognition and last known locations of a long list of people that were deemed "against Russian interests."

The goal was to launch the operation, create chaos, and send China and America and the entire financial system back a hundred years, while Russia ascended and provided aid to the world. Part of the operation was plain old propaganda, now called misinformation, which painted confusing pictures of Senator Seymour and his secret dealings—many of them true—and laundered these stories through mainstream media to give them credibility.

It was difficult to stop this process, even when we knew it was happening.

In the end, I had struggled into DC with the National Guard troops that picked me up, explained again and again who I was. That I had proof of what was happening. Eventually, I played my video to President Chen, and from there, everything came into the open.

The attack against China was halted.

In return, as the dust settled, China re-pegged their currency back to the American dollar. The financial markets restabilized. The world righted itself from the sideways lurch that had almost tipped it into anarchy.

India had never launched the first anti-satellite weapons. It had been Russia, launched from a nuclear submarine parked right off Sriharikota Island. The launches were so close to the Indian facilities that from space-based images it was hard to tell that they hadn't been launched by the Indians themselves.

The Russians had given a whole load of anti-satellite weaponry to the Pakistani government, even people to operate it, and then egged them on to use it when the first anti-satellite weapons were launched against them. Then came the tit-for-tat back and forth that created a debris field in orbit, which created the perfect cover for the next phase of the operation.

To use the GenCorp constellations to begin wrecking everything else in orbit.

Except Russian assets.

They sacrificed a few but maneuvered most of the fleet out of harm's way. Soon afterward, they sent up rockets and claimed they had replaced satellites at an amazing pace. It might not have held up to scrutiny, but at the time, it was total chaos.

They used the confusion at the ports all over America, in Seattle and New Orleans and even New York, to slip in under the wire. Get their commando teams in place, and unload the shipping containers of drones.

Xenon, the mysterious source of information that had spread over the networks just before the attacks, turned out to be part of a Russian psy-ops campaign. Not a real person at all, but propaganda.

We should have known, because we had warnings.

Even six years before, during the CyberStorm, there were reports of unknown drones and aerial objects when the power went down. That was the nascent Operation Star Rise, testing their systems and the limits of our defenses. Over the years, there were reports of UFO sightings all over the country, and even sightings of drones over western Nebraska and eastern Colorado. Nobody even knew who or what they were.

Until now.

"What's Damon doing here? And Babet?" I said as we rounded the corner to Chuck and Susie's. And there were other familiar faces. "And is that Archer?"

Chuck and Susie's place was a three-story Victorian-style home with a wraparound porch and a backyard that spilled down onto the brown waters of the Ohio River.

Terry, my gorilla of a brother, was here. When he showed up, it meant nothing good. He was smiling, though, which made me even more nervous. Thank heavens he hadn't gotten into the car and driven up to the cabin with Oscar, God rest his soul.

I was going to church these days.

The pretty white one we just rebuilt.

I jumped up the stairs and shook hands with everyone, kissed Paulina and Susie on their cheeks. Grandma Babet opened her arms wide and squeezed me tight.

Archer gave me a big bear hug, and I hugged him back. "What are you doing here?"

"Quit the CIA. Started working for Uncle Bigbucks." Archer indicated Damon. "Safer doing security for him. I need a desk job. One that *stays* behind a desk."

A glass of champagne was forced into my hand. "Isn't it a little early to be drinking?" I asked, laughing.

Chuck said to my brother Terry, "Speaking of big bucks, you still owe me fifty."

"Seriously," I asked, "what's the occasion? Did Lauren's bill pass through Congress?"

As one of the leaders of the Battle of Vanceburg, Lauren had earned respect in the halls of Congress. She had created an international tribunal, led by the United States, to outlaw weaponized drones around the world, to stop the targeted extrajudicial killings by any nation, and to limit the use of artificial intelligence in drones and on the battlefield. It was a bit of a difficult endeavor, as that genie was already out of the bottle, but the goal was to stop what just happened here from ever happening again.

The news pundits claimed we had narrowly avoided a fate worse than death—we had averted the creation of an autocratic world power that might have dominated the planet for the rest of this century. But then again, strongmen and autocrats had been the norm for almost all of human history, with democracy and the institutions guarding it surviving only brief periods of time between.

But now was one of those moments.

My wife laughed. "It's not the Bill in Congress."

"Then what?"

Damon grabbed my shoulder. "Paulina and I are getting married."

Salutations and cheers all around the patio. I clinked my glass with everyone but noticed my wife's glass didn't have bubbles in it.

"You're flat," I said to her. "Want a refill?"

Everyone went silent.

"I've kind of already got one." She held her belly.

I was clueless. "Meaning what?"

"I'm pregnant, Mike."

THE END

Author Discussion

Dear Reader,

Thank you so much for coming on this adventure!

As in many of my novels, I like to blend reality with fiction, and in CyberWar, I decided to take the final path along the cyber trail and examine at the impact of artificial intelligence and drones in modern warfare, and I would like to share some of what I researched.

The original CyberStorm novel was inspired by my real-world meetings on cybersecurity in Washington, DC, where I was presenting the intelligence community using my perspective as an info-security contractor for Fortune 500 corporations in my previous life before I became a full-time writer. CyberSpace, the second novel in World War C, was inspired by a second set of meetings I was invited to, again in Washington, discussing the vulnerabilities presented if navigation and timing satellites, notably GPS, were knocked out.

In CyberWar, I took this to its natural conclusion by considering what could happen if drone technology and artificial intelligence were preceded with the events of the first two novels, a coordinated cyberattack with the crippling of space-based assets. In the final analysis, the modern world we live in is surprisingly vulnerable, and the technologies to carry out these attacks are spreading faster than we can contain them.

And this is all based on the incredible rise of drone technologies.

The term "drone" or "UAV" (unmanned aerial vehicle) is somewhat controversial, as all current flying drones require a human operator as well as a supply chain on the ground to maintain their operation, and a vast bureaucratic infrastructure around the supervision of pilots. Typically, they are also intended to be reused, as opposed to the miniature killer bots I portrayed in this novel—but more on this later.

Twenty years ago, there were only a handful of drones in the world, almost all of which were connected to programs in the US military. Today, there are tens of thousands of military drones in operation, from over eighty different countries with active UAV military programs and dozens of independent manufacturers, not to mention the millions of commercial and hobby drones doing everything from filming TV shows to delivering pharmaceuticals.

The term drones, however, doesn't just apply to things that fly.

The most astounding revelation for me was when I read about the US Navy's Overlord uncrewed vessel, a massive two-hundred-foot-long ship that autonomously piloted itself on a 5000-mile journey down the Atlantic coast, through the Panama Canal, and back up through the Pacific. Again, that is a two-hundred-foot-long (!) US Navy robotic ship that piloted itself—without any human help—on a journey almost halfway around the world. The US Navy also has the AN-2 Anaconda gunboat, which is a completely autonomous watercraft equipped with artificial intelligence.

Russia's new T-14 Armata tank is equally or even more frightening. This is a new generation of heavy tank that is being designed to be completely unmanned and even autonomous, meaning it can maneuver and fire without any human intervention. The American military has already launched the new X-47B pilotless autonomous drone combat aircraft from aircraft carriers at sea, which do not require human pilots.

In 2019, the Turkish defense companies STM and Asisguard announced that nation's army will start using their Kargu and Songar drones in 2021, which will have the capability to find, track, and kill people without human intervention. These are fifteen to fifty-pound quadcopters, some of which can be mounted with machine guns, and are intended to be used as parts of a cooperative swarm in combat.

These are entirely different than the drones we began talking about, as these are specifically designed to be autonomous—no human controller required—and operate as combat-ready killing machines.

The difference here is the addition of artificial intelligence.

A few years ago, Google initiated an endeavor called Project Maven in collaboration with the US Department of Defense, which was focused on using AI to enhance or control military drones, with the goal of singling out and attacking enemy human targets. The project was quickly canceled, however, after mass employee outcry.

Of course, the technology is still moving ahead, but now more in the shadows.

The potential for mass atrocities is alarming, especially when hundreds or thousands of these machines may be deployed on a battlefield at once, not to mention the possibility of them being hacked or taken over by bad actors. Nuclear technology is difficult to steal, but the proliferation of artificially intelligent combat machines has almost as much potential for use as weapons of mass destruction, with almost no international treaties governing their control.

China has even recently named its new surveillance system "Skynet," which is the name of the fictious artificial intelligence from the Terminator franchise of movies that wiped out humanity.

This seems to be tempting fate just a little.

With falling birthrates and rising standards of living in almost all industrialized countries, the reluctance to send young people into harm's way in battle has driven governments everywhere to invest in machines that can replace them.

Take a survey in any nation on Earth, and every time the inhabitants will consistently indicate they would prefer sending machines in to fight their battles, rather than their sons and daughters. However, take that same survey and ask if they would prefer to be attacked by machines? An equal percentage is horrified by the idea.

Compared to what I've written in CyberWar, an actual attack by autonomous machines, in a conflict gone wrong, would be far more terrifying than anything I've described on these pages.

There is an ongoing effort at the United Nations to regulate autonomous killer robots, which is backed by people like Elon Musk as well as companies like Google, to create a framework for the banning of this technology, similar to the Chemical Weapons Convention which is a comprehensive and multilateral international ban on the use and possession of chemical weapons. I'm personally optimistic that this diplomatic solution will yield results to contain the spread of autonomous weapons systems, although I'm afraid that it will take a tragedy to wake up the international community to get it done.

With that, I leave you to investigate some of the topics I've brought up. If you haven't come across it yet, I invite you to read my companion novel Darknet, which is was designed as a sequel to CyberStorm, set in the same world a year afterward and deals with the rise of artificial intelligence.

Warmest regards and thanks again for reading!

Matthew Mather

p.s. **If you enjoyed this novel, please don't forget to write a review on Amazon**, not matter how short, because these very much help sales for indie authors like myself. Thanks in advance!

More Books from Matthew Mather

Another connected novel in this world is *Darknet,* which is set in the same universe, but spaced in time between the events in *CyberStorm* and *CyberSpace* (search for *Darknet* on Amazon). This novel is set in New York, and follows one man's journey deep into the tech underworld of Wall Street.

Mr. Damon Vincent Indigo from this series also appears in my *Atopia Chronicles* trilogy. These novels are set fifty years in the future after *CyberStorm,* when Mr. Indigo is an elderly gentleman presiding over a trillion-dollar empire on the island colony of Atopia off the coast of California. *Atopia* was my very first novel, and the style is different—more high-concept sci-fi.

If post-apocalyptic is more your style, then try out my "Science Fiction Book of the Year" award-winning four-book series *Nomad,* where a mysterious deep-space object threatens to destroy the solar system (search for *Nomad* on Amazon). These novels follow the adventures of Jessica Rollins as she protects her family and navigates and new Earth after a truly cataclysmic disaster.

My novel *Polar Vortex,* a new stand-alone title, is about a mysterious aircraft disappearance, and is now under development as a limited TV series (search for *Polar Vortex* on Amazon). This is by far one of my favorite books, and is a great sci-fi mystery from start to finish in an homage to Agatha Christie.

And finally, I have a new sci-fi detective series, the *Delta Devlin Novels,* which follow the career of a rookie New York detective as she faces some harrowing cases. The first in this series is *The Dreaming Tree,* the second book *Meet Your Maker,* with the final book *Out of Time* available as well.

About The Author

Amazon Charts Bestseller Matthew Mather's books have sold millions of copies, accumulated over 70,000 ratings on Goodreads, Audible and Amazon, been translated and published in over 24 countries across the globe, and optioned for multiple movie and television contracts.

He began his career as a researcher at the McGill Center for Intelligent Machines before starting and working in high-tech ventures ranging from nanotechnology to cyber security. He now works as a full-time author of speculative thrillers.

Website:
www.MatthewMather.com
Facebook
www.facebook.com/Author.Matthew.Mather
Email
author.matthew.mather@gmail.com

Made in the USA
Las Vegas, NV
03 August 2022

52581566R10208